I'm Coming to G

It was dark, with the cool feeling of rain coming. He stood just inside the old iron gate on Hensman's Hill, and waited for his luck.

They'd lost the match 11–14, but he'd taken it out on a couple of the opposition. In the cracked communal bath he said he'd see the others in the Greyhound later. He drove back into Bristol, Dire Straits on the tape, the heater on full, and the muscles in his arms and back and legs warm and used. The game had made no difference to the slowly tightening coil inside him. He felt strong, in control. He could do no wrong.

It was the rain that released him. A short line squall from the south-west, travelling fast over the docks and sweeping up the hill to Clifton. When it started battering on the sycamore leaves above him, he felt his mind clear to a hard bright point of action. Now, he thought. Here.

David Ralph Martin began his career as a television scriptwriter and has written for police series from *Z-Cars* to *Heartbeat*. He was born in Birmingham, spent twenty years in Bristol and now lives in Dorset.

I'M COMING TO GET YOU

David Ralph Martin

Mandarin

Lines from 'The Glow Worm' by Lilla Cayley Robinson, as set to music by Paul Lincke and adapted by Paul Mercer, are reprinted by permission of Boosey & Hawkes Music Publishers Ltd. Copyright © 1902 by Apollo Verlag, Berlin. Copyright arrangement 1906 by Hawkes & Son (London) Ltd. Vocal arrangement copyright © 1952 by Hawkes & Son (London) Ltd.

A Mandarin Paperback
I'M COMING TO GET YOU

First published in Great Britain 1995
by Mandarin Paperbacks
an imprint of Reed International Books Ltd
Michelin House, 81 Fulham Road, London SW3 6RB
and Auckland, Melbourne, Singapore and Toronto

Reprinted 1996

Copyright © David Ralph Martin 1995
The author has asserted his moral rights

A CIP catalogue record for this title
is available from the British Library
ISBN 0 7493 1964 X

I'M COMING TO GET YOU is a work of
fiction. Any resemblance to actual events or
persons, living or dead, is entirely coincidental.

Phototypeset by Intype, London
Printed and bound in Great Britain by
BPC Paperbacks Ltd

This book is sold subject to the condition
that it shall not, by way of trade or otherwise,
be lent, resold, hired out, or otherwise circulated
without the publisher's prior consent in any form
of binding or cover other than that in which
it is published and without a similar condition
including this condition being imposed
on the subsequent purchaser.

[faint mirror-image text bleeding through from reverse page]

1

Ellie was a nurse. She was twenty-six years old and came from Birmingham but on the day she was raped she had been living and working in Bristol for three years.

Up until then she had liked Bristol. It wasn't so cold and flat and monotonous as the Midlands where one industrial town blurred and roared and clanked into another. For thirty or forty miles the whole area was strangled with motorways: you could see the individual exhaust palls hanging over the loops and cloverleafs from way out. Birmingham was cars, run by cars and ruined by cars; in Bristol it was wines and spirits and cocoa and chocolate and tobacco, things to do with pleasure, and although all the old money in the city had come from the slave trade, and her flatmates, who were teachers and fiercely liberal, told her that every stone in Georgian Clifton, where they lived, was cemented with the blood and brains and guts of black men and women, Ellie admired the ease and elegant look of the city. To her, Bristolians seemed slower but somehow livelier than Brummies, less beaten down by the business of making a living.

The day she arrived, she walked out of Temple Meads, Isambard Kingdom Brunel's stone cathedral-castle of a railway station, and saw boats and ships in the docks and basins of the harbour. Masts in the middle of a city. Coming from Birmingham where all you got was canals, Ellie thought it was romantic.

Sometimes, walking home in summer from American movies with her flat-mates Marge and Kay, who also came from Birmingham, her head was so full of Technicolor images superimposing themselves on what she felt and saw that she had the idea she'd left somewhere like Detroit or Chicago for somewhere like San Francisco. A hilly, misty city, and from where Ellie lived you could see right across the redbrick saucer of streets and factories and warehouses to the soft green south-west hills beyond.

The Bristol Royal Infirmary, where she worked, was a sprawling mix of old and new buildings close to the centre. On one side lay the commercial heart of the city with its old stone spires and brown glass office blocks, and on the other the run-down Victorian terraces of St Pauls where the black community lived. Some people said the hospital was on the front line, a huge concrete bunker full of the casualties of inner city life, but it reminded Ellie more of a stranded stone liner, almost a city on its own, ploughing on through life and death and humming with electricity and urgency twenty-four hours a day. She was earning close to £18,000 a year and apart from a recent emotional disaster which taught her she wasn't as sensible, cheerful and energetic as she had thought she was, life for Ellie in Bristol was fine. Then she was raped.

The day it happened began as a bright sunny-misty Saturday morning in late November. Ellie came clattering down the four flights of stairs from the attic flat she shared with Marge and Kay out through the double front doors into Cornwallis Crescent. Her car, a black and cream '87 D-reg Citroën 2CV with CHARLESTON written on the bodywork in art deco Twenties lettering, spat, coughed and died. She twisted the key again.

Nothing. She sat back and waited fifteen seconds before trying again. He'd told her to do that, otherwise you flooded the carburettor. Then she saw the little green light on the radio and tape player, and remembered that Janis Joplin's *Greatest Hits* had run out on the way home from work last night. She had forgotten to turn the damn thing off and now the bloody battery was flat. That left less than twenty minutes to walk the steep uphill-downhill mile and a half to the hospital. She tried the key one last time. The only thing that happened was the little green light went out.

And that's your fault too, Doctor Graham bloody Simmons, I hope you rot in hell.

She clamped the pink plastic Krooklok on and set off down Cornwallis Crescent walking fast and arguing with herself, her flat black nurse's shoes clacking and slapping on the wet paving stones. Bloody men, she thought, bloody cars.

It was all his fault, he'd made her buy it, saying I've found just the car for you, Ellie love. Soft top, economical, low insurance, open air motoring all for under £1,500 and a three-month guarantee. That had been in the summer when his wife was away, and what he didn't say was that he wanted Ellie to have a car so he could ride around in it and not get recognised. Yes, well, she realised that now – and my God they said women were devious. She'd even been told it wasn't the first time he'd pulled that particular stroke. There was another nurse, someone Ellie didn't really know, but a nice quiet dark-haired girl apparently, who had left and gone to work in Gloucester. She'd ended up with a Lada.

The trouble was, people, even your friends, only ever told you afterwards. Maybe they saw the madness, that soft, dazed look that made you smile to yourself for no reason when you were walking along the grey hospital corridors, maybe they'd been through it themselves and knew it was no use telling you at the time, but it didn't make it any better afterwards, did it, knowing you were not the One and Only, just the last model off the assembly line.

Rot in hell.

The trouble was, he wouldn't, would he? He'd be there in Casualty, where she was supposed to be in the next fifteen minutes.

She hurried along past the builders' refuse in the iron skips that punctuated the shallow Georgian curve, her mood improving as she moved into the sun. Physically, she wasn't exactly short but her stocky build and the flat black shoes made her look it. She had frizzy soft brown hair, glinting with the mist caught in it, her head bobbing with her quick, determined stride, and clear soft fresh skin pinking up now with the effort. She wore glasses, and although she wasn't bad-looking she wasn't exceptionally good-looking either. Her face was too square, too capable-looking, a face that although it smiled easily, inspired confidence and affection rather than passion or red-hot desire. That was another reason she'd gone overboard for him: a little kindness and smooth, practised attention from a good-looking male and there she was, gone. For a few weeks, when her mind had turned to mush, he'd made her feel as if she'd got the Holy Grail between her legs. God, what a fool, what a pushover – she threw the thought away from her – you bastard – and strode on. Wide shoulders, a good solid bust, a cinched-in waist making her look big-bottomed in the dark blue nurse's raincoat, and strong sturdy legs stepping out in black stockings. A swimmer's body, better naked than

4

clothed, because only then did her magnificent proportions reveal themselves.

Or so that bastard said. Oh yes, she thought, he'd be there all right, smirking away. Good morning Staff, he'd say, as if nothing had happened. She was already rehearsing her reply, Good morning Doctor Simmons, trying to keep her tone cool, distant, neutral, and wondering whether she could manage it.

Up the high-walled steep of Hensman's Hill, past the black iron gate of La Retraite, once a convent school and now a Catholic hospice. Last spring she'd seen a young nun walking in the long garden that looked down over Cornwallis Crescent; the nun had stopped, looked round, quickly picked a daffodil, put it to her nose and then she had eaten it.

She was panting slightly at the top of the hill. Keep going, girl, she told herself, it's just as quick on foot and far better for you. Up again over Clifton Hill and then into the long dark arch of pollarded trees lining the diagonal walk through the old cemetery. There were still a lot of wet dead-looking leaves on the trees, but the grass was bright and fresh and green, well fertilised, she supposed. She had always liked this part of the walk, calm and quiet, with no traffic noise, and table-sized flat-topped Georgian tombs, long shadows in the hazy November sun, and proper old-fashioned black iron railings to keep the dogs out. A couple of tabby and white moggies who looked like mother and daughter were crouching flat in the grass, watching the sparrows and waiting perhaps for some dumb sooty-winged pigeon to come strutting along.

Out into the light and traffic on the corner of Victoria Square, and wondering if she'd be lucky enough to catch a bus. There was nothing in sight, as usual, but at least it was all downhill from here on.

Le plus grand arsehole du monde, ward sister Kate Prosser called him. Well, she should know, she was the last victim but one, before Ellie. They'd both been there, done that, got the bruises. They'd compared notes, rueful and sympathetic at first and then, when they discovered he'd used exactly the same routine, almost word for word, on both of them they'd ended up shrieking and hooting and weeping tears of laughter. Well, almost.

He'd even taken them both to France, Kate Prosser two years ago, Ellie this summer, while his wife was away 'visiting with her folks', as he said, in Maine or Vermont or somewhere. The bastard was probably planning his next hit already, and in a spirit of sisterly solidarity they agreed to look out for the victim and warn her. But would they? Was it worth it?

Three days in the Hôtel du Phare, Barfleur, Kate in numéro sept, Ellie in numéro cinq, and him showing off his table French all the time. *Madame, je vous commande.* And he'd said to both of them this was going to be their three-day honeymoon before he told his wife he couldn't live without them.

Why lie? Ellie had asked Kate, and Kate had replied, Why not? Some men were like that, and they both knew he was married, didn't they? After that one heart-to-heart, Kate and Ellie didn't see much of each other, maybe because they were on different shifts, maybe because neither of them needed to be reminded any more. On balance, Ellie thought that it had helped her get over it, knowing what an unimaginative little shit he was. Well, at least it was another door closed; she just hoped it wasn't going to open again, in ten minutes' time.

She was glad at first when he finally let her down. All that brushing up against each other, quick hot kiss-

6

ing and grabbing in the sluice, sidling out of his flat at six in the morning before the neighbours got up, none of that was really her scene. The strange thing was, he really seemed to enjoy the risk, that carefully organised duplicity; it was almost as if the idea of treachery, of adultery, of licking his lips over it, gave him a buzz, made him feel sexy. Well, he was, the dirty bastard. After he'd given her the push – one phone call: Sorry Eleanor, it's off, I can't do it, I mean, she is my wife but I'd still like to see you some time, love – Ellie had felt clean and relieved until night fell, and then the world caved in on top of her. For two long black summer weeks there was nothing but snivels, misery and long, bleak, bed-rocking endless heartache. Without him there was nothing in the day, and catching sight of him was even worse. Unable to take it any more, she booked a last-minute flight to Corfu on her own and came back ten days later with NSU from a lad called Spiros. At least he'd been nice to her and made her laugh.

Unlike le plus grand arsehole du monde.

Since then, as far as men and sex were concerned, she felt closed up, not uninterested exactly but unwilling. She still went out, to parties, dancing and drinking and letting herself be chatted up but it was more to show herself she wasn't defeated than anything else. She certainly wasn't looking for another new experience, thank you very much. Even though she still liked the feel of a man's arms around her, and their smell and their occasional hardness pushing up against her, something inside her had been knocked flat: the need to give, to bloom, to lay herself open, was replaced by the need to heal herself, to get rid of the fear of being emotionally mugged again. She still used sex at work of course, it was part of the job, it helped cheer up the patients and got them to do what she wanted, but even that got boring and repetitive at the end of a long shift. What Ellie was doing, and knew she was doing, was lying fallow. As far as I'm concerned, she said to Marge and Kay, the House of Love is closed for renovations and repairs.

As October turned into November she found she wasn't just enjoying her celibacy, she was positively exhilarated by it. It gave her so much more time and energy, and she slept better and worked better. On the other hand she found her natural flow of sympathy for her friends' complicated but stunted common-room love-lives becoming tinged with hilarity. How could they get into such a mess, such a steaming tizz, over so little? Then she remembered what she'd been like, and what comfort they'd given her, and felt guilty and tried to make it up to them with motherly hugs and cooking special Thai meals for them.

There was still the problem of Christmas-without-a-boyfriend to face, but even that had its up side. No presents, no sulks, just a couple of days being looked after by her mother and catching up on what had happened to her friends in Brum. That would be enough: just right, in fact.

Then, just as she was beginning to feel really good about things, really back in control, the Management had arbitrarily changed her shift and told her that from now until the New Year she was going to be on Casualty with Doctor Graham Simmons.

She knew what he'd be like. He'd have that way of looking at her that said *I know you, every bit of you, I know what you like, the noises you make*, and then wanting to be sort of mates over it, as if it was nothing but some sodding little holiday they'd been on together.

Going down St Michaels Hill, dodging through the

8

students blearily ploughing up towards her, she could already feel him standing extra close to her, not touching her directly – oh no, he was much too calm and calculated for that – but being familiar with her, as if she were one of the pieces he'd collected, one of the ones he'd made earlier. And then he'd make sure she was watching when he was chatting up the black nurses. You'd think they'd have more sense, knowing what they did about the general fecklessness of men, but no, they still went for it.

Five minutes later, keeping her mind carefully tense and blank, she walked into the Casualty Department of the Bristol Royal Infirmary and there he was. Leaning on the counter, being lazily charming to the huge-eyed Indian receptionist, then starting up guiltily when he saw Ellie striding in.

'Oh hi.' Checking his watch, the bastard.

'Car wouldn't start.' She walked past, feeling nothing but elation. Not a twinge, not a cringe, not the slightest betraying flutter. Nothing but cold, hard elation. She reached the locker room and breathed out deeply and triumphantly. She'd done it. You could never tell until the moment came, and you were finally face to face. But the wound hadn't opened. Even though the scar was still there, the wound hadn't opened. She was whole, she was healed, it was over.

She shook her raincoat, hung it in the locker, pinned on her rectangular plastic ID and became Senior Staff Nurse Eleanor Wilcox.

The walk had done her good.

2

Frank felt like it the moment he woke up. Saturday morning, no work, and his wife Rae standing at the window with the sunlight coming through her nightdress.

'Hey. Come back to bed.'

'Why?' She didn't turn round.

'I feel like it.'

'You always feel like it.'

'You should see this one.' He threw back the duvet. 'See?'

'Frank, I'm looking at the view.' Now he was behind her, lifting up her nightdress, easing it between her buttocks. 'Feel it.'

'Very nice.'

He put his arms around her. 'Come and lie down.'

'I don't want to.' She didn't move. He shoved himself against her. She felt him sucking at her neck and went on looking at the view.

There was mist on the river. It silenced things, like snow. Beyond it, a wall of splintered red rock, then trees, then Georgian terraces, ran up to a clear blue sky. Clifton. She loved it when it looked like this, warm and golden, like the background of an old painting. He said it was better to look at than to live in. They had a cream pebbledash semi in Ashton, on the flat side of Bristol, in the shadow of the flyover.

'Here then, all right, love?' His hand slid over her belly and in between her legs. 'You go on looking out

10

the window. Come on, Rae.' He flexed his knees, tried to get it in. He could see them sideways on in the wardrobe mirror. Their bodies looked good together, some tan left, like a shot in a lovemaking magazine. She twisted away.

'Save it for the match.'

It was then he knew some other woman was going to get it.

It was dark, with the cool feeling of rain coming. He stood just inside the old iron gate on Hensman's Hill, and waited for his luck.

They'd lost the match 11–14, but he'd taken it out on a couple of the opposition. In the cracked communal bath he said he'd see the others in the Greyhound later. He drove back into Bristol, Dire Straits on the tape, the heater on full, and the muscles in his arms and back and legs warm and used. The game had made no difference to the slowly tightening coil inside him. He felt strong, in control. He could do no wrong.

It was the rain that released him. A short line squall from the south-west, travelling fast over the docks and sweeping up the hill to Clifton. When it started battering on the sycamore leaves above him, he felt his mind clear to a hard bright point of action. Now, he thought, here.

The alley behind him led through two walls to the grounds of La Retraite. The nuns would be eating: he could smell cabbage in the clear air. The rain would keep the streets clear for twenty minutes. Now, here.

He heard footsteps coming down the hill. A woman hurrying, half-running. He began to salivate, and tremble, like a springer.

'Shut up and you won't get hurt.' It didn't sound like his voice. 'Struggle and I'll fucking kill you.' She was

11

a stocky girl in her mid-twenties, strong from the feel of her upper arms, in a dark blue raincoat with a hood, wearing thick rain-streaked glasses. She struggled until he hit her across the side of her head with the back of his gloved hand. She went quiet and still, and after that all she did was whimper. He dragged her twenty yards down the alley, turned her face to the wall between a couple of bushes, hauled up her long mac — she was a nurse of some sort, wearing a blue striped dress and a black elastic belt. He forced her head further down the wall so that her white backside stuck out at him. She looked as broad as a shire horse, soft-skinned, solidly muscled, pale blue veins. Rainwater fell from the bushes and gathered in the hollow of her spine, jiggling as he had her. There was a voice inside him laughing for pure joy.

He felt clean, and light, and sorry for her as he tied the belt of her mac round her ankles. She hadn't been as tight as he would have liked, and the difference in their heights had made it awkward. But he'd done it, he'd obeyed, and she'd borne it well. Good girl.

He was changed and in the Greyhound in Princess Victoria Street by twenty-past seven. He had a pint of Courage Directors, phoned his wife and said he'd be back to pick her up about nine and then they'd go for a steak or something at the Anchor in Oldbury. It was fifteen miles out so she'd have to drive back. Was that OK. She said fine, she was just going to have a bath.

Ellie waited until he had gone and then sat up and untied herself. She was numb, wet with cold and shivering uncontrollably. Raindrops glittered and fell from the bushes where he had stuffed her head. She hauled herself on to her hands and knees and forced herself upright. No glasses. Damn. The first thing she did was

12

rethread the belt through the loops of her gabardine raincoat and knot it tight against the cold. The shivery flu-like feeling diminished. She tried to smear the mud and slimy leafmould off herself with her wet dress. Her insides felt as if they were on fire: swollen and bruised dark red, right up to her ovaries. She stumbled around bent double, barely able to move for the pain and the quivering in her thighs, determined to find her black tights and white cotton knickers.

They had been trodden into the mud. She stuffed them into her raincoat pockets and wiped her hands down the gabardine. Where were her bloody glasses? They must have gone flying when he clouted her across the head. She started to trudge up the alley, mud squelching up the sides of her shoes and squirting up her bare legs. Don't think about it. Get home and don't think about it.

Her handbag was where she dropped it when he first grabbed her, right inside the iron gate. No sign of her glasses. Damn and blast. She made her way down the hill holding on to the wall and hoping no one would see her.

When she reached Cornwallis she could hardly walk at all. She had to pull herself along a few steps at a time, clinging to the black spear-points of the basement railings. It felt as if she'd had one rammed up her. She knew she was either bleeding or his come was running out of her, or both. You bastard, she said to herself over and over again, you fucking bastard. Hobbling up the road like an old bag lady, covered in mud, her hair dripping down her face, her shoes slopping and clacking on her feet.

A young couple came out of a house three doors away, looked at her holding on to the railings, leaning against them, and decided she was drunk. They got

13

into the young man's car and drove past her. The girl, pale-faced with long shining hair, gave her a hesitant smile as the car accelerated away. Saturday night: we're going out. Ellie dragged herself on past the parked cars, the black plastic rubbish sacks, the skips full of rubble and plasterboard and old bathroom fittings. Home, get yourself home. There was an old blue mattress on one of the skips, bulging and sodden with its insides ripped out. Peacock blue with gold stitching. It must have been quite expensive once.

She wondered if the others were in. She pictured the pair of them squatting in front of the gas fire, skirts hunched up, making toast. The look of shock when she walked in, the flood of sympathy, the questions, Marge holding her, Kay getting angry. All of them crying. If not, she'd have to phone the police herself. If she had the strength. There was all that to look forward to.

You fucking bastard.

3

Detective Sergeant Vic Hallam was thirty-seven, a big dark-haired man in a baggy dark grey suit with a white shirt and no tie. The tie was in his pocket for later, when they did the late-night clubs and discos. When the phone rang he was lying spark out on top of his six-foot-six-square double bed in his semi-basement flat in lower Cotham, half a mile up the slope from the Jungle. The Jungle was what Bristol Central CID and most of their customers called St Pauls. It wasn't politically correct, but neither were the detectives in Bristol Central Bridewell.

'Hallo?'

'Vic, it's Des.' Detective Sergeant Des Chaffey was the admin and desk man at the Well.

'Bloody hell, Des,' Vic looked at his gold-plated Timex. It was only twenty to eight, for fuck sake.

'You're wanted,' said Des.

'You know what time I finished with Kenny Chen up the Golden Maggot?'

'No,' said Des's voice patiently. 'When was that, Vic?'

'Half-past fucking five, mate.' Vic squinted up at the hanging grey veil of spider's web in the corner of the bedroom and made a rough calculation. 'You know how much sleep I've had in the last twenty-four hours?'

'No Vic,' said Des, still humouring him. 'How much is that?'

'Four and half fucking hours,' said Vic. 'I was round

15

there on the stabbings till eight this morning and back there with the interpreter at twelve – '

'I make that six and a half hours then, Vic.'

'Bollocks.'

'You get a result?'

'Yeah, young Kenny Chen's decided not to press charges.' There had been a triple stabbing at the Golden Market Casino off the top of Park Street. Two Chinese men wounded and a third run off, also believed wounded. 'He thinks the third guy came from Swindon.'

'Why?'

'Because of his fucking Wiltshire accent, why d'you think?' said Vic. 'My guess is they'll find him and that'll be that. Swindon's problem, not ours.'

'Had a complaint from Kenny's dad, Mister Chen.'

'Re what?'

'Your conduct, mate,' said Des. 'He says why you keep calling his place the Golden Maggot?'

'Should try his own fucking prawn spring rolls then, shouldn't he?'

'I can't take it off the sheet, Vic.'

'Fuck it,' said Vic. 'What's one more?'

There was a silence. Des said, 'This is a rape, Vic.'

'Where?'

'Clifton – '

'For Christ's sake, why can't Redland do it, it's their patch – '

'The Chief said you, Vic.'

'It's Saturday night, for fuck sake, Des. I'll be on from half-eight to half-four, what more does he want?'

'If Detective Chief Inspector Barnard says it's you Vic, then it's you, and there's nothing neither you or me nor any other fucker can do about it.'

'He's got the knife in again, hasn't he?'

16

'You could say that.'

'Any idea why?'

'He was muttering about attitude – '

'Fuck off,' said Vic.

'Exactly,' said Des. 'And then he got on to motivation, insubordination, lack of co-operation – '

'He say anything about results?'

'No.'

'No he couldn't, could he? Fucking hell, Des, I've gripped more people than most of 'em have had hot dinners.'

'Yeah, well, you've been at it longer haven't you?'

'He tell you to say that?'

'Just have a word in his shell-like, was how he put it.'

'Anything else?'

'He did mention you failing inspector's twice.' Des's voice paused. 'What he actually said was he didn't think you were being bushy-tailed enough.'

'After an eighteen-hour fucking day? Bushy-fucking tailed? He can stick his nuts up his fucking arse.'

There was another pause, then Des said, 'He thinks you might have lost it, Vic.'

'What?'

'Appetite.'

'Why?'

'Domestic,' said Des shortly.

Neither spoke. Vic reached across the bed for a Marlboro, fumbled awkwardly in his trouser pocket for his gas Imco, lit the cigarette and took a long drag on it. 'Right,' he said, 'whereabouts is this rape case?'

'Cornwallis Crescent. Scene of crime, Hensman's Hill. Cromer's got the details, he's on his way over.'

'Who?'

'Your new kid. Detective Constable Cromer, remember?'

'Oh yeah.' Vic put the phone down, took a couple more drags on the Marlboro, seething with what was by now the familiar rush of anger, hopelessness, self-pity and despair, then stubbed the cigarette and his feelings out at the same time, swung his legs off the bed and shambled into the bathroom to run the Ronson over the day's stubble. Christ, he knew why they all got into dope and crime and fights and stabbings – Christ, he knew what it was to have black and bloody red fucking murder in your heart. My Christ, he fucking knew. Didn't do any fucking good though, did it?

Six months ago his wife Pat, a slim long-legged thin-faced young woman in her early thirties with warm brown eyes and a big Dallas mane of long fair hair, had walked out and left him after eight years of what he had thought was not too bad a marriage. Because, she said, he took the job too seriously, thought more of it than he did of her, never spent any time with her, didn't show her any affection any more – which Vic took to mean he didn't fuck her enough – and all he ever did when he did come home was drink, watch boxing, talk about work and go to bed drunk. All the usual female bullshit, except that when he'd told her to fuck off and leave him alone, she had.

She'd gone to live in London, somewhere in Crickle-wood, she said, when she occasionally rang him up about money or whether her things were still all right in the flat, because she hadn't got time to come and collect them just at the moment. She'd got a job as a secretary in a BMW dealership with a possible chance of doing some delivery driving, she said, because she'd always liked driving. Oh, and she was now calling herself Trish Mitchell, which was her maiden name. It would have been easy enough for him to check up on where she was and who she was with, but he didn't. Wouldn't, to be more accurate.

Now this. Now, apparently, he wasn't taking the job seriously enough. He was losing it. Fucking hell. Jesus Christ. What did they all fucking want? Blood?

Vic looked at himself in the mirror. There were a lot more lines and creases and bags than there should be at his age. A man's character is writ in his face, my son, his old man used to say. Yeah, well, as far as Vic was concerned there were plenty of fucking questions but no fucking answers.

Fuck it, forget about it, shove it in a box like he'd shoved all her stuff, nail down the lid and forget about it. One tea-chest of china and cooking gear, three black plastic sacks of clothes, all piled up by the door in the hall. Ready for you whenever you come down, you've still got the key. Eight years of marriage. Sometimes when he walked out of the door there was a waft of perfume from her clothes. He went on buzzing the razor up and down his neck and tried to think about nothing.

He was pale, with pale eyes and a hard, foxy face, and because he looked like most of his customers, slightly battered with the odd dent here and there, they talked to him. He had an encouraging way of listening, with a faint smile on his face, that made them want to go on, because any minute, they knew, Vic would believe them, and they'd be off the hook and some other poor bastard would be in the shit. He'd been a detective sergeant for fourteen years, which he sometimes thought was a flying start into nowhere and other times felt reasonably comfortable about, and, basically, that

19

was all he did. He listened. You were patient with them, you bought them drinks and gave them cigarettes, and you waited, sympathetically, for them to dig their graves with their teeth. Vic had nice teeth – cleaning them now, spitting into the sink – and a knowing grin, and to a club-owner he looked like a club-owner, and to an Irishman he looked like an Irishman, and to a villain he looked like he might be bent. Or, at least, bendable.

As he changed his shirt and sprayed his armpits with Boots' Man's Natural Balance – no point in putting the victim off before he started – a series of faces flitted through his mind. Des, round and pink, with receding fair hair. Detective Chief Inspector Barnard, a rectangular block of meaty flesh, flinty eyes and a shock of iron grey hair. The young kid Cromer, fresh as a fucking choirboy with big blue watery-looking eyes as if somebody had just shouted at him and a flop of soft brown hair. Vic had left him familiarising himself with the casework on his first night, while he went off to sort out the mess at the Golden Maggot. He'd hardly spoken to the kid, but he didn't look too promising. Too straight by half – although that in itself could be a plus factor if the kid had any nous at all.

His mind backtracked. What had he been like when he started? Dead sharp. Razor keen. Always first in, fists flying, at club chuck-out time – until one old uniformed sergeant had taken him aside and told him not to push it. You'll get there son, but you can't thump it out of people. Wait and watch it dribble out. Well, he had got there: detective sergeant at twenty-three, up for Bramshill Police College not long after – then what happened?

He brushed his dark hair straight back off his forehead, wet his hands and slicked it down. You got too cocky, Hallam, that's what happened.

He failed his first inspector's exam deliberately, more or less, because he'd just got married and didn't fancy being stuck out in the sticks in uniform for five years. Like that other flash git he was up for Bramshill with, what was his name? Warren, Weller, Webber? Yeah, that was it, Webber. First name Dick, or something like that. Rhymed with prick. Actually, so did Vic, so it couldn't be that, but this guy Webber was a real prick. Big, tall, good-looking, four or five years younger than Vic, even more of a high-flyer, a real snotty, superior-looking git, bright, immaculate, good at sports and PT and all that but always brown-nosing round the Brass, which was a dead giveaway as far as Vic was concerned.

They'd hated each other on sight, like two black dogs, and every course they were on together it was either Webber or Vic coming out top. Then there was that final pre-Bramshill test parade. They'd let Webber take it, everybody in uniform, bulled up to the nines, and he came round with his swagger stick and hoiked out Vic's tie. 'There's a cunt at the end of this stick', was what he said. Even now Vic found himself grinning at the memory. Jesus Christ, what a gift. Irresistible.

'Not this end, sergeant.'

But who was it went to Bramshill? Not you, Hallam. The second time he'd failed inspector's was six months ago, just after she'd pushed off. At the time, he'd blamed her —

The doorbell rang. Vic walked down the hall past the plastic sacks and the tea-chest, and there was Cromer in a sports coat and flannels looking like an estate agent. For the life of him Vic couldn't remember the kid's first

21

name. Maybe the DCI was right, maybe he was cracking up. Maybe he already had.

'Drop me off at the SOC and you go on to the house.'

'What?' said Cromer, blue eyes bulging.

'You know what the SOC is, don't you?'

'Scene of the crime, sergeant.'

Holy shit. 'Right, well you drop me there son, and I'll see you later. Anybody with her, is there?'

Cromer looked at his sheet. 'WPC Walford, sergeant.'

'You'll be all right then, won't you?'

The WPC was called Jane something. She sat on Ellie's bed and told her she would be staying with her the whole time. She was a big, neat girl about Ellie's age with bitten-down nails and a blue hat with a chequered band. She kept the hat pulled well down over her eyes and never took it off. It left the back of her neck exposed and you could see where she had shaved the hairline. Ellie supposed it was like the wards: you had to wear your hat to show authority. She couldn't remember whether she'd put her staff nurse's cap in the locker or left it in the office. Never mind.

'You what, love?' Jane was folding her muddy gabardine mac and putting it into a large blue transparent plastic bag.

'Sorry?'

'You said never mind.'

'Did I?'

The first thing that Jane had asked her, after she'd turned the kettle off because Ellie hadn't noticed the kitchen was full of steam, was whether she'd had a bath or washed herself at all. Ellie said no, and Jane said smashing.

After she'd made the 999 call she sat with her head on the kitchen table and couldn't do anything. She still

22

hurt, but sitting down and bent well over, it was more of a dull ache. There was a note on the grey Formica: *Waited 7.30. Gone to pics. Back 11ish.* She was too exhausted to cry much.

As soon as Jane heard she was a nurse she wanted to know if she'd taken anything, any Valium or Librium. Not even aspirin? No. But it felt like that, and she supposed it must look like that to Jane. Everything was distant and woolly and she had to concentrate to catch what Jane said. And then try to think of an answer. Jane said it was shock. You got a lot of it in Casualty. Their eyes followed you round but you could see they weren't registering much. Ellie felt quite calm though. A bit cold, but calm, as if she'd slowed right down. As if the whole world had slowed down, and gone dull. It wasn't what she'd felt at first, only after she'd got into the flat and found it empty.

When Jane helped her into the bedroom to take her uniform off, and her bra, they both saw she was covered with streaks of mud from the waist down, where she'd tried to wipe it off with her dress. Jane looked at her head and her body for marks, moving her round into the light, and asked if she'd been hit across the ear. When she said yes, she could hear her own voice echoing inside her head as if she'd been swimming underwater.

Then Jane had found her some more underclothes and helped her put them on over her dirty legs and arms, then she'd got her dressing gown, then she'd made her sit down on the bed, and given her a cup of tea with too much sugar in it. She'd thought Jane was making too much fuss of her. Then she had asked her what had happened.

Now Jane was asking her something else.

'Ellie love, where's your knicks?'

23

'What?'

'Your knickers, your pants.'

'Aren't they there?'

'I can't see them.' Jane looked at her, concerned. 'You sure you had them on?'

'Course I am.' What did Jane think she was?

He'd pulled them down, and her tights. Then he'd tapped one leg, then the other, as if she was a kid at bath-time, and made her step out of them into the cold mud with her bare feet. She heard herself say, 'I think you'll find they're with the black tights in the right-hand mac pocket.' So there. Her voice sounded like her mother's.

'Smashing.' They were still sopping wet. Jane disentangled them and looked at them carefully. Then she put them in the blue plastic bag.

'I wish I could have a bath, Jane, I feel all sticky.'

'I know, love, it won't be long.' But Jane wasn't looking at her: she was biting her little finger, twisting it round in her mouth and looking at it.

'What's the matter, Jane?'

'Ellie love, d'you think you can stand up for me?'

'Not that weak.'

'Can you turn round, with your back to me?'

'All right.' *I'll do a twirl if you like.*

'Ellie, are you bleeding?'

Ellie looked inside her clean knickers. 'Yes I am, a bit.'

'It's not your period, is it?'

'No it's not.' Serve him right if it was.

'Have you got any STs?'

'In the left-hand drawer.'

Jane found them and gave one to her. 'You'd better take those off and put a new pair on. Don't throw the ST away, will you?'

24

'All right.'

'I think you'd better get into bed and keep warm.'

'Has it come through on to the dressing gown?'

'It'll wash out.'

'It takes ages to dry, being quilted.'

'Into bed now.'

It was nice to get into her bed, even with dirty legs. Jane was fingering her personal radio in her uniform top pocket. 'Look love, I'll be back in a minute.'

'Where are you going?' *Don't leave me.*

'Only in the next room. You all right?'

'Lovely.' *You said you'd stay with me.*

'I've just got a couple of calls to make. You have a bit of a rest now.'

Jane picked up the blue plastic bag and went to the door. There was a dark shape standing outside it, filling the low doorframe. A man in a dark grey jacket. A young man.

Ellie heard herself scream.

Vic was halfway up the stairs, thinking about the nuns at the scene of the crime, lit up black and white by the photographer's flash, chattering like magpies, avid to see the moulds of the footprints being taken, when Cromer came out of the attic flat rubbing his head and holding the blue plastic evidence bag.

'What was all that about?'

'She screamed when she saw me.'

'Why, what did you do?'

'Nothing. I think it was because I was a man.'

Vic wiped the mud off the sides of his shoes on the ratty doormat outside the flat. Kid couldn't be more than twenty-two or three, straight off the training course. Oh well. Vic motioned the way upstairs. 'Let's see what you've got.'

Cromer followed Vic into the sitting room. The baggy

25

suit was shiny from halfway down the jacket to halfway down the trousers. Too much sitting in cars. Cromer had found it harder than he thought switching from days to nights: even just reading through the caseload had left him knackered. Tonight was his first night outside the station as a det-con and he felt tired and keyed-up at the same time. He just hoped he wasn't going to cock it up. 'Watch your head,' he said to Vic. He had already banged his on the sloping ceiling, just after the nurse screamed.

The Put-U-Up convertible settee creaked as Vic sat down. Cromer spread the nurse's clothing out on the coffee table. 'What's she like?' said Vic. 'Pretty?'

Cromer thought of the pale, terrified face. 'Not really.'

'Average?'

'Hard to say. I didn't get much of a look.'

'No.' Vic looked at the bra size. 36B. He tried to think of Cromer's first name. 'But you wouldn't kick her out of bed?'

'I suppose not.'

The kid's face was going red already. Christ Almighty. The name came to him. 'You ever been on a rape case, John?'

'Only house to house, making inquiries.'

'It's a bastard.' Vic picked up the wet knickers and looked at the stained crotch. 'A pain in the arse.'

'I thought we were supposed to take them straight down to Forensic?'

Vic gave him a long look. 'Yeah. But we're going to need the shoes.'

He knocked on the bedroom door. When Jane opened it, the nurse was sitting on the bed with her back to him, bent over, swamped in a thick quilted pink and white dressing gown. He gave Jane a plastic bag con-

26

taining Ellie's spectacles. 'One of the nuns picked these up. Can I have a word with her?'

'I've called an ambulance,' said Jane. 'I think she ought to go to hospital.

4

'Where will she go?'

'Gynae,' said Jane.

'Not Casualty?'

'She hasn't been knocked about enough.'

'Call them again. Say you want a private room.'

'On a Saturday night?'

'I'm not going to get any answers in a ward full of women feeding their kids and having their wombs out, am I?'

'You're not going to get much anyway.'

'Why, what did she tell you?'

'She said he was wearing a stocking mask, a balaclava with eyeslits, a black beret, overalls and driving gloves.'

'What happened to the rug?'

'What?'

'Thanks, Jane.'

He let Cromer drive. Jane went with Ellie in the ambulance. She'd started crying on the way downstairs. Something about not wanting to be seen in the hospital in her dressing gown.

On the way down he radioed in for all outstandings. The girl said did he want inside or outside the family; he said anyone, and shove in all sexual assaults in Clifton. She said she'd see what they'd got. Cromer said the guy sounded more like an armed robber than a rapist. Or maybe he'd got a lot of hair, like a Rasta.

28

The way they stuffed all the dreadlocks in when they wanted to come on normal, or go shoplifting. Vic saw he'd have to keep an eye on Cromer: he'd got the makings of a typical uniformed inspector.

Cromer was all arms and elbows in the maroon Escort, eyes in the mirror every ten seconds, shuffling the wheel through his hands as if he was taking his police test. Any villain would have spotted them a mile off: two men in a small Ford giving everything but hand signals. But at least he knew the way, and it gave Vic time to think. Maybe the faceless look was part of it, what he got off on, made it quicker, more terrifying. Or he could be local, recognisable. Or he could be a genuine nutter. See what the girl said, then stick Cromer on the computer, see if this guy was dressing up anywhere else.

The Man in Black – the *Western Daily Press* would love it.

They went down Clifton Vale and along the black wet slick of Hotwells. There was a lot of Youth about, outside the pubs. Somebody else's problem. Through the Centre. It was scruffier than ever. The aerosol brigade had started spraying the grass and the flowerbeds on the central island. They must have run out of walls.

Up the hill to the Royal Infirmary, the street lighting changed from orange to white. It made the kids on the street look like corpses with black lips. Cromer pulled into a consultant's parking space and said he'd been thinking. The guy could be scarred, or he could have something like a birthmark, or he could be some kind of paramilitary nut. Or, said Cromer, noticing the patient, dead look on Vic's face, he could just be bald.

'That's all we need,' said Vic. 'A bald fucking IRA rapist.'

The sister kept them waiting outside the ward for

twenty-five minutes. Ellie had been sick, apparently, just after she got out of the ambulance, and needed to rest. After ten minutes the sister came out and told Vic off for smoking and said he was exposing patients to passive risk. Cromer kept his nose to the glass, but Vic knew he was grinning to himself. When Vic came out of the staff lavatory where he had dunked his cigarette, Cromer was still at the ward door. 'They're moving two old biddies out, tubes dangling and everything.'

The sister opened the door and asked Vic if he knew he was harassing a patient in a state of shock. Vic apologised and asked the sister how Ellie was.

'She's got a labial tear in her vagina.'

'I see. Has an internal examination been carried out?'

'No, it's quite visible externally.'

'Has she been given any treatment of any sort?'

'No, she has not. We do understand the procedure, sergeant.'

'Then I can talk to her?'

The sister delayed her answer as long as she could. 'You can, until the doctor's ready to examine her.'

'Thank you, sister. One more thing. Can I have an ashtray?'

The two-bed ward still had the sweet dead-flower smell of old ladies. The sister banged down a stainless steel kidney dish on the Formica-topped cabinet, opened a metal window and left. Jane sat on the other side of the bed, one hand stretched out towards Ellie, and Cromer stood with his hands in his jacket pockets, right in Ellie's eyeline.

'Constable, get a chair and sit down somewhere, will you?'

'Sergeant.'

Vic pulled his chair closer to Ellie's bed. She flinched as it scraped across the black vinyl floor. She looked

30

pale, and the skin round her eyes was red. He could feel Jane warning him.

'Ellie, I've got to ask you some questions. If you don't feel up to it, say so. Any time you want to stop, fine by me.'

'I'm all right.'

He took her through it from the beginning. How she'd walked to work because it was a nice morning and her car wouldn't start. Then she'd caught the bus back to Victoria Square after work and walked through the old cemetery with a woman who had an umbrella, down past La Retraite to the iron gate on Hensman's Hill. Where he'd grabbed her.

'Did he touch your handbag at all?'

'No, I threw it away, just inside the gate. I thought that was what he wanted at first. So I chucked it in the bushes. I thought, have it if that's what you want.'

Vic asked her how long she'd lived in Bristol. Three years. Before that she'd done her training at the Queen Elizabeth Hospital in Edgbaston, Birmingham – her family came from Shirley, just down the road. They'd been in the flat in Cornwallis for two years and they thought it was great. The landlords, Mr and Mrs Besant, could get a lot more for the flat if they wanted, but because they were nurses and infant teachers they let them have it for three hundred a month. The others, Marge and Kay, were Brummies too. They'd be worried where she was, when they came back from the pictures. Jane said she'd tell them, and Ellie smiled and said thank you. Vic figured she was relaxed enough now to get things back on track.

'When he grabbed you, could you see his face at all?'

'No, he had the stocking on, and the balaclava and that. He just swung me round inside the gate, and then he got his arm round my neck from behind and told me to shut up and I'd be all right. Then he said "Struggle and I'll fucking kill you." '

'Did you struggle?'

'I did till he hit me. Then, I don't know, I just froze up. I just stopped thinking. I mean, my legs didn't go or anything – you don't understand until it happens to you. We have self-defence, for on the wards. But when you've been hit like that, your mind goes – '

'What about his voice, Ellie?'

'Throaty, sort of rough.'

'Any accent?'

'No, not really.'

'Black?'

'No, it wasn't like that. He wasn't West Indian.'

'How do you know?'

She looked straight at him. 'You can tell, can't you?'

'How can you tell?'

'Well he'd have looked blacker for a start, wouldn't he?'

There was a hint of a smile. 'Even under the stocking he'd have looked dark. He was white all right.'

Vic could hear Cromer's Pentel scratching away. He asked her about her height: five six. Her weight: nine and a half stone. She looked at Jane. 'What they call big-boned.' She said he was a good head taller. His chin, when he was holding her, dug in the top of her head – she touched her scalp, about two inches back from the top of her forehead.

'He pushed me against the wall and shoved my head down in the bushes. And pulled my mac up, and the uniform. Pulled the tights down and the knickers. Then he made me trample them off, one leg at a time. He didn't say anything, he just tapped one leg, then the other, as if I was a kid or something.'

'Then what?'

32

'Then,' she took a breath. 'Then he had to straddle his legs apart. And he pushed my head down further. And poked around for a bit. Fiddled about with himself. And shoved it in.' She looked up at him defiantly. 'Bloody hard.'

'Did you cry out?'

'Probably. I was just trying to keep my head off the wall.'

'Right. What I'm going to ask you now, you'll get asked in court. If we get this bloke. You understand?'

'I think so.'

'Just answer yes or no. Say if you want to pack it in.'

'I'm all right.'

'OK – did he use his fingers at all?'

'No.'

'Did he touch your anus?'

'No.'

'Was there any attempt at anal penetration either with the fingers or the penis or any other object?'

'No.'

'Did he feel your breasts?'

'No.'

'Did he kiss you at all, either before or after?'

'No.'

'Did he ask you to have oral sex with him?'

'No.'

'Did he attempt oral sex on you?'

'No.'

'When he penetrated your vagina, was it only with his penis?'

'Yes.'

'There was no object or objects involved?'

'No.'

'During the period of intercourse did you make any noise for any reason?'

'No – I don't know – I might have.'

'Why might you?'

'Because it hurt. Because of the position, trying to keep my head off the wall.'

'Did he make any noise, or say anything?'

'He said "You fucking cow" once or twice.'

'Why d'you think he said that?'

'Because he couldn't get the angle right. He kept slithering about in the mud. He kept coming out of me, and shoving it back in. That's how he hurt me.'

'When he hurt you did you make any noise?'

'I think I yelled out, but I had the mac over my head.'

'Did he react in any way when you yelled out?'

'He kept saying "Fuck you fuck you fuck you" over and over again.'

'Why was he saying that, d'you think?'

'I think that was when he was ejaculating.'

'Did you feel him ejaculating?'

'No.'

'How long do you think intercourse lasted?'

'I don't know. Two or three minutes.'

'Did you see his penis at all?'

'No.'

'Any part of him?'

'No.'

'If you saw him again, d'you think you'd be able to recognise him?'

'If I heard his voice . . . I don't know.'

'Anything else about him, anything you can remember?'

'He smelled very clean.'

'How d'you mean? Aftershave, deodorant or what?'

'As if he'd just had a bath.'

They went through how he'd tied her ankles together, how he'd walked away, with his hands in his pockets, how she'd looked for her things, got herself home, phoned.

'You smoke?'

'Can I?' Her eyes flicked to the porthole, looking for the sister's face.

'Why not?'

'Thanks.' She leaned forward, squinting at the end of the cigarette as he lit it for her. He watched her inhale and blow the smoke out towards the open window. He put the steel kidney dish on the bed between them and leaned back, letting her think it was all over.

Then he said: 'So you didn't see him, and after he hit you across the head you didn't try to resist?'

'I told you –'

'You're making it all up, aren't you? You're lying, lying through your teeth. You've had a row with your boyfriend, haven't you? All this balaclava stuff is all bollocks. You couldn't see what he looked like because he wasn't there. You made him up –'

She was already screaming at him when she pulled the bedclothes off and opened her legs at him and shouted at him: 'Go on, have a look, is *that* a bloody lie?'

He went out to the corridor so Jane could calm her down. While he was there he attempted to convince the sister that what he was doing was his duty, and he had to do it that way, because although he, personally, was convinced it was a serious case, the rules said that once an officer had heard the witness, it was his job to drive a horse and cart through what she said, and that by calling her a liar to her face he was merely trying to establish her veracity. The sister said she was going to report him and he showed her his warrant card and waited until she had written it all down. When she told him he was as bad as the rapist, if not

35

worse, he was inclined to agree. He still had the image of the blood-soaked bulge inside the paper hospital knickers, and the streaks of mud and dried blood down the insides of her legs when he went back to apologise to her. When she didn't answer and wouldn't look at him he knew he had got through to her. They were aware of each other now in a way that Jane and Cromer were not. It was a breakthrough, of a sort. He looked at her reddened neck.

'Ellie, it's not going to get any easier.'

'Can't get any worse.'

'Yes it can,' he said. 'Did you have a climax?'

'What?'

'An orgasm.'

Jane took hold of her hand. 'Just say yes or no.'

'Jesus Christ.'

'Did you experience any sexual pleasure during intercourse?'

'No.'

'What did you experience?'

'Pain.'

'The whole time?'

'Yes, the whole time.'

'Have you had any previous sexual experience?'

'Can I have another cigarette please? Yes is the answer, by the way.'

'Have you ever been convicted of prostitution or similar related offences?'

'No.'

'Have any sexual offences been committed against you in the past either as an adult or a child?'

'No.'

'When did you first start having sexual intercourse?'

'When I was eighteen.'

36

'How many different partners have you had in that time?'

'God, I don't know. You mean altogether? Every one?' She looked at Jane for help.

'Approximately.'

'About a dozen.'

'Twelve?'

'But only four what you'd call lovers.'

'Do you have a sexual relationship now?'

'No. No I don't.'

'When was the last time?'

'August. Look, how long does this go on for?'

'It can go on for up to twelve hours – not all at once.'

'No wonder people don't bother.'

'What?'

'To report things.' She turned to Jane. 'When do I get a bath?'

'After the internal examination.'

'Great.'

Vic fished a creased list from the back of his pocket-book. 'Just say yes if you've had any of the following. Don't answer if you haven't.' *Your starter for ten*, he thought. 'Syphilis. Gonorrhoea. Trichomoniasis. Herpes. Thrush – '

'Yes.'

'Vaginitis. Cystitis. Crabs. Scabies. Genital warts. Non-specific urethritis.'

'Yes. Any more?'

'Do you have any of these conditions now?'

'No.'

'Good.' Vic folded up his piece of paper. 'Let's hope you don't get any.'

'Let's.'

'Have you had an abortion?'

'No.'

37

'Are you pregnant?'

'I hope not.'

'If you are pregnant as a result of rape –'

'I can get an abortion on the NHS.'

'Yes.'

'Terrific.'

'Plus of course you'll be tested for VD.'

'And I'll get a blood test for AIDS.'

'That's right.'

'The bastard.'

'That's right.'

He started to tell her what was likely to happen in court – since technically she was only a witness, not the complainant, she would not be represented by a barrister or have access to one – when the sister came in. The doctor was ready for her. Ellie asked who it was and the sister said Doctor Chaudhury. Ellie said she was glad it wasn't someone called Simmons. The sister opened the door for Vic to leave. He stood up.

'Ellie, when you said he smelled as if he'd just had a bath, was it any particular kind of smell, one you might recognise?'

'No. He just smelled very clean.'

5

What he really needed was to get obliterated.

He'd had a couple of pints in the Greyhound, then a couple more in the Portcullis. Now he was three-quarters of the way through a bottle of Beaujolais. She'd bitched and nagged when he got home, but she was always like that when she got dressed up. Nervous to get out. Then she'd moaned about his driving on the way to the Anchor, put her face in her hands and said was he trying to kill them or what?

But she'd breezed in, and everybody had turned to look at her in her black dress and her tan shoulders and her cream platinum hair – cut off to swing along the jawline and show the length of her neck – and Nick the barman had given her a big arms-open hello and a kiss, and said she looked like a pint of Guinness. She went for that, and after a couple of gin and tonics, the brittleness left her voice.

Now she was looking at him, her slim grey eyes sliding over him, her back arched on the chair, pushing her tits towards him. He felt her stockinged foot feeling between his legs. She had her chin up and was licking her small teeth with the tip of her tongue. This was another act. Take me, I'm ready. For the benefit of anybody who might be watching. Look at that lovely young couple in the corner, they must be all over each other.

The trouble was he already knew what she'd got inside her knickers.

'Nice,' she said.

'Who, me?'

'The avocado. All yummy and creamy.' She was off on her own again. 'Like come ought to taste but doesn't.'

'Is that right?' He remembered her in a tennis skirt, at Redland, with a dark grey Golf GTI in the car park. How clean she'd looked, how desirable. And underneath was this mess.

'Hey.'

'What?'

'You,' she said. 'You're always looking round.'

'I can't help that.'

'I know you can't.'

'I don't mean that.'

'To see if anything better's come in.'

'How could it?'

'Fresher, then.' She half closed her eyes and blew a thin stream of smoke at him to show she knew him. If only she did. If only she hadn't told him to save it for the match. If only . . .

Periodically, since the nurse, he'd found himself waiting. Waiting for the warm noisy bar to stop dead, for the cold air to come wafting in, for someone he knew to walk up and look at him and say Hello Frank, got a minute? Waiting to drop into cold black water. He should never have sat with his back to the door but she'd done it deliberately. He finished his glass and poured another.

The door opened again. She smiled up as a couple they knew sidled past. The man had his hand cupped closely behind the woman's tight black grosgrain backside. It looked as if he was trying to catch one of her farts.

'You even fancy that, don't you?'

'No I don't.' He took her slim brown hand and

40

grooved his thumbnail across her palm. 'I want to fuck you. You.'

'Don't, Frank.'

'Why not?' he said. 'It's true.'

'You always want to fuck me. Don't you?'

'Yes.'

'Why?' She'd be telling him next men and women were different and not everybody felt like it all the time, so why did he?

'Why not?' he said.

'You think you always will?'

'Always.' He felt part of himself turn to stone.

She leaned back, satisfied. 'Do it to me now.' She looked round, pushed her bottom forward off the chair, inviting him between her legs.

He pushed his chair back. 'All right –'

'No, don't –'

'Why not, we're married.' He started to get down under the table.

'Frank –'

'What?'

'Please don't.' For a moment she looked terrified, and then, when he got back in his chair again, pleased.

He had steak and frites, with mangetouts, she had salmon and small boiled new potatoes which she put in her mouth delicately but whole on the end of her fork as though they were his testicles.

'I wanted to this morning,' she said. 'After you'd gone.'

'Typical,' he said. It was the way everything stopped when you hit a patch of black ice. All you could do was wait and see if you were going to go sideways into the armco. If only – but she'd never liked it much in the morning, and, if he really thought about it, calmly,

41

soberly thought about it, there was no way the nurse could get him. No way. 'So what did you do?'

'Nothing,' she smirked down at her plate. 'I waited.'

He thought of her lying on the bed naked, the sun slanting across her through the curtains. He knew she played with herself when he was out because she told him: knew it excited him. 'Have another drink.'

'I can't.' She was waiting for permission. 'Can I?'

'Let's have another bottle. Let's get smashed.'

'What if we get stopped?'

'We'll go the back way.'

They had Monbazillac with the *crème brûlée*, then two cafés calva. He drank most of hers, paid the bill in a haze and left just before eleven. There'd be no patrol on the back road until half-past.

He was thinking about the bill and she was concentrating on heaving the big Renault round the narrow lanes. Fifty-four quid he'd spent on her, and he still felt sober. He knew why as soon as she pushed the Dire Straits tape in the slot – there was the nurse again, and the rain, and men waiting when he got home. There was only a couple of inches of Scotch left in the cupboard and that was about it. He'd have to give her one – he needed to give her one – he needed to put something between himself and Hensman's Hill. Even if it was only the wife.

Sitting in the car with the heater taking the last slivers of frost off the windscreen, he could still smell the nurse, inside his nose. Oatmeal, like Johnson's Baby Powder, and something else warmer, meatier.

He started to mess around with her. She stared through the windscreen, dissociating her face, acting. His hand closed over the harsh lace front panel, and then, as she wanted him to, he squeezed her protec-

42

tively, and slid his fingers in from one side. He stroked her once, twice, feeling the flattened damp hair, and then she opened up, hot and juicy. He felt her cunt gulping at his finger, and felt sad.

'Frank, I'm going to have to stop.'

'Don't,' he said. 'Keep going. Go on, Rae.'

'Oh God.'

'Do it while you're driving.'

'I can't, I'll crash.'

'No you won't.'

'Frank, I want you.'

'Go on.' He'd got two fingers up her now.

'I want you inside me.' She glanced at him quickly, her eyes dark and hopeless, drowning in whatever it was she felt. 'Please.'

He made her go on until they came to the turning for the brickworks. He'd been here before, but not with her. Oh God, she was saying, Oh God, I want to come Frank, I want to come.

'Pull in now.'

'Christ,' she said, 'I'm glad it's an automatic.' The car rocked as she wrenched the handbrake on.

'Careful, woman.'

'Sorry.'

He pushed his seat back and lowered it while she was hauling her dress and slip above her waist and arching her back to strip off her black french knickers. The white suspender belt glowed faintly in the green light from the key in the ignition. She kicked her shoes off, weaselled herself across underneath him, and pulled her knees up to her chest with her hands so he could get down on the floor. She lay with her head back, wide open to him, looking at the stars.

'Nobody's coming, are they?'

'Not yet they're not.'

43

He eased himself down, stroking the soft flesh inside her thighs, and playing with her, then crouched and spread her more open with her hands and sucked her. He started to get a crick in his neck trying to get his tongue into her, so he nuzzled her up and down with his nose, and then fastened his mouth on her clitoris and sucked it in and out between his lips and tongue. Then, because he sensed she was enjoying it so much she was trying not to come – and the crick in his neck was getting worse – he took it between his teeth and nibbled at it, wanting to bite it, bite it hard, bite it off –

'Frank, Frank, I'm coming.'

He gave her a long flickering lick with his tongue just to make sure she really was, and then reared up over her, his face wet, and pushed it in. Her eyes opened wide, and then grew starry and unfocused. He loved watching her come. The way her mouth widened, and stuck in a grimace that looked like pain at first, or shock, and then slowly lost its tension and became loose, and smiley, and grateful. And her eyes fixed in a long inward-seeing stare, widening only slightly as the waves went through her.

She seemed totally oblivious of the rest of her convulsing away beneath him like a different animal. He envied her that. He liked the sense of power, of covering her, being up her, giving her one, but he wasn't going to come. That was what she wanted, and she'd got enough. Darling, she was saying, darling, darling, darling. It was the only time she called him that, the only time she used that voice. He loved it, loved watching her face, beautiful now she was starting to get into the peace and the satisfaction of it, and he supposed that since he was giving her so much pleasure he must love her.

Or was it guilt over the nurse? He glanced up,

watching for headlights through the back window. The brown grid of the demister looked like a cage.

When she finished and her body collapsed back into the seat, he said 'Good girl', and held on to her until she stopped throbbing. Then she sighed as she always did, as if she'd just had a good meal.

'Oh,' she said, 'I needed that.'

She wasn't bad, really. If she was someone else's wife she'd be terrific.

He drove the rest of the way home, his left hand on top of her head, stroking and lifting her pale hair, cool and heavy as silk, as she sucked him. He glanced down at the back of her neck, and thought of the nurse.

When they got to bed, and Rae turned her back on him and pushed herself sleepily against him, he fucked her from behind, and when he came, he felt miserable and savage and alone. Then she slid into his arms and said she wanted to have his baby.

He turned over on his back and stared at the ceiling.

'Hello Eleanor, how are we then, old girl?' Doctor Chaudhury was his usual self, smelling faintly of Meggezones, a short, bustling man with rough black hair, parted neatly on the side but sticking out at the back. She had done her obstetrics with him, and had often, standing behind him over some poor woman, wanted to get a brush and part his hair properly, higher up, to get rid of the tuft.

'Not too bad.'

'Good-oh.'

She was lying flat on her back on the examination couch. There was a butterfly transfer on the ceiling just behind her head, and if she kept her eyes on it, she couldn't see the stirrups dangling at the other end. When he came into view she saw he was wearing one of his better dark blue suits. Probably going out to dinner.

'Sorry, doctor.'

'Not to worry, not to worry now at all.' Then, looking at her seriously through his square black-rimmed glasses, 'It's the rest of us who are sorry, let me tell you that. If sorry is the word for this – ' He stood by her, taking her pulse. Then he shone a flashlight in her eyes, moved her head gently on to its side and looked into her ear, and felt the hotness of the skin around it.

'Thank you, sister.' He turned away, making a couple of notes with a silver pencil, while the sister lifted Ellie's bare legs into the padded hoops and pulled up the operating gown.

She kept her eyes on the butterfly as he examined her breasts, and the bruising and abrasions on her arms. He felt the palms of her hands, and then prodded her stomach and pushed his fingers into her groin, looking up at her for signs of pain. His fingers were warm and dry, and his voice, now he was working, very gentle and Indian. 'Does that hurt? That? Is this tender here?' He massaged the area of her ovaries and saw her flinch.

'If you could cover up her top please, sister.' She heard him move round to the foot of the couch, and felt herself closing up. There was some metallic clinks and then his face appeared, smiling, between the twin hills of her knees. 'I'm going to have a good look at you, take a couple of pictures, then get some swabs. All right, Eleanor?'

'Yes doctor.' *Don't hurt me.*

'It's going to be the old stainless steel ice-cream cones, I'm afraid.'

'Yes doctor.' It was what he said when he thought women needed distracting. There were a couple of bright white flashes, and then a couple more. The

46

doctor and the sister spoke in low voices, a cupboard door opened and closed; she heard the rustle of the thin plastic examination glove – then fierce red pain ran up inside her and she screamed louder than she had ever thought possible. Her ears rang and her throat burned but the pain was still there.

'You're going to have to try and relax, Eleanor.'

'Sorry.'

There was a long period in which she could feel nothing but pain, and then he said, 'Well, that's it.' She heard the sister breathing out, and him peeling his gloves off.

'It still hurts like bloody hell.'

'Eleanor, listen.' He came round to the side of the bed and sat on it. 'There's no serious internal damage as far as I can see. There is some external bleeding, and you'll feel sore for a couple of days –'

'*Sore?*'

'But that should sort itself out without too much bother, certainly no need for stitching, and we'll have another look at you in the morning. OK?'

Ellie tried not to cry out as the sister removed her legs from the stirrups. 'Yes, doctor.'

'The reason you're in so much pain my dear is that your muscles have gone into spasm. You're like a clenched fist.' He smiled at her, showing his gold tooth. 'But not to worry.'

Vic looked at the two Polaroids Doctor Chaudhury laid on the desk. For a second he thought: so that's what her quim looks like. Then he thought: poor cow.

Like all the medical photographs he'd ever seen, the lighting made the flesh look dead. Pink, bright, glistening, and dead.

'If you will look here, sergeant –' the doctor was

47

pointing with the tip of his silver pencil – 'you will see a slight laceration.' Vic looked, but he could see nothing. There was a faint iron-brown patch to one side of a small lip of flesh, but nothing he would call a laceration. 'Can you see it, just here?' The pencil tapped the curved surface of the Polaroid.

'No doctor, I can't.' It would be no good as evidence – if Vic couldn't see it, the jury never would.

'OK, now look at this one.' The doctor switched pictures and held the second one down firmly with his pencil. 'There, you see the blood?'

'Are these all the pictures you've got, Doctor Chaudhury?'

'Can you see this smear of blood here, or not?'

'No, to be honest.' To Vic, the brown patch, no more than a quarter of an inch long, looked darker but that was all.

'I see.' The doctor looked over his spectacles at Vic. 'Are you familiar with this part of a woman?'

'Not particularly – not to look at.'

'But can you see this brown area?'

'Yes, I can see that.'

'That is the lesion, and the bruising. The flesh is torn there. Where it should be pink, it is liver brown. That is the blood, both on and under the surface.' He put his finger and thumb together and jabbed at the flesh at the base with his silver pencil. 'And that is how it is caused. By the penis being withdrawn, and forcibly re-inserted – in the wrong place.' He rubbed the faint pencil marks away. 'This man was trying to make his own hole, sergeant.'

'I see.'

'You understand it, in those terms?'

'Yes, but would a jury? Would another doctor, another gynaecologist agree?'

'I would think so. This is not the sort of lesion caused during parturition, childbirth – by the baby's head coming out. This is quite, quite different.'

'Could it be caused by some other object?'

'I think there would be likely to be even more damage.'

'Self-inflicted?'

'To cause that sort of pain? No, and the angle is wrong, if you think about it, quite wrong.'

'You would say rape then, would you, doctor?'

'Oh yes.'

'What else have you got?'

Doctor Chaudhury picked up the Polaroids. 'I do have a couple on thirty-five mil, but these have yet to be developed, you understand.'

'Anything else?'

'Unfortunately no, sergeant.' He took off his spectacles and wiped them with a circular lens tissue. 'No sperm, no seminal fluid, no bodily secretions.' He replaced his spectacles and looked sternly at Vic, his purplish lips compressed to a line. 'This swine was a very clean bugger.'

6

'Unlucky my son, it's just started.' Billy Jewel, proprietor of the Kit Kat, had curly gold hair this week. His face, once handsome, now chubby from drink, was a deep sun-bed orange. He wore a blazer, shades, a yellow and red spotted bow-tie, and stood behind the bar with his tanned palms flat on the counter. A gold Rolex dangled loosely from his left wrist, a gold identity bracelet from his right. Without taking his eyes off the rostrum stage on the other side of the room, he reached up, plugged a large thick-bottomed glass twice into the Famous Grouse optic and planted it in front of Vic. 'Ice is off,' he said.

The house lights went down, disco thudded out, and a thin pretty girl with brown eye make-up and skin the colour of chalk walked out under the ropy glitterball, took all her clothes off, writhed about for a minute, and then when the music stopped and the house lights came up she bent down, picked up her clothes, and walked off into the wings, where, in full view of the punters, she put them back on again. Billy picked up the microphone behind the bar and said, 'That was Pauline, ladies and gentlemen and I'm sure you'd all like to give her a nice warm hand on her opening.'

Nobody clapped, nobody moved.

'No seriously, folks, Pauline. I'm sure we're all going to see a lot more of her here at the Kit Kat. Pauline White, ladies and gentlemen, wants to travel and eat people, Pauline is an art student working her way through college, thank you *Pauline*.'

The Kit Kat, off Park Street, had once been the lounge bar of a decent old pub. A series of brewery improvements had driven the customers away, the long narrow room had been stripped out, and Billy Jewel had picked up the last two years of the lease. Now it had a bar at each end and nothing in the middle except the eight-by-four rostrum stage, two badly hung black drapes, a dusty floor and the glitterball. With the house lights on, Vic could see that a large chunk of its mirror glass was missing.

'What happened?'

'Oh, some fucking yob threw a bottle at it.'

'You report it?'

'I wasn't here, was I?'

'Auditioning again?'

'Yeah, again.' Billy looked up and down the bar, leaned forward. 'Mandy was fucking furious. Still, what can you do? We're all led by our dicks.'

'Some more than others.'

'Come on, Vic, they put it on a plate, fucking rude not to eat it. They get paid, they get to do a number.'

'Here?'

'Everybody's got to start somewhere. Look at Elvis.'

'He didn't take his clothes off in front of your missis, did he?'

'Never asked her.'

'They do.'

'Yeah, well life's fucking rough, isn't it? Yours pisses off, mine won't. Same difference.' Billy's arm slung round to the optic, jerked a couple into his highball glass. 'No offence, sergeant – little drop, ease the pain?'

'Why not?' Vic watched him. 'You always do that without looking?'

'You can't take your eye off the punters in a place like this. She still chasing you for money?'

'Haven't heard from her in months.'

'Fucking laughing, then.'

'Does it look it?'

'Yeah well, as the man in the song said.'

'What?'

'It's only a hole with hairs round, but it's made a cunt out of me.'

The lights went down again, and a tall black girl in a Supremes wig walked on to the stage, took off a shiny red dress to a disco version of 'Da Doo Ron Ron', danced in a bored, stoned kind of way, and finally took off her lilac bra and held her small pointed breasts out to the audience. The light played over them for a while. Then, as the music came to an end, she put her bra back on again and bowed. Her wig fell off and lay on the stage like a headless Yorkshire terrier.

'Thank you Suki,' boomed Billy's voice. 'A big hand now for Suki Brown. Next week, Walking the Dog.' He switched off and spoke into Vic's ear. 'Make your eyes water.'

'No thanks.'

'You got it all about you tonight, haven't you? How about Pauline, then? Talk to Pauline, lovely girl, comes from Newcastle under Lyme.'

'I'm working, Billy.'

'I pour fucking good Scotch down his throat, provide him with the finest cabaret this side of Eastville and now I get busted for what — soliciting, right?'

'Rape —'

'Yeah, yellow stuff grows in fields, very pretty —'

'I'm working on a rape case, Billy.'

'No shit.'

'Girl in Clifton. Nurse. Hensman's Hill, some time round seven.'

'I was with the vicar in the vestry getting the come stains off his chaplain. Or was it his chaplet?'

'Billy –'

'You're a bit fucking depressed, old son.'

'Yeah.'

'This is the real bagful of snot, is it?'

'Has the look.'

'Fancy a smoke?'

'No.'

'Come over here.' He started to move round the corner of the bar, then lifted his left arm to look at his Rolex. 'Hang slack.' He picked up the microphone, ejected the cassette and slid in a new one. There was a roll of drums. 'And now ladies and gentlemen, the one, the only, the moment you've been waiting for, the event *de la nuit* down here at the Kit Kat, please welcome on to the floor, by kind permission of the RSPCA, on special release from the vet school across the road, your very own special favourite, the glamorous, the glittering, the great – *Greta Cripple!*'

A big black-haired woman in a sequinned black dress slid herself awkwardly off her bar stool, swayed for a moment, turned to put out a cigarette, and then set off for the rostrum. She walked slowly, flinging her arms out and her head back, sashaying like Shirley Bassey. Greta was about fifty-five and heavily built.

The bouncer, a solemn-faced black guy called Ellard, helped her up on to the stage. The music was, inevitably, 'Big Spender', and as soon as she began it was obvious that she had, once, been a real striptease artist.

'You want to stay and see the tin leg?'

'Not tonight,' said Vic.

The office had a sink, an open catering-size tin of

53

powdered coffee, and a desk scarred with cigarette burns. Billy offered Vic the only chair, metal-framed with a brown Rexine seat, spread a tea towel across the corner of the desk and sat on it.

'Billy Jewel, this is your fucking life,' he said. 'Fucking machine-gunners have repo'd everything. You know they even got fucking female bailiffs now. I don't know why I go on, Vic. I deserve a fucking Arts Council fucking subsidy running this place. Fuck showbusiness.' He lit a Raffles. 'Half the fucking punters'll be gone by the time we get back. See me coming in here with you. More fucking broken glass.'

'This bloke dresses up.'

'What in?'

'Black.'

'Yeah, well that makes sense, but look, Vic – '

'He wears a stocking mask, balaclava and a beret.'

'These mushes here, they couldn't rape their way out of a paper bag. They're AA fucking rejects – you've seen 'em, they're the walking dead as far as women are concerned, that's what they come here to get away from.'

'Somebody must watch the strippers.'

'Yeah, I do.'

'Tall, fairly young, probably, smells very clean.'

'That lets this lot out then.'

'Let me know, will you?'

'If it was GBH or kids shooting up in the toilets, yeah, we don't like that. But we don't get any weirdos in here, Vic, they're all dickheads mostly – I mean, *I* wouldn't come here, would you? This is a naff joint, double armpits no rosettes. *Vaut le détour*. Worth fucking avoiding. We get the occasional Pakamac man but only on rubber nights. Rapists, Jesus, who knows from rapists? I can ask, is all.'

'Thanks Billy.'

'Mandy's into this boarding-kennel shit, she says that's where the money is, but I don't know, taking poodles out to crap. There's got to be another way.'

The thudding stopped, and there was a thin scattering of applause. Billy stood up. 'Good old Greet,' he said. 'And we think we've got it rough. One for the frog and toad?'

Vic felt good in the cold air. The Scotch had warmed him, put some distance between him and Doctor Chaudhury's Polaroids. He had been right to tell Billy. It would be all round the clubs in a couple of hours, and most villains had something on somebody or other. It was part of their stock in trade, to be exchanged for favours. They'd trawl something up. It might not be of any use right now, but it would explain where he'd been for the last hour.

Park Street was empty from top to bottom. He crossed over into Charlotte Street and walked up the hill towards his car. The red air beacon flashed on Cabot Tower, and in the blackness over Brandon Hill he could see a few stars.

In the car his mood changed and he started thinking about Pat. Trish as she was now. Jesus Christ, like a tart's name in a phone box. The last time she had phoned up, about six weeks ago, it was almost as if she wanted his approval for what she'd done, and when he pointed this out, she said why was he always so fucking hard on her and slammed the phone down. Hard. It was nothing to do with hard, it was pride. He was the one who'd been dumped, what was he supposed to do – like it? Ring her up and talk to some fucking secondhand BMW car salesman or whoever it was screwing her and say 'Congratulations, all the best,

55

and what about a spot of golf some time?' Well, fuck it. And her. But what Vic had since found out about pride was that it was only a crust on the same old shit underneath.

He could still see her blonde hair, all scragged up Dallas-fashion, and the curve of her long bare back, but not the rest of her, not her face. Six months, he thought, and nothing in between. Why? In case she came back and started smart-arsing on about all the women he'd been off with? Then making out it was all right because, well, she'd had a good time too. He had bad moments like that, seeing them back together having some cosy chat in some dark lounge bar somewhere, making up, pretending it was all right again. But it wasn't all right. She'd cut his balls off, and if she came back, if she asked and he was cunt enough to let her, it would only be to make her pay, and that was no good. It was over, finished, but he hadn't moved on, he hadn't moved anywhere, he'd just stopped.

He drove slowly round the empty Centre and out towards the Bridewell.

Billy had been very good. No sympathy, just Scotch. Billy didn't want to know and Vic couldn't tell him, not without tears pissing down his face, and he could save all that for the bedroom. Instead, Billy shoved birds at him, but none of them smelled right, or looked right, or was right, and Billy had been through them all anyway.

Besides, he knew Billy, and if he got into that, one day there'd be a price to pay, a favour to perform. The Scotch he could wear, no problem. But it still felt as if some bastard had heaved a television set through a plate-glass window, and six months later he was still full of broken glass.

On the way up in the lift to the fourth floor of the

Well, he thought about the nurse throwing back the bedclothes and saying 'Go on have a look, is *that* a bloody lie?'

All that anger, that pain, coming out of some place you never knew you had inside you. He knew what that felt like. She should hang on to that. He'd tell her the next time he saw her. He wondered if the WPC had rung the Rape Crisis Centre. Poor cow, she didn't know what she was letting herself in for.

Stick with it, girl, we'll get this bastard. He could hear himself saying it. In Vic's mind it was the same man who was screwing his wife.

Whoever that was.

The squad room on the fourth was low and grey with inset daylight strip lighting. There was a smell of tin ashtrays, and underneath it, oil, metal and sweat, like old overalls. All six desks faced inwards so that the customers had only the walls to look at. Two DCs were tapping away, a third was talking to an old dosser with crinkly grey hair and a bandaged hand, Detective Sergeant Des Chaffey had his feet up reading an early copy of the *Mail on Sunday*, and Cromer sat in the far corner, hunched over a Siemens terminal, his face pale green from the glow. He looked up as Vic walked in and noted the time. 01.47. When Vic sat beside him, Cromer smelled his breath.

'How's it going, John?'

'All right.' He sounded sullen.

'Anything from Forensic yet?'

'They sent a prelim.' He pushed the file over, unopened. Inside was a single sheet. Size 10 Nike trainers. No fabric. No hair. No tissue. No semen.

'What about the computer?'

'You want national or local?'

57

'As you wish, John, as you wish.' Maybe Cromer thought he'd missed out, not going to the Kit Kat. On the other hand – Vic looked at the pink cheeks, the slightly protruding blue eyes, the flop of brown hair cut fashionably short at the sides, the pretty little mouth – he looked too much of a mother's boy. But he was definitely pissed off about something. It showed in his tone.

'There's one in Gateshead wears black leather, another in Liverpool dresses up as a priest. Neither reported anywhere else. Plenty of stocking masks, one or two balaclavas. A couple who look like lorry drivers –'

'No berets?'

'No. No berets, no overalls.'

'What about locally?'

'Eight rapes reported, four attempted. All except one inside the family, and the one was a babysitter.' He turned over the page of his notebook. 'Seven assaults in the Clifton area, five since the 28th.'

Vic decided to give him a chance. 'What does that suggest, John?'

'Not a lot. Descriptions don't tally –'

'No, the 28th.'

'It was a Saturday, it was half-term, lot of Halloween parties.'

'It was the day they put the clocks back,' said Vic. 'It gets darker earlier.'

'Oh.'

'What's the matter, John?'

'Nothing.'

'How far have you gone back with the local stuff?'

'Three years.'

'Found anybody you know?'

Cromer looked at the screen. It was page 5 of 6 of an

58

investigating officer's report on the witness's sexual history, including her preferences, and ended with a graphic description of the attack. The witness's name was Miriam Lomax, she was seventy-eight, and she'd been hit over the head with the brass poker from the companion set she'd been given as a wedding present and left with a milk bottle stuck up her. The defendant was a boy of sixteen who claimed his mates had got him drunk on cider.

'I reckon they should be castrated.'

So that was it. For all his fresh-faced blue-eyed-boy look Cromer was one of those. Or if he wasn't he soon would be. Strong views and the funny handshake went together.

'And you'd do it, would you?'

Cromer gestured at the screen. 'Grandfathers with girls of six and seven –'

'We catch this bloke, you'd cut his balls off?'

'No –'

'Why?'

'It's not our job, is it?'

'No, thank fuck.'

Cromer pushed his chair back and folded his arms. 'They can give these guys medical treatment nowadays.'

'Stop them screwing altogether?'

'I wouldn't call it that.'

'I didn't think you would,' said Vic. 'What would you call it?'

The blue eyes were quite cold. 'Part of the punishment.'

'Part of it?'

'Yes.'

'I see.' Vic glanced down at the report, and then

shoved it back to Cromer. 'Not a lot to go on. What do you make of him?'

'I don't know what the doctor said, do I?'

'The doctor said this swine is a very clean bugger.'

'Meaning what?'

'Meaning he did an internal and there was no sign of any sperm but the guy had made the poor cow's cunt bleed.'

'Sergeant –'

'What is it?'

'Do we have to use those terms?'

'Are you a religious man then, John?'

'Yes I am, as it happens.'

'Fair enough,' said Vic. 'What variety?'

'Wesleyan Methodist.'

'Right.' He wouldn't be joining the Lodge then. That was something. 'Sorry, John.'

'That's all right,' said Cromer. 'I knew I'd have to mention it sooner or later.'

'Sooner would have been better. Get a lot of stick over it?'

'To start with.'

'Yeah. I can imagine.' No wonder he looked like a fucking choirboy. 'If this is going to be too difficult for you –'

'That's my problem –'

Yeah, thought Vic, and mine. 'Right, tomorrow you chase up Doctor Chaudhury for a couple of negatives.'

'What of?'

'Damage to the vaginal area.'

'Fine.'

Vic watched him write it down word for word, and wondered how much more he was going to have to spell out. 'Now then according to the witness, this bloke ejaculated, or at least she thought he did, but there's no sperm. What does that suggest?'

'He was using a condom.'

'Have you ever used a condom, John?'

'Yes,' said Cromer, reddening.

'Ever had one burst on you?'

'Yes I have.'

'Doesn't take much, does it?'

'No, it doesn't.' Cromer's face was red from the neck up.

'You get on the vinegar strokes and that's it. Twang.' Vic leaned back in his chair. 'This bloke's didn't.'

'No, you're right.' Cromer was looking at him differently now, paying attention at last.

'Even though he was banging away at her. Bloody hard, as she said. So what do we make of that?'

'He could have been wearing a washable.'

'Mean bugger,' said Vic. 'You ever tried one?'

'No.'

'Me neither.' Vic lit a cigarette and blew smoke at the screen. 'How many of these blokes d'you think use french letters?'

'No idea.'

'None,' said Vic. 'None I've ever come across anyway. They like to stick it up raw, that's part of it.'

'But now they can match the sperm to the bloke –'

'Yeah. This bloke might be weird, but he's not fucking thick.'

'Student?'

'He's not out to get caught is he? Yeah, student's a possibility. What else?'

'He's tall –'

'Size tens –'

'He smells very clean –'

'See if Forensic can give us some idea of weight –'

61

'Right –'

'As if he'd just had a bath,' said Vic. 'Saturday night, though. What about this beret?'

'Something to do with his hair?'

'Bit fucking belt and braces, isn't it? Stocking mask, balaclava and beret –'

'Overalls –'

'All stuff you can burn, see, John. No, it's this fucking Durex. That's his signature. Too mean to part with his own fucking spunk.'

'Or too cunning.'

'You try that on the computer?'

'What, condoms? No –'

'Well you should have,' said Vic.

They spent the next twenty minutes scrolling through the files and pulling out all references to contraceptives, condoms, french letters, Durex, johnnies and rubbers. It was something Cromer was good at, and he tapped away at the keys, muttering instructions to himself. When he got to LIST ALL and TOTAL, out of 481 rape and assault cases, they had only seven mentions and two uses, both assailants arrested.

Vic gazed at the green and black screen. It was page 5 of 6 on Miriam Lomax again. 'You know what they do with all this stuff, John?'

'How d'you mean?' Cromer's eyes were red-rimmed.

'They Xerox it and the screws flog it to the cons to wank over.'

'Fuckin' hell,' said Cromer.

He was putting the cover on the Siemens when Des Chaffey put the phone down and called Vic over. A young woman had been found dead in the bushes by Cabot Tower on Brandon Hill. Her name was Pauline White and it looked as if she'd been murdered, and probably raped. Chaffey wondered if there might be some connection.

In the car on the way up to Brandon Hill Cromer told Vic he was engaged to a girl called Louise who had her own hairdressing salon in Fishponds. It turned out the Methodists didn't go a lot on sex before marriage but if a couple were engaged it was different. Vic said he was separated, and left it at that. He could still see Pauline bending over to pick up her clothes and the vertebrae sticking out under her chalk-white skin. She couldn't have been more than eighteen, and for some reason it made Vic feel as if he'd been punched in the stomach, or just under the heart. Maybe it was seeing her in the Kit Kat less than an hour ago. He wondered what Billy Jewel would have to say this time.

7

She wasn't in the bushes, she was halfway down the slope, her head among the roots and nettles of a wind-shaped hawthorn and the bare fork of her legs pointing up the hill. She looked as if she'd been thrown there. Her face was blotched with blood from her nose, and her body, naked inside an old waxed jacket, looked even whiter under the lights. Around her the grass had frosted to a pale eau-de-nil and was bruised with a dozen sets of footprints.

The photographic assistant was holding a portable sun-gun about three feet above her head and his boss, in a teddy-bear car coat, was on his knees zooming into her face with a Sony camcorder. Her mouth had been forced open by her tongue and the lips were mauve in the blinding light. Teddy Bear got awkwardly to his feet and continued to move his camera down the length of her body, tracked by the assistant with the sun-gun. There were marks on her neck and scratches on her arms and legs. An ambulancewoman stood nearby holding a grey blanket waiting for them to finish. Vic walked round the body, careful not to step on any of the footmarks.

Cromer followed him to the small knot of men standing by the Police Land Rover. A fair-haired kid about twenty in a tartan jacket was being held apart from the others by a uniformed constable. He looked very pale.

'You should be getting used to this, Cromer,' said Vic. 'Stay with the body, watch them do the SOC, and try and have a word with the blond kiddie. The DI turns up, I'll be twenty minutes.'

'Why, where you going?' Cromer looked nervous.

'See the guy she worked for.'

Greta and the tall dark girl, Suki, were sitting on the rostrum in their street clothes. They were holding on to each other and Suki was making short pained noises into the fur collar of Greta's coat. When Vic came into the empty room she stopped and glared up at him. Without the wig, she had a short flat top like a basketball player. Vic smiled and showed his warrant card. 'Good evening, ladies. Detective Sergeant Hallam.'

'Yeah,' said Suki.

'All right, love,' Greta winked at Vic. 'She's upset.'

'Sorry to trouble you –'

'Where the WPC, man? You want to get a woman cop in here.'

'You want to wait and see if one turns up?'

'Now then Suki,' said Greta.

'Hassling me –'

'All I need to know, names and addresses, what time Miss White left, who with. If anybody.'

Neither of them spoke. Greta made a face at Vic: you see what I've got to put up with? Suki had her chin up, showing she wasn't scared. Her eyes were wide and Vic could see she was waiting to be outraged, discriminated against. Hair-trigger ready for it. No wonder black blokes went after white girls.

'Come on, doll.' Greta looked at her watch. 'We can still get in the Dug Out.' Suki made a noise with her teeth. 'The Bamba, then.'

'All I want to know –' said Vic.

'How we know that, how we know you don't want to keep us here till shit flies?'

65

'Because I'm telling you –'

'You always telling us –'

'Look, Miss Brown –'

'Ain't my name.'

'All right, girl,' said Vic. 'Your friend Pauline's dead. She's almost certainly been raped and murdered. You don't want to help, you don't want to help. You want a WPC, we'll get a WPC. You want to go now, what time did she leave?'

'Then we go?'

'Sure.'

'Shit.'

'Suke –' Greta's look said take no notice, she's stoned.

'You believe this man?'

'Course, love. He's a friend of Billy's, isn't he?'

'That's right,' said Vic. 'I'm a friend of Billy's.'

'Ellard!' He came out of the shadows by the stairs, a match between his teeth. 'You know him?'

'Right.'

'Well tell him,' said Suki. 'Tell a man what time Pauline leff.'

'Pauline?' said Ellard. 'She left about ten to two, Mister Hallam. She did her last spot, had a drink at the bar and –'

'Who with?'

'Who she have a drink with?'

'Leave with.'

Ellard removed the match from his teeth, looked at the end, split it and replaced it. 'She got her own kyar in Charlotte Street, she have no trouble walking up there.'

'Not much,' said Vic.

Ellard shrugged. 'What she said.'

'What kind of car?'

66

'Little blue Y reg Mini.'

'Where's Billy?' Ellard's long head wagged in the direction of the office.

Mandy, a good-looking woman whose small face had grown sharp through living with Billy, walked out when Vic walked in. It looked as if she thought he'd finally got what he deserved.

Billy had his hand wrapped round his mouth and chin as though to stop himself being sick on the scarred wooden desk. Vic leaned against the wall.

'Fucked, mate,' said Billy. 'She says she's had enough. Cow. She's pissing off out of it.'

'What you wanted, isn't it?'

'It's all in her fucking name. The flat, motor, the lease and licence on this place.' He pulled a bottle out of the bottom desk drawer. It was a litre bottle with the Famous Grouse label on upside down, ready for the optic. 'Pull up a glass and sit down.'

'No thanks, Billy.'

'Oh shit. You and all.' Billy tipped the bottle up and drank from it, watching Vic as he did so.

'How did you find out, Billy?'

'Ellard. He's outside watching the mushes crawling into their motors on their hands and knees, keeping an eye out for the blue lights, and fuck me there they are, patrol car and ambulance pissing up Charlotte Street. They stop outside the churchyard and he hears one of 'em, one of the ambulance blokes. Where's the fucking stiff, then? They told us Brandon Hill. And all the punters come piling back in here begging for fucking taxis. Next thing I know the patrol car blokes are in here. Do we know anybody answering this description.' Billy's eyes started to water. He took another suck at the neck of the bottle. 'Pauline. Dead.'

'Raped and murdered, Billy.'

67

'Raped?'

'What it looks like. What they do Billy. Strangle 'em to shut 'em up.'

'Fucking hell, Vic.'

'What?'

Billy looked at the bottle, shoved it away from him. 'I walked her up to her car. My car, anyway.'

'Your car? You haven't got a licence.'

'Mand drives, doesn't she? And there's more room in the back.'

'Go on, Billy.'

'I gave her one, didn't I?' Billy tried to smile at Vic. 'She fancies me, I don't know why. I thought, well, you know – I thought it'd help clear the mind –'

'Were you wearing anything?'

'Trousers round me ankles. No french letter, no.'

'You come?'

'As it happens.'

'Inside her?'

'Yes, she's – you know – romantic, in that department.' Billy tried to keep the smile going as he sniffed and blinked and finally wiped the water out of his eyes. 'Was, anyway, poor kid.'

'You're in the shit, Billy.'

'Yeah, I know.' He lit a Raffles. 'You're not going to believe this.'

'Probably not,' said Vic.

'I had the feeling there was somebody watching. We both did. You know, you're going away at it, you suddenly think, hang on –'

'You see anybody?'

'No –'

'Hear anything?'

'Not to swear to. I mean, you stop, have a look round, you're not going to get out the car, are you?'

68

'Have you got the keys?'

Billy unclipped the keys from a gold snake chain on his belt. He offered them to Vic and then hesitated. 'How's Mandy going to get home?'

Cromer was hoping to make himself inconspicuous, watching the Murder Squad and the SOC men, biding his time to talk to the pale young kid who had found the body, but then a car drew up and Detective Chief Inspector Barnard got out and walked up to him. He planted himself right in front of Cromer, meaty-faced and flinty-eyed, hands deep in the pockets of his straight mac. Cromer could smell cigar smoke, and something sweet, like cherry brandy, in the cold air.

'Who are you, son?'

'Constable Cromer, sir. With Sergeant Hallam.'

'Since when?'

'Two days ago, sir.'

'Why?'

'Sorry sir?'

'Why are you here, son, you're not on the squad are you?'

'No sir, we had a rape case earlier sir. Sergeant Chaffey thought there might be some connection –'

'Is there? Was the other one a stripper?'

'No sir. Nurse.'

'Where's Vic?'

'Gone to see the man she works for, sir. He said to stay with the body, have a word with the chap who found her.'

'Have you?'

'No sir.'

'Why not?'

'Waiting for your lads to finish, sir.'

'What's your name again?'

69

'John Cromer, sir.'

'Wait no more, Cromer.' The DCI turned away. 'Tell Vic I'll have a word.'

The PC with the young kid said the DCI had been fetched out of the Lord Mayor's do at the Royal because both DIs were down St Pauls on a stabbing and disturbance. He asked Cromer if he was all right for a smoke. Nobody had ever asked him permission before so he said, OK five minutes. The PC, who was a couple of years older than Cromer, checked to see where the DCI was and sloped off behind the Land Rover.

Cromer took his notebook out. The kid was shivering from the cold. His name was Clive Bartlett, he was nineteen and he lived in Glentworth Road on the other side of Brandon Hill. He'd been coming back from the Watershed on the Docks with a couple of mates when they'd found her. No, they hadn't seen anybody, or heard anything. It must have been about quarter-past two. When Clive rang the police the others buggered off.

'Why did they do that?'

'I don't know,' said Clive. 'I don't know them very well. They said – they said they didn't want any trouble.'

'They dropped you in it didn't they, Clive?'

'Bastards.'

'Can't be very good mates, can they?'

'I told you, I only met them tonight.'

'You'd never met them before and you came up here with them. Wasn't very clever, was it?'

'No, not really.'

'You must have had a reason.'

'It's a short cut. I only live over there.'

'You often come up here at night?'

'If I've been out, yeah.'

'It doesn't worry you?'

'Lived here since I was ten.'

'You know what blokes usually come up here for, don't you?'

'No.' And then he grinned.

'Is that what you were doing, you and your two mates?'

'Bloody hell no –'

'You must know this place well, living here all that time.'

'I told you.'

'Is that what you were doing?'

'What?' Clive was grinning again.

'Come on, Clive, you don't want to end up in the Station all night.'

'What d'you mean?'

'You don't want me going round to see your mother, telling her what you get up to.'

'Haven't been up to anything –'

'Haven't you?'

'Look, I was the one phoned the police. Wasn't for me –'

'We've only got your word for that.'

'Eh?'

'How do we know it wasn't you? You're walking her home, you put it to her –'

'Oh Christ, man –'

'How do we know you were up here with two mates?'

'I told you –'

'You haven't told me anything. Have you?' Cromer waited, but all Clive did was shrug, look at the ground and scuff his trainers on the grass. 'It's not just me Clive, they're all going to have a go at you. If they're not satisfied with what you were doing here you could be down the Bridewell till this time tomorrow night.'

'Playing football tomorrow.'

'Were you?'

'You haven't got a cigarette, have you?'

'Don't smoke. I might be able to scrounge you one.'

'Darren Bingham and Barry Dugdale.'

Cromer wrote the names slowly into his notebook. 'And you were doing what?'

'It wasn't my idea.'

'What wasn't?'

'We'd all had a few pints, and I'd been, you know, telling 'em, and they said come on, let's go up there, see if there's any about. Have a bit of fun.'

'Doing what?'

'You know,' Clive looked up defiantly. 'Poof-bashing.'

Cromer followed the ambulance trolley down the ramp to the post-mortem room in the basement of the Bridewell. The wheels rattled and echoed on the ridged concrete, and once the door closed on the orange-lit car park outside the chill and the smell – Dettol and formalin – settled on him. Another set of double doors and it was even colder. When he helped the ambulance-man and woman transfer the body from trolley to slab he took hold of her feet and found they were still warm. So far, he told himself, aware of the claggy feeling in his throat and not wanting to breathe, so far he had earned £11.33 in overtime.

The surgery was at the other end of the white-bricked corridor. There were two chairs in the small waiting room, a green Formica-top table, a few copies of the *Police Review* and a large pile of colour supplement magazines. Vic was on one chair, Billy on the other. As Cromer came in the police surgeon, a dark balding man in a white coat, opened the door and a uniformed

72

constable hobbled out holding his trousers and boots. His belly and groin were strapped up with padding and four-inch surgical tape. It looked as if he was wearing a nappy.

'What happened to you?'

'Kicked in the bollocks. Some black cunt down the Black and White.'

'What was it like?' said Vic.

'Fucking hurt, didn't it?' said the constable.

'No, the Black and White.'

'Could have been worse. No knives.' The constable looked down at himself. 'God knows how I'm going to piss – '

The police surgeon pushed past Cromer. 'Where the fucking hell's that fucking trolley?'

'Just brought one in – '

'Well tell 'em there's one here to take out – '

The constable leaned against the wall. 'I've got forty-eight fucking sheets already, without tonight's – '

'You're off till Wednesday, son,' said the surgeon.

'You know what,' said the constable, lowering himself on to the trolley. 'Tomorrow'll be the first fucking *Match of the Day* I've seen in thirteen months.'

'Well don't shout too hard,' said the surgeon, 'or you'll give yourself a fucking hernia.' He turned to look at Vic and Billy. 'What's this?'

'Elimination, Mister Calder,' said Vic.

'Name?'

'William Herbert Jewel,' said Billy.

'Herbert,' said the surgeon. 'We don't get many of those in here. What's the case?'

'The one John here's just brought in,' said Vic.

The surgeon looked at Billy over the top of his half-glasses. 'Right,' he said, 'the first thing you should know is that I am a qualified medical practitioner, and

73

the second thing is that it's a lot easier to become a suspect in a rape case than it is to be eliminated from it.'

'Yes doctor,' said Billy. 'I thought it might be.'

'Not to mention murder.' The surgeon gave Billy another searching look. 'I take it you're admitting to intercourse with the deceased?'

'Yeah,' said Billy, shifting in his seat. 'When she was alive.'

'You wouldn't be the first, Mister Jewel, not by any means. How long ago did this intercourse take place?'

'Not more than half an hour before she was found,' said Vic.

'Half an hour?'

'Less,' said Billy.

'Less?' said the surgeon. 'Right, Mister Jewel, the procedure is that you can, if you wish, by signing a consent form, provide me with a sample for purposes of comparison. It does not necessarily, of itself, guarantee elimination. You understand?'

'A sample of what?' said Billy.

'Sperm, and seminal fluid.'

'What,' said Billy, 'now?'

After Billy had had his nails scraped and had gobbed into a sputum bottle, the surgeon clipped a twist of hair from the back of his head and drew off a few ccs of blood from his left arm. By now, Vic noticed, Billy was shivering like a dog left out in the rain.

'I never could stand needles, doc.'

'Look at it like this, Mister Jewel – you're getting a free AIDS and VD test.'

'All I need. I'm not sure about this other thing, this sample.'

The surgeon hunted through a wall cupboard and dug out a government issue condom and a rolled-up copy of *Rogue*. 'Do your best, Mister Jewel. First door on the right.'

'State I'm in, could take all night.'

'No rush.'

Back in the post-mortem room, Cromer wished he had something to cover his face while the surgeon pumped and syringed away at the body on the slab. Another five minutes and his overtime would be up to £16.99. The surgeon chatted away to Vic, more interested in why Vic had pulled Billy in tonight rather than tomorrow. Vic said it was for his own good. Knowing Billy, he was likely to do a runner. Cromer was wondering how much longer he could stand up. The surgeon took a Philips Memorette out of his top pocket and confirmed that due to the presence of petechiae on the lower face and neck and associated suspected damage to the hyoid bone, thyroid and cricoid cartilages, combined with severe localised bruising consistent with heavy pressure being exerted on the larynx, death was due to asphyxia caused by strangulation following a sexual assault.

'It's been years since I had a J. Arthur,' said Billy, holding out the knotted condom. The surgeon held out a small wax paper cup and Billy dropped it in. 'I thought I was going to have a heart attack in there.' The surgeon wrote JEWEL, W. H. on the lid label, and told Billy he'd get results back some time next week.

Cromer sat beside Billy on the back seat. He was silent as Vic drove him back to his flat in York Place. The light was still on at the third-floor window.

'Here we are then, Billy.'

'Hang about. How can they tell who fucked her last?'

'They can't.'

'So what was all that about?'

'Fingernails,' said Vic.

'Eh?'

'If they find any of her tissue under your fingernails or any of yours under hers, you've had it. More or less.'

'Fucking hell,' said Billy. 'Let me know, will you?'

'Don't worry,' said Vic. 'You'll know.'

They watched Billy let himself in. The light in the third-floor window went off. 'Right,' said Vic. 'That's it. Where's your car?' It was 5.27 a.m. The sky was beginning to lighten.

Cromer undressed and climbed quietly into Louise's narrow bed. She turned over to him, jet black hair trailed across her face, her eyes slitty and her mouth swollen from sleep. She was hot and smelled of face cream.

'What's time?'

'Six.'

'You said two.'

'I know – '

'You smell,' she said. 'Awful.' She flopped an arm and a leg over him. 'And I haven't cleaned my teeth.'

'I don't care,' he said. He pushed himself against her. All he wanted to do was to get it in, get it over with and crash out. She took hold of his erection and squeezed it.

'Where'd you get this one?'

'Down town.'

She put it between her legs and rubbed herself with it. 'I've missed you,' she said. Her eyes were open now, gazing at him, waiting. He kissed them, then her mouth. He loved kissing her, more than she did him. She said it roughened her chin, gave her spots. ' – teeth,' she said. 'What've you been doing?'

He circled her nipple with his little finger and felt the dark skin pucker. 'Usual stuff,' he said. If he told her, she'd want to know it all.

76

'I was worried.'

'No need.' He wished she'd stop playing with him.

'What's that smell?'

'Hospital,' he said, and thrust at her.

'Don't be too rough, John.'

'No.' He wanted to shove it right in, deep in, and come, just like that. Just like the rapist.

'John – ' He felt her opening up and rolled on top of her. She guided him in, looking up at him helplessly, but waiting for him to say something.

'Oh love,' he said. Now he was safe. Inside. Home. 'I love you,' he said. 'I love you.' He dug his hands into her buttocks and heaved her against him, trying to get further and deeper inside her.

'There,' he heard her say, 'there. It's all right, love.' As the release started to come, he could feel the murder flooding out of him.

8

Detective Inspector Parnes's office looked out on to the service well. It had dark green walls, a bookcase behind the desk and pot plants, from his wife, on the windowsill. He was younger than Vic, a compact round-headed man with sleeked-down black hair. Since he'd been made inspector he'd grown a moustache. It was lighter, more gingery than the hair on his head, and he was hoping it would grow out dark and lustrous. It was 10.45 on Sunday morning, they'd been called in three hours early and neither Vic nor Cromer had shaved. Cromer was wearing a black leather jacket and jeans, which Vic considered an improvement. He was in the same old baggy suit.

DI Parnes turned the pages of a report from Forensic. 'There's nothing more on the nurse. The DCI wants to know why wasn't she brought in here?'

'Because she was bleeding,' said Vic.

'Bleeding.' The DI made a note, turned the page. 'Lot more on Pauline White. Real name Millward, nineteen, comes from Newcastle under Lyme. Semen found present that of William Herbert Jewel. Also unidentified male suspect, possible non-Caucasian. Hair, skin and tissue fragments ditto – '

'Billy'll be pleased,' said Vic.

'There's another problem with your mate Billy.'

'What?'

'She had at least three lines of coke inside her.'

'Shit,' said Vic.

'Is he into that?'

'Not as far as I know.'

'You should have gripped him, Vic. You should have charged him when you had him.'

'With what?'

'On sus.'

'Did they do his blood?'

'Nothing bar alcohol. Hundred and five milligrams.'

'Fairly normal,' said Vic.

'He could still have slipped her a few lines.'

'So could anybody else.'

'He likes his grumble, your friend Billy.'

'You could say that.'

'Three lines and she'd shag like a rabbit.'

'Apparently she was fond of him,' said Vic.

'Fond? What's fond got to do with it?'

'He said she fancied him. Why coke her up?'

'He says to her, here you are doll, have a snort, she's not going to say no is she?'

'What about this black bloke?'

'Non-Caucasian, Vic.' The DI leafed back through the report. 'AB blood group, and then it's only possible. It says here – ' he opened the *Guide to Forensic Practice and Jurisprudence* – 'ABs form only 4 per cent of the white northern European population, but common in Asia, Africa, Indian subcontinent. He doesn't have to be black – '

'You mean because of last night in St Pauls he doesn't have to be black.'

'That's part of it,' said the DI. 'We're not putting it out that he is or he isn't. Not yet anyway.'

'Whoever he is he could still have offered her a deal. He could have been watching. Billy said there was somebody – '

'He would.'

'This bloke, he's high as a kite, he gives her one, he gets carried away, she starts yelling, hands round the throat, fuck me she's dead.'

'No, Vic.'

'It's a possibility,' said Vic. 'If Billy was into coke, he'd offer me a noseful.'

'Why?'

'He's like that,' said Vic. 'Look, I've known Billy for what, eight, ten years. When he used to be somebody, when he ran a couple of restaurants, when he did know villains, before the banks blew him out. He's not bent, he likes to come on he is because he fancies himself. He's flash, he's shag-happy – '

'And he's a mate.'

'So?'

'So you're sticking up for him.'

'He didn't fucking do it, did he? He wouldn't have told me he was in the car with her – '

'Hang on.' The DI glanced at Cromer. 'Outside a minute.' When Cromer had gone, he took out a Benson and Hedges and rolled it across the desk to Vic. 'What's Billy got on you, Vic?'

'Fuck all, but thanks for asking.'

'You're not doing him any little favours?'

'No.'

'He doing you any?'

Vic shrugged. 'Free Scotch.'

'Birds?'

'Wouldn't touch 'em with yours.'

'But he has offered?'

'I got enough trouble.'

'What's happening on that front?'

'Nothing.'

'Divorce?'

'When I get around to it.'

'Bad times for a copper.'

'Bollocks,' said Vic. 'With all due respect.'

The DI picked up a folder. ' "Tendency to insubordination possibly due to stress".'

'What's that?'

'Your last appraisal.'

'Stress,' said Vic. 'I see.'

'I don't want you to call me fucking sir, mate. I don't give a shit what you call me, but if they come to me, if the DCI comes to me and says what's happening with this fucking nurse, why didn't he pull Billy Jewel and what's he doing always hanging round his fucking club, in and out his fucking office, I've got to have something to tell him, haven't I?'

'I'll consider myself bollocked then.'

'Do that.'

Frank saw the midday news on the TV in the members' lounge. There was a shot of white tape staking off an area round a tree, and then another of a line of uniformeds walking along the flank of the hill. The woman's voice was saying *Police have today launched a full-scale murder hunt after the body of a young woman was found raped and strangled in the early hours of the morning on Brandon Hill in the centre of Bristol. The identity of the young woman, believed to be an art student, is not being released until police have contacted relatives.*

The image changed to the iron gate on Hensman's Hill and zoomed through it down the path to a couple of nuns watching another staked area of white tape. *The murder, described by Detective Chief Inspector Barnard, leading the inquiry, as brutal and senseless is thought to be related to an earlier incident in which another young woman was attacked and raped in the grounds of La Retraite in Clifton. The woman, who was returning from work at seven o'clock last night, is now recovering in hospital. Her assailant is described as tall, well-built, in his twenties or thirties and wearing a stocking mask and balaclava. The police are advising women and children not to walk alone in the area after dark and the public are warned not to approach anyone they consider to be acting in a suspicious manner, but to contact the police on 0117 922 1202 or their local station.* The number was flashed on the screen over another image of the line of police, now including tracker dogs, walking across Brandon Hill, and the woman's voice said programmes would be interrupted by further news flashes as and when.

Frank walked out into the parking area in front of Ashton Court Country Club. There was a fresh smell of pines in the cold air. He dropped his new squash bag in the boot of the Renault and took out the old one with the broken zip. He locked the boot and double-checked it. If they thought the cases were related, he was home and dry, no problem. But they could be just saying that to put the shits up people. He walked round the car, trying the doors. The little bastards had started to come in on motorbikes, rip out a radio and away. White kids mainly, the blacks wouldn't dare come up here, too far away from home.

It was very pleasant walking through the car park, under the pines, very pleasant. The whoosh of air in the tops, the blue sky through the green needles, the resin. Soft underfoot, springy, and the cars looked good. Plenty of new reg, couple of Porsches, half a dozen Toyota and Nissan coupés, plenty of XR3s, old Arnold's S1 Bentley. What he should do was chop in the Renault, get one with a Plip key.

It probably was bullshit, about the two cases. Keep

82

people off the streets. But it could be panic. Bound to be falling downstairs time. Press conferences, overtime, phones going berserk. One thing for sure, it had fucked up a lot of golf and family life. Rape and murder. They'd be buzzing like blue-arsed flies down there.

It could turn out a bit of a bastard. One rape outstanding was par. Two rapes and a fucking murder meant all kinds of hoohah. Thousands of interviews, no stone unturned, house to house, all that bollocks. They'd have WPC decoys out, everything. As he turned round behind the swimming pool block and heard the women and kids screaming and yelling inside, he began to get the thrill again. Risk. A fat juicy feeling in the mouth, and the adrenalin surge in the blood, running through him, making him feel light and speedy.

He watched a couple of old dears waddle across from the golf shop to the bar, golf shoes in identical Dingles bags. When the brown glass door hissed shut behind them, he slipped round the back of the professional's hut. It was like being a kid again. His trainers flew him down the twenty yards of cinder track to the breeze-block boiler and filtration plant. Holding the old Puma bag with the gear high to stop the nettles getting his hands, he worked his way round the side of the wire mesh ventilation window. Within seconds he was inside, dropping on his feet like a cat. The boiler furnace whuffled and roared as he opened the door with the metal bar and slung the bag in. He saw it land flat on the orange-white bed, and slammed the door shut. His face and eyeballs felt seared by the heat.

A minute later, on his way to the bar, he glanced up at the boiler chimney. The shimmer above it was barely discoloured. In the bar they were talking about rape and murder. The men thought the girl who'd been done in was asking for it. Brandon Hill at two in the morning.

The women thought it was terrible. They had withdrawn from the men into their own group and were telling each other about the time it had nearly happened to them.

One barrel-shaped old bugger in a blazer with a nose like the tail on a pig carcass was leaning on the bar telling his cronies how Barney Barnard had belled him to cancel the foursome. You could tell there was a big flap on. Everybody felt sorry for the police. A sales manager for Honda bought Frank a drink. They talked about discounts and he felt great.

Detective Chief Inspector Barnard was having trouble with the remote. The TV monitor, mounted at head height so the forty or so CID men could see it, showed a white shaking image of Pauline's body. It was stuck on freeze-frame. 'How d'you fast-forward this bloody thing?'

The police photographer, Teddy Bear's assistant, stepped forward. 'You have to point it at the VCR, sir, not the screen.' The VCR was on a makeshift three-quarter-inch ply platform two feet below the monitor.

Apart from Vic and Cromer, who stood at the back with the detective sergeants from other divisions, most of the CID men were in Sunday morning gear. Only a few, the DIs from the Murder and Drug Squads already on duty, were in suits. DCI Barnard was wearing a shiny grey three-piece, Italian in cut, that looked too tight for his thick body. The white blur of Pauline's body sped forward on the screen to a close-up of her left hand. The DCI straightened, and pushed a hand through his shock of swept-back grey hair.

'Right,' he said, pleased to have mastered the machine. 'No clothes except the wax jacket, no underclothes, no handbag. Now look at the left hand. No rings, no watch. All traceable items, and when this feller comes to his senses, he may realise that. Alternatively, if he's got a habit, he may be tempted to sell. All we need is sight of one, and descriptions have been issued. We're not pressing the black issue, for reasons you will know. He could just as well be Indian, Chinese, or any mixture of all three. Or,' he paused, 'he could even be white. We don't know. What we are pushing, for the moment, for public safety, is that the two rapes may be related. And they may be.' Again he stopped, chin up, looking for disagreement.

'But the chances are, since the first comedian left the nurse's handbag behind, they are not. He could of course have had a lager personality change in the intervening period, but we think not, due to evidence of shoe size.' He sped the image forward again to a staked and taped imprint on the frozen grass. 'Given that we have several sets of prints, including the lads who found her, and that a print on grass is not the best we could hope for, the second bloke was wearing a size eight and a half to nine with a cuban or cowboy boot heel. Rapist number one had size ten trainers, that we do know. So, gentlemen, the two investigations will continue in parallel, but not I hope in isolation. What I am hoping, as I am sure all you lads are, is that the murder factor is going to knock any would-be copycats on the head. If it doesn't I need hardly remind you we're in deep shit.' He pointed the remote control at the VCR and the screen went blank.

'Vic.' It was the DI. 'He wants a word.' They made their way through the small groups, followed by Cromer, notebook in hand. The DCI was talking to a uniformed Chief Super about press conferences. He looked up and saw Cromer.

'Not you, son.'

Cromer reddened. 'Sorry sir –'

The DCI waited until Cromer was out of earshot. 'Vic, I gather you've had one bollocking.'

'Yes, sir.'

'Right. Here's another. You've already failed inspector's twice. Don't let it happen a third time or you could be looking at early retirement. You don't want that, do you?'

'No sir.'

'Neither do I.' When he smiled, the DCI pulled in his lips so that all you saw was the crease widen across the flesh. 'Now, you know Billy Jewel.'

'Yes sir.'

'And you know this nurse.'

'Well –'

'Stick to the nurse, Vic.'

Vic drove the maroon Escort hard through the empty streets, taking it out on the gearbox while he argued with himself. Three bollockings in twenty-four hours, all of them saying the same thing. You've lost it, you're too bolshy, you're too thick with Billy Jewel. Maybe he should have been more like that cunt whatsisname, Webber, and arselicked his way up. Well, fuck it, he'd been doing the job his way for fourteen years, his arrest record was as good as anybody's, better on the serious stuff, Parnesy knew that, so did Barnard, so why the sudden pressure? They could have pushed him for inspector at any time, but they knew he was more use on the street, and besides, who wants to sit in a fucking office all day? Now they wanted him to drop Billy in it. Why? So they could pin Pauline on him? Set him up for the sake of a quick arrest? By the time they got to York Place, Vic had convinced himself he was right, and even if he wasn't, he was doing it anyway. Whatever Billy may or may not have done, Vic knew he hadn't topped Pauline, so they could all get fucked. Billy was a mate. He got out of the car and slammed the door. A black cat shot down the basement steps. He'd show the bastards.

Ten years ago, Billy's living room had been all white. Now the thick Indian carpet was cigarette-ash grey, pocked with burns and stains and the paint had turned pale brown. Smoke hung in layers in the dusty room, and sunlight did it no good at all. Billy sat in the nubble tweed oatmeal settee, legs apart, facing the 26-inch TV set. He waved Vic to a chair with the drink in his hand.

'Shit, man, I've just had three hours of your lot.'

'Where's Mandy?'

'Out.' He tried to reach for the bottle of Grouse. 'Little heart-starter?'

'Too early.'

Billy squinted up at Cromer, who was standing by the window, making a hole in the sunlight. 'How about your mate?'

'No thank you, sir.'

'Do me a favour, son. Sit down will you?' Billy's tan, in the morning light, had faded to a hepatitis yellow.

'What did they want to know?'

'Ins and outs of the cat's arse. Who she was, where she came from, how long I'd known her, what she was wearing, what she was like – '

'What was she like?'

'I don't know, I only fucked her, didn't I? You don't listen to all that crap do you? They don't mean it any more than we do. I mean, "you do love me don't you?" All leg-over chat – ' He took a drink and swirled the glass round in the sunlight. 'Poor cow.'

'She liked you,' said Vic. 'You like her?'

87

'Yeah. She had a lovely sweet little twat. Just like the coral on a scallop – you know?'

'John here's a Methodist, Billy.'

'More fool him.'

'It's all right,' said Cromer.

'It's more than all right, son, it's the seafood of the gods.' He blew out smoke in a long thin stream. 'Anyway, she was a nice kid. I mean, she wanted it all at once, but she wasn't, you know, fucking calculating all the time.'

'Was she into coke?'

'Anything, yeah. She wanted me to fuck her on Ecstasy, but I wouldn't have it. You got to draw the line somewhere, Vic –' He reached for the bottle of Grouse, grunting as he bent over, and this time he made it. 'The old Low Flyer's good enough for me.' He poured in one slurp, then another. 'Both wings, as the man said. You sure, Vic?'

'Sure.'

'I suppose I shall miss her, but when you're in the shit yourself, you don't give a rat's left nacker, do you? I thought I was nicked for sure. Half-past seven, I'm only in bed hour, and Mandy, she's been giving it that –' he made the quacking-duck sign. 'Ratatatat – three blokes, you know, one by the door. Mister Jewel? Yeah. We're the Murder Squad. Fuck me. Well it's ring-palpitation time isn't it?'

'Tell me about the girl.'

'I told Mandy. Had to, didn't I? How it had only been the once, I was pissed, she led me on, I was worried sick about the business, all that shit.'

'She believe it?'

'Would you? Anyway, if she wants to fucking go, let her. That's what they do, isn't it? Wait till you're down

88

and kick you in the bollocks. Women. You married, son?'

'No,' said Cromer.

'He's engaged,' said Vic.

'Very nice. Best of luck. Then I had to tell them. Lot more than I told her too. I been knocking her off for a year Vic, off and on. Life, love and the pursuit of cunt. What can you do?' It was the first time Vic had seen Billy sigh. 'Just when I get her to come and work — blam.'

'You do that because it turns you on?'

'Yeah. Yes it does, actually.'

'Seeing her perform in front of Mandy?'

'And the rest of 'em. Watching all those toerags and thinking yes and I'm the one that's going to whop it up her.'

'Weird.'

'Yeah, well it's not very nice, but everybody's fucking weird, Vic. Nobody's perfect, and very few are fucking normal.'

'What about Pauline?' said Vic.

'She wanted me to leave Mand. Yeah, you know, pack it all in, go round the world with her. In a VW Camper — you imagine, me in a VW Camper, like some latter-day fucking hippie, for Christ sake. She goes on, the smell of sage, thyme, orange groves, lemon groves, moonlight swims and olive root barbecues, and all financed by a fucking fortnight's fucking grape-picking down some poxy farm in Provence. Barking mad, Vic. That or fucking television. Then I'm saying yeah, yeah, yeah, lovely, because, well, you saw, she's got a lovely little arse, skin like fucking marshmallow –' Billy stared into space. 'She was lovely, Vic. Anyway, I'm forty fucking eight, man. You got to say you love 'em, they're the best thing ever happened – and she goes, one night she goes, fucking prime-ministerial tension or something, well if you won't Billy, Nigel will.'

'Nigel?'

'Only her day fuck, isn't it? Some half-assed fucking nineteen-year-old anarchist with his trousers hanging out and stainless steel fucking split-ring through his nose. Yeah, she goes, Nigel'll go with me.' Billy took an aggrieved sip. 'Cunt.'

'You tell these other lads that?' said Vic.

'Did I bollocks,' said Billy. 'Big enough prat already.'

Vic watched Cromer scribbling away, and waited for him to catch up. It was something he wanted to get straight, and Billy could run out a few more yards of line. 'They say why they weren't pulling you in?'

'Apart from my natural charm?'

'Apart from that.'

'All down to Ellard, apparently. He clocked me coming back in. Ten-past two. They said that put me out the frame.'

'You sure that's what they said?'

'Yeah, Ellard. Now he'll want a fucking rise.'

There was something going on. It wasn't TOD that exonerated Billy, it was Forensic. Vic decided that if he owed Billy one, now was the time. 'They didn't pull you in because they didn't want to pull you in.' Vic could see that didn't go down too well with Cromer. 'Time of Death's got nothing to do with it.'

Billy shrugged. 'What they said.'

'I got bollocked for letting you go.' That went down even less well. Cromer was looking at him as if he'd blown it.

'What's going on, Vic?'

'Well Billy. I reckon it's a case of let's wind up King Kong and see where he goes tonight.'

'Fucking hell.' Billy looked worried. It was time to reel him in.

'What was this other bloke's name?'

'You mean Nigel?'

'Nigel who?'

'Reject,' said Billy. 'That's what she called him. Nigel the Reject. It's all over the back of his jacket.'

'What in, studs?'

'No, paint, he's a fucking anarchist, man. Spray-paint the world, all that shit.'

'Should you have done that?' Cromer was driving. In Dingles a couple of display kids were laying red felt in the windows, ready for Christmas.

'How d'you think Pauline's parents are going to feel?' said Vic.

'I don't know,' said Cromer. 'I meant telling him they were letting him run.'

'You ever have to do a doorstep after a fatal traffic accident?'

'No, but –'

'This is worse than a fucking accident. Yes that's right officer, she's studying art in Bristol. Why, what is it? Your daughter's been raped and murdered, Mrs Millward. Some young copper about your age.'

'Why did you have to tell him, Vic? If I'm supposed to be working with you – '

'And then there's things like, will Billy go to the funeral.'

'We weren't even supposed to go and see him, and you as good as tell him they've got him on obbo – '

'You understand what I'm telling you, John?'

'No I don't.'

'No, you don't.' Vic turned in his seat to face Cromer.

91

'You don't get very far thinking like a copper all the time.'

'Well you haven't got very far, have you?'

Cromer was getting ratty. Good, about time. 'Did you have a jump last night, John?'

'What?'

'A jump. With whatsername, Louise.'

'What's that got to do with you?'

'Hasn't put you in a very good mood, has it?'

'I just want to know where I am, that's all.'

Wind him up a bit more. 'Halfway down Park Street,' said Vic, 'up there on Brandon Hill, there'll be a little crowd, some of 'em just out of church, walking past the white tapes, gawking. And standing in front of 'em, moving 'em along, there'll be a young copper. If you'd sooner be doing that John, say the word.'

'I didn't mean —'

'Just say the word, John, and we'll go down the Station, sort out the fucking transfer here and now. Because I don't need some kid pissballing me about telling me what I should and shouldn't do. I don't tell you what a cunt you are, do I?'

'Hang on,' said Cromer. 'I'm stopping the car.' He pulled in next to the Christian bookshop, his ears and face flaming.

'You're too near the crossing.'

'Fuck it.' He saw Vic grinning at him. 'I didn't ask to be put with you —'

'Likewise —'

'But since I am I've got a right to know what's going on, haven't I? One minute you tell me we're off the murder and the DCI has told you to stick with the nurse, the next we're off to see Billy —'

'That's right,' said Vic. 'He's a mate —'

'Deliberately putting us both in the shit —'

92

'Thinking like a copper – '

'I *am* a copper, for Christ's sake – '

'Exactly.'

'What?' Cromer saw an old dosser watching them from the steps of the Masonic Hall. He stood up, put his flagon of Whiteways Cyder in his overcoat pocket and shuffled off.

'You're trying too hard,' said Vic. 'It's no good *disapproving* of all this shit because it's not going to fucking go away, you got to get down there in amongst it – '

'Look, when I was in uniform – '

'When you were in uniform, you were in uniform.'

'I still got stuck in – '

'This isn't a Saturday night punch-up, John, I'm not talking about that, it's this attitude, this constant fucking *disapproval* of what I do and how I do it – '

'Because I don't fucking understand!' Cromer was yelling at Vic, 'And you don't fucking tell me – '

'And I don't need fucking nagging, and pursed lips, like a monkey's arse, and tut-tut-fucking-tutting all the time. I've had nagging, had it, up to here. I'm pissed off with it.'

'So am I.'

Vic took out a cigarette and lit it. Cromer thought about opening the window but decided not to. 'Right,' said Vic. 'I went to see Billy because he's a mate, and because he's a mate, he talks to me. He needs to talk to me because he's scared, he's had three blokes on his back, and when he talks to me he tells me something he didn't tell them, because he knows I'm not going to jump all over his face. So I figure I owe him one and I tell him they could be watching him. And he's still grateful, see? You get it? He's still biddable, still a mate.'

Vic wound his own window down and blew smoke

out. 'You listen, and you think like them. Are you with me so far?'

'You mean this Nigel character.'

'John, I'm not here to help you on your way to Chief Superintendent of fucking Traffic, or whatever your ultimate ambition might be, so if you want to find out how it's done, how I do it, fucking watch, OK, and don't interrupt.'

Cromer thought about it, and restarted the engine. 'Where to?'

'You take me to the hospital, and then see if you can track down friend Nigel.'

'Right,' said Cromer. 'How?'

God give me strength, thought Vic. 'How would you go about it?'

'Try the girl's house?'

'Be full of fingerprint men. You know Kensington Road, in Cotham?'

'Where the travellers' buses park up?'

'Try the red and green one. It's got Dreamstalker painted on the front.' Vic looked at his watch. 'They should be up.'

On the way to the hospital, Vic said, 'The last jump I had was six months ago. I don't know whether it makes you more sane or less.'

9

She was dozing, her head back on the pillow, hospital headphones round her throat, mouth open. Vic let himself look at her. A sleeping woman, her face relaxed, pink in the hospital warmth, her bare arms resting on her stomach, the fingertips just overlapping. She had a nice mouth. Wide and full. He could see the glint of alloy fillings in the back. He moved his head away and knocked on the glass.

She woke and saw his fist in the circular panel.

He said he just wanted to warn her. Later on she'd have to make a statement. And also they'd need details of her sexual history. With names and addresses. But there'd be a WPC present, and she could have a friend if she wanted. She said she didn't know if she did or she didn't. There wasn't that much to tell. He smiled but looked tired and said he wanted just to check one more point. The last time she had sexual intercourse. Was that in August? Yes, she said, in Corfu, but when she got back to England she found she'd got NSU.

'I haven't bothered since.'

'Not since August?'

'No, that's it.'

She leaned back against the pillows and put her hands behind her head. They looked at each other. About ten weeks. It wasn't that long. She felt a trickle of sweat run down her armpit, and saw him watching it.

The girl was pale and thin, in a brown Oxfam dress

with a rainbow-stripe cardigan which was frayed at the elbows and belled at the wrists. Her hair looked as if she'd tried to Rasta it in dried mud, and she had a silver ring through her right nostril and several more in one ear. She smelled of woodsmoke and patchouli oil, and stood on the steps of the bus, not letting Cromer in. What sounded like Jack Russells were yipping and scratching at the hardboard door behind her.

'Hang on a minute, will you?' She squeezed through the door, shushing at the dogs. Cromer stood back, just in case. There were four vehicles parked by the side of the old railway line. Two single-decker buses, painted red and green and blue, a Dormobile, and an old Post Office wagon with a four-man cab and a flat front tyre.

'Hi, man.' A tall youth with matted hair, a waistcoat and collarless shirt climbed slowly down the steps of the bus and collapsed into a sitting position on the bottom step. He pushed the hair off his face and peered up at Cromer. 'What's the problem?'

'I'm looking for this guy called Nigel. He wears a jacket with Reject on the back.'

'Yah, Nigel.' The youth scratched himself inside his waistcoat. 'Have you got a card, you know, or something?'

Cromer showed his warrant card. 'You know where he might be?'

'Look, I'm not trying to be difficult, right, but if Nigel gets busted and he comes down on me –'

The girl stuck her head round the door. 'Don't tell him anything Ol.'

'It's cool, it's OK.' The youth waved the back of his hand at her, sending her back inside, but she took no notice. 'What's all this about? I mean, you know, why Nigel?'

'Investigation of a serious crime.' It was a lot easier

in uniform talking to kids like these. 'We think he might be able to help us.'

'But it's not him, right? He's not directly involved?'

'Don't tell him anything. Ask him what it is.'

'I just did, man –'

The girl came down the steps and confronted Cromer. 'What d'you want to see Nigel for?'

Cromer said, 'We're investigating two rapes and a murder. An art student named Pauline Millward –'

'Pauline. Shit, man.' The youth put his head on his knees and rocked to and fro. The girl sank down on the steps to join him, and they put their arms round each other.

'You know her?' There was no reply. 'Did you know her?'

When the girl looked up there were tear streaks on her face. 'Yes,' she said. 'Why? Why do people do these things?'

Nigel's squat was in Montpelier, and looked out over the Jungle. There was a length of motorcycle chain across the bedroom door.

'Yes?' A face with a tight mouth just above the level of the chain. A savage crewcut and alert grey eyes behind Lennon glasses. He looked to be a foot shorter than Cromer.

The squat was fanatically bare. A rubber sleeping mat was laid out exactly parallel to the boards. There was a tightly rolled olive-green sleeping bag at its head and an orange box of books beside it. On top of the box, laid out like army kit, a mug, toothbrush, razor, soap and flannel. The rest of his belongings were in a jungle-pattern 75-litre rucksack hanging from a shiny six-inch nail splintered into the middle upright of the door.

Even standing in one spot, he found it impossible to keep still. His fists, buried in the pockets of his combat trousers, clenched and unclenched. From time to time, as Cromer told him about Pauline, he rolled his shoulders, and his head, and braced back his knees, flexing and unflexing his thigh muscles. It was like watching Canadian Air Force exercises. He was slightly built, and wore high-laced para boots, and a camouflage jacket with *Nigel the Reject* painted in black Gothic lettering on the back. He listened to Cromer with small birdlike jerks and nods of his head. The sense of his pent-up energy, his tension, filled the room. As soon as he could he began to pace the floorboards in a strict rectangular pattern.

Yes he did know Pauline. Yes he had slept with her. He wasn't aware that was a crime. Apart from an abrupt pause in front of the window, where he stood with shoulders hunched like a small, brooding bird of prey, he showed no signs of concern. No, he didn't know Billy Jewel, nor did he want to. Yes, he knew Pauline took cocaine. He didn't. Never had, never would. Nor anything else. He'd got too much self-respect. He'd told Pauline she was poisoning her brain and rotting her septum but she was weak. His real name was Nigel Evens — two e's. Yes he could say where he was on Saturday night. He could explain exactly. And with witnesses. Now he wasn't going to answer any more questions with nobody else present.

'If you want me to come down the station, fair enough. Otherwise Detective Constable Cromer you and your fucking fascist police state can get fucked. Clear?'

Cromer found it difficult not to smile. 'Thank you, sir.'

'Don't fucking sir me.' He ran down the stairs like a

para. For a moment Cromer thought he might go on running, and panicked. Suppose it was him? Suppose he'd caught him and let him go? He'd be bloody difficult to catch – these little buggers always were –

He was waiting at the bottom, boots apart, thumbs hooked into his belt, stiff with contempt as Cromer picked his way down the broken staircase.

'What car you got?'

'What–?'

'What car? You tell me what it is and I'll meet you there.'

'Why?'

'I've got to lock up, haven't I?' The grey eyes glared. 'Make this place secure.'

'He did what?'

'He came out the bathroom window and down the drainpipe.'

'How's he get in?' asked Vic.

'Same way,' said Cromer. Vic looked into the interview room. All he could see was the top of the crewcut. Nigel had his arms folded and his face about six inches away from an illustrated wide-format book on the interview table. Between his knees under the table was the jungle-pattern rucksack. Vic closed the door.

'What's the book?'

'The *Official SAS Survival Handbook*,' said Cromer.

'Did you tell him to bring his gear?'

'No, he says he has to have it with him.'

'You've done well, John.'

Cromer wasn't so sure. 'Are we going to hand him over?'

'Yeah,' said Vic. 'Later.'

'Where you from, Nigel?'

'I live outside the system.'

'What system's that,' said Vic. 'The solar system?'

'No.' The voice was disinterested. 'The capitalist system.'

'You're on the dole you mean?'

'No.' Now he was being bored, but patient.

'Parents, then. They give you money?'

'I don't have any parents.' Take it or leave it.

'You mean they're dead, or what?'

'I mean I'm over eighteen. I choose not to recognise them.'

'What do they choose?'

He tried to stare Vic out. Cromer, who was standing to one side and behind him, noticed that he kept squeezing the rucksack between his knees.

'Up to them.' The shrug was an afterthought. 'In a free society any child should have the right to divorce his parents.'

'Fair enough,' said Vic. 'So how d'you live?'

'There's no shortage of food in an urban environment.'

'The skips at the back of Gateways? Stuff past its sell-by date?'

'Not necessarily.' A thin, insolent smile.

'You know that's technically stealing?'

Cromer watched him pull his feet back to lean closer to Vic. 'By whose laws?'

'You got to have laws, Nigel. Otherwise John and me'd be out of a job.'

'Everybody should make up his own –'

'They do, son, they do round here anyway.'

'There's no such thing as The Law.' He pushed his glasses back up his nose. 'You know what the Rule of Law is, don't you?'

'You tell me, Nige.'

'Keep the people down. That's the only rule there is. Repression.'

'Correct me if I'm wrong,' said Vic, 'but you came here of your own accord didn't you? Your own free will –'

'Of course.'

'Why did you do that, Nigel?'

'I was being interrogated without a witness.'

'We don't interrogate –'

'As soon as he told me –' he jerked his head towards Cromer – 'I knew I'd have to get you people off my back.'

'You've been in trouble before?'

'I don't have to answer that.'

'This is nothing to do with Pauline, then?'

'Of course it's to do with her –'

'But it's basically to save your own neck?'

He nodded. 'Basically.'

'You're a selfish little bastard, aren't you?'

'We're all on our own. Sergeant.'

'Arrogant too.'

'If you mean do I think I'm your equal, yes, I do.'

'I think you think you're my fucking superior, son.'

'Think what you fucking well like,' said Nigel.

'Thanks,' said Vic. 'I will. What I think is this. I think you're an intelligent, well-educated, middle-class arsehole.' He waited for the response. Nothing. 'A girl's dead, a girl you knew, liked presumably. You slept with her, you fucked her –'

'Fucking's got nothing to do with feelings –'

'You haven't got any feelings, Nigel. Have you?'

There was a pause. A long stare. 'What you call feelings, aren't.'

'I give up,' said Vic. 'Look at you, you're dressed like some urban terrorist, some street guerilla. You live in

a squat with motorcycle chains on the doors, you climb down the fucking drainpipe, you bring this in here –'
Vic prodded the rucksack with his toe.

'*Don't!*'

'What?'

The voice returned to normal. 'Kick it.'

'Why, what's inside?'

'I just don't like having my stuff – knocked about.'

'Something breakable?'

Nigel reached down and pulled the rucksack towards him, protectively. After he had settled it under his chair, he said, 'What you call feelings are urges.'

'What's the difference then?'

'An urge is what you want to do to somebody.' Another pause. 'Feelings are what should stop you.'

Vic nodded. 'Yeah, I go along with that. So what's all this Nigel the Reject stuff?'

He smiled. 'It keeps people away.'

Vic took Cromer outside. 'What d'you think's happened to this kid?'

'Had a row, left home –'

'More than that,' said Vic.

'You think he did it?'

'It'd be nice,' said Vic. 'You're his age, you talk to him. I want to see if there's anything on him.'

There was. Unlawful assembly, Stonehenge. Resisting arrest, Marlborough. Destruction of police property, Bristol. All over the space of three days in June. He was the only one in a cell of fifteen who admitted to ripping the covers off the mattresses. His defence was he was cold. Nobody turned up with bail. The other fourteen got bound over. He got ten days. There was an address in Reading, but no follow-up. When Vic got back to the interview room, he had turned his chair to face the wall, and had his rucksack on his lap with his arms round it. Vic looked at Cromer. Has he said anything? Cromer shook his head.

'Were you on the Peace Convoy, Nigel?'

'There was no Peace Convoy.' Then he turned his chair round. 'You saw to that.'

'I wasn't there.'

'One of your lads threw a baby off a bus.'

'Really?'

'Through a broken windscreen.'

'Did you report it?'

'Yes.'

'What happened?'

'Nothing. The kid was trespassing.'

'Was the kid hurt?'

'His mother caught him.' The start of a smile. 'Funnily enough.'

'And you've been in Bristol ever since?'

'Off and on, yes.'

'What about Saturday night?'

'I was in the Kensington.'

'You have much to drink?'

'About four pints.'

'Beer or cider?'

'Water.'

'What, Perrier?'

'No, tap water. You get it from the tap in the Gents.'

'Landlord must have been pleased to see you.'

'Put Lea and Perrins in, they think it's beer.'

'Where d'you get the Lea and Perrins?'

'Off the counter. They don't notice when the bar's full.'

'Must taste pretty vile.'

'Yeah, but –'

'What?'

'I told you. I like to stay in control.'

After that, he said, he went back to one of the buses and stayed there until half-three. There were half a dozen people there: Cosmo, Dice, Ben, George, Earl, Ollie and Nell. They listened to some sounds. He thought Pauline might turn up but when she didn't he pushed off home.

'At half-past three?'

'About that.'

'You have anything to drink?'

'Tea.'

'Smoke?'

'I don't.'

'What about the others?'

'You'll have to ask them, won't you?'

'You know Pauline was raped before she was murdered?'

'I don't *know* that, no.' He jerked his head at Cromer. 'He told me she was.'

'Would you have any objection to having your fingerprints taken?'

'You've already got them.'

'What about a blood sample?'

'I shall have to think about that.'

'Think about it now,' said Vic.

He straightened his back, stretched and refolded his arms and stared at the surface of the table. Then he looked up from the mug rings and said, 'This is to eliminate me from the inquiry?'

'To get us off your back, yeah.'

'They have boxes of disposable syringes, right?'

'Right.'

'If I can pick the syringe, and watch the guy put it together, OK.'

'Why would you want to do that?'

104

'Look, man, I came here voluntarily, to *help*. So is it a deal?'

'I'll see what I can do.'

'Not good enough'

'Why not?'

'I want a guarantee, otherwise forget it.'

'All right, Nigel. You tell me why and we'll do it.'

'Christ, man, isn't it obvious?' He showed his small yellowish teeth. 'I don't trust anything you bastards do.'

'And I'm asking you why.'

'Because I've *seen* what you do to people.'

'Seen what, exactly?'

'You're doing it now, man. Hassle. It's one long hassle with you people, you're all the same, it's what you do. You hassle people. I don't need it. All I want to do – I want to live my life the way I want to live it. It's different because I'm different – but because it's different it's not wrong. But you guys, you come and trash our vans and kick our heads in. You shove us in jail, man, you do it for a fucking pastime, for a fucking laugh. I've seen it, I was there – and you expect us to trust you? Dream on, man.'

'Look Nigel – '

'I'll help you because of Pauline, but that's it. You understand? That's *it*.'

'Fair enough,' said Vic. 'When did you last see her?'

'Saturday. Lunchtime.'

'What did you do?'

'Argued.'

'What about?'

'This strip deal.'

'You didn't like it?'

'Her life, she can do what she wants – '

'But you were jealous?'

105

'It's cheap shit, man.'

'Did you know she was seeing Billy Jewel?'

'Look, my point was if you want to tits and ass about in front of a bunch of pissheads fine, but ten quid? Forget it.'

'Did you know she was going out with him?'

'I found out, didn't I?'

'She told you? In the course of this argument?'

'I don't like – contamination, being contaminated. Especially by that old cunt –'

'You said you didn't know Billy.'

'I know of him. She told me about him.'

'That she was sleeping with him?'

'It's her life, her body.' He took off his glasses and wiped them. 'She should have told me. She should have told me *first* –'

'You were pretty annoyed?'

'She knew how I felt. She wants to fuck somebody else, fine. But I *need to know* –'

'Why? Because you're jealous, possessive?'

He shook his head. 'I don't need it, man.'

'And that's why you were angry?'

'I don't want my body full of old men's shit diseases.'

'Did you hit her?' said Vic.

'What for?'

'Women sometimes do that, try and make you hit them.'

'What good does it do?'

'It makes you feel guilty instead of them.'

'Something else I can do without.'

'You didn't hit her, what did you do?'

'I talked to her.'

'What did she do?'

'Cried. Said she was sorry, stupid. All that shit.'

'You go to bed with her?'

'In the end, yeah. Yes I did.'

'And you waited for her, with your friends, until half-past three.'

'That's right.'

'Why?'

'That's where I said I'd be. She said she'd –' he breathed in deeply through his nose – 'said she'd come back there.'

'Did you talk to these friends about it?'

'I talked to Nell and Ollie.'

'What did they say?'

'Nell said I was better off without her. Ollie just kept saying she'll turn up, she was probably making a score, stuff like that –'

'Waiting for the man?' said Vic.

'Right.'

'Which man?'

'Some bunch of black kids from the Jungle.'

'Grosvenor Road, City Road?'

'I don't know. All she said was they've got a car with a car phone.'

'And they tell her where to meet?'

'Something like that.'

'Fine,' said Vic. 'Thanks very much.'

'That's it? I can go?'

'Like to show me what's in the rucksack?'

'No.'

'Why?'

'You don't have a reason.'

'I don't need a reason son. It's called Stop and Search, you want to see the book?'

'This is just more fucking hassle, right?'

'This is a murder inquiry, Nigel. Just open it up. It's all I'm interested in.'

He unpacked it item by item, squaring each one up

107

with the edges of the table. There were four tubs of Flora margarine, some packs of longlife milk, a large bag of muesli inside another, resealable bag, and a box of eggs. In another compartment were a dozen dog-eared s-f paperbacks, a pair of green rubber-cased 8 × 50 binoculars, OS maps and a prismatic compass. In the bottom section, wrapped in plastic, fifteen exercise books, all filled with small, very neat handwriting. Vic flicked through one. It was full of words like ontology and cosmos. It was called 'The Exploding of Superman'.

'What's this?'

'It's a book I'm writing.'

'About Superman?'

'No. Nietzsche.'

When they took him down for a blood test, it turned out AB positive.

10

The car!

Going straight at her – in the *shopping precinct* –

Eight-thirty Monday morning and Frank in his street gear of padded canvas blouson, green with blue shoulder shooting patches that looked like Next but was off a stall, dark grey flannels and black Clarks semi-brogues, was coming out of the Bedminster Sainsbury's with a smoked trout and a white Beaune and thinking how rough it used to be –

Then this car, this X-reg blue Ford Granada, coming screaming off the cinder car park – first gear, all over the place – down past Currys, Hepworths, Jean Jeanies – into the central piazza, the dead fountain, the inlaid cobbles – straight at this old girl waddling along, head-scarf and bottle-green coat, two big bags of shopping – Jesus Christ –

She must be fucking deaf –

'Watch out!' Frank was sprinting across the paving, bottle thumping in his pocket. He hit the woman with his shoulder, heard the whouf, the breath being knocked out of her, both of them rolling in the empty cement bowl of the fountain with the grit and old crisp packets – dough-white flesh at the top of her legs –

He was up before she started screaming and on to the parapet. A glimpse of a scared black face looking through the steering wheel. The car slewed, skidding round the fountain. The back wheels scrabbling for grip on the cobbles. The boot slamming into a paper-back stand. The books flying like ducks –

And Frank launched himself – shit, now what have I done – off the parapet on to the bonnet. He felt it buckle, and grabbed for the wipers. One came off straight away –

'You cunt!' he shouted at the dark oval head behind the windscreen. The kid couldn't be more than fifteen. 'Stop the fucking car!'

Shouts, thuds, a blast of music from Jean Jeanie dop-plered past. 'Stop the fucking thing!' One second the kid's face was scared shitless, the next a gob of thick white phlegm hit the inside of the windscreen. Auto-matically Frank ducked, grabbed for the edge of the bonnet. Now the kid was shouting, mouthing 'shithead' and 'fuck off' through the glass and they were out into the black cinder car park. 'You stupid fucking idiot – '

Seeing himself with space again, the kid flung the wheel this way and that. Frank felt his body swerving across the lumpy dented bonnet. Still looking at the black face, the jutting jaw, the two lines down between the eyebrows. . . .

He felt warm blood coming out of the top of his clenched fist round the wiper. Now the little bastard was operating the wipers. Jesus, my fucking knuckles –

Frank's foot hit something. The wing mirror. Thank Christ. He pushed himself closer to the screen. Hauled himself forward on the wiper. Block his view. Face to face through the glass –

'Stop the fucking car!'

'Fuck you!' The mouth had snarled back showing the pink inside of the lips and the gappy white teeth. 'Shithead!'

'You fucking little – '

The impact of the crash – the Granada hit the low

110

concrete flower tubs on the edge of the car park – threw Frank off. He came up with the wiper blade in his hand, blood running down it but no pain. He staggered to the car, wrenched open the passenger door. The kid was trying to squeeze out the driver's side, but it was jammed tight against another car. People were beginning to run up. He grabbed hold of one white trainer. The other foot lashed out at his face. He seized it, heaved the kid back in, kicking and gobbing, and put an arm across his throat. Bodies surrounded the car, blocking out the light.

'Police,' said Frank. 'I'm a police officer –'

Bedminster nick. Frank's adrenalin still going, the kid dragging along beside him down the corridor like an empty sack, his face greying. They went through the rigmarole. The circumstances were that at 8.30 this morning. . . . The kid said his name was Daniel Smith and he was fifteen. The desk sergeant laid his pen flat on the charge-sheet.

'You're not going anywhere, son. Apart from downstairs. You can forget bail, mother, phone calls. Now then –'

This time the kid was Winston Travis Winters and he was seventeen and a half.

'Name of arresting officer?' said the desk sergeant.

'Inspector Frank Webber.'

'Shhhhh-yit,' said the kid.

'Exactly,' said the sergeant. 'Name of station, sir?'

'Thornbury.'

'What he doing down here, man?' said the kid.

'Looking for little bastards like you,' said the sergeant.

By the time Frank got to the hospital, the surge had gone and his mind was banging about between suppose and what-if. Suppose it was a commendation. Suppose he was interviewed. What if it was on telly? What if the nurse was watching? Suppose she could tell it was him? Jesus Christ, she could even be here in the hospital. . . .

Why the fuck had he done it?

He could hear the voice laughing. *Oh boy,* it was saying, *oh boy, have you done it. Have you done it now.* He told himself to get a grip.

The sister, a heavy-duty brown piece in her forties, big smile, quite nice-looking, was strapping some thin silky material across the palm of his left hand telling him it would give and breathe. He nodded and kept himself still but his hand, his whole arm, was shaking. Tension, she said. It had to come out some time. 'As a hactress said.'

Then she patted him on the head like his mother, and shuffled over to the treatment room door. She had a wide swaying arse like some prime tan Jersey milker. The creases and dark patches in her skin, knuckles, neck, knees and ankles varied in shade from oxblood to charcoal. So did the outside and inside of her lips. The panic Frank was in, he wanted to fuck her, bury himself in her, take the sleepy-lidded smile off that face and forget it all in rolls of satin-smooth brown fat.

Here, said the voice, *now —*

Here, among the sharp shiny things on the stainless steel dishes. Now, on the high grey plastic examination couch. That'll make her fat ass squeak. Go on. There's a lock on the door. Go on. She'll love it —

She must have seen the look in his eyes because when she opened the door to Casualty she tipped her head back and clicked her gorgeous veal-pink tongue in disapproval.

Nice-lookin' white boy like you eyein' me like some

112

City Road bug-eye no-chance Rastaman – you too bold for your own good, y'hear – you mine I keep you lock' up, chain' to the bedpost. That's what the voice said she said.

There was an orange-striped traffic Carlton waiting outside. The PR mob wanted him. The traffic blokes grinned at each other. Thornbury. The sticks get macho. But they loved this hanging-on-the-wipers-sliding-off-the-bonnet-you're-nicked-dinge stuff. They all did. He did. Image. Now he'd got himself fucked by the fucking image.

The co-driver got out and said he'd bring Frank's car round for him. Frank said thanks and the co-driver saluted. Holy shit. On the way there was a message on the radio. Mr Perry was going to try and be there. The CC. Chief Constable Royston Perry. Despite himself, Frank started rehearsing.

It was instinct, sir, pure instinct. Any copper would have done the same. Thank you, sir.

What a cunt, said the voice.

'More promotion,' said the driver.

'I shouldn't think so,' said Frank.

'So what was it like then, sir?'

'Tell you the truth, I was shitting myself.'

The driver grinned at the windscreen, placated.

You still are, said the voice.

The PR boys had the bottles out on a stained white linen tablecloth. Being morning, it was sherry, courtesy Morans of Bristol, and thin salty Chinese biscuits. Bob, the chief PR bloke, with steamy jamjar-bottom glasses and a Newport, Mon accent he faked up Bristol-posh, said Wally the Flash was still doing mug-shots down the morgue, and what would Frank take for it,

Manzanilla? The word came out 'mantha-neeliya'. Frank said a small fino.

Bob was asking him questions in the all-mates-no-bullshit way civvy PR blokes had, and a busty, shiny-brown-faced twenty-year-old brunette called Nina in a black and white check dress was taking it down in shorthand and letting her eyes crawl·over his face and giving him a mental gobble, when the CC came in with DCI Barnard, and the noise fell. The CC and DCI offered congratulations and accepted amontillados. Frank saw the CC, a hard-faced old-fashioned Fishponds Presbyterian in his fifties who kept flexing his knobbly hands in an attempt to relax, looking at the clutch of bottles and the schooners in the fists of the PR men and said, 'Right, if we could have a word, chaps.' Bob opened the door for Nina and all the men breathed in through their noses as she took her bottom through it.

'Somebody's daughter,' said the DCI curtly.

'They all are,' said the CC. 'You want to kick off, Barney?'

Twenty minutes later, the drinks were being locked away, Nina was typing up details of Frank's forthcoming second commendation and he'd had four minutes of inter-rank respectful joshing with the DCI and the CC himself. One of the youngest inspectors they'd got. DCI saying he'd have to watch out or Frank'd be sitting in his chair and he'd be growing chrysanths the rest of his natural. Frank pulled his rugger-club porcine aviation line and they both laughed. The derelict old farts. Then the CC said something about keeping his nose clean and Frank felt his sphincter tighten and his palms sweat – but the CC went droning on and the DCI was feeling for nose-hairs. There wasn't much chance of anything else at Thornbury – as if he didn't know – but we all have to

114

do our time in the sticks, all-round experience, increase in rural violence, all that.

'But a good bright, clean-cut type like you, lad, somebody who holds himself well, somebody who actually looks like a good copper instead of some shambolic shiny-arsed pool-hall villain, if you can handle the bullshit that's what we're looking for.' Then the magic first name came. 'Not too long now and you'll be there or thereabouts for Chief Inspector. What lodge are you, Frank?'

As if he didn't know.

Another minute's chat, the speed of these old farts' decisions startling Frank, and it was all settled. With all this race crap in St Pauls and the contingency of two rapes, one murder, the DCI said best to play it down, keep Frank's heroics out of the papers, off the box, keep it in the drawer for now, till when they needed it. As they fucking well inevitably would, said the DCI. The CC said he hoped Frank wouldn't mind. It'd all redound to his satisfaction eventually. Redound, thought Frank. Fucking A. It was all very warm, very friendly for four minutes, music in his ears, and for an hour it shut the voice up.

Then he was back on his own in his office in Thornbury, ten miles outside Bristol, sitting very still, trying to hang on to his mind.

Wally the Flash had finished down the morgue and could he take some pictures? It transpired, said Wally, in the interim, the DCI and the CC decided it would do no harm to have something on the record ready to shove out when they needed it. No, Wally couldn't say when, all he was told was get some ten by eight smudgies, make the inspector look good. You old fart-breaths, thought Frank. That was the way they did it. He should have known. First the butter then the red-hot poker.

He was in his parade uniform, his hat and baton set parallel on the desk in front of him, his hands, bandaged inside black leather gloves, resting on the edge of the desk. Behind him the window and the trees. In front, he could see himself in the reflection of the framed photograph of his passing-out do at Bramshill. He looked calm enough.

'Great,' said Wally the Flash. 'Nice bit of back lighting there.'

As Wally hunched and stooped round the office for a properly obsequious angle, Frank could hear himself hammering on the bars of his self-control. In the wheezing silence the voice inside him screamed like a maniac.

Why? Why do it? Why let it happen? Get rid of this fat ugly lump of shit before he signs your fucking death warrant –

The flash jolted him upright in the chair.

'Brilliant, great, sorry about that. Thanks, Inspector Webber. Now just a couple with the hat on.'

'What? Oh right.' He watched his two gloved hands reach forward and pick it up, smelling the comforting mixture of hair and the waterproof oilskin-like material inside it. He was aware of examining the shiny black peak for fingermarks, of part of him saying fine while the maniac inside him raged and cursed, and then settling the blue-black cap squarely on his head.

'Jaw up a touch. Touch more. So I can get the eyes.' The photographer squatted and squinted into his old Mamiya reflex. Flash. 'One more, looking away.' Flash. 'Fine, lovely, great, terrific.'

'Is that it?'

You vain bastard, said the voice. *You prat.*

'Just one more, standing this time. Let's see,' said Wally the Flash, venturing a yellow grin. 'Let's do it naval style, starboard profile.' He was an old *Mirror* man, he said, turning Frank this way and that, now freelancing from Gloucester down as far as Yeovil. He didn't go a lot on Yeovil. Frank could smell the stale beer on him. He was well into his fifties, in a baggy jacket with leather elbows, maroon cardigan, shiny trousers and scuffed pale grey shoes. Flash. 'Smashing. You couldn't give me a bit of bio, could you?'

Inspector at twenty-eight. Now thirty-two. One previous commendation. Tackling an assailant threatening a young woman with a carving knife. He didn't say the guy was sixty-three and rolling drunk, or that he fucked the girl himself after. Yes, Bristol born and bred. Married. No children.

Wally scribbled it all down and gave Frank his card. WALLACE HALLETT, PRESS, WEDDING, INDUSTRIAL. There was an address in Thornbury, Avon. 'Any extra prints give us a bell direct.' He drove off in a beige F-reg Cavalier, and Frank noted the number on a sticky yellow SelloNote.

Nemesis, said the voice. *It's started*.

Bollocks, said Frank, and rang jamjar Bob in PR. No there were no plans for any releases as far as Bob knew. Mind you, he laughed, only par for the course, Bob being the last to know. But no, Wally the Flash wouldn't pull anything *vis-à-vis* the tabloids on his own, he'd lose the morgue job. Then Bob said that if this double rape and murder hit the fan they'd dig Frank out the drawer and wheel him on to the catwalk. Show the watching millions what a decent clean-cut copper looked like. Frank knew how it worked, news management. I tell you what, Frank, said Bob, Day-Off Cop Risks Life to Save White Pensioner from Black

Mugger. Writes itself, said Bob. But not to worry, Bob would keep Frank posted, TV or not TV-wise. Any case Frank, it can only redound to your credit.

Frank put the phone down. Dig him out the drawer. Decent, clean-cut. Redound. They'd already been talking to each other. Why? What could they know? Nothing. Nothing from Forensic. Nothing from the witness. Nothing from the two mushes on the case.

Time to get paranoid, said the voice.

Frank started thinking about the nurse. The oatmeal baby-powder smell of her. The white skin under the rain. The noise she made when he shoved it up her. It started a hard-on rising.

He wanted to fuck her again. Fuck her and kill her.

Yes, that was the answer.

A couple of hours later, Nina from PR walked into the squad room on the fourth floor of the Well and dropped a red-tabbed PR release labelled FOR INTERNAL INFORMATION ONLY in Des Chaffey's in-tray. Vic stopped tapping away at his progress report and watched Des watching Nina's black and white checked bottom walking out again. Des's fat pink cheeks blew out like a trumpet player's, exhaling a thoughtful, hopeless lust.

'It's a good job your missis can't read your mind,' said Vic.

'She can,' said Des. 'That's the trouble.' He picked up the PR release. 'I tell you, if the rest of this place was as quick off the mark as those pissheads in PR there wouldn't be any fucking crime problem.' He walked over to Vic's desk, reading the three-paragraph report. 'Here you are,' he said, dropping it in front of Vic, 'your old mate's covered himself in glory again.'

'What old mate?'

'Webber,' said Des.

Vic glanced at the heading.

CAR THIEF FOILED ON DAY OFF.
INSPECTOR FRANK WEBBER TO RECEIVE
SECOND COMMENDATION.

Frank, thought Vic. Yeah, that was his name. Of
course it was. Rhymed with wank.

11

Vic didn't say who he was but that didn't stop the sister from Gynae. She was even shittier on the phone than face to face. Staff Nurse Wilcox wasn't technically ill. She'd been sent home Sunday teatime. Health Trust policy on beds. No she hadn't informed the police. No she didn't know when she'd be back on the wards. Not her department. But while she was on the subject she was going to take the opportunity to register the strongest possible complaint concerning the extremely rude and offensive behaviour of one of the officers on the case with regard not only to patient harassment but also to the Trust's strict Anti-Smoking Rule. She'd taken his name, rank and number – Vic put the phone down while she was still speaking and saw Cromer looking down at him across the squad-room desk. More fucking disapproval.

'Sit down, John, you're not in uniform.' It was Monday lunchtime, Vic's third day on the rape case and fifth day of Cromer. 'What's the matter now?'

Cromer remained standing, arms behind his back, feet at ten to two. 'I don't think we should have let Evens go.'

'Who's Evens?'

'Nigel. The Reject.'

'John,' said Vic, 'this is the third and last time I'm asking you to sit down. D'you know why?'

'No.' Cromer didn't move.

'Because it intimidates people.' Vic stood up and

moved the grey metal chair to the back of Cromer's knees. 'When you intimidate people, they do not talk to you. When you stand between them and the light and look them directly in the eye you're threatening them, you're saying I am here to control you. I don't need it, John. Especially not from you.'

Cromer thought about it, took his time, sat down.

'Thank you,' said Vic.

'He was AB positive,' said Cromer.

'That's right.'

'He refused a sperm test.'

'That's right.'

'We could have held him on sus.'

'Right again.'

'Refusal to co-operate, wasting police time.'

'You're dying to do somebody, aren't you John?'

'I think we should have gripped him, yes.'

'Six kids say he was on the bus with them till half-three.'

'Travellers,' said Cromer.

'Scum of the earth, aren't they, John?'

'Suppose he does a runner?'

'If we'd banged him up for the night he would have done a runner.'

Cromer said nothing, neither agreeing nor disagreeing, still looking boyish and sullen. Maybe it meant he was thinking. That would be something, some fucking progress made; so far it was two steps forward and three steps back. That was the trouble with all these bright kids like Cromer. They knew all the rules and thought all you had to do was apply them and bang, you got a result. If only, thought Vic.

'I signed him out though, didn't I?' said Cromer.

'What's that supposed to mean?'

'Me they jump on.'

So that was it. The kid was already protecting his arse. Like some fifty-year-old fucking desk sergeant out in fucking Fyfield or somewhere.

'You're too straight for this job, son.'

'How?'

'Rules are there to be bent.'

Vic watched Cromer redden up and waited. Out it came.

'That may be all right for you,' said Cromer. 'Seems to be your chief aim in life – '

'What's that?'

'Going round antagonising people – '

'You, you mean?'

'No I don't mean me. The DI, the DCI, anybody. You seem to want to go round antagonising people just because they're your fucking superiors – '

'Seniors,' said Vic. 'Not superiors – '

'There you go, you see.' Cromer was looking at him like his fucking uncle. 'That's what got you where you are today. Thirty-eight and still a sergeant.'

Vic grinned at Cromer. 'Thirty-seven actually. Always try and get the facts right, John.' Egg him on.

'It's not just Nigel the fucking Reject, it's your mate Billy fucking Jewel and neither of them are our fucking case. You were told to stick to the fucking girl – '

'Well,' said Vic, 'at least you're getting hold of the vocabulary.'

'Bollocks.'

Vic let the grin drop. 'Who told you, John? Who told you the DCI said stick to the girl?' Got you, you little bastard.

Cromer swallowed. 'I overheard.'

'You mean you were earholing.'

'If you like.'

'Thank fuck you've learned something.' Vic stood up. 'You know what a three-legged sack race is?'

'Yeah.'

'What?'

'Two blokes and they each have one leg tied together inside a sack. Why?'

'That's what this is like.'

Vic left Cromer to start offender-profiling on Ellie's sexual history. Any of her previous blokes had any form Cromer would dig it out. Driving without a seatbelt, anything. That's what the kid was good at. He'd got to be good at something with four A levels. Better than four Os and City and Guilds in metalwork.

On the way up from the Well to Clifton Vic drove along the docks. The water was glittering with a light southwesterly driving sets of small diagonal waves. Across the water Brunel's six-masted *Great Britain* lay wedged in its dry dock, fully restored now and gleaming in black and white and gold, but somehow trapped-looking, like Gulliver, overrun by tourists and schoolchildren. His old man had taught him the names of the masts and told him it was always good for a bet on a pint in a pub. Vic had waited thirty years for someone to ask him. No one ever had, but he still remembered the names. Fore, main, mizzen, jigger, driver and striker.

He drove on up through Hotwells, wondering what would have happened if he had followed his old man into the Navy. He'd probably be out by now. Little pension, fishing boat somewhere, few pigeons, and a wife who hadn't fucked off to fucking Cricklewood because she said he was never there.

Ellie was in her quilted pink and white dressing gown having a French-style Leek and Potato Cup-a-Soup with

123

Croutons. She asked Vic if he'd like one. He watched her pad across the small kitchen to the gas stove. Her bare feet and ankles were very pink and clean, just out of the bath by the look, and after a night's rest her face had lost the pale tense angularity he had seen in the hospital. She looked softer, more feminine, more relaxed, and her hair, tied back off her face with a band of rainbow-coloured velvet, let him see the creamy white skin of her neck.

Ellie, tipping the contents of the Cup-a-Soup sachet into a hospital mug, felt him looking at her. She was glad she'd asked the WPC, Jane, about him. She knew he was separated, and should have been promoted, but hadn't been because he was thought to be too bolshy. He'd certainly been straight enough with her in hospital, direct but not unsympathetic, apart from when he called her a liar, but then he'd explained and apologised about that, and she hadn't been particularly lady-like either. Oh well. Anyway, they were stuck in this together for the time being, so try and make the best of it. He wasn't exactly unattractive, a bit battered perhaps, and although part of her said Oh my God not another married man, not another loser, another part of her – the nurse part, she supposed – wanted to know more, what had gone wrong, where did it hurt? Still, she couldn't help her nature, and apart from anything else, he seemed to be on her side, and most of all she felt safe with him. Maybe that was all she needed for now. It was curious, she thought, a bit like being a patient with a doctor, like being with a stranger you had to help, a stranger who had intimate rights over you.

She thought he looked pretty worn out, same old baggy suit, maybe the soup would perk him up a bit.

124

'How are you?' he said, clearing his throat after the climb up the stairs.

'Well, I'm still a bit sore but I'm much better than I was, I can tell you.' That's it, girl, start off brisk and keep it going.

'You look a lot better. You sleep well?'

'Better than you did, by the look of you.'

He pushed his thick dark hair back, combing his fingers through it. 'Yeah, well, you know, weekends are always worse.' Vic had already decided not to tell her about Pauline: it was better if they thought they had your undivided attention. He watched how she struck the match, holding the big kitchen box well away from her. She lit the dented old kettle, blew the match out and dropped it in a bowl with a neatly crayoned sticky-paper label reading 'Matches' in rounded classroom lettering. She saw him looking. 'Marge and Kay use them at school, in projects.'

'Oh, right.' He made a mental note to send the WPC round to check with Marge and Kay that Ellie was telling the truth about her sex life or whether there was some bloke she had conveniently left out.

'She was here yesterday evening.' It was as if she'd read his mind.

'Who was?'

'Jane,' said Ellie. 'The WPC. She's nice, I like her. She came round just after I got back from Gynae.'

'That sister of yours had a right old go at me again.'

'What for?' Ellie tipped boiling water into the whitish powder and stirred it vigorously with a teaspoon. The tinkling noise reminded Vic of coming home from school and his mother making Bovril; he realised it was a long time since he'd watched a woman doing things in the kitchen, even if it was only making Cup-a-Soup. 'You have to give it a good stir,' said Ellie, 'to get rid of the lumps. What was she on about this time?'

'Oh, patient harassment, smoking, my attitude in general, you name it.' The smell of the steam in the air was nice.

'It's supposed to have garlic in it.' She put the Bristol Royal Infirmary mug in front of him. On the back it said 'Not To Be Removed From This Canteen'. 'Don't look at the china,' she said. 'It'll be too hot to drink for five minutes.'

'Thanks. Certainly smells good.' It was always the same, you had to pussyfoot around for a couple of minutes, vamp till ready, give the customer a chance to relax.

She sat down opposite him, elbows on the narrow blue-check Formica table. 'The thing about Sister Bowden is her husband's got pulmonary cancer, poor man.'

'I didn't know that.'

'No, but you can see why she gets a bit fierce.'

'Maybe I should give her a ring.' Knowing he wouldn't.

She spooned a few quarter-inch-square croutons out of her mug, put them in her mouth and licked her lips. 'That's the funny thing about working on Gynae, looking after women all the time, it does make you extra-ratty for some reason, I don't know whether it's all the hormones flying about, but she can be a cow if she's got it in for you.'

'How about you when you go back?'

'Oh, I shall be on Casualty.' She didn't look very happy about the idea. 'But it doesn't worry me. I stand up to her when I am on Gynae. I can stick up for myself, you know. Well usually I can.' She looked down at her lap, pulled fussily at the dressing gown to cover her legs

126

more, made a face at him that said only too clearly, What's happened has happened and there's nothing anybody can do about it.

'Look. I'm sorry about this,' he began.

'I know you are. So am I, believe me.' She was looking him straight in the eye, face to face, no more than eighteen inches away across the table. It could be co-operation, it could be confrontation; the only thing to do was wait and see. 'At least I haven't started dreaming about it,' she went on. 'Not so far anyway, so that's one good thing.'

'Did Jane mention the Rape Crisis Centre?'

'To be honest I don't think I can face it.'

'You mean telling more strangers?'

She nodded. 'We can get counselling at the hospital.'

'I think you might be better off.'

'That's what Jane said.'

'When do you go back?'

'I've got to see old Chaudhury Wednesday.'

'The Indian guy?'

She glanced up at him over her spectacles. 'Sri Lankan, actually. And then if it's healing all right, no infection, I'm due to go back on Thursday, on nights.' She spooned up a few more croutons. 'Which is quite good, really. It'll suit me better.'

'Why, because it's quieter?'

'On Casualty? Hardly. No it's because there's somebody there I'd sooner not see.'

'Fair enough.' Vic could see it was something she wanted to talk about, which was good, it meant she was opening up, but it was one to follow up later, when she wasn't expecting it. For the moment he wanted to keep it impersonal, to get her to trust him on that level before going any deeper and laying on her what he'd

127

really come for. 'How long are you going to be on nights?'

She smiled at him. 'Nobody would guess you were a copper really, would they?'

He smiled back. 'What d'you mean?'

'It's just one question after another, isn't it? Must be like living with the third degree.'

'No, what I meant was, I might need to get in touch with you.' Nights was good. She would be free in the day.

'Oh, I see. Well, it should be ten nights on the trot and then four nights off but if anybody on days is off sick, they can call you in.' She took a slurpy sip at the soup. Either she didn't care that Vic was there, or she felt at home with him. He found himself comparing her with his wife, who had always nagged him about his table manners. Don't suck your teeth like that. Don't do that to your ears. Get your elbows off the table and stop holding your knife like a pen.

Maybe Northern girls, Midlanders, were less fussy, more straightforward. This one certainly was. She was straight, she'd been doing a decent job, rougher than most, and she'd been raped. Now she was going to have to go through it again. Raped in the name of the law. Vic felt he should be saying sorry in advance, but what was the point? He was going to do it anyway. 'Let me know, will you?'

'Yes I will.'

Time to move along. 'How did you get on with Jane?'

'You mean the story of my riotous sex life?'

'That's right.' Vic waited, watching her bite her bottom lip, and wanting to say to her, look, forget it, let's go and have a drink and something to eat, and maybe a couple of laughs and see what happens. 'You don't have to talk to me without a WPC present if that's

128

what you'd prefer.' There, straight out of the book and a real downer.

'No, it's all right. There's nothing much to tell anyway.' But the warmth had gone. He'd applied the rules, and she'd gone back from being friendly to being a victim. He could see it in her eyes. Oh well, one up for the rules. 'Jane said she'd be faxing you a copy of the list.'

'That's right. It came this morning.'

'It's not much, is it, I mean, when it's all written down.' She was trying to smile, make a rueful joke out of it, but really she was looking to him for reassurance.

'Nobody's is.' The soup was still too hot and tasted like sweetened white cardboard, but at least the delay gave him a chance to work out how to get some sort of contact back on track. 'You could put mine on the back of a betting slip.'

'What, win or lose?'

'What do you think?'

Ellie waited for him to continue; when he didn't, she put it down to male pride and said, 'Oh well, join the club.'

She put both hands round her mug as if to warm them. Vic did the same and they looked at each other across the table, staring directly and deliberately into each other's eyes. It couldn't have been more than about four seconds, but it made him feel as if the sun had suddenly come out, and gave her a warm feeling in the stomach. Her eyes, he noticed now, had little flecks of gold in amongst the blue-grey, with dark curved lashes behind the glasses. She thought his were pale as ice. He could smell the cream she'd put on her face, and another, warmer, oatmealy smell. She made a sad little grimace, disconnecting them, that could have meant Here we go again, or, more likely, What a pair of losers.

As she leaned back from the table, mug still in both hands, the moment of intimacy vanished and real sound came back into the world. 'Actually,' she said, 'we had quite a laugh about it, in the end.'

'Who did?'

'Jane. Me and Jane. She's very easy to get on with, isn't she? Don't you think?'

'Yeah, she's OK.' Personally, he thought she was too big and lumpy, but women didn't see each other like that. He told himself to get Jane's version.

'She's more my age than Marge or Kay, or maybe it's just something to do with the sort of jobs we both do, I don't know. I mean, infant teachers, they spend all day with little kids and other teachers, they don't see the sort of things we do, do they?' She was away now, freed, he thought, by what had happened, by the look between them, uncrossing her legs and leaning her full breasts on the table top, treating him more or less as she had probably treated Jane, with some sort of confidence. It would come in useful if he managed not to break it.

'I think they were, I don't know, sort of po-faced, a bit prissy, shocked really, me just coming out of hospital after – after being raped. . . .' She cocked her head at him to see what he made of her using the word. He nodded encouragingly, it was progress, she'd come out with it, the recognition of what had happened to her. Good. Then he told himself he was going soft in his old age and tried to ignore the slight swelling inside his trousers. You bastard, he thought.

'Shocked at what?' he said, sipping his Cup-a-Soup. It tasted all right now, pleasantly warming.

She smiled at him knowingly, almost flirtatiously for

130

the first time. 'Oh, you know, me and Jane laughing and joking about men and their little ways.'

'Such as?'

'None of your business. Women's talk.' She pulled herself up straight and tried to sound sensible. 'It was only to get over the embarrassment. You know, all that business of having to say what you've done, who with and where. . . .' She shook her head and looked down, trying to suppress the memory, but when she looked up again her eyes were wet and sparkling. 'My God, you do get into some funny situations though, don't you?' She was grinning and biting her lip at the same time, eyeing him with a sort of frank but secretive delight. Then whatever it was she was remembering got the better of her and she burst out laughing, pushed her chair back and grabbed for a sheet of kitchen towel to wipe her eyes. Vic could see the swell of her breast where the thick quilted material of her dressing gown bent open. 'I'm sorry,' she said, 'I shall have to go to the loo.'

As she padded out of the kitchen Vic saw the small brown scrubbed and smudged bloodstain on the seat of the dressing gown. Saturday, when he helped her into the ambulance, it had been a bright red patch.

She was dressed when she came back. No make-up, a loose blue-striped denim shirt, jeans and flat black shoes. She asked him if he would like some toast.

The grill lit with a soft blue plop. While she waited for it to glow red she placed four slices of thin white Tesco bread on the bars of the grey enamelled pan and reached down a tub of low-fat spread. Vic hadn't had toast in the afternoon for years. 'Actually,' she said, 'I couldn't remember all their names or addresses, so it's not much help really, is it?'

There had been about fifteen names on the greasy fax sheet Vic had left with Cromer. Over half were just first names and districts in and around Birmingham.

'A lot of the boys were just, you know, students, medics and that, from when I was a student nurse at QEH. People you met at parties, nothing really serious, just part of growing up.'

She bent over to turn the toast. Vic found himself watching the centre seam of her jeans where it curved between her buttocks. She certainly had a good solid backside. The trouble was, the more he found himself liking her the worse he felt about what he had to do to her.

'The Nurses' Home was this huge brick prison block opposite the hospital. The more they lock you up the more determined you are to get out, aren't you?' She turned round to him. 'Well at that age you are. I've got an old address book with my things at home if you really need it, but I didn't really want to tell Mum, she's had enough to worry about since Dad died.'

'When was that?'

'Eighteen months ago, he had a stroke and just went, but she's still, you know, lost.'

'Yeah,' said Vic. 'That's what happens.'

'What about your parents?'

'The old man went about five years ago, the old lady the year after.' He offered her a cigarette. She shook her head, but put a Present from Ilfracombe ashtray in front of him. 'Thanks. You don't have to tell your mother, not yet anyway, but we might need the addresses when and if it comes to the trial.'

'When they try to make out I'm just another old slag?'

'They'll try anything, Ellie.'

'What about the others?'

132

'Any of them bear you a grudge, write you threatening letters?'

'What, you mean "If I can't have you nobody else will" sort of thing?'

'Yeah, that sort of thing.'

'Not really, no.' She was smiling at the thought. 'I don't really seem to be the *femme fatale* type. Why d'you want to know?'

'We'd have to have them in and interview them, especially if they've got any form.' There was no point in telling her that was what Cromer was doing at that very moment. 'Otherwise we just check their records. Discreetly, they won't know.'

'Good.'

'What about the last one?'

'What, Spiros?'

'No, before him, Doctor Whatsisname, Simmons.'

She turned away from him, back to the grill and took the toast out. 'He was the reason I went to Corfu and ended up with NSU.'

'What happened?'

'In Corfu?' She was trying to dodge him. Before, she'd wanted to talk about it. Now she didn't. He must have got the timing wrong somewhere.

'No, I mean before you went away.'

She turned round to face him. 'He was married.' There was a new defiance about her. 'His wife came back.'

'Had they split up?'

'No.' She busied herself with setting out a couple of blue and white Woolworth's plates. 'She'd been in America, visiting her family. I was just a fill-in. One of the many, as it turned out. I didn't think so at the time, but I shouldn't have been so bloody stupid, should I?'

'We're all bloody stupid,' said Vic.

133

'I didn't think I was.' Vic waited, knowing there was more to come. 'Some men lie to you so much you end up lying to yourself, you know that?'

It made Vic feel even less comfortable about what he'd come to do but there was no way out. 'Now what?' he asked.

'I call him Doctor and he calls me Staff.' She tried to shrug it off and failed.

'So it's all over?'

'Absolutely.' She looked as if she meant it. 'We all make one big mistake.'

'You're telling me,' said Vic.

'Anyway, it's all over now.'

'We still might have to see him, Ellie.' Let Cromer do it. There was no point in getting hard with some guy he'd never met just because he'd shafted her. Maybe the kid was right, maybe he did like to antagonise people. Rile them into saying something useful.

'Why?' said Ellie. 'He's got nothing to do with this.'

'We have to see him in case he's called as a witness.'

She frowned. 'Who by?'

'The defence.'

Vic watched the expressions move across her face. Bafflement. Anger. Feeling trapped. A dawning sense of what she'd got herself into through no fault of her own. 'You mean it's all – the whole thing could come out in court?'

'If the defence so choose.'

'Oh my God.'

'What?'

'I don't care about him, but it's hardly fair on his wife, is it?'

'Maybe it won't come to that.'

'I hope not.'

Vic decided to lie. 'I shouldn't be telling you this,

134

but you can always leave his name out, if you want to.'
It was already too late, the list was already on file, but
if it made her grateful, made her think he was bending
the rules for her, it would make the next stage easier.

She thought for a while. She had only seen the wife
a couple of times. A slim blonde woman with small
features and long straight fair hair, and a sort of vague,
startled air as if she didn't quite know where she was,
as if she'd been born prematurely and the shock had
never worn off. Whichever way you looked at it, it
wasn't her fault, and Ellie felt a sudden protective rush
towards the woman, and a consequent gratitude
towards Vic. 'Thanks,' she said, pushing the tub of low-
fat spread towards him. 'It's not butter and there's only
one knife, I'm afraid.'

'No problem,' said Vic.

'You've had a bust-up as well, haven't you?'

'As it happens.' He spread both slices of toast, taking
his time about it and wondering how she'd found that
out. He wiped the knife on the back of one of the slices
before handing the knife to her, handle first. 'Who told
you?'

'I asked Jane about you.' So there, said her look.

'Why?'

'Why shouldn't I? I mean, you know all about me,
don't you?'

'That's part of the job.'

'Even so, it doesn't make it any easier for me, you
know.'

'No, I suppose not.' Part of him wanted to tell her;
the other part was already wondering how he could
use it. 'We were married for eight years and she pushed
off about six months ago.'

'Jane said you were separated.'

'Not officially.'

135

'You think you'll get back together, then?'

Vic bit the corner off a slice of toast. 'No.'

Ellie spread her slices thickly and cut them into triangles. 'Good,' she said, taking a hefty bite out of one.

'Why's that?'

She chewed away thoughtfully, and then, when she had finished, she smiled at him but didn't say anything. Vic figured it was time to spring the trap.

'Ellie, I want to ask you something.'

She licked her lips all around like a child. 'Go on, then.'

'I want you to come back with me to the SOC.'

'What's that?'

'Scene of the crime.'

He drove her along Cornwallis and parked on the short straight in the middle of Hensman's Hill.

'You're blocking the traffic.'

He put the POLICE sign in the rear window. 'Tough.'

He could see she thought he was showing off. Maybe he was. The important thing was to keep her sweet until it came to pushing her over the edge.

It was the smell that brought it back to her, the smell of dead leaves and wet earth. He stood aside to let her pass through the narrow iron gate first. She hesitated and glanced up at him, hands deep inside her old blue duffel coat, holding on to herself to stop the sudden cold shivery feeling in her stomach.

'Come on, Ellie,' he said, groping for something inside his suit jacket, 'let's get it over with, shall we?'

She took a couple of quick steps through the gate, not liking the feeling of him behind her, not liking it at all, and swung round to face him. He had his black

136

pocket-book out and was looking straight past her down the path. The blue and white POLICE DO NOT CROSS tapes had gone. Three days, he thought, and she was already history. Although it was a cold day and her cheeks had had a just-out-of-the-bath glow in the flat, out here she had gone pale. Vic hoped she was going to be up to it; even if she wasn't it was too late now.

'I want you to show me exactly what he did, where, and what he said.'

There was a cold, hard edge to his voice that made her feel wobbly and panicky, unaccountably afraid of him. She took a breath to control herself. 'This is you being a copper now, isn't it?'

'Look, Ellie –' he tried to sound friendly and warm but he knew he was getting too close to the push to fake it successfully – 'if you think it's going to be too much for you, if you don't want to, you don't have to, but we're going to have to go through with it sooner or later, and the fresher it is in your mind the better.'

She stood for a moment, looking at the black mud and leaves between her feet, then shot him a look that was sullen with betrayal. 'Better for who?'

'The reason we're doing this,' he said patiently, 'is because the defence are going to try to nail you to the wall on every single minor detail in any way they can.'

'All right.' She hunched herself up inside her duffel coat, took a step towards the stone gate pillar, stopped, and said in a low dull voice, 'This is where he got me from behind, round the neck.' She walked a couple of paces across the path to the other side of the gate. 'This is where I threw my bag –'

'What did he say?'

'What did he say?' He wasn't even looking at her.

He had his pocket-book open and his black ballpoint ready.

'The exact words.' He waited. 'If you can't remember, Ellie, just say so.'

'He said shut up and you won't get hurt, struggle and I'll – struggle and I'll fucking kill you.'

'Then what?'

She moved down the path and off another couple of paces into the wet shrubbery. 'I tried to get away, break his grip on me, and he hit me across the side of the head.' She looked up defiantly. 'Somewhere round here.'

'Thanks.' He paced out the distance carefully and made a note. 'Did you say anything? Scream, anything?'

'I couldn't, could I? I mean, I must have tried – '

'You don't remember?'

'He'd got me round the throat, just here.' She pointed to the base of her neck, just above the collarbone. A smudge of bruise was still there.

'Any thought of self-defence?'

'One smack round the head and all that's gone – you can't think of anything – '

Vic nodded. 'That happens, the first time.'

The first time? What did he have to say that for? Once is enough, she thought, more than enough. The fear started to come back. She felt the hot sour taste of bile rising and thought, *he's as bad as the rapist.*

He pointed the way down the path with his ballpoint. 'I want you to go first and show me exactly where you think the assault occurred.' She walked off, stumbling once, and stopped after about twenty yards, facing the wall, staring at the gap between the bushes. 'Are you sure?' he called.

'Yes!' Her voice was unsteady. 'Yes I am.' She watched him walk up to her. He kept his eyes on the

138

path, counting off the paces, glancing from one side of the path to the other. He stopped a couple of yards from her. If he was trying not to threaten her it wasn't working. He flipped open the pocket-book.

'Go on.'

'He bent me over –' There were two spots of red on her cheeks and her eyes had gone glittery.

'You don't have to do that.' He flipped over a page, and she saw he was checking her story against what she had said in hospital. 'Just say what he said.'

'He said fuck you fuck you fuck you over and over again. While he was doing it.'

She watched him make another note, as if he was marking her homework. Any second now, she thought, and he'll lick the end of his ballpoint. 'Good girl,' he said. It was all there, word for word. She would make a good witness –

Out of the blue she was flying at him, nails out for his face, lunging a kick at his groin. 'You bastard!' she was screaming at him, 'You rotten bastard! You're all the same!'

The notebook flew through the air and landed in one of the bushes, showering raindrops. Shit. If he had to scrap it and copy the whole bloody thing out again they'd be on to him for falsifying evidence –

She lunged at him again, screaming herself hoarse. Vic wondered if any of the nuns were watching. He caught her by the coat sleeve and pulled her to one side. When controlling disorderly or hysterical women, it said in the book, the officer should avoid disturbing or damaging their clothing or, for obvious reasons, injuring or touching their breasts. Something like that, anyway –

She felt her arm twist up behind her back and

smelled the tobacco on him. 'You bastards – all the same –'

'No we're not, Ellie –'

She tried to pull her arm out of the sleeve. 'You are! You know you are! Bringing me up here! All this!' She flailed her free arm at his head. 'Then you say exactly the same thing he said –'

He caught her by the wrist, and spun her right round, facing him but unable to lash out at him, holding her fast in his arms. 'What was that?' She went weak, heavy as a sack of wet sand. He kept hold of her. 'What was that, Ellie? What did he say? What same thing? Ellie?'

She lifted her face up to him, glaring at him. He could smell her soft frizzy hair.

'Good girl. You called me good girl. When you finished with me you called me good girl.' She started sobbing against him. He held on to her, comforting her, trying to work it out.

'Is that what he did? Ellie, is that what he did?'

'Yes.' A meek voice, like a hurt child's.

'You never mentioned that before, Ellie.'

She twisted round in his arms, her face smeary with tears, accusing him. 'You bastard.'

'No I'm not, love.'

She put her head against his chest. He could feel the solid warmth of her convulsing and sobbing against him and once more thought about any nuns watching.

'Yes you are,' she said.

After he had taken her home, he drove the maroon Escort out of sight along the curve of Cornwallis Crescent, then pulled in and stopped. He took out the wet pocket-book, checked that the ballpoint ink hadn't run, and put paper tissues between the pages. Then he made another entry. *Good girl. Possible trademark.* When he looked in the rear-view mirror to straighten his hair he saw a faint, slightly cocky, killer's grin looking back at him.

I'm coming to get you, you fucker.

Frank squirted the litre-size Badedas into the bath and watched the heavy liquid lasso out on to the white enamel. It looked like fluorescent green come.

While it foamed up under the water he posed his long smooth not-hairy-enough body this way and that in front of the mirror. Broad across the shoulders, still not deep enough in the chest but plenty there on the thighs. Too bad the tan was going so fast. Every day at least once he stood in front of the long bathroom mirror, always expecting his reflection to have somehow improved. But every day it turned out the same, although some days it looked better than others. As a general rule, the less he drank the better it looked – unless he'd been off drinking and screwing, which always seemed to tone up the definition. The trouble was, the older you got the more you drank; it was inevitable as you went up the police ladder. When he made Chief Inspector, for example, he would have to cut down on the extramaritals – to start with, anyway.

On the other hand, the more promotion you pulled the more silence you bought. Everybody had little deals going – discounts, free dinners, thirds off here and there. Compared to screwing, little deals could do a lot more damage in the end. Frank thanked God he'd always kept his nose clean in that respect. So it could work out. The thing was to get more on them than they had on you. A simple matter of contacts, really.

The thighs were good, though. He made the long

double muscles jump and tense, alternating them. His prick joggled up and down, then started to elongate under his gaze. He'd lost the horizontal ridges on his stomach unless he yoga'd them back by swirling his abdominals with that exercise Rae used to tighten the walls of her cunt.

At least there was no gut yet. Still washboard flat. His prick nodded agreement, starting to rise. Down boy. And down it went. He smiled, showing his white teeth to himself. Not many people can do that. Then he thought, you dickhead –

Rae said he was in love with himself. Well, so what, so was she. If you don't like yourself, an old girlfriend had once told him, black-haired and a big spreading black bush with a line of it right up to her belly-button like a bloke, nobody else will. What was her name? Big dark Irish piece. Never mind, it would come to him in the bath when he went through the parade of old fucks, one two three and four star.

'If you don't like yourself nobody else will.'

Mave. Mavis something. Conley. Yeah, that was it, soft skin, said 'Oh Jesus' a lot. He tilted the line of his jaw at his reflection. People had always seemed to like looking at him, in or out of uniform. He grinned and arched one eyebrow at his reflection. You big handsome fucker.

Early in their relationship when she still had the GTI, still played tennis at Redland, Rae had once peroxided his short and curlies to make them look sun-bleached. It had stung like a bitch at the time. She said it made him look like a Greek god. Later he found out one acrid wine-sodden evening it was to remind herself of some blond Australian git she'd fucked brainless on Kos.

If you had money you could always have a better

143

time. She'd always had more than him. She still had – and kept two-thirds of the house in her name. That was all down to her parents putting a third in, a fact that her old man never ceased to mention. Never mind, he'd had his own back since. A bit of fresh at least once a month for the last three years – including most of her mates. He looked out the window to see if any of the neighbours' wives were on watch. No, they would be picking their kids up from school. Anyway, he'd had all the ones that were halfway decent. Only the ugly buggers left. They could be the best shags, though. Forget it, there was work to do. He always thought well in the bath and this was important.

Steam filmed the window then slowly filled the mirror. It was just on four when he climbed into the white foam and soft green slimy water. Ahhhh! Too hot. Lobster bollocks again. He toed some cold in. Rae said all these hot baths would make him impotent. That'd be the fucking day.

Now then, how to kill the nurse.

It was a quarter to six when Rae came in.

'Frank?'

'In the bath.' He heard her heels tick-tock into the kitchen to dump the shopping. Good. He'd been waiting for her. The water was blood-warm now and after all the thinking he'd put in he felt like giving her one. He'd worked out a couple of alternative procedures and a method of operation; until he got a rundown on the nurse's movements that was enough for one day. He could get all that, plus all the other reports, straight off the terminal. Thank Christ for electronics; it meant he could stay one jump ahead and put it down as all part of the day's work. There would be no traces, and even if there were, all he had to say was he was keeping

144

up to speed on area workloads, and the Brandon Hill rape and murder was still there as cover. The other thing was to talk to the lads, get the current shit on that no-no Hallam. There were a lot of guys like Hallam, Frank thought; start off like a rocket, come down like a burnt stick. Hallam had certainly had it all about him ten years ago on that Selection Board course but he'd turned out too cocky, too cocky by half. Too, what was the word, abrasive. It took more than grit to rise up through the ranks: soft soap for one, the ability to kiss arse and still come up smelling of roses. There was no difference between men and women, basically: they all had their points of vanity, their areas of weakness, and if you had to butter up the Top Brass, so be it. It was part of the job, they all knew it, the only difference was they called it respect and you called it arselicking.

'Not long now and you'll be there or thereabouts for Chief Inspector.'

Frank felt pleasantly relaxed, and after reviewing a score or so cases from the old fucks file, half-hard and ready for a bit.

'Who's my big hero, then?' She was in her long red jacket and little silk sleeveless black top. He could smell the outdoors still on her, a whiff of white wine and traffic fumes. Her slim grey eyes, he noticed, went straight to his groin. He had deliberately positioned the last foam island over it. Now he blew it away and let the monster rise from the deep.

'How did you know?'

'Some of our PR guys met your friend Bob in Kelly's Wine Bar.'

Rae was senior receptionist at APR, a Queen Square ad agency. She had been for years, the size of her old man's TV Rentals account had got her the job. That and her legs. She put her hand in the green water and, knuckles looking like an alligator head, swam it round his knob and squeezed. 'Mmm,' she said. 'And how long have you been in here?'

'Hour and half. Get in.'

'Let some out then and put more hot in.' She was already out of her jacket. Her bare arms were browner than his. He pulled the French plug thing up with his toes and then turned the mixer lever on.

'You haven't been drinking again?'

Her eyes flicked up guiltily as her short red skirt dropped to the cork floor. 'Only one. Jim had some Sauternes in from Phillips.' She hauled her black silk top off to hide her face. He examined the tops of her thighs for desk-bruises. She was wearing her red suspender belt, high-cut black knickers and stockings. Jim was her boss, a red-faced white-bearded pisshead who wore spotted silk shirts and striped bow-ties. She said she liked him but couldn't fancy him, who could. Even so the old cunt had got her pissed in his office more than once.

'Bottle or glass?' She'd already had one drink-driving this year and got stroppy when he refused to do anything to get her off. As he'd told her straight, that's one thing I don't do, not for you or anybody else.

'Glass.' She peeled off her knickers, fluffed up her mott, gave him that funny don't-hit-me smile and got in. He played with her with his big toe and then stuck it up her and wriggled it about. She lay back, eyes half-closed, lipsticked mouth still a little tight, but tits jiggling nicely in the water. After a while she opened her eyes and said, 'What happened to your hand anyway?'

'I cut it on that little black bastard's wiper.'

'Have you had it seen to?'

146

'Yeah.' He wondered what the big black nurse was doing, how many toes he could get up her.

She leaned forward, moving his foot away. 'They all think you're terrific.'

'I am now. It was shit or bust at the time.'

'Apparently your friend Bob was going pear-shaped he couldn't get it on the early evening news.'

'Yeah, well they're like you, aren't they?'

'What?'

'They're saving it.'

'Oh love.'

'What?'

'I can't do it in ten seconds flat, can I?'

Once he'd made her come, just with his toe and looking at her. Maybe once was all you got with Rae. Carefully, she knelt up, leaned forward and kissed him. He could taste the wine on her tongue. Sweet then brassy. 'Why move my fucking foot then?'

'Because,' she said, pulling back and swinging her nipples across his chest, 'it's not as good as the real thing.' Then she slid backwards, he knees between his, curled her body into an egg shape and dipped her mouth on to his cock. Her straight blonde hair hung over him, just touching the water on his raised-up belly. Perfect. Beautiful. He felt her nibbling and sucking and licking her tongue up the cleft on the underside of his knob. She was good at the old gam business. He wondered as he always did where she got that from. Or, more to the point, who. Then she was going deeper and deeper on him. He ran his bandaged hand down the bumps of her spine and round the curve of her bottom. She was juicy as a fig.

'Good girl, Rae. Good girl.'

For the first time in their married life he felt his penis

147

touch the soft red flesh at the back of her throat. Holy shit. Holy holy shit. Trying to hold back. Failing –

'There,' she said, after she had taken it, swallowed it or gobbed it out he didn't know. Lifting up her dripping mouth, face and hair. 'How's my little hero now, then?' He held her tight against him and for the next five minutes loved her with all his cold stone lump of a heart.

Right down to the fucking tonsils, he thought. Brilliant. She lifted her head from his chest. 'What d'you fancy?'

'There's some white Beaune in the fridge.'

He lay there staring at the ceiling, waiting for the tall, cold, long-stemmed condensation-misted tulip glass to be brought to him. He stretched, hands behind his head. Now that he had decided on the alternatives for the nurse he felt a new, peculiarly warm, childlike affection for Rae, as if she were some kind of soft protective shield between him and the world. She would be his alibi, his own personal fucking airbag in case of accident. He listened to her slim bare feet coming up the stairs and felt grateful for being alive.

King of the fucking castle, kid.

13

Tailored deep blue shirt, canary yellow tie clipped with
a bit of silver chain, tight grey trousers, basketweave
burgundy loafers, short brown hair going thin on top,
Mansell-type moustache, trim build around five-ten,
thin hairy hands spread wide apart on Vic's desk and
head very close to Cromer's. Christ, Vic could smell
the aftershave from the squad-room door. He had come
in at quarter to six and found Des Chaffey and the rest
having pie and chips down the canteen. No wonder
they'd started taking the piss: they knew the guy was
there. The civilian social worker, Paul Pooley by name,
stood back as Vic approached, wiped his palms
together and bared his big white teeth.

'Oh.' Nervously. 'Hi there – '

'Sod off, ducky it's your hometime and we're
working.'

'Well, thanks a bunch.' Paul Pooley went, flinging
the door shut behind him. Cromer was giving him a
mixture of there you go again and where've you been
you never take me for a walk.

'What did Paula want?'

'Why hadn't Ellie been to the Rape Crisis Centre?'

'And you said because of people like him.'

'No I didn't.'

'Then you told him it wasn't obligatory.'

'I didn't say that either.'

'You ever been to the RCC?'

'No I haven't.'

149

'Apart from the doctors it's full of agony freaks getting their rocks off. If there is anybody normal you can bet they're divorced and haven't been fucked for years. All going tut tut and where did he stick it then dear.'

'I think that's a load of crap,' said Cromer.

'I knew you would, John, but I've been there and you haven't. Guys like that are useless, they know they are, we know they are and they know we know. Hi there, you hear that? Hi there. He knows who I fucking am –'

'You fucking CID blokes –'

'*You're a fucking CID bloke, Cromer!*' The bellow shot Cromer back in his seat. Good. Vic waved his arm round the empty room. 'They're all fucking CID blokes! Why d'you think they all fucking walked out when he walked in?'

'Because they're all fucking idiot fucking chauvinists like you!'

Vic loved it, wanted to laugh. How could anybody be so innocent-fucking-stupid? He was quite getting to like Cromer, he was a challenge, a relief, but even so the kid had to have the shit kicked out of him or he'd be fucking useless for fucking ever. And that, Vic reminded himself, was a waste, a waste of Cromer, a waste of Vic and who knows possibly even a waste of some fucking hidden talent – talent for what, though, being a total fucking prat?

Time to cool it, try and get through.

'No, John, we're not all fucking chauvinists, we all have to *act* like fucking chauvinists because we're surrounded by useless wankers like that little dipshit. And you're sitting in my seat.'

Cromer moved. 'Can I ask you something, then?'

'Feel free.' Vic sat down. The plastic was unpleasantly warm.

'We're supposed to keep in contact, in close personal contact, with all sections of the community.'

Vic lit a cigarette. 'For information, yes John.'

'Including gays, right?'

'Yes John.'

'How?'

'Well John, the world out there is full of gays, blacks, women, kids, cats, dogs and budgerigars. But we don't want them in here, in this squad room. This is *our* gaff. See?' Was he getting through? Possibly. 'If you look in the book it's under Esprit de fucking Corps. It only looks like a load of fucking chauvinist crap. See?' He *was* getting through. 'To belong to the fucking Corps you got to have the fucking Esprit. See? Bad language, piss-ups, arrogance, antagonising people, all part of it my son.' Now for it. 'And that particular fairy is a fucking menace and a real – and I mean real – pain in the arse. You follow?'

'No, I don't.'

'He loves coppers. Am I making it clear enough for you? He. Loves. Coppers.'

'Oh.' Cromer went red and pushed his silly cow-flop of soft brown hair off his forehead. There was a bit of recycled purple card sticking out from under the edge of Vic's blotter.

'What's this?'

'It's a comp.'

Vic turned the card over. THIS INVITATION ENTITLES HOLDER AND FRIEND TO TWO SET MEALS AT SUNNI'S. MALAYAN SURINAM SPECIALTIES. WINE NOT INCLUDED. A drawing of a couple of temple statues legovering in a standing position and an address off the Whiteladies main drag.

'He give you this?'

'Yes.' Still sounding hurt. 'It's a friend's of his.'

'Yeah,' said Vic. 'It would be.'

151

'They've just opened.'

'Good. When we going, then?' said Vic.

'He said it was for me and Louise.'

'You told him you were engaged, did you?'

'He asked me if I was single.'

'Funny that,' said Vic. Then he ripped the card in half and dropped it in the square grey waste bin. 'Comps is another thing we don't do.'

'Not what I heard about CID –'

'We,' said Vic, 'meaning you and me. Anyway it's all shit mostly.'

'Oh yeah?'

'Yeah.'

'What about Billy Jewel, then?' Gotcha.

'Billy's a mate,' said Vic. 'My mate.' The kid was right though. Well, half right. The trouble with Billy was you didn't take his Scotch you didn't get the rest of it.

'Course,' said Cromer, nodding. 'That's different.'

'It is if I say it is,' said Vic. 'And while we're on the subject, your Louise is a hairdresser, isn't she? Got her own salon up Fishponds, right?'

'Yes.'

'Well get her to cut your fucking hair, John, it irritates me to buggery and if you're doing the rounds with me I don't want shirtlifters buzzing round us like flies round shit. Get her to cut it off, sweep it back, gel it, any fucking thing only try to start looking like something out of *Taxi Driver* instead of some Saturday night boy tart down the YMCA.'

Cromer was measuring Vic up. Scratching his knuckles, thinking of throwing one. Then he walked away, glanced through the slatted window blind and listened to the Monday night rush building up four floors below. People going home. He walked back to Vic's desk. 'Anything else?'

'Yeah,' said Vic. 'How'd you get on, John?'

Cromer shrugged and pushed the fax of Ellie's list across to Vic. 'Nothing much on that but there was a development on Pauline White just before you came in.'

'Such as?'

'Billy's done a runner. So has Nigel Evens.'

Suck that, smartass.

They were on the same InterCity but Billy didn't know that at first because as they pulled out of Bristol Temple Meads Platform 5 there on the opposite track steaming in and travelling level with Billy for a good two hundred yards was *King Edward I*. Gleaming and smoking in full green and gold Great Western livery pulling the old maroon Torbay Express. Fuck me. The King of the King Class. And there she was less than twenty yards away sliding in under Brunel's curved glass and iron roof cool as a fucking cucumber. He put his Readers' Wives Special down, rushed to the window and clung on just looking. Fuck me. There was a God, there were miracles, there was every fucking thing. Even for a cunt like me, Billy Jewel. Torbay Express on the front, *King Edward I* in black and gold over the wheel arch, massive green and gold boiler – Jesus he'd forgotten how fucking big and huge and daunting and magnificent these fucking things were – two blokes in proper greasy black in the cab, and there on the tender in wide-spaced old-fashioned shadowed gold lettering the initials G W. The engine, the whole train, just slid in, no fancy stuff, no great shouts of steam, just a few wisps and a shimmer of blue-grey smoke almost as dull as diesel, but what a fucking great stunning thing it

153

was, maroon coaches with the old British Rail lion-in-a-circle logo, CHRISTMAS EXCURSION stickers in the windows and a load of bald-headed mushes with beards, sports jackets and camcorders hanging out the windows grinning like fifty-year-old schoolkids. Fucking A.

Billy's own engine he had noticed, as he stumbled, touch of gout, along the platform in his best navy one and a half inch chalk-stripe and a trenchcoat some pissed-up telly bloke had left behind in the Kit Kat, was called ASSOCIATED NEWSPAPERS LIMITED.

Said it all, really.

Billy was in First on the remains of Mandy's Gold Card so they were past Filton-Home-of-Concorde before he saw Nigel. He'd only clocked him once before, hanging round in the rain glaring up at Pauline's ratty net curtains, but it was him all right. The jungle greens, the fast leaning-forward walk, the butting carpet-tile head, the mad glint off the wire glasses, the rucksack towering over the slight frame, arms swinging low and yomping along the corridor like Son of Quasimodo. Christ, all I need. He craned his head forward, saw Nigel cramming himself into the toilet as the guard came up the other way. Typical. The little bastard was trying to wing it. But where the fuck was he going? Billy had a good idea and hoped he was wrong. The more he thought about it he knew he wasn't. Shit and double shit. Billy buried his head in the open frankfurter-coloured legs of the Readers' Wives but they were no help. All big heavy-duty pieces, lying on their backs trying to smile at both ends. He wondered why their blokes always dragged the mattresses downstairs to take their dozy pictures. Maybe they thought they should show off the lounge at the same time.

'Tickets, please.' The guard was a black bloke, neat

154

grey suit moustache and glasses, like a young Trevor McDonald in a bus conductor's hat. He put the Readers' Wives in his lap and kept one hand over Mrs Deirdre Vowles from Plymouth while holding out his ticket with the other.

Clip. 'Change at Birmin'ham and Stafford.'

'Ta, mate.'

'Any good?' said the guard.

'What's that, mate?'

The guard nodded at Billy's lap. 'Quimspotter's Monthly.'

After the guard had gone, Billy put his feet up. Who said they'd got no sense of humour? All fucking equal anyway, though why the poor bastards wanted to live in England and take all that Union Jack lager shit he'd never know. Still good luck to 'em, he'd done his bit for the cause. He'd run a couple of their clubs for them, the Palm Grove and the Salamander, back in the old days when their guys couldn't get a licence. Christ all that goat curry. Yeah, they were all right, same philosophy as him basically – live love get stoned and be happy. Where he'd met Vic, holy shit he was a right tearaway them days. All right, yeah, a tearaway on a leash, had to be, but still a tearaway. Take no shit and take no prisoners. Until he goes and gets married. And then what happens? She goes and pisses off and now old Vic's gone all heavy and dismal and painful. Not like the old days but then nothing is.

Not like when he used to come down the old Salamander to keep an eye on the white trendies. Same old business even then, CID didn't give a fuck about the blacks so long as the white kids stayed out of bother. Not that they were any trouble. All them backcombed scrawny Dusty Springfield lookalikes up Cotham and Clifton liked their bit of black. Not to mention ganja.

Up to Billy, he'd legalise it. No fuck me he'd fucking nationalise it, make it compulsory, stop this fucking trouble all this race stuff all this crack shit. Mind you that was down to the kids off the estates now. Yeah, he had a good scene going down the Jungle till the riots knocked it on the head. He remembered the night, cars in flames and a white mob with hammers and spanners and jack handles coming in saying, from now on it's blacks out, whites only, free curry and a colour bar. The only bar in this place mate is the one I'm standing behind, he'd told one ginger-haired Megadeth-shirted Knowle no-neck and if you don't like it you can fuck off. What they didn't know and Billy did was the Salamander Sports and Social Club was having their weekly cricket meeting upstairs and some of those guys were seriously large. What? Fucking mayhem. Billy smiled to himself and looked out at red-roofed north Bristol. That was the end of it, though.

He only hoped Ellard was up to running the Kit Kat till Wednesday because where Mand was God alone knew. Round her sister Chrissie's was the usual bolt-hole but he wouldn't bet on it this time. This time she'd really got it on her. This time he'd really shit and fell back in it. Anyway, think about all that when he'd irradiated her Gold Card over the next forty-eight hours. She'd go fucking spare when she found out what he'd used it for. But then she always fucking did and there was no getting out of this one. Poor old Pauline. Good old Mand. What a rotten life she'd had. Even before she'd met him. Married to that midnight roofer. What was his name? Sid. Came out after doing four years aggravated in Horfield and fucked off with some middle-aged middle-class hatchet-faced tweed-wearing fucking prison visitor. Then she'd met Billy. Said he made her laugh. Poor old Mand. Ten minutes later the Readers' Wives depressed him so much he made the mistake of going for a drink.

Nigel, cornered in the buffet, giving the guard a load of grief. No he hadn't got a ticket. No he wasn't going to pay. He hadn't got any money, he didn't believe in money, he believed in freedom. Capitalism was slavery and you had to live in peace with your conscience. If the system was oppressive you had a duty to resist it. The guard ought to know that. Passengers at both ends and the guard and Nigel in the middle. Rucksack between his combat boots, standing sideways, feet at ninety degrees, arms folded, one elbow tilted up towards the guard and palms straight out and stiffened. Oh shit, it's Kung Fu Nigel. The buffet attendant rattled the metal shutter down.

'You don' have a valid ticket or the means to buy one, is that right, sir?'

'I've already explained that.'

The guard turned slowly to the back of his ticket book. 'Can I have your name and address please, sir?'

'You don't have that authority.'

'I'm sorry but I do –'

'No,' said Nigel. 'You don't have my authority.'

Billy saw one or two passengers begin to smile, siding with the little bastard. The guard felt it too. 'Will you give your name and address please, sir?'

'No.'

'Take his number, mate,' said a lanky thin-faced kid to Nigel.

'For the las' time I am askin' you for your name and address.' The guard was getting more West Indian every second. Nigel put his chin up, said nothing. The guard closed his book, glanced idly round at both sets of passengers, sucked his teeth and spoke so everyone could hear. 'I'm goin' to have to stop the train at the next station and ask you to leave.' Murmurs of Oh No. 'Do you understand, sir?'

'Yes,' said Nigel. 'Fine.'

'Thank you, sir.'

'And then I'll get on again.'

Oh shit, thought Billy. So did most of the passengers. 'Good for you, mate,' said the thin-faced kid.

'And I'll keep on doing it. Every station up the line.'

'No you won't,' said the guard.

Nigel advanced his front combat boot, knee bent and ready. Any second now thought Billy. How did the little bastard get so packed full of aggro?

'You try and stop me I'll deck you.'

'Not me, son,' said the guard. 'All I do is call the Railway Police.' As he turned away Billy was moving forward, feeling for his wallet, thinking, what a prat, what a prat you are, Billy Jewel.

'I'll pay.'

Well anyway Mand would.

He was staring out the window when Billy handed him his written-out ticket. 'Here. Stoke-on-Trent return. You and I got to have a talk.' Nigel took the paper, looked at it, folded it rapidly until it was no bigger than a postage stamp and pocketed it without a word.

'Just tell me one thing,' said Billy. 'Why not just fucking hitch it?'

'What d'you think I am,' said Nigel, 'a fucking beggar?'

14

Mandy was out and the travellers had moved so Vic and Cromer finally got round to Ellard's place off City Road just after a quarter to seven. His mother let them in. She was a woman not much older than Vic with deep sunk liverish eyes and a once-generous mouth now turned down tight. Everything about her said, I've kept Ellard out of trouble for as long as I can; now it's up to him. She told Vic he'd gone to bottle up the club but Suki and Greta were upstairs. 'In that room a theirs.' This was news to Vic. He asked Ellard's mother to keep an eye on the Escort. She gave him a what did your last servant die of look and went back to watching Channel 4 from a pale blue velour Thunderbirds armchair.

Suki Brown and Greta were in bed together under a black and white dazzle-pattern duvet with Greta's plastic leg propped up against the doilied bedside table. There was a thick incense-patchouli-pot smell and smoke was still twirling out of a Red Stripe can.

'What is this,' said Suki pushing herself upright in bed and showing her small pointy breasts, 'a bust?'

'No, Miss Brown,' said Vic.

'Ain't my name.'

Greta levered herself up more awkwardly. She too was showing her breasts, big and blue veined with erect dark-ringed nipples. Vic could feel the heat coming off Cromer.

159

'Yeah,' said Greta, 'because if it is you're gonna have to take us in as we are.'

'Right,' said Suki. 'Cool.' She and Greta put their arms around each other, stuck their pursed lips together went mmmmm and broke up, laughing at the two men.

'This is DC John Cromer, ladies,' said Vic. 'They do this to embarrass us, John.'

'Kid looks too clean for a copper,' said Greta.

'Go on,' said Vic. 'Talk to them, John.'

'What? Oh right.' Cromer took out his notebook. 'If I could have your names please, ladies.' Vic began to despair.

'Kiss me harse,' said Suki.

'What's all this about, son?' said Greta.

'We're trying to establish the present whereabouts of Mister Jewel.' What a plonker.

'Never yeard of him,' said Suki.

Greta looked at Vic. 'He talking about Billy?' Vic waited for Cromer.

'We have reason to believe that you work for him on a part-time basis at the Kit Kat Club.' Reason to believe? Part-time basis? Like some dozy fucking DSS desk clerk. Come on Cromer even you can do better than this. Vic moved round to Suki's side of the bed and picked up the can of Red Stripe. Cromer was still standing square-on at the end of the bed clicking his stainless steel ballpoint and trying not to look at their tits. 'So if I could just have your names, please.'

'What's this Mister Jewel supposed to have done, son?' asked Greta.

'What a man does his own affair.' Suki was eyeing the Red Stripe can in Vic's fist. 'Comin' in here botherin' us.'

Vic sniffed the can. 'Tell you what, girls. Ellard's old

160

lady won't go much on it if we get the drugs mob in, will she? You two'll be out on your jacksies for a start.' He put the can down hard. 'Won't you?'

The two women looked at each other, waiting to see who led off. Suki pulled the duvet up over her breasts, lay back and closed her eyes. Greta followed suit but kept her eyes on the mottled anaglypta ceiling. Time to push now before they got too stubborn or resigned.

'There's a dead joint in that can, John.' Cromer was hypnotised by the three feet sticking out at the other end of the bed. Two brown with pearlescent emerald nail varnish, one white with blood red. 'Don't write it down yet though, let's see if we can work something out.' That got Greta looking at him. 'Ellard's mum says he's gone down to bottle up. He say anything to you, did he?'

'Monday's our night off,' said Greta.

'For restin'.'

'We're sorry about that, aren't we, John?' Say something, Cromer.

'Yes we are. Sorry, ladies.' He moved to look out of the looped and swagged pink and white lace curtains. Better. Trying to divide their attention.

'So what did Ellard say, Greet?'

'I only saw him on the stairs, didn't I? Coming out the bathroom all showered and shaved and that so I goes, Christ Ellard this is early.' She nudged Suki to cue her in. 'That gas boiler's got terrible water-hammer, annit Suke?' Your turn girl.

'Yeah,' said Suki, eyes closed not interested.

Greta made her older woman it's-always-me face. 'So anyway he goes, I got to go down the club haven' I? Billy's orf. I go, what Billy, he's not sick is he? And he goes, no he's takin' off for a couple a days, and I go, what, with Mand? Because I know they've had this

161

bust up over . . . you know, all that . . . and Ellard says no, Billy don' know where she is and will Ellard do the club. Till he comes back like.'

'Yeah,' said Vic nodding, letting the pause drag on. 'So where is he, then? Where is Billy?'

Greta, considering she had done enough, elbowed Suki. She half opened her eyes, looked from Vic to Cromer and then up at the ceiling.

'Man gone to Pauline funeral. Show a bit a respect for once his life.'

'So now you know,' said Greta. She waited for Vic to make a goodnight ladies move for the door. When he didn't, as if to excuse herself in her own mind for being forced to drop Billy in it, she said, 'He was very fond of Pauline, in his own way.' Looking up at Vic, the woman daring the copper to deny it, to scoff at the possibility of Billy loving anybody or anything. Vic did nothing of the sort. He'd got what he wanted; he might well need to see them again; it was time to look human.

'Yeah,' he said. 'He told me.'

'So were we, weren't we Suke?' Greta bit her lip. 'We all loved that kid. Poor cow – ' She rolled over into Suki's arms and the two women held on to each other.

When Vic and Cromer got downstairs all three wipers had gone off the Escort.

'What d'you think?' said Vic. Cromer driving, turning left out of the Jungle on to Stokes Croft and back towards the Well.

'I don't think I did very well, did I?'

'No,' said Vic.

'I couldn't handle it, just couldn't handle it.'

Christ Cromer what is this, humility? 'What was it,' said Vic. 'The tits?'

'No,' said Cromer. 'The leg.'

162

Drizzle was misting up the screen and starring the streetlights. If Cromer bent the Escort they'd both be even further up shit creek. Plus the leg possibility hadn't even occurred to Vic. To get them both off the hook he said, 'They say if you rub it with half a potato it keeps it clear.'

Cromer frowned, took a quick glance out the side window to see if they'd passed the last of the Jungle greengrocers. 'What about yams?'

A series of wheezing and coughing sounds like an asthmatic dog trying to bark. Cromer realised he had never heard Vic laugh before.

They walked straight into mad hour. Uniformeds clattering up and down the stairs struggling into flak jackets, phones echoing in empty rooms, bodies rushing in and out and doors banging up and down the Well, DI Parnes and DCI Barnard storming round their offices fucking and blinding down several phones at once, the squad room full of smoke, metallic sweat, faces staring into terminals and shouting down mouthpieces with one hand over their ears to keep out the rest of the racket.

'Whose arse in the bacon slicer now?' asked Vic.

'Where the fuck have you been?' Des Chaffey was wrestling a duplicator loading tray and his armpits were wet with sweat.

'St Pauls.'

'What?'

'You know, the Jungle. City Road.'

Des pointing to Parnes's office. 'Get in there!'

DI Parnes was bollocking them over the wipers and re-bollocking them for not radioing when DCI Barnard came in and gave them another for being down the Jungle and not seeing anything. Vic put on his stolid copper's face. It made the DCI run his hands through his thick grey hair like a man demented.

'You must have seen something, Hallam, you were driving round the fucking place for forty-five minutes, for Christ sake!'

'No, Chief.'

'What d'you mean no?'

'I mean no we weren't down the Jungle for that entire period of time.'

'Where were you then, down the fucking bingo?'

'No, Chief we were interviewing witnesses.'

The DI chipped in. 'How long were you down City Road?'

'Twenty minutes all told.'

The DCI waved a sheaf of faxes. 'We get intelligence reports, phone calls, stuff off the street saying a crack war's about to break out and you didn't see anything?'

'Straight in straight out no bother, that right John?'

'Yes, sergeant.' Thank Christ Cromer was backing him up.

'No white kids, no joyriders, nothing?' said the DCI.

'No, Chief,' said Vic.

'Why?'

Vic shrugged. 'We didn't have any wipers.'

'You're pushing it, Hallam.'

Another half-hour and it was all over. Apparently some black kid Winston Winters out on bail got beaten up by a bunch of white kids. Then three transit vans full of white youths were seen cruising St Pauls and the balloon had gone up.

'What was it then, Des?'

'Basketball teams looking for the Community Centre. Area semi-finals.'

'A tenner says St Pauls'll walk it.'

'Be more fucking trouble if they don't,' said Des.

164

When the stragglers had all got back the DCI appeared, calmed down and hair combed, and said the operation had been a success, the rapid response was excellent and all in all it was fucking good exercise for the real thing. Which was he need hardly remind them well on the cards this time of year. 'Christmas Eve, knowing our luck. It only needs one black tealeaf, one white pisshead, City to lose at home and bang, all Christmas leave cancelled.' A groan. He advised them all to shop early and pray for rain. 'A fucking three-day torrential fucking downpour for preference, keep all the comedians at home kicking shit out the wife and kids instead.'

Vic and Cromer were still trying to locate anybody who knew anything at Temple Meads but it was shift changeover and they weren't having much luck or paying any attention to the DCI until he came to the end of his summing up, walked over and put his hand on the top of Vic's terminal. 'In fact the whole operation was carried out with only the loss of three windscreen wipers, wasn't it, Hallam?'

'Yes sir.'

Gratified by the ragged cheer this got, DCI Barnard smiled his tight little smile, winked got you Hallam you bastard and walked out stiffly in his tight Italian suit.

'We don't even know he's on the train,' said Cromer. 'He's got no licence, he can't hire a car, he's not going to walk and there's no airport in Stoke. Try London, Birmingham, Glasgow, Manchester, anywhere.' Use your initiative Cromer not fucking excuses. Don't tell me, show me. Jesus Christ. It was either getting harder or he was getting more irritable. Not enough blood sugar. Not enough fun, more like. Or enough fucks. Not enough fucking *peace* even. Or progress. When was there ever? You went grinding and pressuring on day after day and you'd either given up, moved on or more or less forgot and a case would just suddenly crack open of its own accord. Sweet as a nut.

Sometimes.

Vic got to Calder the police surgeon on his home number. He sounded half-pissed and swaggering. Guests there, probably. Earholing. Giving old Calder the chance to play the great pathologist. Yes, sergeant he had done the post-mortem. Yes the coroner was happy yes he had kept all the right bits and yes the body release had been signed. Now if the CID didn't mind he had a gigot to carve.

'What the fuck's a jiggo, Des?' Des liked to get his face in the trough and his gut showed it.

'Frog for lamb.' Des was battering out the St Pauls report. 'What I can't understand is, why bail this Winters nipper.'

'Yeah,' said Vic. 'Funny thing to do to a black kid.'

Des went on reading. 'Ah, here we are. Drugs mob got their fucking finger in. Bail recommended for purposes of observation. Law to their fucking selves they are.'

'Yeah,' said Vic. 'How you doing, John?'

Cromer was looking into the earpiece of the phone. 'I've got some woman calls herself night relief.'

'Wish I had,' said Vic.

'Gang of Hartcliffe lads jumped Winters in the bus station,' said Des.

His fat fingers spidered over the keyboard. He was a really fast typist was Des. And a good admin man. Too fat for much else but everybody was good at something. Come on, Cromer. The kid was writing stuff down and looking eager. Des hit PRINT. 'Bust Winters' jaw, wiring him up in the BRI. Here endeth tonight's lesson.'

When Des said BRI Vic wanted to ring Ellie.

Des was saying Winters said the Hartcliffe kids had guns and knives and big rocks of crack and told him they were going to team up and roll over all the black dealers so the Drugs mob went into overdrive and thus tonight's little bundle in the Jungle.'It's our arse in the volcano, Vic.'

'Yeah well if you keep poking sticks in the antheap the ants are bound to get fucking humpty, aren't they?'

'What would you do then, send 'em all back to Africah?'

'No. Leave the poor bastards alone.'

Trouble was he couldn't think of anything to ring Ellie for. Not from here anyway. Day off tomorrow. Do it then. But would he feel like it then or like shit after the piss-up he felt coming on, and was there any point anyway? Plus the fact she was the witness and – oh sod it, sod it all –

Cromer on his feet, fixated on the fax machine like a fucking pointer.

'What is it, John?'

'I think I might have a result,' said Cromer. Tearing off the fax page, trying to decipher the smudged reprint of an imprint of a credit card, squinting so hard he didn't notice the fax machine still jerking out line after line. 'Fuck it.' Cromer looked really pissed off. Crestfallen, even.

'What's up, John?'

'They said they took a note of a bloke because they don't get many Gold Cards going north. But this is A. M. Crawley, first-class return Stoke-on-Trent, stupid bastards.'

'Good old Billy.'

'What?'

'You have got a result, John. Fucking brilliant.'

167

Cromer was smiling without knowing why. 'He's only using Mand's card. And going first class, the cunt.' It was a pleasure to watch the relief bloom over Cromer. 'What's the other one, John?'

'Eh?'

'In the machine.'

'Oh.' Cromer tore it off. 'Some incident report, filed ex-Birmingham New Street and one of those white tickets they do.' Scrutinising it. 'Fuck me, it's Nigel Evens. On the same Gold Card—'

'Mand'll crucify him,' said Vic. 'What time's the train due in Stoke?'

Vic could hear the Tannoy echoing round the station. *Would Mister William Jewel travelling from Bristol please contact the Stationmaster's Office on Platform One. Mister William Jewel please ....* Clatter of a receiver being fumbled and the breathing of someone coming in at a run.

'Hallo, Billy.'

'Hallo?' Very nervous.

'Vic here.'

The voice suddenly closer. 'Jesus, Vic. Frightened the life out of me.' Breath being expelled close to the mouthpiece. 'I thought they'd sussed the fucking card.'

'They didn't, Billy, we did.'

'Oh.' Billy waiting. Let him dangle.

'Yeah,' said Vic. 'Me and my mate John.' Throw the kid a bone. Cromer looking delighted. 'You remember John, don't you?'

'Dopy-looking dickhead of a choirboy.'

'That's John. He rang your number straight off.'

'Did he? How?'

'Ever heard of computers?'

'Oh. Yeah, well,' Billy relaxing now. 'Real fucking

168

long arm of the law stuff, innit. Give him my regards, the cunt.'

'I will.'

'How you doing anyway, Vic?'

Now stick it to him. 'Why didn't you tell me, Billy?' Harder. Right in. 'You're a fucking murder witness for fuck sake, DCI has anything to do with it you're suspect number fucking one –'

'Oh shit, Vic –'

'It's your fucking head or my fucking arse Billy. I got Brass here queuing up with red-hot fucking pokers and I'm not getting shafted on your account, not any fucking more I'm not. Am I making myself plain, mate?'

'Oh Christ. Oh shit.' Crumbling nicely, starting to gabble. 'Sorry Vic I never thought with you know Mand pissing off and everything piling up and oh Christ oh fucking hell mate what can I say?' Vic waited. 'I was only –'

'Only what, Billy?'

'Well, you know. Do the right thing by Pauline.'

'Yeah I heard,' said Vic. 'Well from now on you do the right thing by me and you fucking tell me what you're going to do and I'll fucking tell you whether you can do it or not. Clear? Because you're one step from throw away the key, old son.'

'Yeah. Thanks Vic. Sorry, mate.' Billy was soft as shit under the flash: one reason Vic liked him.

'So where you staying?'

'Nearest fucking four-star I can find, mate.'

'Ring me when you do.'

'Yeah, yeah I will, mate.'

'Before you hit the Low Flyers.

'Yeah, sure, Vic. First off –'

Now slip another one in. 'And Nigel?' He could hear

Billy's mind shifting gear thinking, thank fuck, out the frame.

'Longdogging it out the station soon as you had my name called. Kid's a fucking fruitcake, Vic, I mean he's serious bad news, can't you get him arrested or something because he really does need fucking long-term parking —'

'You bought him his ticket, Billy.'

'Eh?'

'You bought him his ticket.' Cromer was grinning all over his face. Watch and learn, kid.

'Yeah well I'm like that, aren't I?'

'Are you? I don't know, Billy. I'm beginning to wonder.'

'Shit, Vic he was going to stick one on the guard.'

'And now he's gone.'

'Thank fuck. I've had Gandhi I've had Buddha, maharishi'd up to the fucking eyeballs. Love and fucking freedom and all the time he's looking at you like he'd sooner fucking top you. I've had that as well. Quickest way's with a fucking steel guitar fucking E string apparently —'

'Where?'

'What do you mean where?'

'I mean where's he gone?'

'Fuck knows, some squat somewhere, I mean kids these days they take all that in with their fucking school milk, don't they, where to roll up where to crash out. Said he'd be at the funeral though, Christ knows what he'll do there —'

'You see him Billy you tell him to get his arse back down here double fucking quick.'

'Oh he's coming back all right.'

'How do you know?'

170

'Said he's got some business or other and besides – you'll never guess this, Vic – '

'What?'

'He says he's worried about the security of that fucking gaff of his, Christ, there's nothing fucking there – '

'How d'you know that, Billy?'

'Eh?' Nervous again.

'I said how d'you know that?'

'Pauline told me, all fucking bare boards. Who's going to turn that over?'

'Pauline told you?'

'Yeah. Why?'

'Thanks, Billy. Have a nice day tomorrow.' Vic put the phone down. Cromer was still trying to figure it out. 'Never leave 'em laughing, John.' Vic looked as if he meant it. He did.

Billy's call came through in twenty minutes. Vic told the desk to say he was out but take the hotel name, telephone and room number. Then it was pie and mash in the canteen and write up the notes later.

Cromer had two lots of crumble and yellow custard and Vic had a second mug of tea and a fag. He sat and watched Cromer eat: fork and spoon for Christ sake, like the fucking vicar.

Vic pushed his chair back, blew smoke out and spooled back through the day. He'd dropped a real bollock on Billy and Nigel. Definite case of losing his touch there. Managed to pull it back though. Well, so far –

'Shit.' Thinking about Ellie in the nuns' garden.

'What?' Cromer took the spoon out of his mouth.

'Mind like a fucking sieve.' He dropped his fag end in the mug, saw Cromer wince. 'I took Ellie back to the

171

SOC this afternoon. She said this geezer called her good girl.'

'Good girl?'

Vic took out his pocket-book. 'Wallops her, says shut up you won't get hurt, struggle I'll fucking kill you. Then he rapes her going fuck you fuck you fuck you. And when he's finished, when he's shot his load, presumably – ' Cromer pushing half a bowl of thick yellow custard away, placing spoon and fork neatly together at six o'clock – 'he calls her good girl. What do these guys usually do?'

'What, ordinary rapists?'

'So to speak.'

'Usually they hit 'em about, sometimes they do 'em in, to shut 'em up. Like Pauline.'

'Yeah.' Vic leafed back through the pocket-book. 'What did that doctor say?'

'The Indian bloke?'

'Sri Lankan actually.' He had a flash of Ellie looking at him over her glasses. 'Here we are. Doctor Chaudhury. "This swine is a very clean bugger." That say anything to you?'

Cromer put his elbows on the table and contemplated the stained Formica. 'If he said good girl – '

'Which she says he did – '

You could see the wheels going round. The kid was still anxious about making a prat of himself. 'Spit it out, John.' We're used to all sorts of bollocks in this business.

'No I was just thinking. If he said good girl, it doesn't sound much like a student, does it?'

Straight out of left field. 'Why's that John?'

'Well if Ellie's twenty-six, and you were a student, eighteen, twenty-one, you wouldn't call her good girl, would you? I mean, I wouldn't.'

172

Fuck me. Good old Cromer. 'No you're right, you probably wouldn't. Makes sense.' Go on give him some credit. 'I hadn't thought of that, John.' Not too much or the silly cunt'll start thinking he's a detective. 'I tell you what I had thought, though.'

'What?'

'He smells very clean, he's a very clean bugger, knows enough to dress up and wear industrial-strength french letters and he calls her good girl when he's finished.' Vic tapped the table with his lighter. 'This character's a well-brought-up kiddy. Like you, John.'

'Thanks.'

'And I reckon good girl could be his signature, his sign-off, something he says to all the girls, probably doesn't even know he's saying it.'

Cromer, considering. 'Trouble is he hasn't raped anybody else, has he?'

'Not yet John no – '

'So even if it is his signature – '

'Chances are he will if he gets away with it, gets a taste for it – '

'Yeah but you can't put it on house to house can you? I mean, good morning madam, what does your husband-stroke-boyfriend call you after intercourse?'

'What do you say to Louise when you've just given her one?'

'Eh?'

'You don't say thank you and goodnight petal, do you? Not every time anyway. You sort of lie there, don't you?' Feeling better most of the time. In the early days anyway. 'And you have a bit of a cuddle, don't you. Tell 'em you love 'em and all that shit.'

'Yeah, usually.'

'Say daft things like chucklebum and pussycat. Don't you?'

'Yes you do.'

'You don't start spitting the hairs out until the light's off, do you?' Vic looked at his watch and stood up. 'But good girl. What would Louise say, you called her good girl?'

'Well, I mean it's the sort of thing you say to a kid, isn't it?'

'I hope to fuck it's not, John.' Vic had to think about that one in the lift.

Good girl. Yeah, it was a fucking possibility. But blokes who went for kids usually stuck with kids, didn't they? Usually. A nonce was a nonce. Usually. But as a possible future development it was fucking frightening. Fucking terrifying. He could see Cromer was thinking the same thing. To get their minds off it he said, 'What else would she say?'

'What, if I called her good girl?' Going down the corridor, a thought every couple of paces. 'Bit patronising. Bit non-PC. Bit fucking chauvinist.'

Chauvinist. Yeah, chauvinist was more comforting. Put chauvinist on the profile. But remember the other.

Tall white middle-class fucking chauvinist in his late twenties, early thirties.

Christ, there was a long way to go.

15

It was half-ten before Vic switched his monitor off. 'Come on John we're going to get wrecked.'

'Hang on I'll just finish this.'

Vic walked out as if he hadn't heard and Cromer checked Paedophilia as a possible on the multiple-choice prelim chart, entered DISTRIBUTE ALL LISTS and put the blue plastic cover on. Sod it. It was his idea. And Vic should have waited. Tell him in the bar.

On the way up he phoned Louise to ask her if it was all right and she'd said yes of course love, ring me when you want fetching. Nice as pie.

A wall of smoke and noise and bodies. Cromer had to shove his way sideways into the packed bar. The St Pauls adrenalin. No outlet there so get rid of it here, lads. Men he knew only by sight as hard grey serious faces under artificial daylight were now looking pink and shiny. Knocking it back, laughing, shouting, elbows on each other's shoulders, pints knuckled back to chests, heads together for the joke then throwing their heads back in big all-together roars.

One or two grinning or nodding at him. Most looking who the fuck are you. Vic and Des Chaffey at one end of the bar, the middle held by the DCI and his grey-haired cronies from the districts, the other end by the DI and his mates. The merest glint from the DCI, clocking the new kid, who he was with.

Hierarchy. Territory. Shop talk. Gossip. Fucking blacks fucking yobs fucking women. *Esprit de Corps* at full fucking blast. 'What you want, John?' Don't say medium white spritzer and don't say half.

'Oh. Cider top.' The way Vic hunched to put his hand in his pocket probably meant he should have said lager no top.

'On the scrump then, John.' It was the first time Des had called him John. They were both on Directors and Bell's chasers. Oh shit.

'You put Paedo on the sheet,' Des had turned back to Vic, 'media get hold of it, they'll go fucking berserk.'

'Fuck 'em. Let 'em. Fuck 'em, eh John?' Vic unperturbed, handing Cromer his pint.

'I meant to tell you – '

'Cheers.' Vic's jaw like a trap. Shut the fuck up. 'If we think it's a possibility it's a possibility, that right, John?' Cromer was a prat for not mentioning it but he didn't want Des to know that and anyway the kid might have done right by accident. 'If it gets out and annoys this bastard, great. If I thought it'd do any good I'd say he was the illegitimate bum-fucked son of a syphilitic Mongolian abbot – '

'Not the point,' said Des, 'starting a panic – '

'And wait for his letter of complaint – '

'Too fucking reckless – '

'Fuck off,' said Vic.

'Have another pint,' said Des.

They had three before they let Cromer buy one and then it was only halves, no chasers, John. Hierarchy. When the DCI left, the party started to break up. Protocol. It was after 11.30 and Cromer was looking forward to ringing Louise and getting into bed nicely pissed. Vic and Des were talking to half a dozen sergeants and older DCs. 'Come on John,' he said, 'we're all going for a nosh up the Apollo.'

Esprit de Corps. And no way out.

It was just up the hill off Stokes Croft on the edge of the Jungle, a late-night caff that had been busted so many times it was now a club, Private Members Only, with painted-out windows. It was the first time Cromer had been to a place where somebody slid a black metal rectangle to one side and looked at them through squared wired glass before letting them in. Then it was up a flight of thick greasy carpet through a red chenille curtain that looked like somebody's bedspread and into an empty upstairs room with unlit red candles and matching paper tablecloths with murals of cypresses and mountains painted directly on to plastic pine-effect tongue and groove wall cladding and framed in nailed gold-sprayed lath. There were a couple more steps up into the matt-black dancing area at the back. A table for eight was already laid opposite what had been a bandstand but was now a karaoke set-up booming out bouzouki.

'Allo Angelo,' said Vic to a dark thin young bloke in a DJ, 'Come sta? Va bene?' Angelo shrugged and murmured something, eyes sliding dully over Cromer. 'It's Greek Cypriot Italian,' Vic said, 'but they do a fair old mixed grill if you don't mind eyeballs.' Angelo, who had once been good-looking but now just looked worn out, rubbed his veined hands, showed them deftly to their places and left. 'The needle,' said Vic. 'We won't see him again.'

Bottles of white Demestika and Cyprus Rouge appeared by the double handful and the next time Cromer looked at his watch it was half-past one and the place had filled up and there was dancing going on and women's backsides in red and green Lurex were bumping into the back of his chair and the table was covered in plates and candlewax and everybody was reaching out and eating bits of this and that. People he didn't know were coming up and sitting next to him, opposite him, on both sides of him and muttering then laughing out loud to Vic and Des and the others as if it was some kind of chaotic midnight wedding do: one side white-shirted black-tied Greek and Italian croupiers and blackjack dealers and club girls in black dresses with immaculate make-up and dead glittery eyes, and the other older lot bull-necked shaven-headed moustached demolition contractors and scrap metal dealers in baggy gabardine suits who walked with their shoulders and whole upper bodies swinging, followed by their raucous heavy-set brick-faced wives in shiny peacock dresses who took no notice of the men whatsoever. They even danced with each other, fags held out in bent-back fingers.

Cromer, head swimming, got up from the wreckage of screwed-up paper napkins, dead bottles, overturned glasses, spilled wine, bread ends and cigarette-laden plates to find the loo and the phone. Vic and Des and the others had scattered by now and were talking and smoking and dancing and putting their arms round the shoulders of anybody and everybody all mates together and fuck Northern Cyprus we could take it out tomorrow, how's Jacko managing, Alli still there is she, what about Julio and Ari they sorted it out yet, any word on turkeys so far, you heard about Billy did you, yeah Mutchy's still in, Ford Open or some fucking where. Whole stories, lives, crimes Cromer knew nothing about, passing Vic swaying in the arms of some forty-year-old frizzy-haired piece in a shirred red dress, 'Night off, kid, fuck it!' and then winking at him through her black frizzy hair. *Esprit de Corps* and be nice to the customers' ladies.

He found the loo but not the phone, and when he came back the karaoke room was packed and it was

178

Cromer where the fuck you been and right lads who's on 'Blue Suede Shoes'? and after that it turned into an all-singing all-dancing here we go Christ-I'm-out-me-fucking-head hellofagoodfuckingnightmate blur with the occasional memorable bit sticking up here and there out of the nightmarish feedback and bass turned up so high it went straight through your chest and shimmered the wine out of the glasses.

Vic saying, 'What makes it John see, what makes it see, is the ability to remember things when drunk, when pissed, when arseholed totally fucking witless. That right Des?'

Des saying Yes what was the question and falling over and everybody shouting Penalty Forfeit and Do the Glow Worm and Lights Out and Des up on the stage turning his back on them and shaking his fat arse and doing something with his flies. Vic with tears rolling down his face and then Des turning round with one of those kids' luminescent plastic tubes sticking out of his trousers with a pink Durex on the end, for fuck sake and everybody falling about as Des went waggling it up to one woman after another singing 'Glow Little Glow Worm Glow and Glimmer Fly through the Sea of Night Little Swimmer' and then everybody pissing themselves and joining in with 'When You Gotta Glow You Gotta Glow, Glow Little Glow Worm Glow' as he got it up some woman's dress so you could see the pink glow coming through the backside of her skirt.

She was taken home shortly after that.

And then in the middle of 'La Paloma Blanca' when it was getting towards the end around four and he'd finally found the phone and he was sitting down with Vic and Des who'd stuck the plastic tube in one of the bottles so it lit them up like a scene off a Christmas card, Vic was saying, 'What it amounts to is, would

179

you like your telly nicked and thrown back through the window? No you wouldn't, John, you wouldn't like *your* Jag *your* Roller *your* fucking GTI nicked and wrecked and parked up outside your house with a big fucking notice on it What A Load of Crap, your most precious possession, would you?' And him grinning and going no waiting for the punchline and Vic looking dead serious and going, 'Well that's women and rape, John, they're vulnerable, they got their sense of honour, their most precious possession same as you or I or Des here and suddenly it's fucked – mirrors smashed, seat ripped, no fucking aerial no fucking radio and some-body's pissed in their petrol tank. You're raped, defiled, fuck-all you can do about it or want to say about it, all you want to do is crawl into a hole and fucking die, sexually die, and no cunt cares. Like you having your dick cut off and you're wandering around bleeding to fucking death and no cunt cares. All sorts of rape, John. Like your old man fucks off one day and never comes back, the old lady goes on the piss and comes down the street with her drawers in her hand come all over her shoes and she says she found fifteen quid. Oh yeah everybody's looking through the curtains but no cunt gives a fuck, and then she's arrested and you're doing your O levels and it's all a terrible inconvenience and later on she dies incontinent and all these things fuck-ing happen, John, you've seen them I've seen them he's seen them all these things fucking happen and it's all fucking rape and no cunt cares. You've got no work, no hope, your best girl's fucked off with a second-hand car dealer and you're out on the street with fourpence and no cunt cares. All rape, all the same. No cunt cares. Only us, John.' Vic leaned back and lit a fag. 'And we're all fucking arseholes anyway.'

Vic and Des found this so funny they both slid under

the table and rolled among the bread and wine and fag ends shouting 'Anklebiters! Watch out! Anklebiters!' then crawled about trying to nip the feet of the last women left dancing.

That was when Louise finally got let in.

After the bath Frank and Rae had slobbed around in their dressing gowns having the smoked trout with the rest of the Beaune and a bottle of blood-coloured Sliven with some breaded veal, broccoli and oven chips. Rae had a Safeway's profiterole and he stuck to port and instant espresso. They watched television, messed around and finally fucked on the floor with a loose cushion underneath her arse during *News at Ten*. Then she'd yawned off to bed and he'd gone on to three-star Martell for a nightcap, flicking channels to see if anything was getting its tits out. Some Paki thing about irrigation and jealous mothers-in-law, so by 01.07 on the red digital he was in bed beside Rae's hot body, drifting off feeling warm and fireproof. At 04.19 he fell, jolt, foot through the floorboards, out of deep unconsciousness into black icy water again.

Thudding panic. He held on to his pulse with his left hand, his heart with his right. The drink, that's what it was, it had to be. Port, caffeine and brandy, sending his heart racing and tripping all over the place. The blackness came washing over him again; but this time it wasn't just fear, it was sanity, the realisation of what he'd done giving him a weak shitty feeling in his gut. Oh God, he prayed, oh God, please God, say it never happened, say the nurse never existed, say it was a nightmare. Oh please God wipe the tape. Obliterate it. Make it never happen. Please God it's me, Frank, I'm only little. Help me.

More blackness, taking him down.

An image of Rae's face, hearing about the rape. Shocked, pale, full of disbelief at first, then changing, hardening, knowing it was true, knowing it was what he was like. Her voice, Oh Christ Frank what have you done? Other faces, police faces, laughing, sniggering. Hey, you hear about Webber, then? And then seeing himself, on TV, a blanket over his head, a couple of plainclothes dragging him up steps into court. More voices, accusing, witnessing, sentencing. The words like doors slamming. Rape. Despicable. Police officer. Trust. Guilty. The nurse's face watching him go down –

He tried to hold on, to fix his mind on the nurse, to recall the smell, the feel of her. But all he could smell was Rae. That was the trouble, he thought: one fuck wiped out another and the net result was you started to lose your bottle. He should have kept it, saved it for the nurse. But what could you do when it was there, lying there, asking for it, squirming for it? He turned to look at Rae. Spark out, jaw dropped, little teeth showing, night-creamed face looking completely fucking ga-ga.

Outside on the flyover and the Portway, he could hear the occasional car and truck tyres ripping and swishing over wet black tarmac. People going somewhere, men and women laughing, groping, half-pissed, trying not to drive too fast. He pushed his hand between Rae's legs but she mumbled, pawed him off, turned over and left him feeling even rattier and shittier.

04.58. He began playing with his prick, trying to flog up a flicker of interest in the old fucks file. It usually sent him off like counting sheep but tonight his mind kept flitting off, outwitting him, running away from him until he no longer knew whether he was sleeping or waking or switching channels between the two. Now

182

it was showing him walking through some huge blank concrete Costa del Sol joint, somewhere he knew he had never been. He was padding along this endless carpeted hotel corridor, and all the women he'd ever had, they were all there, each one in a different room, all with their doors and legs open but none of them worth the fucking bother – all he wanted to do was get out of the fucking place –

His mind twisted, turned on him again, out of his grasp, out of his control. Holy shit, the fucking voice –

They're not the fucking victims. You are, Frank. You, Frank Webber. Poncing about like some fucking dickhead disco Spic waiter porkswording endless mounds of hot pink dunlopillo flesh and all they do is wake up and spew all over you. Thank you Franco –

That's what they do, Frank. They let you get them exactly where they want you. Up their manky greedy little chuffs. You're the cheap fuck, you're the sex object, you're the walking prick, you're Mister Easy Lay number fucking one, all they have to do is look, smile and you're up there panting and licking like some mad legfucking terrier. Aren't you? Gobble gobble gobble. All you are. A servant of the orifice, no more no less. Itinerant sexual plumber to a bunch of assorted cunts.

What does that make you, Frank? The biggest cunt of all or what?

It took Frank some considerable time to work through it. When he did the voice was there again, with the mocking spiteful all too self-evident truth:

So they deserve everything they fucking well get, don't they, Frank? Not just fucking but fucking and killing –

It was what he'd thought before but it made more sense now because he'd worked out what they'd done to him, using him, conning him, sucking the juice out

183

of him then chucking him away: goodbye fuckface. Christ it was fucking criminal and they called it fucking love.

He began to feel better. The drink, all it was. He should have had something to line his stomach. *Do it now, Frank.*

He was up at half-five shovelling down Rae's special muesli and watching the jerky second-hand on the kitchen clock. Stuff tasted like cow's breath. He daren't turn on any of the machines or wash or shit or shave or have coffee or anything because she'd hear, ears like a bat, wired up to every fucking room in the house. Coming down wanting to know why. What is it den coulden sleep? Come on back to bed, love have a cuddle. Fucking voracious cow. Told him she'd wanted his kid again. Holy fuck.

A big, panicky, heating-up sweat came over him, filling the small kitchen with the rank smell of onions. It was followed by another shivery flu-like bout of black wet despair. He sat head in hands at the kitchen table, listening to the whoffle and purr of the central heating boiler and looking at the condensation running down the inside of the double glazing. He felt as if he was sitting inside a never-ending, rising scream – he knew he'd fucking kill her if she came creeping down yawning and fucking smiling. . . .

He left a note. 'Lot on. Back late, love F.'

He did a hundred and ten up the M5, the old Renault flat out and his foot hard down, waiting for something to happen. When it didn't he slowed down into Michael Wood Services for the brain-dead camaraderie of men, bacon and silent shuffling disinterested Indian women. It was the end of night and everybody looked as if they had cancer. He had the full breakfast and a

184

decent shit and by the time he drove off he had put the night behind him.

He shaved and showered at the Station and was in uniform in the safety of his office by 0647 on his green malachite presentation desk alarm.

They were used to his sudden comings and goings, thought he did it to keep them on their toes. He did the hours because when the chance arose it meant he could occasionally get a three-hour lunchtime fuck in.

But not today. He keyed in and spent the next hour or so getting up to speed, scrolling through St Pauls, the nurse and Pauline White-stroke-Millward. Interviews, medical reports, house to house inquiries. There was some sloppy work on Pauline White, losing and finding the two male witnesses and still not gripping them. Stoke-on-Trent, for Christ sake. All down to that no-no Hallam and his sidekick Cromer. Frank felt a momentary glow of warmth and security; Hallam had really lost it this time, and it wasn't just because his wife had fucked off either. He was falling apart all over the place, as the assessments clearly showed. Good on casework and arrest record but poor on discipline and co-operation. Failed two inspector's, and the notes indicated the third would be his last. Good. Frank played through the files to see if there was anything on Cromer. It was too soon to expect anything much, but there was a brief progress report. Intelligent but immature, query CID material. He paged down through the St Pauls business looking for the nurse. More interviews, more house to house, but nothing he didn't know and nothing to get concerned about. The whole thing was going nowhere; in a week or so it would be just another unsolved. Frank was beginning to feel really good when he came across the profile.

Good girl.

Vic woke about nine. It was Tuesday morning and his day off. He felt fine in bed but as he shambled naked into the bathroom a weak light-headedness flashed over him. He sat down heavily, staring at the patterns in the grey and gold flecked Cushionflor between his feet. He couldn't tell whether the patterns were moving or if it was something wrong with his eyes. He lifted his head. The same little wriggly things were swarming up over the damp and black mould patches on the walls and ceiling.

It was going to be one of those. Another day off fucked.

Well he'd had them before and the only thing really was back to bed. He sat on the bevel-edged black lavatory bowl, the seat up, the porcelain cold and hard as ice, waiting for the strength to stand up again.

Grey and black, he thought, the whole bathroom grey and black. That was another of her ideas, another legacy from his ex, another attempt to upmarket their lifestyle into the BMW-driving classes. Now the seat was cracked and testicle-threatening, the goldplated dolphin taps didn't turn off or on properly and greeny-coppery-limestain beards hung down the black Italian porcelain. What a mess. All her fault.

Yes, it was going to be one of those, all right. One of those where temper and self-pity got worse as the day went on. Maybe he should have kept the cleaning firm on but he couldn't stand being woken up by the sound of the Hoover, one reason he'd left home in the first place. It was all too, what was the word, reminiscent. Yeah, reminiscent.

Thank Christ he managed to shout down the Victorian red cedar conservatory. Ecologically harvested and lifetime rot treated or not I've never been a member of the fucking conservatory party and I'm not starting now. He didn't mean to say conservatory party but then he thought it was funny and she didn't and started screaming mental cruelty and holding her ears. It had only made him shout louder. On a semi-basement flat in the arse end of Cotham, for Christ sake? Who the fuck are we trying to impress? Shit it'd be fucking pergolas next, where she think they fucking lived? Ealing? Give me a fucking break, woman –

Well she had. Yeah.

Ealing was where she originally came but now Cricklewood was all she could afford, or so she said on the phone. Actually, he didn't feel too bad on the emotional/mental/psychological front. He'd let the rat out and the tension, the pressure, the bash-bash-bash trying to remember everything and still at the end of the day feeling massively depressed had gone. He felt weak but freed up. And while we're on the subject, Hallam, get the facts right. She's not your ex. Not legally she's not. Not yet, but hooray for fucking Cricklewood.

Then there was Ellie. Oh shit.

The last thing he'd sworn to do before he'd hit the bed, bounced and passed out was to phone her first thing. Now he felt too dishonest, disloyal, wasted. Instead he looked at the faces in the Cushionflor, men with beards and berets, women with hats and breasts. Under the heated towel rail opposite was a dead woodlouse curled up into a ball. Did they all do that? The faces started moving, changing shape. He levered himself up, avoided looking in the bronze-tinted mirror, made an attempt to smear toothpaste on his splayed-out brush and tried to clean the shit out of his mouth. A red wine belch came up his throat with a strong aftertaste of garlic and battered squid. He lowered himself back into bed and wondered how Cromer was managing.

Cromer had been sick all night, or so Louise was telling him as she pulled on her black working slacks over her high-waisted no-nonsense white knickers, face as long as a pine box. 'I don't know how you can do that to yourselves, John I really don't, I just can't see the fun in it, you've started swearing worse than you ever did, the bedroom smells like a brewery and as for the bathroom –'

Go away, thought Cromer. Don't say anything, just go to work. Please. Love.

' – you can finish it. Pick me up at twelve and don't forget we're going shopping.'

'Bye love.' She didn't kiss him. Don't forget meant get some money out. It was going to be expensive. Like that bloody piss-up. The door slammed and Cromer flinched. All his overtime money gone, and more. And Vic had hardly let him put his hand in his pocket until they got to the Apollo. At least he'd paid his whack there. At least he'd got Louise out of bed at four in the morning to run them both home. At least he hadn't been sick in the car. Not quite. He sipped his hot weak tea and while he was throwing up again he wondered into the diced carrot and tomato-skinned brown mess in the bottom of the pan whether he was cut out for life in the CID.

Good girl. That had been a real smack in the face at first, but by quarter to one Frank was on top of his Station work and drafting out contingency plans for the nurse. Plan A home. Plan B hospital. *Good girl* was still a bastard though. So was *lower middle/professional/query*. They were guessing, but pinning him

188

down. He'd thought all the effing and blinding he'd done would have covered that but then everybody effed and blinded nowadays. Two slips, one big, one little. And they'd got the age and the weight and the height, all that. Guesses, but sound guesses, decent close work starting from nothing. Hallam had really got his finger out on this one. But *good girl*. . . . Had he really said it? Did he always say it? Hell, there was always less time than you thought –

Watch it, Frank, slow down.

Right. All the psycho guff about fear/dislike of women, possible interest in pornography, paedophilia, dirty jokes, chauvinist attitudes, possible loner, possible failed interpersonal relationships, all that was straight out of the Boys' Book of Higher Bullshit. This was that new cheapo try-out system from the Met, three out of ten success rate. Some civilian titbrain makes up a prelim psycho profile chart and then it gets left to some kid like Cromer to tick it in. Paedophilia for Christ sake, all because he'd said *good girl*. Guys who went in for that should be shot.

He toothcombed through the reports again. The nurse off till Thursday, then on nights. Perfect for Plan B. Plan A still favourite though, nice little in-house number. Her mates infant school teachers, Backwell and Old Sodbury. Well out in the sticks, so that would give him another half-hour. Frank began to build up a picture. The nurse on her own all day. The layout of the flat. The other tenants. The owners, the Besants, him in the University Biology Department, her in some bookshop. No kids in the joint. Lock on the front door? On all the flats? Bound to be. What about the rest of the street? Parking? What time did it get dark? Dark. Was that the window he was looking for?

No rush. Chill out, man.

Right, but suppose it's not all down here? Just how sloppy is Hallam? Pretty naff on Pauline White but sound enough on the nurse. But did he put it all down anyway? Very few CID did: daren't in a lot of cases, too much hard graft in others. Which was Hallam? Both, probably. Cromer was no bother, the kid had to get it all written up, word for word or get one bollocking after another. But Hallam. Did he need to get closer? How?

Getting dangerous, old son.

He paged back up to the St Pauls thing, went through it again, looking for Hallam's involvement. Nothing, bar a note from DCI Barnard suggesting him and Cromer had been there earlier and cocked it up on obbo. He trawled on – and yes, Christ, there it was staring at him. There it was, if he wanted it. The link: Winston Winters, the black kid with the busted jaw. Frank could row himself in on that no trouble, re-interviewing, just doing his job. Yeah that was it if he needed it, a way to get close and stay under cover, no sweat.

The rest, the nurse, was just good police work.

He checked his schedule, mentioned Winston to the desk, back around five, changed back into civvies and then out into the fresh wet air. The car radio said there was more rain forecast. Good. He'd already got overalls and stuff in the boot if he needed it. By half-one Frank was walking along Royal York Crescent in Clifton looking down on Cornwallis.

Little recce, little obbo, then we'll see.

16

Come on Frank.

He was standing on top of Royal York, high above it
all, looking out over Bristol to the green hills beyond.
He pulled his shiny dark blue car coat round him,
feeling one second hidden, the next exposed and
naked, as if the whole city down below was watching,
grinning, waiting for him to make a prat of himself and
get arrested –

This is it, Frank.

Then feeling cool, feeling high, feeling so alive he
frightened himself. It had to be what villains felt:
mouth watering, full of juice, the whole system well
tuned up and full of power. Frank began to feel lucky,
like the first time, on Hensman's Hill – and then it was
all going, draining away, and his guts were turning to
water –

You great big fucking babby.

Shit man, I'm on the fucking edge.

You can do it, Frank.

Don't push me.

You can do it. All you have to do is go for it.

Oh yeah?

*Yeah. Go for it but don't go at it blind, mad-headed,
like a villain. Think about it, you're supposed to be a
cop, for Christ sake. Work out your quit points. Ways
in, ways out. Always have an alternative, always have
a quit point. If you're seen, stopped, challenged, recognised. The unexpected you can expect. Be ready. Have*

191

*a quit point. You get all the way up there, four, five
flights of stairs, and you're knocking on the door and
it's one of her mates – what then?*

Frank tried to work it out.

You walk away, Frank.

Walk away?

*You get your answer ready, double glazing, home
improvements, doing a survey, police, what the fuck.
And you walk away. Fucking easy, man. Come on,
Frank. You've got three hours. Three hours. How long
does it take, twenty minutes? You can do it, Frank. You
want to do it, you've got to do it, so stop pissing about
and go for it.*

Frank looked out over the city. A young mother in a
long dress that looked as if it were made out of brown
curtains was pushing a kid and a bright blue bagload
of washing up the steep slope out of Granby Hill. Traffic
noise rose from the flyover and the Portway. He was
alone, on high, above it all. If only he could fucking
fly. If he could fucking fly he'd swoop down and grab
that young mother and fuck her on the wing.

*Pissing about, Frank. Never mind fucking flying. Just
remember, you can always walk away.*

Right, he could always walk away. He could always
quit at any point. Until she was actually there naked
before him. He wanted her naked this time.

To know her every fucking mole.

From where Frank stood this end of Clifton collapsed
down the hill to the docks like one side of a squashed
wedding cake. Stone Georgian and early Victorian
terraces skewed left, right and centre, slate roofs ran
up, down and sideways. Cornwallis was one of the
biggest, a third of the way down and completely surrounded by houses. Row upon row, tall narrow tight-

packed, stacking up all round it. Upwards of a thousand windows staring right at it, right at the nurse's flat, saying, We're watching you, sunshine.

All it needed was one nosy idle old biddy with nothing better to do than stare out of her net curtains all day long – and Christ knows there were enough of those in Clifton, so forget it. Walk away now, forget it.

You're losing it, Frank. Nobody saw you before, nobody'll see you this time. This is Clifton, for Christ sake. Everybody's on the mooch.

He moved higher up the worn steps until he could see right along the dormers and double roofs of Cornwallis. In the middle of the shallow M-shape made by the roofs lay the central valley gutter.

That's it, man. You get in there you're invisible.

Frank walked along Cornwallis counting the skips and FOR SALE boards. Make an appointment, use that as a way to get in? No, it would take too long, be too fucking obvious, he'd leave a description. There were four skips though. The place was always falling down, being rebuilt, converted. One of the skips was only two houses away from the nurse but there was no sign of life. Probably be some mean DIY bloke who couldn't stand his wife and did it all at weekends. The other skip was fifty yards away outside a house with dirty empty-looking windows and a load of scaffold planks reared up in the basement area. There was a builder's van outside and an electric hoist on the stone parapet.

Keep going, Frank. Bear it in mind. Notice everything. Forget nothing. Not even dogshit. Remember. Anything can bring you down.

Thanks a bunch.

Halfway along, Cornwallis split in two. A couple of Victorian semis and an alley then dark solid five-storey Georgian terracing started again. He vaguely remembered some tale about the original builders running out of money and having to leave a gap. Some things never changed.

He went down the alley. It was steep, and slippery with leaves. There was another iron gate, like the one on Hensman's Hill. This one led into Cornwallis Crescent communal gardens. He turned right along the narrow lane that bordered the gardens. Down below lay The Polygon, another curved terrace, but with smaller houses. He looked over the wall into the communal gardens. Plenty of bushes, trees, lawns and borders, sloping up to a gravel path in front of the raised and balustraded terrace. The coach-houses under the terrace had long since had their arches cemented and breeze-blocked in. Short lines of washing hung limp in the damp air. Frank walked along, counting the houses. The builders were round the back as well. A mixer, two piles of sand and gravel. A pile of padlocks and scaffolding lying on the floor. He craned his neck to scan the roofline. On the first floor, ornamental cast-iron balconies, some painted and copper canopied, some bare and rusting. There were no curtains in the windows of the builders' house and Radio 1 echoed through its empty rooms. On the roof there was another stone parapet, about two foot high and running the full length of the Crescent. Parapets front and back; either one would give good enough cover. Frank decided the rear was probably best. He would be in view climbing over the chimney dividers that separated one house from the next, but even then he'd be in dark blue against wet slates. There were dormer windows behind the parapet, but no lights, which meant everybody was still at work or picking up kids.

Place with the builders in was favourite. Decision number one.

Frank. Think about getting out. Getting in is easy, getting out can be as long as the rest of your life.

Christ what was was he looking at, twenty years? Fifteen minimum. Fifteen cuntless years. Oh shit.

Frank. You're making it too difficult. You go in, you do her, you get out. Just like last time. You can do it, Frank.

He walked back. The mixer stood in the open doorway of the blocked-up arch. From what Frank knew of the toerags round Clifton and Hotwells the builders would have to drag it inside at night. There was only an old plank door on the coach-house, probably with no more than a couple of rusty old bolts on the inside, a household Yale at most. The front door would be security-locked against squatters by the builders when they left; even so he could still come down through the empty house, out through the plank door, into the bushes, over the wall and off. Say twenty seconds. Another forty, in the car and away. He started pacing it out down the narrow lane.

That's good, Frank. Walk, don't run.

The wall was higher this end, the lane dipping down and narrowing, hiding him from sight. The sky was darkening with rain. He hurried on, feeling stronger, tougher, more secure every step of the way. Yea though I walk through the valley of the shadow of death and I know that you are with me it's not me that's going to get it sunshine, you are.

More like it, Frank.

Now he was passing the nurse's house. There was a light in the back dormer. Not overhead but soft and pinkish, probably coming through the shade of a bedside lamp. Frank began imagining her. The bed, the room, the furniture, rosebud wallpaper, everything. As the air turned colder before the rain he recalled the

oatmeal smell of her. And saw it all. Slamming into
the warm-lit bedroom. Struggling punching kicking
screaming gobbing and then *whack* blood everywhere,
up the walls across the white candlewick, all over her
naked body everywhere, and her all slippery with it
yelling red bloody murder, like shagging a bird with
the rags on. Only better. Perfect, in fact.

Don't get carried away, Frank.

He raced the start of the rain up the steps at the
Granby Hill end of Cornwallis and piled into his car
just as the first freezing drops came lancing and battering down. It was on, he was going for it.

He drove down to the BRI and covered himself by
making an appointment to see Winston Winters at 4.45.
He called Thornbury from the hospital car park.
Nothing untoward, said the desk. He drove up St
Michael's Hill through rain streaming down and back
over Whiteladies into Clifton. He changed into his overalls and dark blue deck shoes in the multi-storey and
by 4.05 he was back on obbo in Cornwallis, under the
wall at the end where the punters parked their no-tax
motors, nicely hidden behind a skip but with a good
sight of the shallow curve. He rolled his balaclava up
to look like a builder's woolly and waited. It was all
but dark now, the car windows were well fugged up,
and the rain made a misty yellow ball of light round
the old street lamp opposite the nurse's house. Looking
at the light, he felt comforted.

Tell me the quit points, Frank.

One, here. Anybody comes up, I flash the card, I'm
on obbo, end of story.

Next?

Two, the builders. Same thing. They see me, I'm
investigating theft of materials.

In overalls?

196

Keep the car coat on until I'm in.

If you're seen on the roof?

Saw some oik Breaking and Entering, went after him.

And the nurse?

Frank thinking about it, hardening.

Frank, I'm asking you about the nurse.

Seeing her, ample, solid, splayed out, helpless.

Stop wanking on about it, Frank.

Frank ran through all the permutations, quit points, accidents, unforeseen. Yeah. Well. It's shit or bust, basically.

Yes, old son. Basically it's shit or bust.

He sat, fiddled with his gloves, listened to the rain. One or two cars pulled up and women rushed their kids into houses further up the street. None of them so much as glanced in his direction. A couple of builders came out and dumped blue plastic fertiliser sacks of plaster and lath rubble in the skip. With their outside work rained off, Frank figured they were getting ready to jack in early.

4.15. Time to make a move. He pulled out his mobile, pressed in the nurse's number.

Ellie was in bed when the phone rang. She padded barefoot into the hall, thinking it would be Marge or Kay wanting to know what shopping to get.

'Hallo?' There was a hiss of static and then nothing. Just as she was getting back into bed it rang again.

'Yesss?' She let enough irritation into her voice to deter a nuisance caller.

'It's me, Vic.'

'Oh.'

'What d'you mean, Oh?' His voice sounded early morning rough but – she looked at her watch – it was quarter-past four in the afternoon. She found herself wondering if he'd got a cold, or flu or something, and then told herself not to be such a nurse, such a mother all the time. He was big enough to look after himself, and besides, she didn't want to have to go through the whole thing again, certainly not standing on the cold floor, talking into the phone. It made her instantly want to go for a pee.

'You didn't just ring, did you,' she said. 'Just this second?'

'No, why?'

'I was in bed, and as soon as I answered it, it went dead.'

'Sorry about that. It wasn't me.' A pause, waiting for her to say something. She looked in the hall mirror. Her hair was a haystack, all spread out and cock-eyed from lying on her side, reading, and then nodding off. She was surprised to see her eyes looking so bright: she must be getting back to normal. His voice was asking her how she was.

'Oh I'm all right. Well, I'm half asleep actually, if you really want to know.'

'Me too.'

'What?'

'I only just got up.'

'Why, what's the matter?'

'Nothing. I went out last night.'

'Oh.' Then, more tartly, unable to help herself, she said, 'Did you have a nice time?'

'Had a late-night nosh up the Apollo with a few of the lads.'

That explained the voice. Some men seemed to be so proud of their hangovers. 'Then they let you stay in bed all day, do they?'

'It's my day off. I meant to call earlier –'

'I'm glad you didn't.'

198

'Why?'

'I told you, I was asleep.'

'So was I.' Another pause. Thinking of each other in bed, miles apart. She didn't even know where he lived. She said she was trying to switch her hours round, get her system ready for nights. 'It never works though.'

'No,' he said. 'It still gets you at four in the morning.'

'That's low blood sugar.'

'Is it?' Another pause. What was he up to? 'Listen, would you like to come out and have something to eat tonight?'

So that was it. Well well well. Her thoughts starting to race, she looked in the mirror again, and shoved her hand through her hair, trying, unsuccessfully, to tidy it. 'I'm supposed to be cooking for Marge and Kay.' Pasta and tuna. She wondered whether she should ask him round. For pasta and tuna, with Marge and Kay? She couldn't see that one working out at all. 'What time?' she said.

She could hear him blowing smoke out before committing himself. 'Eight, half-past?' He didn't sound too sure.

'Make it eight.'

'I'll be round.'

'It's not posh, is it?'

'Not if they let people like me in.' He cleared his throat. 'Italian all right?'

'Fine.'

'Right.' Another cough, then his voice changed. 'This phantom phone call. Get many?' There he was, back to being a cop again.

'Oh, you know, one or two a week. Everybody does round here.'

'You get a better class of burglar in Clifton.'

'What d'you mean?'

'They call to see if you're out.'

'All I did was say Hallo, then it sort of hissed and went dead.'

'OK.' Very abrupt. 'I'll see you.'

'Vic.' Saying his name for the first time.

'What?'

'Don't expect anything too lively will you?'

'Against the rules.'

'What rules?'

'You're still a witness, Ellie.' And that was that.

She went back into the bedroom and looked at the rain slanting hard into the dormer window then streaming down the reflection of her face. You're still a witness. She wished he hadn't said that. One minute he was taking her out, the next she was still a witness. He always seemed to be manoeuvring her on to the wrong foot. She couldn't quite make out whether it was because he never stopped working, force of habit like her being a nurse, or whether he just found it hard to be naturally straight. There were a lot of men like that, who found it hard to be themselves, and had to put on some sort of act to show they were in control, on top, even when they weren't. The insecure type, frightened of being warm or open, frightened to death of touching or being touched – until the last minute, when they jumped on you.

Vic didn't strike her as insecure, so perhaps he was just protecting himself, staying on the defensive. On the other hand, he had already led her up the garden path once – literally – and that still rankled. For a moment fierce again, she was glad she'd had a go at him. But then he'd held her, calmed her down; she remembered the feel of him, his arms, his whole body hard, plank-like, unyielding.

Perhaps he'd soften up over a bottle of wine. She'd

never been out with anyone in the police before, let alone a detective sergeant. He must be well into his thirties, she thought, old enough to be crafty, not to give himself away if he didn't want to. And in addition, she told herself firmly, he was still married, and we don't want any of that again thank you very much. What was he really after? Company? Lonely on his day off? Sex? Well that was out for a start, too sore, too all sorts of things. He wouldn't dare try it on, would he? Not from what he just said anyway. She turned her face from side to side in the wardrobe mirror, glancing at her jawline and beginning to wonder what sort of clothes to wear, and hoped he didn't want to witter on about his wife all the time.

Anyway, he'd asked her out and if he wasn't supposed to that must mean something. Oh sod it, she thought finally, a date was a date. It had come straight out of the blue, she hadn't angled for it, not in the least, and it was the first for God knows how long, so why not, what else was there to do on a wet Tuesday night? And at the very least it would be something to tell Marge and Kay about, before and after. She began to smile to herself; something funny was bound to happen, something they could have a good laugh about later. They'd be bound to disapprove at first of course, but so what, they weren't going out with him, she was.

Twenty-past four. Plenty of time for a bath before they came home. She pulled her nightie off and put her arms up to twist her hair back.

The front door of the builders' house was open. A glance up and down and he was in, out of the rain. The outer door had a Chubb deadlock newly fitted. In front of him the inner front door was also standing open; to the left of it was the door to the basement flat.

He made sure it was on the latch, then stepped into the hall and listened. The radio was still going, somewhere right up at the top of the house. Cloudy shuttering plastic on the floor, newspapers on the stairs, a smell of damp plaster, thinners and new-sawn pine. He looked up the well of the staircase. There was a full-width two-door cupboard on the half-landing, which was probably the old lavatory and cloakroom. An alloy extending ladder stood on the first floor and paint-sheets protected the fluted mahogany banister rail.

Frank went springing up the stairs two at a time, light as a cat.

'Oy!' A voice echoed down. Frank flattened himself against the wall. 'You ready, Tone?'

'Almost,' replied an older voice.

'Well come on.' Boots began clumping down and the noise of the radio grew louder. Frank dived into the half-landing cupboard. Full of rags, paint, sacks of pink plaster, yellow five-gallon cans of proofer. He crammed himself into the six-inch space between the frame and the door. One, two, three pairs of workboots, the clank of a toolbox, the radio.

'Turn the fucking thing off,' said the older voice.

'Bollocks.' Then it went off.

The feet stopped at the half-landing. The door opened, pushing against his face. Fucked, he thought, totally fucked at the first attempt and no way out. So much for fucking quit points –

'Give us it then.' He saw an arm in a red plaid shirt, the back of a head, matted tow-coloured hair, a darker sideburn, an ear with a spot of pink plaster on it. The smell of Golden Virginia. Frank held his breath, making himself nothing, inert, dead as wood, stone, plaster. Holding back. See me and I'll kill you I'll fucking kill you. And at the same time knowing he wouldn't, and

202

couldn't: absolutely no way he could get away with it against three of them –

He watched the toolbox being clanked down then the arm reaching back round the door and placing a paint-splattered radio on the floorboards between his feet. Touching his shoes. Holy shit. He spread his feet fractionally to let the radio rest –

'All right?' The older voice.

'Hang on.' The hand, thick-fingered and black-nailed, less than an inch from his overalls, checking the radio was off, then disappearing, drawing the door shut behind it.

Three pairs of workboots banging down the stairs. Frank with his eyes shut, straining his ears. The inside door slamming shut, then the front. A key turning twice in the deadlock. The van starting, driving off. Silence. Rain. Breathing out, swallowing hard.

Your lucky day, Frank.

He slipped a short-bladed one-inch chisel in the ruler pocket of the overalls and moved down the stairs to check the back way out. The basement door was still on the latch. Down a rickety flight of wooden stairs into a flagstoned hall smelling of damp and cat piss. Through the back door out into heavy, splattering rain. The rear basement area was topped with spiked black railings, the walls thick with fern and black mould. The coach-house under the terrace had been partitioned into an whitewashed brick coal cellar and some kind of wash-house, piled with sawn-off joist ends. There was a fungus smell of wet and dry rot, and little white distemper stalactites hung from the arched ceiling. The mixer was butted up against the plank door. Frank squeezed past and gave the door a heave. The hinges dropped but it would open with a pull.

Back up, all the way through the empty house full

of the sound of heavy rain. Two vast rooms on the first floor, sixteen- or seventeen-foot ceilings, floors newly planked and sanded. Frank understood all of a sudden why villains shat on the floor: it wasn't simply spite, it was the feeling of being alone, illegal, in someone else's gaff, nerves making you want to void your bowels.

When he made it up to the top flat, he found all the ceilings were down. There were new rafters in the V of the double roof with water collecting in pot-bellied swags of plastic where the builders had removed the lead guttering and slates to bed the rafters in. Fucking cowboys, he thought, they never put things back right.

He chinned himself up through the new sealed-unit double-glazed skylight. It was like walking out on to the top deck of a ferry in a full gale. Rain smacked horizontally at his face, wind ripped at his coat, and the valley gutter was inches thick with leaf slime and black-grey sludge. He made his way forward into the lee of the chimney stack and looked up for handholds.

Holy shit, now he was up here the stack was a lot higher than he thought: a black greasy brick pile towering fifteen foot above the gutter. Even at the roofline it was a good eight. He would have to jump for it – with no decent footing – in the middle of a howling gale. . . .

Don't, Frank. One loose slate and you're nackered. Get back inside and think again.

Ellie sank into the bath and started to plan what to wear. She had bought an expensive steel-blue bra in Dingles' summer sale, and then gone back the next day for the matching camisole and french knickers. Wearing them always made Ellie feel good; the cool feel of the silk and lace against her skin somehow made

204

her think she was taller, slimmer, lighter, more model-like. Then, on top of that, it would have to be something dark; the long black satin top made her creamy skin look good, and then she could wear her new black baggy pants underneath. But what shoes? Shoes were always a problem – she would need heels, because of Vic's height, and not wanting to look dumpy tagging along beside him – but on the other hand, she didn't want to look tarty either, and she was inclined to think that pants and heels did look a bit *Dynasty*. Flat black pumps were best, but then – she listened to the rain, and the wind howling in the vent stack – she didn't want to sit around all night with sopping wet feet. Maybe her old granny boots would be best, but inside or outside the trousers? Or should she try another outfit altogether? The long blue-grey tweed skirt? She lay back, letting her mind drift through her wardrobe, pleasantly luxuriating in the problem and looking forward to the night to come. Perfume, she thought, which perfume to wear?

Frank, stripped to his overalls now, writhed his long body out of the dormer window into the gutter below the parapet. The lead flashing was washed clean by rain. He knelt up and looked over the edge of the parapet. Jesus it was a hell of a drop, straight on to the black spiked railings of the basement area. He imagined himself slipping and falling end over end on to the blunt ornamental spikes. Small muscles were starting to jump in his arms and legs, and his teeth wanted to chatter under the cold smack of rain. A wave of giddiness passed over him, his gloved fingers dug into the parapet, and he spent long seconds frozen with vertigo, unable not to look down. Water was falling and blowing out of a cracked down-pipe splattering on to the terrace, smashing itself to pieces –

Move, you dumb bugger.

Inching forward on hands and knees, head down below the parapet level, safer now he couldn't see the drop, feeling the rain hitting like steel rods on his back, Frank crept up to the dividing wall. He tested the slab of coping stone on top for looseness, then squirmed over it, his heart lumping up into his throat and all his limbs quivering like a wet dog. He subsided into the gutter on all fours, his chest heaving and his pulse hammering. Christ. Flattening himself to belly-crawl past the next dormer window. No light but you never knew. The next divider. The coping stone loose, wobbling in his soaked gloves. Holy shit. Standing up, feeling the wind pulling and sucking at him. Leaning into the roof, stepping over, his throat closed tight, wind and rain ripping through the overalls plastering themselves to his skin, don't let me fall, please God.

He'd made it. He'd done it. Crouching, a couple of breaths to let his heart slow down and he began to feel invincible. Jesus Christ if I wanted to I could stand up and dance along the fucking parapet –

No you couldn't, Frank. Crawl.

Left arm, right arm, left leg, right leg. Getting into the rhythm now. Three to go. Fuck the rain.

Ellie came drifting back out of her childhood in the small modern semi with the stained-glass sailing ship set in the front door oval, and pulled the bath plug. She had decided on the black, and was going to set it off with that bright turquoise blue Peruvian enamel combined necklace and pendant thing Graham bloody Simmons had given her when he told her his wife was coming back from America. She had never worn it before, but she would tonight; the decision made her feel extraordinarily free and high-spirited. She coupled the shower attachment on to the taps, fiddled with the mixture until it was cool but not icy cold, stood up and began to spray herself.

Frank was crouching under her bedroom window, pulling the balaclava down over his face, lifting his head, fraction by fraction, to peer into the room. Seeing the warmth of it, the unmade bed, the lamp, the white nightie thrown on the floor. But no nurse. What the fuck –

She walked into the room pink and naked, rubbing at her hair with a towel. Him grinning. I can't believe this, I can't believe I'm getting all this. She'd got terrific tits and a nice big damp fluffy-looking snatch, then down went the towel, and she stood there listening to something he couldn't hear because of the rain, posed like some big pink and white marble fucking statue, and then she was turning her back to grab for some quilted dressing gown thing and she was gone. Oh God what an arse. Oh God I want you.

He put the chisel to the window and slid it up to release the catch. Nothing. Forcing it, using the full strength of both arms, his neck reddening and throbbing with the strain. Still nothing. The fucking window. Come on come on. What was the matter with the fucking thing? He peered into the join: the fucking window frame was fucking rebated. Fuck it fuck it fuck it. Unjamming the chisel. Now what?

The roof, Frank.

He stood up. Mad. Mad for it, mad for her. The strength of madness pouring through him driving him up over the roof through the blinding rain like a pelted cat and down the other side into the central valley gutter. As he paused to get his breath he realised he was growling, actually growling, like a fucking lion or a bear or a wolf or some fucking animal. Jesus Christ, he was so fucking quick and lithe and powerful and silent he was a fucking dynamo, unbelievable, absolutely fucking irresistible – fuck yes kill yes thank you yes – oh God yes –

Don't blow it now, Frank. Slow down.

The skylight. It wasn't like the new double-glazed affair on the builders' house; this was old with a loosely nailed chickenwire cover to stop leaves blocking the drainhole next to it. He prised the wire off and set it to one side. Remember. Put it back later. Underneath lay a wood frame set with four panes of glass. The putty was cracked and green with algae, the wood split and warped. The bastard thing was only held together by mould. He slid the chisel along the putty, steel squealing on glass. Take out the pane, unfasten the strut, in. The pane slipping between his wet gloved fingers. Falling. Grabbing for it, catching it, lurching off balance, recovering in a flash. Jesus Christ he was fast. Like greased fucking lightning. He laid the pane flat in the sludgy leafmould and reached down for the strut, rust crumbling orange under the swollen black paint. Easing it back, lifting the skylight slowly up and over. Chisel back in ruler pocket and dropping silently 'in. Like that bloke. All because the lady likes Milk Tray. You're going to get a lot more than Milk Tray, girl – any fucking second now –

She wasn't there. Tearing round looking through every door. She wasn't there. The bathwater still swilling down the sodding plug hole and she wasn't fucking there. Down below the noise of a heavy front door slamming shut in the wind and then a gust of it coming right up the house and out through the skylight. Then voices, a man and a woman. Feet on the stairs four

208

flights down. She wasn't fucking there and she fucking ought to be –

Out, Frank. Out out out!

Pulling himself up, even remembering to put the pane of glass back. And the chickenwire. Brilliant. It had taken ages, fucking years, getting there, now he was out, flying, gone.

Frank sat in his car heaving with joy. What a buzz, what a terrific fucking buzz. As good as doing it, going through with it. No wonder villains got hooked on it. He could feel his soul laughing and singing and dancing inside him. Oh boy oh boy oh boy oh boy oh boy –

Then he felt the chisel hard against his thigh, still inside the ruler pocket.

17

'Well,' Ellie closed the flat door, pulled her dressing gown round her and looked Vic up and down. 'You're keen I must say.'

'What d'you mean?' said Vic. He was wearing a new suit; it was exactly the same as the other one, just as baggy, but less shiny.

'I've heard of early, but three hours –'

'I put the phone down and I thought why not, I've got nothing else to do –'

'You really know how to make a person feel good, don't you?' He wasn't listening; he was looking at the water on the floor in the hall. 'I just got out of the bath –'

'What I meant was, I thought we could go for a drink first.'

'At five o'clock?'

'The Portcullis opens at half-past. I thought it might take you that long to get ready.'

'Did you?' He seemed to be taking a lot of things about her for granted. It wasn't that she minded going out early – it would save her cooking for Marge and Kay, and she could easily leave them a note – but she might as well show him she wasn't going to be pushed into dropping everything for his benefit, just because he'd got nothing to do for a couple of hours. Apart from anything else, she thought, he could have phoned first and asked instead of just walking in and telling her. She moved away from him into the sitting room

210

to give herself time to think what to say, then turned to face him. 'Can I ask you something, Vic?'

'Sure.'

'We're not going to talk about this case all night, are we? Because if we are, well, I don't want to hurt your feelings, but to be honest, I'd rather not go.'

'I see.' He looked at his shoes as if he was thinking of all the time he had wasted polishing them; Ellie had a brief glimpse of the disappointed boy inside the man and immediately – knowing it was stupid, knowing it was her being a nurse again – began to feel sorry for him.

'It's not that I don't want to go out with you, I do. I was looking forward to it, I haven't been out for ages – '

'Me neither.'

'You liar,' she said, trying to lighten it, 'you went out last night.'

'Only to get wrecked with the lads.'

'Anyway,' she said, 'I don't want to go over it again and again and again, I've had enough of it, and apart from anything else I thought this would be a chance to talk to each other, you know, normally for once, instead of this constant, endless interrogation.' His pale steady gaze had not shifted from her face for an instant; she pushed her hair back, starting to feel flustered by him, but determined to stick to her point. 'I mean, I don't exactly know very much about you, do I?'

'Not much to know,' said Vic. He took out a pack of Marlboro, looked at it, looked at her, then put it away again, thoughtfully. 'But fair enough, I see what you mean, I do get a bit one-track about things.' He put his hands deep into his trouser pockets and hunched his shoulders up and down. She hoped he wasn't going to start jingling his keys, or his loose change. 'Tell you the truth Ellie, I'm not used to this – in fact I'd say I'm

211

more nervous than you are, I mean, I haven't been out with anybody – well, you know, like this – for years.'

'I should hope not,' she said briskly, moving past him out into the hall. 'You can smoke if you like.'

'Thanks,' he said. 'Anyway, if the worst comes to the worst, we can always talk about what's wrong with Bristol Rovers' back four. That should keep us going till midnight.'

Ellie walked into her bedroom with a faint, pleased smile on her face.

Winston Winters was feigning sleep, bandages round his head and jaw, wire just visible between his big white teeth. Old men lay asleep on either side, their skin like parchment. One had a tube running out of him into a bottle under the bed the colour of raspberry jam. A slim Indian in hospital whites pulled the over-head-rail floral orange screen past their eyeline and disappeared. Frank sat down on a grey plastic chair and scraped it up close to the bed. Winston had one eye bruised and closed; the other opened slowly and took Frank unwillingly in. He used the smile and the warm voice.

'Hallo Winston. How you doing?' The kid stretched open his grey-looking lips to show the wire. 'You remember me, don't you?' Getting the ID out. 'Frank Webber.' No Inspector, just keep smiling. 'Don't try and speak, Winston, you've had a rough time. Just nod or shake your head. Listen,' leaning forward, 'I'm not here to give you any hassle, what's done is done son, no stress. OK?' He took hold of Winston's limp dry hand, squeezed it and let go. 'Now what I've come to say is I'm willing to help you. If you're interested.' Winston simply looked at him, old beyond his years.

The funny thing was after that business on the roof,

the buzz of it, Frank felt pretty close to the kid. He'd had the luck, the kid hadn't; that was all it was, that was the only difference. The poor little bastard had got his head kicked in and Frank had got away with it. It made him feel warm and sympathetic towards the kid; now then, he thought, how to use it.

'I said are you interested Winston? I mean it.' He bent forward, giving it to him straight, man to man. 'All right, so I'm police and you're black and we're not generally known for helping each other out but I reckon I owe you one Winston. Which is why I'm here. Let me explain something.' The little bastard wasn't going for it. Well fuck him, keep after him and he will. 'I nick you, I get a commendation. Commendation means promotion and promotion can mean an extra five or six grand a year. Now that's what I'm looking at, what are you looking at? I'll tell you what you're looking at, Winston. You're looking at two years minimum. Taking and driving away, dangerous driving, assaulting a police officer. Me, in point of fact. Now you're not dumb, Winston, you're not stupid. To do what you do takes nerve. To do what I did took nerve.' Now give him the grin. 'I tell you I was shitting myself when I jumped your motor.' The wired-up jaw prevented any response. 'So if I say I owe you one, you don't want to think what is all this white cop shit you want to listen first, then make up your mind. Understand?' The kid looking wary but no longer coming on with that me-I'm-so-black-I'm-brain-dead act. 'Now because it *is* me, my say so, I can get you a suspended or I can send you down the steps. Now you can nod if you like or alternatively you can shake your head and I'll walk away. No witnesses, it never happened. Up to you.'

Winston looked up at the ceiling. Then out through the screens to the other side of the ward. Frank turned to see. Across the ward was a lank-haired white youth with his leg up in plaster, watching.

'Know him?' Winston shook his head. Frank got up, pulled the orange screen right across. 'Well?'

A nod like a little old man hanging on to his dignity, down and then up, once. Got you, you little bastard.

'Now I'll tell you something else. Whatever you and your mates might think, not everybody in this Force is dead against you or anybody else in the black community. What you have to put up with is very similar to what we have to put up with. Drunkenness, violence and abuse from a load of pig-ignorant white bastards.' Don't overdo the official fucking sympathy, or you'll turn him off. 'But at least we get paid for it, so in that sense we got the sweet end and you got the shitty end. And because of that you know there's nothing for nothing in this life. This is a deal, Winston, and it's the best you'll get, son. So are you still interested?'

A wait, then another nod, somewhere between genuinely wary and acting bored.

'Now you know this as well as I do. St Pauls we can live with, no problem. You know what the Man says. Years they pass away and a rude boy come a good boy.' A flicker of contempt from Winston, the look saying Don't give me that I-know-reggae shit. Ignore him Frank, keep going. 'But these white yobs off the estates, the simple truth of the matter is, Winston, there's too many of 'em for us to deal with. I mean, you've got kids leaving school one week with no GCSEs, and the next week they're chemical bloody geniuses with a spoon and a can of Camping Gaz. "What you want, Mister, crack, H, speed, E or what? OK come back in ten minutes." They're the ones we want, not you. The ones we want Winston are the same assholes done you. That's point one. Now have the Drugs boys been to see

214

you?' Another nod. 'And you told them nothing. Me no coco, right?'

Almost a grin there. So go for it.

'Point two. These yobs, these assholes, they didn't kick your head in because they didn't like your face, did they? They knew who you were and they knew what you'd done. They got you lined up all the way from Bedminster nick to the bus station. And when they did you, they did you close enough to the Front Line to mean something, right?'

No reaction. The kid seeing himself as a black dog-soldier. Fighting for the Cause. Time to wrap it up.

'This is territory, right? Soon be fucking war, Winston. You heard what happened down the Jungle, those basketball kids. Whole place is a pool of petrol waiting for a match. And if they do team up and come looking for you and your mates that'll be it, and we won't be able to put it out and you won't be able to put it out and they won't be able to put it out.' Jesus Christ he was almost beginning to believe this. 'But this, you, this is territory. This is you pissing on their patch. This is you taking it to them, this is you giving them the finger, doing it for a reason, right?'

A shake of the head. Not me, man.

'Who told you to nick a Granada? Nice big old motor, plenty of 'em, plenty of room in the back, good dealer's car. Isn't it, Winston? Who put the order in?'

No nod, no shake of the head. Just evenly staring each other out. Stalemate. Except that I know I've won, kid.

'Somebody out of wheels, isn't it, Winston? Some guy with no motor who needs a motor, a motor we don't know.' Watching the eyes. Just a blink then the kid's head turned to look at the orange flowers on the screen. 'See you in court, son. Thanks for your help, I'll see that it's appreciated, so don't worry. Take care now.'

Frank walked out through the swing doors of the fracture ward thinking Christ what a cop he was. He called Traffic from the car park, and asked them to fax Thornbury with last week's Lost and Stolen Vehicle list. Then back up the hill and following the signs for GYNAECOLOGY, checking the staff laundry and locker rooms until he found a door marked DOCTOR G. CHAUDHURY.

That was where she would be tomorrow.

When he got back to Thornbury there were a couple of sheets on his desk from Traffic. On one was a report of an incident between the M32 and M4 Junction 19. Some black kids had a burn-out in a 1985 B-reg BMW 728i early last Saturday night. Frank phoned the Drugs Squad with the name of the registered owner and mentioned Winston. Then he leaned back in his chair and felt he'd justified his afternoon jaunt. There was still the chisel but he'd be rid of that after tomorrow.

While Ellie changed, Vic wandered round the sitting room, tried to watch television, lit a cigarette, couldn't find an ashtray, and wandered out into the hall to look in the kitchen. Ellie had mopped the water up from her bath, but now there was an even bigger pool under the skylight. And rain dripping into it. He moved underneath and looked up. The bar was fastened but there was new rust showing under the black paint blisters. And the pane where the water was coming through, how'd it get all that roof shit on the inside? Fuck it, he thought, it's not my job, let the landlord sort it out. He went to put his cigarette out in the sink. The rain was still pissing down. He glanced out through the kitchen dormer. To the right, where the parapet met the dividing wall, one of the slates was cracked right across. It had slipped a couple of inches to show a slice of the roof batten. It was soaked a bright yellowy-orange. Unweathered.

He took a kitchen chair and stood it under the skylight. From a few inches away he could see the old dirt-line where the skylight had been shut, probably for months if not years. Where it shut now was a good three-eighths of an inch above that. Down again. On with a pair of yellow kitchen gloves. Back up on the chair. The pane lifted as soon as he touched it. No putty. He pressed his fingers against the other panes. Firm, no movement.

The skylight went up easily. Too easily. Usually the bastard things swelled and warped until they jammed solid. Some sort of chickenwire arrangement slid off the skylight as Vic stuck his head out into the rain. Shielding his lighter and turning the gas up to maximum flame he looked along the valley gutter. Plenty of gritty sludge and black leaves from the big copper beech in the garden but with the rain battering down for God knows how long it was hard to say whether there was recent disturbance. There were grooves and hollows where somebody could have been kneeling or scraping their feet, but they were softened and filled with rain, and they could be shapes made by the water flow anyway –

But not that toe-print.

Under the overhang where the slates jutted out over the flashing the lead was dry. On it was the wet black mud imprint of the sole of a shoe from the toe to roughly the ball of the foot. Somebody getting purchase to step up the angle of the roof. He looked up the wet slates. No other signs, all washed off. Sooner you than me, sunshine. Now the fucking lighter was burning his fingers through the glove –

A hexagonal pattern like they have on sailing wellies –

Vic peeled off the glove and shoved it under the slate overhang hoping to protect the print from the rain, ducked back in and lowered the skylight, slotting the loose pane back in under the rusty ends of the half-inch nails. If anything he'd made the leak worse, but fuck it, not his problem.

He had just put the bucket underneath when Ellie appeared in one of those long black fisherman's oilskin things they sold in surplus shops.

'It's not mine.'

'You got another leak.' He saw her looking disappointed. She'd made her eyes and face up. It was the first time he'd seen her with eye-shadow and lipstick and smelling of perfume. His heart sank. 'You look nice,' he said.

'Thank you,' she said. 'It's always a bit of a mess when I do it myself because I can't see properly close up.'

'Looks fine.' Lying because it was less trouble, but it wasn't her. It made her look older, harder, further off. But that was what they all did, going out. 'What's the smell?'

'*Lou Lou*,' she said. 'And it's not a smell it's a perfume.'

He bent closer to her. Not too close, but close enough to look gallant, and interested. 'Nice,' he said, his eyes watering, trying not to sneeze. Christ he was out of practice.

She looked up at the skylight. 'Oh leave it, let them deal with it.'

'What I thought.'

218

They went downstairs in a trail of perfume and Vic
started to warm to it. But this other thing. What the
fuck was he going to tell her? Should he tell her at all?
How could he avoid it? How would she take it? Plus
he should have picked up the phone and reported it
straight away.

Christ I need a drink.

They were the first in. He hadn't said anything in the
car in the short drive up, although he had glanced and
smiled at her while he was backing the Escort into a
space opposite the pub door. She thought he looked as
if he were still not quite sure he was doing the right
thing, and felt like saying Look mate if you don't want
to, say so I can always go back and cook but I don't
need three hours' male bloody moody, thanks very
much. But then he held the door open for her against
the slamming gusts of wind; it had gone round to the
north-west now and the rain was so cold it had a metal
scent of sleet in it, a feel of bringing down all the heat
and fumes and grit the city had put up during the day.
Crossing the road she heard him swear to himself as a
car slashed downhill past them. Temper temper. She
hoped he wasn't going to drink and sulk all night.

There was a good fire going in the stove at the far
end but he led her straight to the window seat behind
the entrance door, saying he liked to see who came in.
She said, thinking to ease things into the start of a
conversation, to get him talking about his family, his
parents – she didn't even know whether he had any
brothers or sisters yet – her dad would never drink
with his back to the door either, something to do with
fights in the Army, she thought. There, that's a bit about
my family, what about yours? But he said nothing, just
nodded and took her slicker. He wasn't being sullen or

anything, but he certainly wasn't relaxed, not in a million years; she felt herself growing hot, awkward, nervous, and hoped she wouldn't knock her glass over, or do anything similarly stupid. But he definitely wasn't being the person he had been in the flat; she could tell he felt more or less at home there, and had done ever since that first Cup-a-Soup. It was as if he was distracted by being out with her, in the pub with her; it wasn't that he was scared of being seen out with her because he was still married, but he was somehow being careful with her, wary of her. She felt like telling him, I'm not glass you know, I won't break. Then she told herself, trying to get into whatever he might be feeling, it was, after all, the first time he'd seen her dolled up. Usually he had turned up when she was just slouching around in her dressing gown, so maybe it was the clothes and the make-up and everything that was creating the distance between them. Something was, anyway, something she couldn't put her finger on. Perhaps he had told her the truth, perhaps he was more nervous than she was, but whatever it was it was certainly affecting her. Why did he keep prowling around, why didn't he just come and sit next to her, look at her, smile at her, say something? She watched him move to the bar, digging into his back pocket for money.

He had about seventy quid cash. Plenty, even allowing for a taxi back to Cotham if he drank too much. But what the fuck was he going to tell her? Maybe after he'd had a couple it would just come out. That bastard, whoever he was. Screwing up what was meant to be a perfectly decent ordinary meal out, no intention of anything else. Not yet anyway, she was going to old Chaudhury tomorrow. Maybe not ever. But any rate getting to know her, be normal, as she said, straight with her, and try to relax like a couple of ordinary human beings for a couple of hours. Now this. It was either a break-in or the bastard was still after her. And a break-in was stretching it. What time had it started to rain? He had no idea. Oh shit, forget it, wait. It was what he usually did. But how the fuck was he going to tell her?

It was a snug low-ceilinged bar, built under the raised pavement, clean, smelling of polish, with a fine display of warm-lit malts. Nice. Warm and cheery after the rain. Perfect in fact. Except that there was no bugger behind the bar.

She watched him walk away from her down the length of the bar to the stairs at the end, glancing from side to side, taking everything in. Till, prints, brewery mirrors, state of the fire, even looking over the bar to see if there was anybody underneath. At this moment Ellie you don't exist, you're completely absent from his mind. Then he strolled back looking at everything but her, not even bothering to sit down but leaning himself on the corner of the bar. He was about ten feet away from her and she felt totally disconnected from him, as if he were a stranger who'd just come in on his own.

'Welcome to the *Marie Celeste*,' he said. It wasn't enough to deserve an answer and it didn't get one.

A pair of long legs came down the stairs then a black leather miniskirt followed by a waistcoat and see-through look-no-bra white chiffon top decorated with a big floppy cream and black striped bow-tie. Instead of turning his head to look, he asked Ellie what time it had started to rain.

'Rain?'

'Yeah.'

'Well. Let me think. It was quarter past four when

221

you phoned because I looked at my watch to see if I had time for a bath. It was raining then.'

'Thanks.' Some time between four and five.

The barmaid was one of those long slow self-absorbed tawny willowy light gold tan things about nineteen and five foot ten who still had names like Sara and went skiing and did cordon bleu courses and probably had a yah-right drawl and certainly had a hair flick problem. Nose not quite right though. Ellie hated her on sight and felt wet and windblown and frumpish. Now what would he do, gawp at her tits? Most would. Instead he went on looking at his watch, tapping the dial, working something out.

Then he turned, clocking the barmaid. She went on languidly laying out bar cloths, perfect pearl silver nails on long fingers and no rings. Ellie watched his reaction. Still baggy and patient, but with that way of looking faintly amused when he was actually quite pissed off.

'Anybody in?' he said.

'Oh right,' said the barmaid, laying out another cloth, turning her back.

'Any danger of getting a drink then, Maureen?'

'Actually my name's not Maureen.'

'And mine's not Job, darling.' He caught Ellie's eye in one of the framed brewery mirrors and gave her a big straight-up builder's lorry driver wink and a shake of his head and a smile that said Don't worry I've got this one sorted, only a slight inconvenience, we will have a good time I'll look after you I promise you, but bear with me for a moment while I deal with this because it's you I'm out with, kid.

Ellie felt herself slipping, falling, stomach going like the first big drop on a rollercoaster, wits all over the place and starting to shake, arms, legs and insides, in case he came and sat down next to her. Then she told herself not to be so bloody silly; all he'd done was wink at her, and she'd gone all trembly, like a schoolgirl. She began to feel warmer, and happier.

Two large Black Labels in tall glasses full of crushed ice were being set down in front of her. He was leaning over her, and giving her a big grin which made her feel even more like a rabbit. Vic, seeing how funny and pale she looked, moved close to her, clinked glasses and said drink up, here's to us and Bristol Rovers. For the first time she felt some sort of warmth flowing out of him, enveloping her in a pleasant woody masculine smoky smell that made her like him even more.

He waited for the barmaid to swing herself and her hair and her pert little tick-tock leather-clad bum haughtily back upstairs and then looked at her seriously for a few seconds, squinting one eye against his cigarette smoke. He didn't say anything, just went on looking at her, making her feel like a child. Did he know? Was he aware of what she was feeling? If he was, why was he treating it like a bloody wake? He sat and swirled his glass, taking big morose swigs at it. She was still too nervous and frightened to look at him for long and just sipped at hers.

'We might as well be married.' It just leapt out, she wasn't thinking of that, only of something to break the silence. 'Me looking out the window, you staring into your drink, neither of us saying anything, just like some gloomy old pair who've been married for forty years.'

He took another swig and said, 'Your life's in danger, Ellie.'

The door slammed open and the cold wind roared in and then half a dozen noisy big redfaced pinstriped men with complexions like babies rolled in after it, shaking themselves and going brrr and suddenly the pub was full of lawyers.

Outside the rain had stopped and there was a fine soft layer of sleet on the raised pavement but not on the road below. As they walked up towards Princess Victoria Street he took hold of her hand and put it in his coat pocket.

'Fuck the rules,' he said.

Everything, the street lights, the Suspension Bridge lit for Christmas, the sleet on the grass, the softness of their footfalls and the weaving set of prints they left made Ellie feel warm and silly and glad. They turned the corner out of the wind, their hands gripping each other tight inside his coat pocket, walking shoulder to shoulder. Then thinking it's shock my girl, drunk and delirious after one large Scotch. Your life's in danger, Ellie. Oh sod it why shouldn't I be happy?

In the restaurant, a cool pale green place with brass ceiling fans, she knew she was half drunk as soon as she hit the heat and the *pregos* and the *grazies*. He left to make a couple of phone calls and a pink fizzy bitter drink the waiter said was Punt e Mes and soda appeared in a textured green glass like an upside-down empty pyramid with a cherry in it and olives and stick biscuits in paper on a side plate. When he came back her cheeks were burning red and she knew she was being pathetic for clutching at his hand when he didn't want her to because he was trying to explain, but she couldn't help it. All she heard was his voice, keeping low and dull and deliberately monotonous until right at the end he said, 'Don't worry girl, you're with me now.'

His eyes were as pale as ever, but in the wheeling, scattered state her thoughts were in, like a flock of pigeons, she felt they were saying, I won't let you down, I'll take care of you, I promise, and she lurched even more towards being in love with him, if that was what it was, a feeling of being half drunk, dependent, grateful, wanting to be held, looked after, made safe. She wanted to let go, move into his arms and cry on him, but at the same time she was too frightened, not just of what might happen, but of him. Also there were other people looking.

The more he drank the more sober he felt. She'd gone, she was off the scale for some reason. Well, he'd done what he was supposed to do, and that was that. He'd phoned Redland first because it was their patch, saying just a possible attempted B and E, then the Well to get Forensic moving and some sort of protection rota and phone trace organised, God knows how long that would take, but telling them where he was so they could phone him back. But for the moment it was all down to him and he knew from her wobbly loose eat-me-now look and the way her eyes were crawling over him while they were both trying to eat he could have her under the table if he wanted or even Jesus Christ on top, the way it was pouring out of her.

But it wasn't real, was it, it was just her way of reacting – help me, don't leave me – which was all very well, but putting the whole thing on him. As per fucking usual. Then thinking: Come on for Christ's sake, this is what you're getting paid for. Even if it is your night off.

'Ellie.'

'What?'

'I think I should take you home.'

'I don't want to go home, I like being out, I like being here, it's nice.' Looking at him, drinking him in. 'Don't worry I'm OK, I'm fine.'

225

The worst thing was she thought she was, poor kid.

Eight-thirty and still no phone call. On the puddings now. Jesus, she could eat. She finished her zabaglione then his while he had an amoretto and a couple of large espressos. The sweet stuff seemed to calm her down and she started to look tired, blinking her eyes more. She was managing to hang on to it, which was good but as an evening out it was a bit of a disaster, a bit of a weepie, her clutching his hand and the waiters thinking he'd pulled her. That was what was wrong with this bloody job, you started off helping someone, got to know them and soon as you got interested you ended up responsible for them and there you were lumbered. *And* she was still a witness. But none of that was the point, the point was what happened next....

And he didn't fucking know.

Four young lads came in, big lads, hair cut floppy on top, short round the side, bit like Cromer, all carrying sports bags, all looking at least half-cut, and sat at the next table piling notes into a kitty and asking the waiter for two carafes house red, four spag bogs pronto —

'Vic.' Pulling at him.

'What?'

'That smell, Vic.' Her voice rough and urgent. 'That's it. That's the smell he had.'

'You sure?' He leaned back. One of the lads was directly behind him. The smell was half medicated like a dandruff shampoo, half pine like ordinary foam bath.

'Sure?' Glaring at him now. Christ what was this, was it real or was she drunk or hysterical or getting that way or trying to get him into a fight or what?

'You've got to be sure, Ellie.'

'You think I'd forget it? Would you?' So much for don't worry I'll look after you; she tried to hold on to

226

herself, forcing herself to sound calm, sane, rational, while all she could register was that cool clean sickening smell, and her head swimming as the whole assault came rushing back at her. 'It *is* the same, Vic. I *know* it is.'

'Right.' He pulled out a cigarette, lit it, took one drag and stubbed it out. 'You go to the Ladies.'

'Why?'

'Because I'm telling you to. Come on, Ellie.' He stood up to let her pass and watched her walk through the restaurant. She looked steady enough, but her shoulders had gone up, and her back was so straight he knew she was tensing herself and could collapse any second. He watched her go through the door marked TOILETS and hoped there was a fair old queue.

Now then. There were about seven ways to play this. There always were. Good evening lads. Good evening gentlemen. Out with the ID and then hope. That was the way it was supposed to work and eight times out of ten it did. But there were four of them, all big, and given their half-cut state and sports bags they could easily turn out truculent, and there was only one of him, and no back-up. Suppose this bastard was one of them, he could lie, could bolt, he could fight. And then his mates could join in. Knives, bottles, glasses were all there waiting. He glanced round the other tables. Two parties of four and three couples, all peaceful now but in seconds any one of them could go down covered in blood for having had nothing to do with it. Mention rape, or just making inquiries? Ask the questions inside or outside? And what if she'd got it all wrong?

He listened. Boys' names. Girls' names. Cars. Work. Party Friday, Alison and Claire's. You going? Hell no, wouldn't touch her with yours. Where's the spag I'm

227

fucking starving. Hunger, drink and aggro. The wrong time to go wading in. He went to the bar. Alberto please. *Momento.* Alberto, plump, pale, thinning black hair, hurrying in smiling and rubbing his hands. Good evening, Mister Hallam you and the lady enjoy yourselves? You see that table sitting next to us. *Si.* You seen them before? Oh yes, once, maybe twice a month they come in here. They any trouble? Trouble? No, Mister Hallam we don't have no trouble. Vic giving him the look. OK, noisy sometimes, you know Saturday nights. Last Saturday night, Alberto? Alberto scratching behind one ear, thinking back. No, not last Saturday, definitely no. Right, thanks. You want me to do anything, Mister Hallam? making a circular phone-dialling gesture. No not yet Alberto, just see if their order's ready. Waiting. Alberto's kitchen voice, a rattling blast of high-speed Italian and then three waiters hurrying out. Two with two plates each, a third with a pepper mill the size of a truncheon. *Grazie*, Alberto.

Vic walked slowly back to the table, putting himself reluctantly between them and the door. He leaned on the back of his chair while the waiters finished serving, smiling at no one in particular. Four big hungry lads. The waiters moved back but not away. Here we go.

'Good evening lads, everything all right?' Showing the ID quickly round the table watching their eyes then out with it all in one: 'Bristol CID Detective Sergeant Hallam sorry to interrupt may I join you for a moment?' Sitting down anyway. 'Don't let me stop you eating, gentlemen, this won't take long.' I hope. Three of them either starting to eat or looking apprehensively at the big blond lad opposite Vic; he must be the leader.

'What's all this about then, sergeant?' Pushing a hand back through his floppy hair, showing a hell of a lot of

228

teeth in a big Schwarzenegger jaw. 'None of us are driving.'

'No need to worry about that, sir, I'm just hoping you can help us with one of our inquiries, that's all.'

'What sort of inquiry's that, sergeant?'

Skate round it. 'I was just wondering if you could tell me where you've been tonight.'

'Dirty Duck, Greyhound, here.'

'And before that, sir?'

'Before that, sergeant we were running round in the dark.'

The others grinning. Vic joined in, leaning his elbows on the table. Nobody using a knife. 'Bit like me then. Doing what exactly? Territorials?'

'Christ no. Training.'

'Where?'

'Clifton Rugby Club.'

'All together?'

'One for all, sergeant.'

'Right, thanks very much.' Vic stood up.

'And are we now, what is it?'

'Eliminated from our inquiries? Yes, sir. Thanks very much everybody. Have a good time.'

'We will.'

'Oh there is one thing. Did you all have a shower or a bath afterwards?'

'Communal bath, sergeant. Why, we don't smell that bad, do we?' The blond lad leaning back, relaxed now, showing the others he was in control.

Vic acted dumb, dogged, boring. 'I'm sorry sir, there's been a lot of theft from golf clubs, country clubs, Long Ashton, places like that.' It didn't add up but they wouldn't figure that yet, if at all. 'Any of you miss anything while you were on the field, or in the bar, or in the showers?'

'Bath, sergeant. No, nothing, nothing so far anyway.'
Schwarzenegger checked his wallet. The others followed suit.

'Good. My apologies, gentlemen, goodnight and thanks again.' Now for it. 'You couldn't tell me who was playing last Saturday, could you?'

A big roar, startling him. All four guffawed their hearty yahoo rugger laughs, reminding him of cops. Other tables were glancing over to see what was going on. Ellie was standing by the door marked TOILETS.

'Oh Christ,' said one.

'Bugger me,' said another.

'World's greatest fan, obviously,' said the third.

'You honestly don't know, sergeant?'

'No sir.'

'Last Saturday was your lot against Cardiff.'

All he told her on the way back was, Yes it was a possible lead. As soon as he got her in the flat he started cancelling everything to stop this fucker, whoever he was or might be, from finding out he was on to him. He told Redland it was a false alarm, called off Forensic until he could talk someone into keeping it off the books and doing it as a favour. The protection request and phone trace were still on hold, which meant, he knew, he would have a hell of a lot of explaining to do.

Marge and Kay were watching television. One full-faced, the other one thinner, and darker. They were both attractive pleasant smiley young women, younger than Ellie, and he knew they were being nice to him because of her. He'd already told her to say nothing otherwise he could have all three going hysterical on him. Ellie saw him to the door, her eyes searching his face, wanting him to kiss her or touch her or do some

230

damn thing. Show some sign of affection he supposed. 'Sorry Ellie. The night out's over. Don't let anybody in and don't answer the phone. I'll be back in half an hour or so. Watch for me out the window.'

He drove fast down to the Well seeing the blond lad's face, hearing his voice, the whole thing banging round and round inside his head. *Last Saturday was your lot against Cardiff.*

Bristol Police v. Cardiff Police. It had to be a mistake, there had to be other games. It couldn't be a copper. Anybody could smell like that. It couldn't be a copper. But how many people had communal baths and smelled like that – just like that – on Saturday nights?

Vic parked in the Well and looked at the uniformeds and the plainclothes walking in and out. When you came down to it, and hit the bump-stops, there was only one question. Why couldn't it be a copper? Vic walked in, wishing he hadn't had so much to drink – and then thinking if he hadn't, how would he have found out about the fucking smell in the first place?

18

DCI Barnard's desk was laid out end to end with home-made pangas, cleavers, bayonets and ground-down breadknives with adhesive tape handles.

'I made a cock-up, sir,' said Vic.

'Not the first time, is it Hallam?' The DCI set down a three-page PR brief printed in oversized type. Flinty eyes in a meaty face said I've had enough of you son, and to make it obvious he reached out a hand to adjust the angle of one of the bayonets in the fan facing Vic.

'No sir.'

'You've been drinking.'

'Yes sir.'

'I can smell it from here.' He plucked a nose-hair and rolled its triangular section between finger and thumb. 'You're in deep shit then, aren't you?'

'No sir. Day off sir.'

'Give me strength — what the *fuck* you come in here for?'

'I thought there'd been a break-in, sir.' He tried not to sound too plausible; both of them knew that was what villains did, how you knew they were lying. 'In Cornwallis, same place as the nurse in the rape case.' Don't ask me why I was there.

'And?'

'It was the landlord, sir.' Keep the sir level up. 'Mister Besant getting the sludge out of the gutters.'

'Really?'

'I'm afraid I over-reacted, put in a protection and trace request.'

'You over-reacted?'

'Yes sir.'

Bullshit, said the look. DCI Barnard indicated the deskful of knives. 'You see this lot? I've got to go on television tomorrow morning and say we picked these up off white kids in the street last night. Hartcliffe, Eastville, Knowle. Ten-, twelve-, fourteen-year-olds. Using kit like this on each other, proving themselves, before they graduate to getting given guns. Or so it says here.' He read off a list of subheads: 'Gang wars. Drug wars. Risk to officers, members of the public. Your co-operation vital.' He laid the PR brief on top of the knives. 'You know where we got most of these? Last year, down the Jungle, St Pauls. We all have to lie, sergeant.'

The DCI lifted a panga, picked up a page of perforated internal printout, tore it in half and handed it to Vic. It was the protection and trace request. 'It wouldn't have gone through. No resources. Not after tomorrow anyway. You get my drift, do I make myself clear?'

'Yes sir. Thank you, sir.'

'Fuck off, Hallam.' The DCI put his half-rims on, went back to looking over his piece to camera. 'And watch it.'

Vic walked down the long grey corridors to the squad room. He'd screwed up and been let off. So what was going on? It could be a show of force, a publicity blitz with Top Brass on telly and stab-victim shock-horror pictures in the papers to scare the public. Or it could be the real thing with everybody including Vic involved. Another rumble in the Jungle or more duff undercover stuff? Meanwhile this bastard, this rapist who could be a cop and could be a killer otherwise why go for her twice, was on the loose with a clear run. On a big operation he could have a field day. Nobody ever knew where any other fucker was until it was all over.

Another corridor another corner.

If tonight proved this bastard was or even could be a cop, what then? Esprit de fucking Corps, that's what. The whole investigation well fucked arsehole to breakfast time by Esprit de fucking Corps. He'd seen it in Operation Countryman, the West Midlands thing, everyfuckingwhere. For a start nobody would believe him and as soon as anybody showed any sign of doing so the ranks would close, above, below, everywhere, drawbridges going up, portcullises clanging down, alibis multiplying like fucking mushrooms and by then he'd be in fucking Coventry and it would be too late anyway. Probably. Oh shit. A detective sergeant on his way home walked past. 'Cheer up, Vic.'

If it was a cop and he did get through all the Esprit de Corps shit, and he was believed, as soon as he told anybody the bastard was bound to find out and lie low until he could get to her, do her, shut her up once and for all. Holy fuck. Basically he was fucked both ways. Utterly and totally fucked by fucking Esprit de fucking Corps.

Through the squad-room door. The drink was wearing off. Less than an hour ago he had been sitting in Alberto's, nothing exactly perfect but at least everything more or less organised. Protection, Forensic and a real chance of getting the bastard. Now, because this fucker probably was a copper, it had all turned to shit. Par for the fucking course maybe but it was still a fucking pain. All of it, the grey paint, the work smell, the nicotine-edged fins on the daylight strip lighting – and now for fuck sake there was some Drug Squad git

234

sitting at his desk in his chair using his fucking terminal for fuck sake – what the fucking hell –

Striding between the desks, zeroing in on this fucking weirdo. What a fucking poser. Biker's black leather jacket, triple Flash Gordon shoulder flanges, elbow ribbing, body quilting, riddled with zips, studs and chains, knee-ripped jeans, calf-length tooled motorcycle boots, gelled swept-back jet black hair with big steel comb marks through it, a pair of fake alloy-rimmed Aviators with gold reflector lenses – in the fucking office for Christ sake, at night –

Getting closer. The dickhead keeping his head well down, as well he might. Quadruple silver earrings, LOVE on one set of knuckles, DETH on the other, and a pair of nick-tattoo bluebirds between each thumb and forefinger – Christ who does this fucking goon think he is? Because whoever he is he's going to get it –

The head coming up the Aviators coming off and Christ it was fucking Cromer – grinning all over his fucking face.

'What the fuck?'

'Hallo Vic. What d'you think?'

'The fuck you think you are?'

'What you told me to do.'

'Me?'

'You told me to get my fucking hair cut.' Still grinning. 'Louise did it.'

'Holy shit.'

'It's only transfers and hair dye.' Pulling the earrings off. 'And a bit of soldering wire.'

'This gear?' Vic fingered the jacket, got a smell of Castrol X on his fingers.

'Twenty-six quid the lot. Unredeemed pledge down Old Market. You ought to get one. You don't have to hang 'em up, they just stand there on their own.'

'You fucking idiot.'

'You fucking told me.'

'Yeah.' Yesterday lunchtime. It all seemed a fucking long time ago but thank God there were some fucking idiots left in the world. 'Put the glasses on again.'

'Should see the way the girls look at you.'

'What, hookers?'

'No, all sorts,' Cromer still grinning, all gold reflectors and white teeth. They suited him. 'They all like a bit of rough, you know.'

After they'd gone shopping and Louise had finished his hair, she put on some old sixties gear she'd bought and they had one of the best and funniest fucks of their lives. It was like cutting loose and discovering America and even if it was only dressing up and pretending you were someone else it didn't half put some fucking zip in it, ripping that puce ruched minidress off her. It had only cost a quid and Cromer considered it a pound well spent; he couldn't wait to get home to find out whether it worked twice or whether it had to be new stuff –

'What are you doing here anyway, John?'

'They tried to call you and couldn't so they called me.' Louise wasn't overpleased, she was covered in Vitamin E Creme at the time.

'The lying bastards. I rang in, when? Half-seven at the latest.'

'Nobody told me that.'

'What did they say?'

'You mean you don't know?'

'Why I'm fucking asking you, John.' Christ he hadn't changed that much.

'They had Billy and Nigel picked up at Temple Meads.'

236

'Oh.' Then a long gap. 'They say why?'

Cromer shrugged. The Flash Gordon shoulder flanges stayed in mid-air until he pulled them down. 'Further questioning. A lead from Drugs via Traffic. We know 'em so the DCI said we should do it.'

The DCI. Who never so much as fucking mentioned Billy and Nigel. 'He say anything about the nurse?' Don't call her Ellie.

'No. Why?'

'I'm going for a piss. While I'm gone – '

'What?'

'No it's all right, forget it.'

Back down the corridor. He had been going to ask Cromer to dial up keyholders for Clifton Rugby Club, trace whoever it was supplied the stuff they put in the communal bath. Or did they all bring their own? But how could they? The stuff had to be medicated to buggery. Then he realised he couldn't trust any fucker.

DCI Barnard's door was shut but the light was still on. What was the old bastard playing at, telling Cromer one thing, him another? It was time to get a few things sorted. But have a piss first, think about it. He checked his watch. He'd told Ellie he'd be back in ten minutes. Oh well she'd have to get used to it.

Not that the last one ever did.

The DCI was on the phone, from the oily smile in his voice talking to a woman. 'Well I expect he's on his way. Yes if you could. We shall need to wheel him out at the conference tomorrow and the cameras'll be there, tell him. Yes down here, ten o'clock sharp.' He smiled reflectively to himself as he put the phone down.

'Me again sir.'

'I thought it might be.' No smile now. No lips even. 'You've spoken to DC Cromer, I take it?'

'Yes sir. I'd like to know what's going on.'

'So would I, Hallam.' The DCI moved to the door and locked it. 'Sit down, Vic.' He pulled his chair round and placed it opposite Vic, knee to knee. 'You jamstrangling young bastard.'

Wait for it, see where he's going. 'I don't follow you, sir.'

'Don't push your luck, sergeant.'

'I'm not, sir.'

'If you hadn't come in tonight you'd have found yourself suspended in the morning.'

'What for?'

'This Jewel thing. This Billy Jewel business stinks, Hallam.' One second sergeant, the next Vic, then Hallam. Standard stuff. 'Not to put too fine a point on it, you're bent son. Bent as a wickerwork bicycle. In my book and as of this moment.' The DCI leaned back, looking for a reaction.

'Not in mine, sir.'

'You tell him the Murder Squad's got him on obbo, you let him go when you should have gripped him, you even phone him up in Stoke on fucking Trent, for Christ sake, you're always up his arse –'

'He's a mate of mine –'

'You don't have any mates, Hallam.'

'A source of information –'

'You're a police officer and he's a major fucking suspect –'

'Not to me –'

'He is to me, Hallam, so is this toerag Evens.'

Go for it. 'Picking them up was a mistake.'

'I tell you what would have been a mistake, Hallam. Going along and interviewing 'em.'

So that was it. He'd laid one and waited for Vic to walk into it. 'Not quite with you, sir.'

'Yes you fucking are. Luckily for you, you didn't. You came in here to have it out. Which is just about the only thing in your fucking favour so you might as well say what you've got to say and I hope for your sake it makes sense.'

'Why tell Cromer, why call him in and not me? You knew where I was –'

'I needed,' said DCI Barnard slowly, folding his hands across his tight-suited paunch, 'to see if he was bent. To see if you'd bent him.'

'Fucking arseholes.'

'Now we're getting somewhere.' Counting one two three on his thumb and fingers. 'Jewel. Evens. The nurse, Eleanor Wilcox. Ellie, as we seem to call her.' He bent forward, gripped Vic hard with both hands, just above the knees. 'What's going on, Vic?' Giving him the little lipless smile, come on son, you can tell me, because if you don't I'll have you anyway. Close enough for Vic to smell his sour pipe-tobacco breath.

'Nothing.'

'If you're giving her one you're fucked, Hallam.'

'I am aware of that, sir.'

'Funny fucking way of showing it.' The DCI let go and leaned back. 'St Pauls about to go up in flames and you don't even notice, two murder suspects running all round the country and you're fiddling about in some Italian fucking restaurant with the chief witness in a rape case – one minute you're calling for protection, Forensic and God knows what, the next it's all out the window and you come all the way down here on your night off to tell me you've made a cock-up. It's not good enough, Vic. If you want some fanny you can fuck my granny but you'll get no arse off me. For the last time what the fuck is going on?'

All Vic had to say was he'd got a lead on the rape

239

case; he didn't even need to mention the possibility of it being a cop. Ellie would get protection and that would be that. But in the first place it wouldn't work. And in the second place he wouldn't get the fucker. 'Nothing sir,' he said.

The DCI stood up, went to the door and unlocked it. 'Possible lead on Pauline Millward from Drugs via Traffic. Some black dealer. This toerag Evens mentioned black kids with a car phone. Your mate Billy's been with Evens for the last twenty-four hours. Up to you.'

'Thank you sir.'

DCI Barnard held the door open. 'Your last chance, sergeant, don't menstruate all over it.'

Frank was so cheerful when he came home just before ten Rae said he'd been off with another woman. Frank said, 'Strangely enough, my work gives me pleasure.'

'You've been up since five.' She was halfway down a bottle of Black Tower.

'One of those days.'

'You've got another one tomorrow.'

'How?' Seafood pizza so fucking dried-up when he tried to cut it it skidded off the plate.

'DCI Barnard rang. Actually I think he fancies me.'

'Wife like a brick shithouse.'

She pushed over a telephone message with I JUST CALLED TO SAY printed across the top. 'He wants you down the Well tomorrow.' A stone falling right through him splash into black water. 'Press conference. They want to wheel you out in front of the cameras.'

'What time?'

'Ten o'clock sharp.'

In bed, she sneaked her hand through his legs from behind and started massaging him. 'Come on love,

240

come on, I want you to fuck me Frank I've been waiting thinking about it, I want you Frank I'm lonely,' breathing sweet white wine down his ear and sticking her tongue down it. 'Come on Frank I want you to go on TV and be famous and fuck me, fuck the arse off me, come on love I want it I want it, oh I love it I love it I love it.'

Pawing at him, squeezing him, going down under the bedclothes on him and all he could think about was the nurse. The nurse walking into her room fresh from the bath, rubbing her hair with the towel, her magnificent tits jiggling and the water droplets nestling in her big damp snatch, and then turning and her wonderful arse all pink from the hot water. It was her he wanted. Her. Not Rae. Her. Big, solid, pure, like Venus and the Virgin Mary rolled into one. Her. Not this slim greedy little fuckrat squirming all over him, sitting up on him and biting her lip and frowning as she tried to cram his prick up her –

For the first time ever as far as he could remember he failed to get it up; as he was fingering her and she was crying and saying it was her fault and she knew he was too tired and she was sorry she was just being selfish and maundering on about wanting his baby he realised he just didn't fucking care. It was the nurse he wanted and as he lay next to Rae wanking away at her, stonily listening to her trying to come, all he could think was tomorrow, tomorrow, tomorrow.

Vic sent Cromer down to see Nigel, dialled up Keyholders and got through to the Rugby Club caretaker. The caretaker put him on to the physio who put him on to some old guy on the committee who came up with the name of one of the players. Chap called Linley, some sort of chemist, worked for Avonmouth Pharmaceuticals, got the stuff through the firm.

'Through the firm' meaning nicked, from the guarded tone of Linley's voice. Vic could hear the telly on in the background and Linley telling his missis it was work and put the extension down please, Carol. Vic told him not to worry this was unofficial, the soccer boys had heard of it and he'd been asked if they could get hold of some, order any, and whether Linley supplied it to any other sports organisations.

Linley started to open up then, relief making him run away with himself, and said, Well no it wasn't actually on the market yet in fact it was a new formulation of a foamer, an emulsifier and this new unchlorinated antibacterial agent they'd been developing for leisure parks and swimming pools and a group of them were thinking of maybe marketing it themselves if the company didn't take it up but hadn't got round to it yet because he was still doing what you might call a test run on the lads to see if any of them got pimples on the marley bag, if Vic saw what he meant, but so far there'd been no adverse reactions in fact quite the opposite, it seemed to be effective on all sorts of minor cuts, rashes and abrasion infections so if Vic would like to leave a few details he'd get a sample over to him a.s.a.p. Vic thanked him, gave Cromer's name and address and put the phone down.

That narrowed it to a minimum of thirty, half of them Welsh, all of them coppers.

On the way down to see Billy he stopped at the Sports and Social noticeboard. Next week's team was up, last week's was gone. Not that he could phone anybody up without seriously blowing it and in any case there was a 50 per cent statistical possibility the bastard was Welsh. Vic hoped so, but doubted it. What was left was a chance he might worm something out of one of the lads in the bar. Who was playing, what they did after, was it a good night, did the Cardiff boyos stay on, where did they all go boozing. Working it round to who was where at seven o'clock last Saturday night. And more important, who wasn't.

Then there was the break-in at four o'clock this afternoon. Difficult. He could chat one of the accounts girls into doing a search through timesheets, say he was doing an internal on overtime claims. But how long would that take and would anything show up? Anybody could lose an hour. He did, often.

Your last chance, sergeant.

Every lie, every bent and dodgy move, was taking him further up shit creek. Fuck it, he was as good as there already.

So. Stick to Saturday. After the game what was favourite? Everybody in the club bar, no option. Esprit de Corps again. Wives and girlfriends turning up half-six to seven, coach drivers hanging about smoking and looking pissed-off and hangdog. Everybody well out of it by nine, all bellowing out 'Sospan Bach' and 'We're Off to See the Wild West Show the Elephant and the Kangaroo-oo-oo-oo'. Big sweaty thick-necked lads standing on tables mooning their hairy arses at each other and the women shouting 'Off-Off-Off'. Anybody AWOL from that lot would need looking at. Hard. Find out who, have a chat, and then casually slip in something about four o'clock this afternoon. The fucker was bound to have some excuse but Vic reckoned he was old enough to know who was shitting bricks and who wasn't. A simple matter of elimination. Elimination being the operative word.

I want you you fucker. And I'm coming to get you.

Good. Getting somewhere. He checked his watch.

Not so good. He was twenty minutes over the time he said he'd be back at Ellie's and he couldn't even phone her. You're never as clever as you think, Hallam. Remember that.

A bang-bang-bang from the cells and Cromer standing in the corridor with some young kid off Traffic. Why did their hats always look too big? Bang-bang-bang regular as clockwork, some doolally punter trying to kick the cell door down.

'Nigel,' said Cromer.

'He's been doing it on and off since we brought him in,' said the PC.

'You got his bootlaces?'

'It doesn't stop him.'

'You know what will, don't you?'

'What?'

'Letting him out,' said Vic. 'Take him down the other interview room, John, give him a cup of tea or something.'

'I've tried that,' said Cromer. 'He just sits there with his arms folded, says he's not touching any fascist shit-poison.'

'I don't give a fuck,' said Vic. 'I can't talk to Billy with that fucking row going on.'

'Christ, it's rough up North, Vic,' said Billy. 'I thought you know have a look-round, any opportunities, but there's nothing there. They've done up the canal front-ages for the funny-hat crowd on the barges in the summer but behind that it's fucking death.'

Vic switched on the microphones and checked the twin tape deck was rolling. This interview timed at 22.28. The young PC standing behind him.

'We're in the crematorium car park and it's pissing down,' said Billy. 'This old geezer with a brolly, all the

244

spokes sticking out, gaunt as fuck and coughing his lungs up, I tell you it was hardly worth him going home unless it was his idea of a good day out. And there's Nigel in a suit. No coat but he's got this suit, this brown suit with big fucking lapels.' Billy shook his head. 'Are you family or just friends, says this old bloke and then who are we, turns out he's the undertaker's runner wants our names for the paper so every bugger can see who's turned up and who hasn't. And Nigel says Nigel the Reject. Poor old Pauline, eh? Her mum and dad looked fucking belted. All right on the outside but fucking wiped out on the inside. What a fucking waste. And you know Nigel, what a cunt he is, he goes up to them and he's nice as pie. What a wonderful talented young woman she was. Oh shit. Then we all sang "For Those in Peril on the Sea". I don't get it, Vic I just don't get it, any of it.' The tears had started pouring down his face but he was still trying to blag his way through it.

'Everybody goes quiet, the little grey velvet curtains open up, in she rolls and that's it. What a life, eh? And I'm standing there thinking Christ I hope they've got enough shillings in the – meter – ' He cracked, and stopped, and looked helplessly at Vic through wet china-blue eyes. 'Oh fucking hell, Vic.'

Vic let the tape go on rolling while he lit a couple of fags and passed one to Billy.

'Ta mate. I should have emigrated when I had the fucking chance.' He blew the smoke out in a long thin stream. 'Then we come out and there's another lot waiting to go in, looking up at the fucking chimney. And the old geezer's still there with the brolly in the pouring rain. All chimneys round here once he said, all belching smoke, pottery capital of the world. Now look at it he said, this here's the only fucking factory going for

245

miles. You can't beat it, Vic.' Crying again but not bothered by it. 'I could have kissed the old bastard. Christ it takes some fucking guts living up there. Unsung fucking heroes they are. Not a light bulb over forty watts. No wonder the poor kid came down here. Pauline.'

'Yeah.'

'Then we all went back to their front room and had cold ham and lettuce and raw onion rings in a bowl of vinegar. And her mother told us there were cans of Bass for them that wanted it.'

'What did Nigel do?'

'Oh he was very nice, very polite, very bland. And all the time there's white sort of foam coming out of the shoulders of this terrible brown suit he's got, stuff like soap or something, somebody said it was fuller's earth, they know about stuff like that up there, but he didn't give a monkey's. He's completely blanked out, man. Shtumm all the way down on the train, sitting there with his eyes closed and his arms folded and his legs crossed, and then when he gets off he goes, You'll be relieved to know she didn't die in vain. And I'm thinking what the fuck. And he says, his words Vic, The people should own the means of production, death included. He thinks he's Clint fucking Eastwood man, four foot eight and a half in NHS glasses, he believes all this shit he comes out with, that's what's so fucking frightening.' Billy shook his head and stubbed out his cigarette in the screwed-down tin ashtray. 'Who d'you think he's talking about?'

'Who?'

'Me, Vic. He says it's me, my fault. We're walking along the platform, me on the train side, Mind The Gap, and he's saying if I'd paid her there and then, this black cunt wouldn't have come up offering her three lines for a fuck—'

'What black cunt?'

'This black cunt he reckons fucked her and killed her then took her fucking handbag.'

'He say who?'

'Vic, I'm walking along the edge of the platform, one nudge and I'm under the six-fifteen to fucking Plymouth. Then suddenly there's there four of your mushes in car coats, two in front and two behind and thank fuck we're lifted—'

'Billy.'

'What?'

'Does he know this kiddy?'

'Only by sight.'

'Big deal.'

'We're in the van coming down here. Don't worry, he goes, I know 'em by sight.'

'Them?'

'Three or four of 'em, one with a car phone. How she used to score, apparently.'

'Yeah.' They made you get in the car while they counted the money. Some of the bastards even had a fucking Forgefinder plugged into the lighter socket. If it wasn't right you didn't get out until they rolled you out. 'Then what?'

'They they bring him in here and he goes raving mad and starts kicking the door down. You can't do this to me, freedom, I know my rights, all that. I tell you Vic he's a one-man band that kiddy but God knows what the music is.'

Vic got through to the DCI on the internal in the corridor outside the interview rooms.

'Apparently Evens knows them by sight, sir.'

'What does Evens say?'

'I haven't asked him yet, sir.'

'What the fuck you talking to me for then?'

'He's not going to recognise them in here is he, sir?'

There was a long pause. 'You want him released into your custody?'

'Yes sir.'

Another long pause. 'I'm writing this down, Hallam.'

'Yes sir.'

'When? Now?'

'Too dark sir.'

'Don't fucking smartarse me, Hallam.'

'No sir, sorry sir.'

'You lose him you're out you know that, Hallam?'

'Yes sir.'

'You screw this up and drop this department in it again I shall personally see to it that your future employment prospects are permanently fucked.'

'Yes sir. Thank you sir.'

Cromer vacated the chair as soon as Vic walked in. Nigel sat with his arms folded, his mouth shut and his jaw tensed.

'He wants to ring Amnesty International,' said Cromer.

Vic switched on the tape deck. This interview timed at 22.53. Holy shit. He forced Ellie to the back of his mind. 'Mister Evens has expressed a wish to call Amnesty International. Interview begins. Why's that, Nigel?'

'I'm allowed to call a lawyer am I not?'

'You are, yes.'

'In which case I wish to say I'm being held by a State that refuses to recognise my rights as an individual.'

'According to the Police and Criminal Evidence Act commonly known as PACE we can detain on suspicion

248

for up to forty-eight hours and on application to a magistrate for another forty-eight, and then another twenty-four and so on. Five days just on sus. Did you know that, Nigel?'

'Yes I did actually.'

'So what's all this Amnesty crap then?'

'Nobody informed me of my rights under the Act.'

'You already fucking know all your fucking rights – '

'So fucking what? I wasn't fucking told, was I?'

Vic looked at Cromer. Cromer shrugged. Not my fault.

'Your complaint has been recorded during this interview and will be formally looked into,' said Vic. 'That satisfy you?'

'No. Wrongful detention, immediate release – '

'You don't like being locked up, do you Nigel?'

'Would you?'

'At least I'd get some fucking peace. I wouldn't spend three hours wrecking my fucking toecaps. I'd just lie there.'

'Good for you.'

'But you get all twitchy, don't you? You start losing it.'

'According to you, not according to me.'

He was going to clam up any second. 'I can get you out of here, Nigel.'

'When? Now?'

'Tomorrow morning.'

Kicking the table leg. 'Why not now?' The red needles on the double tape deck jumping all over the place.

'We can't see 'em now Nigel, it's too dark.' The kid took off his glasses and wiped them on the bottom of his khaki T-shirt. Without them he looked even younger, even more defenceless. Pupils half the size, blinking, probably half-blind. 'You said you knew these

249

black kids used to feed Pauline. You told Billy you knew them by sight.' Nigel put his glasses back on and the overlarge glare returned.

'He blubbed all the way through that stupid service, you know that? God. What an embarrassment he ever is.'

Blubbed. 'He's an emotional man is Billy,' said Vic. 'He hasn't had the benefit of your public school education.'

'Bollocks,' said Nigel. 'Psychological bollocks.'

'You should know, Nigel.'

'I do.'

'Anyway, we want this bloke, you want this bloke. Tomorrow we start riding around until we find him. That's the deal.'

She was watching for him through the curtains. He got out of his car and stood under the lamp-post. She pulled back the curtains so he could see her.

'He's here.'

'About time too,' said Marge.

'We shall be listening for the bedsprings,' said Kay.

'Fat chance,' said Ellie.

Marge was picking up her knitting and her marking and Kay was taking the cocoa cups out and going on about whether or not we should condone adultery under this roof of ours but Ellie was already out of the door, glancing in the mirror and halfway down the stairs when Kay called after her to don't forget to send him in to her when she'd finished with him and Marge was shouting, and me and me.

He looked grey and worn-out and not half as attractive as she'd been imagining he was. On the way up he said he was sorry he was late but things had got complicated. He smelt too. Sweat, petrol, cigarettes and

250

disinfectant. Almost the same as the first time she saw him, when he'd helped her into the ambulance in her dressing gown.

He walked round the small dormered sitting room, touched the top of the 16-inch telly to see if it was still warm and looked closely at the cushions and loose covers on the Ercol sofa and armchairs. Oh Lord, she thought, was he always going to be like this?

'Where are the others?'

'Oh, they're being tactful – they've gone to bed.'

'When?'

'Just. You want a drink?'

'Not particularly.'

'I got Kay to go up to Oddbins to get me half a bottle of Scotch.'

He was looking at her sharply. 'She get back all right?'

'Course she did.'

'Good.' She watched him relax, hitch his trousers up, sniff, look round for a chair to sit down on.

'They didn't have Black Label.' They did, but not in halves, and Ellie wasn't paying nineteen-pound-odd for a bottle of whisky.

'Anything.'

'Ice?'

'Please.'

When she came back with a flat half-bottle of Stewarts and two glasses, hers nearly all ice and water, he was standing at the window with the light off and the curtains open.

'Vic?'

'What?'

'What have you put the light out for?'

'Just looking.'

'You're frightening me.'

His dark outline moved towards her and when he

251

bent to switch the cone-shaded table lamp on again his shadow leapt up the wall as if it was strangling a nun.

He said, 'Ellie, I'm going to have to stay here.'

Without thinking she said. 'Not with me you're not.'

'Sit down a minute.'

'Why?'

'I think this guy's a cop.'

19

Ellie listened as Vic took her through it. Implications, possibilities, risks. Her position, his position, the legal position, the police position, the rapist's position – and what Vic called the question of his timing.

After a while it became clear to Ellie that he was holding something back. One minute he was himself, the next he was back to being a copper again, telling her only as much as he thought was good for her. It was what he did, what he'd always done right from the start: he held something back, pretended to be looking after you and then, when he'd got you nicely softened up, wallop.

Now the drink and the excitement had worn off, and she had had an hour or so in the warmth of the flat with Marge and Kay, drinking cocoa and being normal, she realised she'd come round to a different way of looking at him. It wasn't that she'd gone off him exactly, far from it; she liked him, liked walking along the sleety pavements with her hand in his pocket, liked him saying Fuck the rules and looking after her and being straight with her. But after the restaurant, he'd changed: she was no longer the main item on the agenda. It wasn't even the rapist, or the danger she was in, although he kept telling her it was. No, there was something else, a whole different way of looking at things. It was only when he got on to the evidence that she started to realise how big the difference between them was.

'Look at what we've got so far. Two footprints and a fucking smell, for Christ sake.' Even the swearing was part of it, conscious or not, pulling, drawing, bullying you into his world, his game. Every word, even the tone of his voice, flat and heavy, leaning on you, forcing you to think, this may be depressing girl but this is the way it is, so you better listen because this is real. But it wasn't, life wasn't all crime and bloody punishment, there had to be some joy in it –

She felt herself quietly coming to the boil. You, what are you? A man that's all, the usual bossy boring oppressive I know it all, where's my dinner, I'm your father eat that up or you'll get it tomorrow, I work I pay so you do what I say, what time do you call this, don't you dare contradict me my girl or you'll feel the back of my hand – the same old everlasting voice of male authority. Well, she wasn't having it, no matter what sort of danger she was in; it was like an emergency on the wards, you had to be in control of the situation to make the decision – and he was trying to take that control away from her, to blindfold her. My God, she wanted to shout at him, It's my life, you know, I've seen as much blood and mess and pain as you, if not more, so what's going on? I'm not a kid –

Not that he would tell her; whether he knew it or not, he seemed to need something to hold over her, some club behind his back. Was it him, or what the job did to all of them?

'All right,' he was saying, 'there may be something else on the roof, if we can find it.' He was really getting into it now, not talking to her so much as thinking out loud, off on his own, perfectly happy wandering about in the wasteland he had inside his head. What was it? The urge to win, hunt, kill? There was a blunt-edged singlemindedness about him, a cold doggedness, which made him go for what he wanted and to hell with anybody else's feelings.

It was something like that anyway, similar to the bull-headed way most of them went about sex, like half-mad testosterone-driven animals, unaware there was anyone on the receiving end – like the rapist, in fact. Maybe that was it, she thought, maybe that was the link, what he was trying to hide from her: the fact that coppers or not, they were all rapists.

On and on he went, looking at her without seeing her. 'But that could take days because we don't even know how he got in or out yet, and unless there are any prints, fingerprints that is, which there won't be judging by last time, or clothing, and it's got blood on it or hair or skin and it hasn't all been pissed down the gutters by the fucking rain, none of it'll be any good. So if we do narrow it down and you do recognise his voice, one voice out of thirty minimum and God knows how we do that, we might as well tell him we're on to him, even then what have we got? Nothing concrete, it's all subjective, it's you Ellie, your say-so, nobody else's. Your word against his. None of it'll stand up in court and if this guy is a copper it won't even get to court.' He took a long swig at his glass. 'And that basically is what we're up against. I'll be out on my fucking ear and he'll know he can get you where and when he likes, at his fucking leisure, girl. Unless we get him first – '

'That's it, that's it, isn't it?'

'What? What you don't seem to realise – '

'This is nothing to do with me, is it?'

'What you don't seem able to take on board – '

'This is you, isn't it? You – '

He was shouting at her. 'This bastard's tried it once,

he'll try it again – he's out to kill you, for fuck sake woman!'

Now she was shouting back, 'It's you! You're as bad as he is! It's nothing to do with me! Not any more! This is you! You don't care what I feel, you couldn't care less, you're out to get this bloke, you Vic, for some reason, God knows what, you're out to get him and you're using me!' She knew she was yelling and screaming at him but she couldn't stop it, couldn't help it; she hoped Marge and Kay would hear her and come in, and be with her, and stick up for her, because she couldn't stand it any more –

'You are, you're using me, and you have been from the start and that makes you ten times worse than him because you made it your business to get to know me and all this be nice come and have a drink I'll look after you, all that's lies, because it's all for you, your sake, your benefit, your satisfaction because that's what you're like, what you're all like, so why don't you just fuck off and leave me alone? Go on! Fuck off! Leave me alone!' She collapsed back in the armchair, not looking at him, breast heaving, face and throat mottled red and burning.

In they came, in their dressing gowns, sleepy and angry-eyed. A glance at him to make sure he was staying put and then both of them moving straight to Ellie.

'You all right, love?'

Vic watched them fussing over her and hugging her and kissing her and kneeling one on each side of her and getting her to drink water until she stopped sniffing. Then three pairs of eyes turned on him.

Kay stood up, looked down her nose at him, put on her sniffiest you-lump-of-shit voice. 'I think you ought to leave. She's had enough for one night.'

Marge put her arms around Ellie again. 'More than enough.'

Vic finished the dregs in his glass and set it down. 'I'm not going, Ellie.'

She eased herself out of Marge's embrace to take a blue-edged handkerchief from her sleeve and blew her nose hard. 'You'd better tell them then.'

Now the other two were there and she was hearing it for the second time Ellie felt able to stay calm and detached, comforting Marge when she began to shake and telling her not to worry. She felt as if she had been anaesthetised, above it all, watching the others from on high even though it was her life they were talking about. Kay's eyes never left his face, judging him first and then considering him. Marge kept hold of her hand and didn't seem to be able to look at Vic for very long, glancing constantly up to Ellie for reassurance.

Although there was a lot of all coppers are bastards and all men are rapists still in the air Vic felt himself moving slowly through their minds from some sort of bully to some sort of protector. The question was, how long would they keep their mouths shut? Ellie would, and probably Kay, but Marge was softer and more emotional and would almost certainly feel the need to blab. So it was her he laid it on at the end, looking at her hard.

'If you so much as mention any of this information, to the Besants or anybody, you're putting your own lives at risk. Because if he gets to know I've told you, you two will be next on his list.' Marge was biting her lips, telling herself to keep her mouth shut. Then, in an attempt to end things more amicably, he said, 'Apart from anything else, if anyone finds out I spent the night here, or even suggested I should, Ellie's case'll be fucked and so for that matter will my future employment prospects. Permanently. So if you still want me to go, I'll go.'

Then it was their turn to ask questions. Very mild at first, tentative and baffled and in some way motherly even, now they'd got hold of the risks, full of What I don't understand and Could you just explain this. And then what did he think about this and feel about that, about his job, about Ellie and why did he think the police were like that and why couldn't he tell Cromer and did he think he'd got a chip on his shoulder and was it anything to do with his marriage, and what did he think the rapist was like really?

Holy shit.

It was all to do with feelings, relationships, that whole fucking miasma like some hot meaty cunty African fucking swamp, and they were the fucking experts at navigating their way through it, that was their game, and he was just some overgrown fucking five-year-old they could nibble their soft-mouthed way at but were still a little bit wary of in case he had some unexploded bomb about his person.

Oh yeah.

They were interrogating him all right. In their soft and gentle way it was Strip Jack Naked. Sorry I'm a bit slow and I don't really understand, but don't you think? Like being slowly bludgeoned into submission with marshmallows, some of which were embedded with razor blades. There was a warm sly undercurrent of sex too, all serious and responsible on the surface but underneath when they weren't asking him some daft thing or other Marge and Kay were shifting themselves about inside their nightdresses and dressing gowns letting him know, God knows fucking how and maybe it was all in his mind, that they were naked underneath. Unprotected. Available even, in some weird non-available female fucking way. Even Ellie was posing at him now and again, blowing down the front of her black shirt and then checking to see if he was looking at her or one of the others.

Actually, Kay looked a bit of a goer, she'd got that sharp challenging If-you're-so-fucking-good-show-me air about her. Marge looked as if she was just biding her time before making somebody a good little wife and mother out on some new estate in the sticks somewhere but she could just as easily be a demon gobbler on a one-night stand. The question was, without being some mindless fucking animal like this fucking rapist and wanting to shove it up everything you saw, how could you ever tell? By the time you found out you were in too deep anyway, led by your prick as Billy said, and most of them were too cunning, they'd been training up for this particular guerilla war for years, it was their territory, and they'd got you sussed from the word go.

Then it came to him that was what they were doing to him. Estimating him for some possible future use. From fucking to wallpapering or maybe even friend.

Just before he got fed up with it – they'd been at it for well over an hour, and sometimes they had that way of talking among themselves that even though he was only two or three feet away and trying to listen to them he couldn't really catch what they were saying – he came to the conclusion that they'd all be fucking brilliant at offender profiling. Maybe all women would. Maybe he ought to suggest it to somebody some time.

Then he'd suddenly had enough. It was after three and he just couldn't stand any more meandering fucking female conversation. He stood up, his balls uncomfortably hot from facing the gas fire but telling himself not to rearrange himself at their eye level. 'Well

I'm sorry, ladies but what I'd like to do is go to bed, what you do is up to you, but in the end this rape business is just a question of physical strength, and that's basically why I'm here. I can't help it but that's the way it is and whatever you may happen to think I've got in the back of my mind, whether I'm as bad as or worse than the rapist, I consider myself to be in this flat entirely and solely for your protection. At considerable risk to myself, I might point out. So if you just show me I'll doss down wherever you like.'

For once all three of them seemed to be quite happy to have their minds made up and be told what to do, so they trooped into Ellie's room to split the bed. He could hear them talking among themselves, even laughing in that light quiet way women had when they were doing things together.

He had just finished off the last half-inch of Scotch when Kay came briskly in and told him he could use the bathroom now if he wanted, there was a new toothbrush put out on the shelf above the sink.

Marge and Kay were waiting with Ellie in the hall when he came out of the bathroom. Ellie was already in her nightdress and dressing gown. Marge and Kay kissed him on the cheek like aunts, and then, when they'd gone, Ellie smiled broadly at him, opened her bedroom door wide and said, 'Come on in.'

The two halves of the bed were about six feet apart, hers against the wall, his by the door. He undressed to his underpants and T-shirt and she hung her dressing gown on the back of the door. Then she turned to him and kissed him on the mouth. She didn't part her lips so there was none of that falling down the liftshaft feeling, otherwise he knew he'd be gone beyond recall. 'Goodnight Vic.' They held on to each other for a moment and he could feel the hot heaviness of her breasts through his T-shirt. A hard-on immediately started to rise. They moved apart but kept hold of each other's hands. She was looking straight at it with that amused-pleased-self-satisfied way they had. Then she came back into his arms and pressed herself against it.

'Look,' he said, pushing her away, 'I'm sorry about this, and I feel a right dick but –'

'So do I.' Grinning up at him. No shame these bloody nurses. Then she kissed him again, on the cheek, and moved herself away from him. 'Don't worry there'll be plenty of time.'

Lying in bed. Oh Christ I hope so.

Then she put the bedside light out and they said goodnight again in the dark. Stupid really, but what the fuck. Twenty-past three. Vic lay on his back, listening to the traffic and waiting for the hard-on to die down, then drifted into a tense alert oblivion dreaming he was still awake.

Frank woke up at 06.24 feeling cup final good. The wind had blown itself out in the night, there was frost on the bare branches of the flowering cherry in the front garden and the sun was coming out. Rae had a hangover. He ran downstairs naked to put the kettle on and was back up in the shower while she was still moaning and groaning to herself. This'll be the day. Buddy Holly and Don McLean running through his mind as the hot water blasted him thoroughly awake. Risk yes, but what a reward. Oh boy. This'll be the day. Oh boy. Yeah. This'll be the day-yay-yay that you die –

'Frank!'

'What?'

'The kettle's boiling. And please stop singing will you, my head's splitting and I feel like death and all you're doing is making it worse.'

The sky was red with long rags of grey cloud. This Could Be the Last Time You Don't Know. Oh No. Oh boy. Oh boy oh boy oh boy oh boy oh boy. He was going to be on TV, he was going to fuck the nurse and kill her and then he was going to ride off into the sunset with her magnificent naked corpse across his saddle, her wonderful arse smiling up at him and she was going to come alive again so he could fuck her and kill her again for ever and ever –

Grow up, Frank.

Dree-ee-ee-eam. Dream Dream Dream. He made the coffee, drank his and took hers up. She was still in bed looking pale and bilious.

'Thanks love. I feel awful. Oh God.' Sipping, holding the cup with both hands. 'Oh thank God. What time will you be doing your bit?'

'I don't know, any time between ten and one I should imagine. I've got to get my parade kit from the office first.'

'Will it be on the lunchtime news?'

'I shouldn't think so.'

It better not be, Frank.

'Will you be back by six, then?' Her face yellowish, her slim grey eyes practically invisible without make-up trying to focus on him, pleading with him, please be back, please come home.

'Course I will.'

'We can watch it together, can we?'

'Yeah. Bye love.' He kissed her shitty morning mouth and was off. He was free.

Up over the Downs in the early morning sun, no traffic, the bare trees glittering like brides and the clumps of long grass stiff as bunches of white knives. Great.

Two things to check, Frank. What are they?

One, what do they call it, transmission time. If they don't finish till around one and then there's bound to be some kind of reception, the Brass and TV blokes smarming up to each other, it's not very likely it's going to be on the lunchtime news, is it? Be some sort of Special Report thing early evening and then a repeat later unless something else happens. Which by then of course it will have — she'll be dead. . . .

You've still got to check, Frank.

I'll be fucking glad when you're off my fucking back, you know that?

Don't count on it.

What the fuck's that supposed to mean?

All I'm saying is if she sees you on TV and recognises your voice you're fucked.

Yeah. But she won't, will she? She'll be gone by then.

Good boy. What about the other thing?

Check her appointment for 2.15.

You know what these things are like, Frank. You can wait around for hours.

No I can't. I've waited long enough.

So have I Frank, so have I.

Vic woke up to the smell of tea. 'Time is it?' he said to a pair of square healthy-looking feet with gaps between all the toes and no nail varnish. A few hairs on the legs from the ankle up.

'Fine bloody guard dog you are.' She knelt on the mattress beside him, towering over him, the drape of her nightdress tightening over her breasts. 'We could all have been raped and murdered in our beds.'

'Yeah.' He blew into the steam coming off the mug to open his eyes. 'So what time is it?'

'Ten to eight. The others have gone.' Then she was lying on him, all over him on top of the bedclothes, legs apart, face in his neck and hot tea slopping over his wrist. 'Hallo,' she said. God she was solid, practically crushing the breath out of him. He set the mug down and put his arms round her. Her mouth tasted of toothpaste. She said, 'You snore, you know that?'

'Yeah, so do you.'

'The others think you're all right. Fact I think Kay fancies you, said you were battered but hunky. Cow.'

'Good. Can I breathe now?'

She rolled off to one side and Jesus she was sliding her hand down his boxers over his belly hair after his dick. Christ, was she always like this in the morning? He grabbed hold of her wrist. 'Hey. No interfering with the truncheon.'

'Boasting again.'

'You want to get arrested?'

'How about if I said I'll come quietly?'

'No chance.' He sat up and sipped the orange smoky-flavoured tea. Her nightdress was up round her thighs, big smooth muscles and creamy skin, one pale translucent blue vein running up the inside of each leg. Holy shit. 'Nice tea.'

'Lapsang and Typhoo. Marge makes it.' She plonked a heavy leg across him, pinning him down, and put her head on his chest. He stroked her hair and with his heart melting and his prick stiff as a poker gazed at the curves of her flanks and buttocks. Oh God if You made anything better You kept it for Yourself. Feeling as if he was committing suicide he said, 'You're a great-looking woman, Ellie but I wish you'd cover yourself up.'

'Why, what time d'you have to be at work?'

'Half-eight. What time's your appointment again?'

'Quarter-past two.'

'Right. We'd better get moving then.'

'What?'

'You're coming with me.'

'When?'

'Now. All day.'

'Why?'

'So I can keep an eye on you.'

'Oh.' The bounce going right out of her. 'Oh God.'

'Yeah. I know.' It was all he could think of, and he was bound to get another bollocking which could even be the last but fuck it, it was either that or take her down the nick and book her for shoplifting and even there he couldn't depend on her being one hundred per cent secure. The other alternatives, letting her stay in the flat or leaving her to wander about on her own, were complete non-starters. He clapped his hand on her gloriously morning-warm bare arse. 'Come on, girl.'

She hung on to him. 'I want you, Vic.'

'Lucky old me.'

'Oh fuck you –'

'You got an examination, Ellie.'

'You think you're so fucking hard, don't you?'

'No. No I don't. Funnily enough.'

'Sad. Sad then.'

'Disappointed. Temporarily.'

'Why? Why Vic?'

'Why d'you think? Any chance of any toast?'

She hauled herself up and stalked off over him so he could look right up her if he wanted to. He did, but he didn't.

'Make it yourself,' she said.

While she was in the bathroom he wandered round getting dressed and looking at the weather. The sun was melting a line across the frost on the grass. There were new chisel marks in the wood around the window.

20

Ellie's D-reg 2CV wouldn't start and when Vic said it was a fucking deathtrap with the worst accident record in the UK and bodywork you could punch holes in with your bare hands she got stroppy, so he ended up taking the plugs out, scraping the black off with her nailfile and warming them up with his lighter then finally spraying everything with some poxy French version of Dampstart; even then he needed the jump leads from the Escort before it banged away on one cylinder, shaking itself like a wet dog until finally the second one came in. Vic listened to the engine racketing away like a bag of nails; when Ellie said He didn't like the winter Vic knew it was going to be one of those days. How could you call a 2CV He? What happened to them once they got out of bed?

He stayed three cars behind her on the way down to the BRI but nobody pulled out to follow. He got nothing out of Winston who went grey as a sheet as soon as he showed him his ID, so he asked the sister if the poor kid had had any visitors. She said yes two young blacks last night; when he asked her what they were like she said it had been a busy night on the ward and they hadn't stayed more than five minutes, but she thought one was darker and shorter than the other. One of those days. They left Ellie's car in the staff car park so that she would have transport to get to wherever Vic was after her appointment, then he drove her down to the Well.

Cromer was waiting at the desk looking at his watch. He was still in his leather gear and didn't go a lot on dragging Ellie round the Jungle all day when they were supposed to be doing Nigel. When he started on about putting her at risk and sounded as if he was going to get on to rules and regulations and use of police time and vehicles Vic told him it was still one step forward and two steps back with you, John so put a fucking sock in it and follow her even if she goes for a piss you sit in the next cubicle, got it? One of those days.

Billy was no better. He said the three heavy mushes from the Murder Squad had given him another four and a half hours' fucking verbals, threatening to charge him with Pauline and he hadn't had a wink of sleep what with Nigel banging away and some old dosser got the screaming habdabs and what the fuck was this all about, Vic I thought you were a mate? Vic said he'd find out, and did he want a lift home. Billy said he wasn't going to get a cab with nothing but a red hot Gold Card, was he?

Then Des finally put the tin hat on it and said everything was cancelled, there was a sweep on. It was partly PR to coincide with the press conference upstairs but it was also masonic pressure from the Chamber of Commerce pushing Let's Keep Christmas Shopping Clean and Decent and they wanted some arrests. Mostly whites but they'd need to pull in some blacks to make it look even for the media. Vic had drawn City Road so he could carry on with the Pauline job as per normal.

'What d'you mean as per fucking normal? One unmarked car full of short-haired white blokes driving down City Road and there won't be a fucking black dealer on the streets by ten o'clock this morning. Whose fucking stupid idea is this?'

A shadow fell across the desk and Des looked up

over Vic's shoulder. 'Mine,' said DCI Barnard. He was wearing his best dark blue shiny Italian suit with a cream shirt and a spotted red and blue tie. 'And don't say I didn't fucking warn you, Hallam because I fucking did, didn't I? Last fucking night.'

'Yes sir. You did, sir.'

'Chaffey I want you and all the admin men you can spare in the conference suite otherwise it'll be all fucking uniforms and I'm not having that.'

'No sir,' said Des.

'Not you Hallam you're too fucking busy.' The DCI tossed a file at Vic. 'That's what they got out of your mate last night. I'm charging William Herbert Jewel with the murder of Pauline White-stroke-Millward.'

'You're what?'

'You heard.'

'He's got a fucking alibi, a witness to the time, he doesn't do cocaine – '

'You should have been a fucking social worker Hallam.'

'Not to mention the sperm test, the fact he's the wrong fucking blood group – '

'Jesus Christ Hallam are you in love with the cunt or what?'

'And what about this black bloke, this dealer?'

'Never mind black fucking dealers, we can't pin everything on the blacks with no fucking evidence, can we? Well not any more we can't.' A lipless smile and a waft of Eau Sauvage as DCI Barnard leaned his thick red paws on the desk. 'Your mate's admitted he was scared shitless of his missis finding out Pauline wanted him to fuck off down France with her, he was in the car giving her one, she was coked up, he was pissed up and he's big enough and strong enough to strangle her. Motive, opportunity, means.'

'Bollocks,' said Vic.

'You heard that Chaffey.'

'Yes sir.'

'He didn't fucking do it,' said Vic.

DCI Barnard leaned even closer. 'They you better find the black-enamelled junglebunny fucking shit-shifter who did or you're all in shtuck, aren't you? Especially you, Hallam.'

'Yes sir.'

The DCI stood up. 'I thought that'd put a firecracker up your arse.'

They watched the tight-packed Italian suit and the meaty grey head butt across the squad-room floor, stiff little arms pistoning just like Cagney. Out through the door and slam.

'Holy shit,' said Vic.

'He's a bit nervous this morning,' said Des. 'He's on telly.'

'Big deal.'

'You seen that tableload of knives he's got?'

'Yeah.'

'He's had it all laid out on green baize,' said Des. 'Face like that and a suit like that, give him a fez and he's Tommy Cooper.'

Vic read through the file on the way down to see Billy. Billy sat on the cell bed looking down at his crotch. 'I should have had it cut off years ago.'

'Too late now old son,' said Vic. All this and that bastard still prowling round after Ellie. Oh shit. 'Look Billy, I don't find this dealer we've had it. Both of us. You and me.'

'Little black cunt,' said Billy. He was getting morose. Soon he'd be no fucking use at all.

269

'Come on, mate, you used to work their clubs. You must know somebody.'

'That was then, Vic. That was ganja. Now it's all kids and E and all that shit.'

'What about Ellard then? Or what's her name, Suki? You used to knock her off, didn't you?'

'Christ Vic, you want me to drop 'em all in it?'

'For fuck sake, Billy look at the alternatives –'

'For Christ sake, Vic Pauline's bad enough –'

'All right then, fuck you.' Vic stood up. 'You can rot on remand in fucking Horfield reminiscing about what went wrong with your fucking life for fucking months for all I care.'

'Hang about,' said Billy. 'Fuck that for a game of soldiers.'

Vic offered him the file and a ballpoint. 'Write something down I can show Ellard.'

Billy frowned and then wrote in large capital letters on the inside of the file, DEAR EL AND SUKE AM IN SERIOUS DEEP SHIT MAN PLEASE TELL VICK HERE ALL HE WANTS AND ONLY THE GILTY PARTY WILL GET IT OTHERWISE WE ALL WILL MOST OF ALL ME AND YOU WONT GET THE BIG RISES I AM HEREBY PROMISING YOU BOTH YOURS LOVE BILLY

PS AND GREET TOO IF SHE WANTS IT BUT DONT FUCK ME ABOUT

He read it through and then signed and dated it. 'What's the time, Vic?'

'Ten-past nine.'

'That all?' He noted it down and passed the file and ballpoint back to Vic. 'Feels like fucking midday in here.'

At the Picton Street traffic lights on Stokes Croft, with Cromer driving and Nigel beside him and Vic and Ellie in the back, Nigel suddenly pointed to a couple of young blacks in overcoats and woolly tam-o'-shanters standing in a doorway on the other side of the road. 'There!' It was the first word he'd spoken since the nick. As they all looked to the right and Cromer pulled up to the kerb, Nigel was out on to the pavement and off like a shot across the road, sideslipping through the traffic and away down Picton Street into the Jungle.

'Go on then, John!'

'What?'

'Run you dumb fucker!'

Cromer switched off and piled out.

'Don't take the fucking key, for Christ sake!'

'Sorry – '

It was 9.40, Ellie looked as if she was trying not to wet herself laughing, Nigel had legged it, the job was fucked and the Escort was causing a traffic jam. One of those days.

Frank walked into the Well at 9.50 with his uniform in a long red-edged plastic clothes bag. On his way up to the sixth floor he stopped off at the fourth, walked along the corridors till he found an empty office and rang the hospital. Chaudhury's secretary said new Trust rules on security meant she had to check and ring back and hoped he'd understand. Frank said of course and gave the name on the office door. Collins, extension 3232. He changed while he waited. If anybody came in and asked, that was all he was doing. The phone rang again and the secretary said No the appointment had not been changed and as far as she could tell by looking at Doctor Chaudhury's list it was mostly just examinations so there shouldn't be any delay. Frank thanked her and walked out into the corridor and took the lift up to the sixth floor. Easy. Like swimming downstream.

The Chief Constable Royston Perry got in at the fifth.

'Morning sir.'

'Morning Frank.' The Chief Constable checking Frank's kit from the shoes up. 'How are you?'

'Fine thank you, sir.'

'Ready for the ordeal?'

'I think so, sir.'

'Do your best.'

'I shall, sir.'

Frank and the Chief Constable walked into the conference room side by side. Everybody turned round and stared. They were of a height and in step. A couple of stills guys flashed the moment. Me and the CC. Another stroke of luck.

The Chief Constable strode on through the salutes and mornings and sirs up to the dais, leaving Frank to watch from the sidelines. They were all there, Deputies, Supers, Chiefs, Inspectors from the districts, all standing tall in their best dark blue and silver, the blue looking black under the blinding TV lights and some of the older guys already red in the face from the heat.

A TV director who couldn't stop tugging at his scruffy ginger beard took the Chief Constable's arm and ushered him to the miked-up maple lectern. The rest of the Serious Brass were already seated along a couple of grey-draped trestle tables behind him. His big knuckly hands gripped the sides of the lectern, keeping his head up and his body ramrod straight while the director bloke fussed about with a white reflector board trying to throw some light up on to the Chief Constable's raw-boned face so his peaked cap wouldn't shade his eyes and make him look like something out of the SS.

Frank checked out the three four-man TV crews, one from each channel and a bunch of ponytailed independents. Machine-tooled aluminium video cases were piled against the back wall and a busty woman PA in a sharply tailored trouser suit and cowboy boots was talking earnestly to Bob from PR about lunch and what sort of white wine was it.

Then DCI Barnard came bustling in and strode over to a small group of CID guys lounging around in leather jackets trying to look like *Hill Street Blues*. Frank followed him. The DCI bounded up on to the dais and started trying to shift a green baize table full of knives. Frank leapt up to help him.

'Oh thanks, Webber. Apparently they want this lot sideways on and back a bit, they're getting too much fucking bounce and glitter.' They began moving the table an inch at a time for the bloke with the ginger beard until it was practically offstage. Clusters of sweat had sprung up on DCI Barnard's temples and streaks of it were running down his thick red neck behind his ears. 'I hate all this shit.' Pulling a sheaf of printouts from his back pocket to show Frank how important he was. 'Three pages of the fucking stuff straight to camera. Had to memorise the bastard lot. Not nervous, are you?'

'Not so far.'

DCI Barnard wiped the sweat off his face and neck with a red and blue spotted handkerchief. 'Thing is not to let them get you rattled or the bastards'll go for you.'

'Right.' Frank didn't feel a thing and couldn't give a shit. It was like diving into Clifton open-air pool on a hot August Bank Holiday as a kid. As soon as you hit the water all the heat and yelling and shrieking went and there was only a cool underwater silence.

Maybe it was because most of him wasn't there, but waiting somewhere else. Waiting for the nurse.

'They told you anything?'

'Not so far.'

'Typical.' DCI Barnard shuffled through the pages. 'What it says here it's the CC, me, then you.'

'Right.

'I saw you coming in with him. He say anything?'

You cunning old bastard. 'Don't screw up, basically.' *You better not, Frank. Not with this bloke.*

'How's the Pauline Millward thing going?' Steer it round to the nurse later if he got the chance. 'You get that touch I put through on the Winters lad?'

'In the end I did. Next time don't go through Drugs and Traffic, come straight to me.'

'Right, I will. Did it lead anywhere?'

'I can tell you one thing, Frank.' DCI Barnard looked carefully over both shoulders for eavesdroppers. 'If it doesn't somebody's going to be out on their arse pretty fucking quick.'

'Like that is it?'

'You ever have anything to do with this bloke Jewel?'

'Can't say I have, no.'

'Take my advice and don't,' said DCI Barnard. 'Otherwise you could end up drummed right out the fucking Brownies.' Another look round. 'And when I say out I mean seriously out.'

It had to be Hallam. Had to be. It was music in Frank's ears. 'Sorry to hear that.'

'It all reflects back on the man in charge.' The DCI plucked at his nose-hairs and then decided to blow his nose. 'Shit sticks, Frank.' He took some time wiping his nose extra clean and looking into his handkerchief before glancing sharply up at Frank. 'As we know.'

Don't say another word, Frank.

The Chief Constable tapped the face of his watch irritably. 'Ten ten, can we start please?'

The director with the ginger beard conferred with his opposite numbers. 'Ready when you are, sir.' Frank noticed the camera crews smirking at this remark, then the Chief Constable gave a short bark of a cough and everything went silent. Little red lights began winking on the sides of the cameras.

The Chief Constable's address was stolid, cold and abrupt. One Society, yes. But Duty and the Law Must Come First. Families. Drugs. Peril. Our Young People. Most of whom were fine upstanding et cetera. But. The criminal minority. Black and White. Must be Swept from the Streets. Are being at this very moment. A city-wide purge. The Future of this Great City. Your Co-operation Vital. The Serious Brass applauded heartily and so did Frank, thinking as far as the human face of the Force was concerned the CC would have done better to have stuck a sprig of holly up his arse and called himself a Christmas turkey. Bob from PR was scribbling away and the TV mob were eyeing each other quietly and stroking their noses. Frank could see they all thought it was the same old stuff, nothing new, and not a soundbite in sight.

Things livened up for DCI Barnard's performance with the knives but the DCI's accent grew more and more Bristolian until in the end he got totally carried away and picked up a panga and waved it about saying We got to eradicate this idea of violence from our society once and for all.

Frank saw the ginger-bearded guy shaking his head at Bob from PR, who stood up and passed a note to the Chief Constable and then sat down scribbling away furiously. The Chief Constable thanked DCI Barnard and took another page of notes from Bob from PR;

he gripped the lectern hard and spoke close to the microphones. It made his voice sound deeper and less raspy. 'If I could just say this. Operation Clean Sweep as we are calling this exercise in community policing means one thing and one thing only. We were all children once, unlikely as that may seem, and it is to the children of Bristol that I would like to put this question. If the chimney is dirty and filthy and all blocked up, how can Santa Claus get down it to deliver his presents? Equally, how can the people of Bristol enjoy the good things of Christmas in a city made filthy and unsafe by the presence of drugs and crime? The success of this operation means that we can all, all of us young and old, celebrate this festival in the spirit in which it was meant, a spirit of love, and peace, and harmony, and goodwill to all men whatsoever their race, colour or creed.' The Chief Constable's Presbyterian nostrils flared. 'A true Christian needs no other drug. Thank you.'

Bob from PR was beaming and sweating so much his jamjar-bottom glasses were steaming up. The Chamber of Commerce was going to love it. The director bloke was stroking his beard, pacing about and pondering. His PA woman was watching and waiting. 'We can use it,' he said finally. 'We can use this and lose the rest, make this the lead. But forget the true Christian bit.'

Bob from PR went over to DCI Barnard and they reshot the end of his piece without the panga-waving. Then it was Frank's turn to shake the ginger-bearded director's sweaty little hand.

'Hi, my name's Terry and this is Maggi Reed.' A young woman Frank hadn't seen before stepped forward and shook hands with long leather gloves on. The leather felt cold so she must have just walked in. She was wearing a flared and fur-trimmed Russian greatcoat

276

and high boots; they made her look bulkier than she was and reminded Frank briefly of the nurse. Then she took her fur hat off and scuffed up her short fair hair and Frank recognised her. Bob from PR and DCI Barnard and even the Chief Constable began to gather round. She flashed Frank a lightning-quick professional smile and glanced first at one side of his face then at the other. 'Right,' she said. 'Terry, can we do this one outside? I mean, you know, one to one? Let the other crews pick up on him later. Is that a possibility, on the roof, say, Bob, or is that a problem for you? I see this as a separate piece, Terry. Don't you think?' Flashing Frank another smile. 'I mean you know the inspector here's got a jaw and cheekbones to die for.'

There was a delay in which Frank heard himself described as a piece they could send up the line to *News at Ten* and then Terry caved in and Bob caved in and the CC and the DCI caved in, all of them melting to slush in front of this small assertive young woman with her pointy little face, her spiky blonde hair and her slanty cat-like eyes. 'D'you mind?' she said to Frank.

'Whatever you like.'

'Good. Good voice but remember I'm a lot shorter than you so we'll need to watch the eyelines. Thanks.' Another millisecond smile and she was gone with the camera crew.

Frank thought she was like all those other nightmare women waiting to suck him dry and then chuck him. Added to which she was all bright-eyed hard-faced needle-sharp ambition: he couldn't even force himself to fancy her. Maybe it was the nurse but he didn't give a shit about anything, least of all being interviewed.

Stay cool, Frank. Stay ice fucking cool.

There was still frost on the roof but it went well once

277

they got it set up and baffled off the traffic noise. It took about twenty minutes and he blew it a couple of times but so did she. All the time they were eyeing each other like knives but nobody else seemed to notice and when she blew it a third time she said, Oh fuck it I'll do that on cutaway.

In the second half, after he'd said Well it was his day off and he was just doing a bit of shopping for his wife Rae who was out at work, to which she gave him a huge bug-eyed silent-mouthed Great, he saw that the Chief Constable and DCI Barnard had come up on to the roof and were standing in the background watching, checking out his performance.

'So the car's coming right at you, then what?'

'Well, all I did, you know, basically, was react.'

'You didn't think about the danger?'

'Didn't have time, I mean there was the old lady — and well —'

'Go on, Inspector.'

'Well, anybody, any normal fairly young guy anyway, would have done the same thing, wouldn't they?' He remembered to grin and shrug at the same time, looking modest, then looking off as if thinking back but in reality giving the camera a bit of profile, showing he was embarrassed but on the whole quietly proud of himself. Fuck it. He couldn't give a toss.

Don't knock it, Frank. It's something you can do.

'Would they, Inspector? Would most people these days risk their lives to save an old lady, a pensioner?'

'Well I think so. At least I hope they would.' Would they fuck.

'And then?'

'I just sort of jumped on the vehicle, on the bonnet, and hung on more or less, on to the wipers actually.'

'Which were working at the time?'

'They had been operated by then, yes.'

'So you were hanging on by the windscreen wipers, knuckles jammed and bleeding against the windscreen, careering at high speed round and round a pedestrian precinct?'

'Well yes, more or less. Not that it was that high a speed, obviously.'

'It all sounds wildly Hollywood, Inspector.'

'I can assure you, Miss Reed it didn't feel like it at the time.'

'How did it feel?'

'Well I did think for a moment there might be a slight underwear problem.'

'Keep rolling, we'll run that again.' She didn't even blink and her intonation and expression stayed exactly the same. 'How did it feel?'

'To be honest I was scared witless.'

'Until the car crashed?'

'Well until it was stopped forcibly by a bollard, yes.'

'With you still on it, still hanging across the bonnet, with the wipers still going?'

'Well yes I suppose they were.'

'And you still made your arrest?'

'The driver was detained, yes.'

Using a different tone of voice she said, 'Thanks Frank, now if you would just look slowly out over the city to your right, distant gaze, long focus, that's it and now back slowly again, back to me and hold it on me one two three and now on you go left, travelling over to the left and hold it there, chin up and slight smile, keep it going because this is my voiceover finish on your big close-up, try not to blink and . . . right that's it, thank you very much Frank, ace wonderful smashing. How was that for you, Terry?'

'The usual thrill.'

There was another delay while she and Terry and
the camera and sound guys went into a huddle and then
the busty PA woman came over and asked if it would
possibly be possible to have a shot of Frank's hands in
bandages.

21

Vic was going spare. He'd lost Nigel, lost Cromer, Ellard and Suki and Greet hadn't come home from the Kit Kat and now he was in Nigel's squat with Ellie, listening to Nigel's feet very quietly and very slowly coming up the broken staircase.

He was pretty sure he could deal with him but he was a quick slippery little bugger and he'd have to get the arm on him first time or they'd be all over the place. Having Ellie there wasn't going to help. Especially if she froze or screamed or lost it or generally got in the fucking way –

The feet stopped outside the door, stepped back two paces, three. Silence. Vic eyed the length of motorcycle chain across the door. He'd climbed in the way Cromer said Nigel did, up the drainpipe and through the window. Then he'd taken the chain off, brought Ellie in, replaced the chain and considered he'd out-manoeuvred the little bugger. But had he? Billy had said on the phone the kid was worried about what he called the security of the fucking place but God knows why because it was all bare boards, so what was he up to? Something about business too but what fucking business? Come on Nigel, what the fuck are you doing, casing the joint? Suppose he was, suppose he'd got it all out of that SAS book, cotton across the door jamb, hairs on the locks, all that shit – Vic with his heart starting to trip-hammer, glancing behind him making sure Ellie hadn't moved, still had her arms up over her face –

With a Godalmighty double-footed crash, the door-post splintered, the chain lashed back and a body came hurtling through feet first shouting *Police*!

Ellie was standing in the corner of the room with her arms folded, shaking her head in quiet disbelief as Vic and Cromer got to their feet wheezing and laughing and leaning on each other and dusting each other down.

'Fuck me, John – '

'Fucking hell – '

'You all right?'

'Fucking elbow, man – '

'Thought you were fucking Nigel – '

'I thought *you* fucking were – '

'When you jumped me – '

'I was shitting myself – '

'I thought oh shit – '

They were grinning at each other like a couple of kids, enjoying it. She could understand they needed to discharge the aggression but why did they seem to love it so much? She might just as well not be there. 'Don't mind me,' she said.

'Oh,' said Cromer. 'Sorry.'

'So what happened,' said Vic on the way down the stairs, 'you see him at all?'

'No. He can run, that kid.'

'He'll need to if he stays in the fucking Jungle.'

'I thought he was bound to come back here.'

'Yeah, me too.' Vic looked round the wrecked hall, the sodden mattresses, the piles of plaster and broken bricks. 'God knows what for though.'

'I tell you what I did see.'

'What?'

'Carload of our blokes.'

'CID?'

'Plainclothes. I flagged them, gave them Nigel's description.'

'What were they doing?'

'Gridironing. Up City Road, down Grosvenor Road, across, back, up, down.'

'It's started, then.'

'Looks like it.'

'We might as well pack up and go home, John. We're not going to see anything on the street now, Nigel or no Nigel.'

In the car, Cromer driving, Vic next to him looking out the window, Ellie found herself stuck in the back, ignored. She wished she were back at work and thought to herself who in their right minds would want to do this all day? Driving around in heavy traffic, street after sullen street, the heater blasting the car full of smog, scanning everybody, watching everything, bored to death and looking for violence but Vic seemed to love it. So did Cromer. They weren't just fascinated, she thought, they were obsessed, like dogs with other dogs' messes, and they seemed to regard the rest of the human race with a joky, patient contempt that made Ellie want to bang their male heads together –

'Why do a runner in the first place?' Cromer was saying. 'I mean you got him out the nick, he's supposed to be looking for the same lot we are –'

She watched Vic reach out his notebook, flick through it until he found the page he wanted. ' "Urges are what you want to do to people, feelings are what should stop you." The thoughts of Chairman Nigel.' Vic closed the notebook and glanced back at Ellie. 'Another fucking loony on the loose.'

You included, said her look.

'What's he going to do?' said Cromer.

Vic glanced at her in the mirror and turned the radio up to make it difficult for her to hear. You pig, she thought. Ellie decided that whether Vic knew it or not the job had got him. No wonder his wife had left; there was no room in his life for anything as normal as a relationship, the bloody job had got him in its grip, and that was it, basically. It was hateful, and so was he, particularly when he was being like this, treating her with no more consideration than a bloody parcel. She slumped down and stared out of the window trying not to listen to idiot static and incomprehensible police messages. All she could see was the side of his face talking to Cromer.

'I'll tell you what he's going to do. Thinks he's going to do because he's all gee'd up at the moment. He thinks he's on the run, he thinks he's a fucking hero, he thinks he can probably take out these four guys on his own, same way he thinks he's a fucking genius, same way he thinks he can fucking invade Stonehenge with his fucking toerag army, same way he's going to start the fucking revolution, hang the Prime Minister, shoot the Queen, and live in love and peace and freedom for ever fucking more. That's what he thinks he's going to do. But what he's really going to do is end up as a fucking accountant.' Vic took out a packet of cigarettes, ripped the cellophane off and held it over the back to Ellie.

'No thanks.'

'The problem with kids like Nigel is we don't know what they're going to do because they don't either. It's called being young, John. You're young, she's young, I don't think I'm that fucking old, but we're not fighting the entire fucking world on our own because of something that happened in the fucking sandpit. But he is.

284

He's fucking young and he's fucking angry. He's fucking stupid and he's fucking clever and he's fucking daft and he's fucking cunning all at the same time.' Vic lit his cigarette with the car lighter. 'Actually I quite like the little bastard.'

'Why?'

'He reminds me of you.'

'Fuck's that supposed to mean?'

'Needs the shit kicked out of him.'

'Thanks.' She watched them grinning at each other, being all buddy-buddy, leaving her right out of it, deliberately, or so she thought. On and on they went, Ashley Road into Lower Ashley, right into Tudor Road, left into Newfoundland; three white people in a car watching and being watched by black people on the street, and no friendliness anywhere.

'If he does catch up with these black kids,' said Vic, 'he'll get more than shit kicked out of him. Unless he has a sudden fit of sanity and realises where he is and what he's trying to do, we'll be round mopping up the blood and picking up the fucking pieces and it'll all be our fault as usual.'

'You think he is a nutter?'

'He's well on the fucking way.' Vic ground the cigarette out in the car ashtray. It was full and started burning, filling the car with the acrid smell of dead dog-ends. Neither of them seemed to notice. 'The best thing,' said Vic, 'would be to let him have the fucking breakdown, get pumped full of tranks for a few weeks then spend the rest of his days sitting in some dozy fucking office punching a calculator and wondering what happened to the real Nigel.'

'If he does go for these black bastards,' said Cromer, 'they could fucking kill him.'

'Yeah. Easy.'

'But you don't think he will?'

'I don't fucking know, John. Could be he's just doing it to annoy us.'

'I don't get it,' said Cromer. 'It's not just us, the Filth, it's everybody.'

'He said he saw some uniform throw a baby through a van window. Doesn't fucking help, does it?'

Ellie said, 'Can I say something?'

'What?' said Vic.

'I think all he's doing is running away.'

'Who from?'

'You.'

'Meaning me?'

'Yes.'

'Why?'

'You're mad. You're all mad.'

'And Nigel isn't?'

'You know what I mean.'

Cromer said, 'What's she talking about?'

'Tell him,' said Ellie.

'No,' said Vic.

'Why?'

'All I'm interested in at the moment, strange as it may seem to you, is what Nigel's up to.'

'Is it?'

'Yes.'

'Well thanks.'

'Oh bollocks.'

'And you.'

'For Christ sake Ellie –'

'Can I get out now?'

'No you can't.'

'Why not?'

'It's my fucking job, woman!' A moment's silence. 'You're not the only fucking one, you know.'

'I gathered that.'

'Good.'

'What the fuck's going on?' said Cromer, 'I can't drive with all this shit – '

'Time you learned,' said Vic.

'He thinks – '

'Shut the fuck up – '

'Holy shit,' said Cromer.

'He thinks,' said Ellie, 'the rapist, the person that raped me – '

'We all know what a rapist is,' said Vic, 'so shut up.'

'Do you?' Ellie's voice rising to a scream. 'Do you?'

'What the fuck,' said Cromer.

'Will you fucking shut up, woman?'

'No I will not fucking shut up – '

'You stupid cow – '

'I'm going to have to stop the car,' said Cromer.

'Take no notice,' said Vic, 'she's fucking hysterical.'

'I am not hysterical!' screamed Ellie.

'Well stop fucking screaming then!'

Ellie took a deep breath. 'He thinks,' she said to Cromer, 'the rapist is one of you lot. A copper. Don't you?'

'Yeah,' said Vic. 'Well, we're not going to find Nigel driving round in fucking circles are we, John?'

'Doesn't look like it,' said Cromer. 'Where to now?'

'Ellard's,' said Vic.

She might just as well not exist.

Ellard's mum was standing on the doorstep with her big slack-skinned arms folded across her bust and wearing a loosely crocheted blue hat against the cold. 'Ellard is a man free, black and over twenty-one,' she said. 'I done what I could for him and I don' have a

287

strength or inclination to do no more so if he gone off partyin' he gone off partyin' – '

'Yeah but where's he gone off partying?' said Vic.

Ellard's mum hunched her big bony shoulders up round her ears and slowly closed her eyes to make Vic disappear. When she opened them and he was still there, she clicked her tongue against her teeth at him. 'Somewhere to forget the cold that live in the heart of this damn country.'

Vic turned away, not to go but to make sure Cromer was watching him from the Escort. There were two or three women with shopping bags twenty yards away and men's shapes behind the net curtains on both sides of the narrow cul-de-sac.

At least Cromer had got the car facing the right way. It was worth a try. 'Ellard!' he shouted past her big gaunt frame. 'I've got something to show you from Billy! If you don't come down you won't have a job tonight and nor will anybody else!' Especially me.

Ellard's mum closed the front door in his face. Seconds later an upstairs window rattled up and Ellard's long bleary-eyed face appeared. 'Wait there now, Mister Hallam.' Vic heard Ellard's mum's voice echoing up the hallway and Ellard mumbling in reply then the front door opened again. Ellard was in a T-shirt and boxers, looking wrecked and coughing in the cold morning air. Vic glanced over his shoulder. There were men standing in the doorways now. Ellard got the message and smacked his two hands down and then up on Vic's and stood aside, openly inviting Vic in.

'No problem, Mister Hallam.'

'That's what you think, Ellard.' They went into the TV room; Vic showed him the file and waited while Ellard read Billy's message. 'We're looking for someone deals from a car.'

'Who don't?'

'Car with a car phone or a mobile.'

'People offering that stuff all the time.'

'Young kids.'

'They're the worst.'

'Three or four of 'em. The dealer probably older. Was a black BMW seven series.'

'Nice motor.'

'Not any more.'

'Why not?'

'Burn-out.'

'You got a man's name on the computer.'

'Not the registered owner.' Vic took the file back. 'Come on Ellard, we can play this game all day and all fucking night. Four black kids, dealing with whites, no wheels on a Saturday night, an important night. Cocaine, possibly crack, and they know this kid Winston, got his jaw broke. Come on Ellard, you know who deals and who doesn't. Who the fuck is it?' Ellard slowly closing his eyes, Vic thinking it must run in the fucking family. 'What wheels have they got now?'

Ellard opening his eyes, the whites red from God knows what. 'Mister Jewel say something about a raise. He say how big?'

'For fuck sake Ellard.'

Ellard leaned forward in the powder blue armchair, steepled his fingers and looked at Vic through the hole. 'Let me put it to you like this, Mister Hallam. Let's say you the opposite of me, and you work for a black man. One day the black man says one of your bad-ass white brothers do something wrong but you don' know he's telling you the troot or not because all black men motherfucking liars you know? Always putting you down and keeping you down and ripping you off, man.

289

You going to tell him the name your bad-ass fucking white brother?'

'We all got problems, son.' Wondering what Ellie was telling Cromer out in the car. 'It's Billy's neck, Ellard.'

Ellard stood up, swaying. 'What about mine, Mister Hallam?'

'Come on Ellard, you can take care of yourself.'

'Yeah but I ain't fucking bulletproof.'

'Guns,' said Vic, getting in the Escort. 'All we fucking need.'

'He say anything else?' said Cromer.

'Would you?' He looked round at Ellie. She'd been crying. Oh fuck. 'She put you in the picture?'

'Yes.'

'And?'

'Circumstantial, isn't it?'

Vic turned round to Ellie. 'See what I mean?' To Cromer he said, 'Any other great thoughts?'

'Well, if you don't mine me saying so – '

'No I don't mind you saying so, John – '

'You fucked the case by staying the night.'

'Thanks for your support, John. Try not to tell the world.'

'It's true though isn't it? All I'm saying – '

'I know it's fucking true!'

'There is one good thing though,' said Cromer, pulling away.

'Duck!' shouted Vic, reaching back to push Ellie's head down. Half a brick came sailing over the remains of a privet hedge. Cromer swerved and the brick hit the door instead of the windscreen. 'Go like fuck!' Cromer put his foot down and the front tyres yelped and squealed and laid wavy black rubber lines all the way down the cul-de-sac until he sawed the fucking thing straight and heaved and yawed and scrabbled it round the corner and gunned it flat out up towards City Road.

'You can change out of second now,' said Vic.

'Oh yeah,' said Cromer. 'Do we go back?'

'Like fuck,' said Vic. They reached the lights at the junction. 'Christ I wish we could leave these people alone.'

Back on Stokes Croft, Vic radioed the incident through then said, 'What good thing?'

'What?'

'You said there was one good thing. Before the brick.'

'Oh yeah,' said Cromer. 'Ellie was talking about the hospital, this Winters kid.'

'What about him?'

Ellie said, 'We were talking about visitors and I said if you wanted to know anything it was no good asking the staff, you should ask the patients who haven't got any.'

'Any what?'

'Visitors?'

'Why?'

'Because they're lonely and they're nosy and they've got nothing else to do.'

'Thanks for telling me earlier,' said Vic.

'You were in a bad mood,' said Ellie.

Seconds after Pauline's coffin slid through the grey velvet curtains she had appeared to Nigel dressed in billowing white and yellow flames, her palms out, her feet sailing off the ground, her face smiling down on him, forgiving him, and he knew what it was he had to do.

Telling the police there were four of them instead of just one was only part of it. They'd lied to him, they'd locked him in that hellhole knowing he couldn't stand being locked in for Christ sake, then they'd bust the squat while he watched from the back garden, so fuck them. They'd lied to him, he'd lied to them. That was one part of the equation. Now for the other part. It was right. It was only right. It was not only right it was justice. Yes.

He took the things he needed from his rucksack and stashed it in the foxhole and escape tunnel he'd dug under the mass of brambles at the foot of the squat garden. There was frost still on the dead ground inside and as he squirmed flat on his belly through the dead gingery thorns out to the back alley he caught a rank whiff of fresh fox-piss. My brother.

He dropped into the alley and came down through the gardens and allotments out of Montpelier into St Pauls.

Into the Jungle.

Through bent rusted railings into the slimy brick culvert under the road and out into the cutting.

It was a dank narrow steep-sided swamp of a place even in summer, about fifteen foot deep, no wider than a pram at the bottom and completely overgrown with loosestrife, convolvulus, juicy bright green hart's-tongue and that stuff that looked like giant prehistoric rhubarb. All dead now, the hairy frostbitten leaves cracking like poppadoms into the mush under his feet. Threading his way through, planting his combat boots carefully so as not to pop the brittle stalks. Nigel in his element, slipping and sliding through the dead yellow and black jungle like a shadow. Soon to emerge into the light.

On the right a high dripping stone wall topped with half-round bluish railway bricks. On the left the backs of sheds and board fences snagged with loops of barbed

292

wire. At the end a brick arch cinderblocked off and covered with graffiti. It had once been a narrow-gauge quarry line but the track and sleepers and even the bedding gravel had long since gone. The local kids called it the Sewer and terrified their younger brothers and sisters by threatening to shove them down it among the old bedsteads, used syringes, dead dogs and black rats and big green adders they said lived down there.

He climbed up the angle between the end wall and the slope, found a place where the bottom fence boards had rotted in the ground and crawled through into the guy's narrow back garden.

The guy had tried to grow hemp in the space between his shed and the fence and half a dozen stripped plants lay rotting in an old tin bath.

There was a concealing bank of long whitish-yellow feathery grass like bamboo, now laid over flat by the gales like swaths of matted blond hair. Beyond that a stuccoed flat-roofed kitchen extension with a square stainless steel central heating vent sticking out of it. And beyond that, the back door.

An old woman came out and hung up a few bits of washing and then slip-slopped back inside. She looked tired. Never mind her. She was innocent. They all were. Yes.

He moved up along the fence to the side of the extension. There was an old coalhouse or shithouse he could use for cover if she came out again. He listened. A door banged inside the house. It couldn't be the door into the kitchen: there was too much echo. It had to be a door off the hall, nearer the front of the house. Yes. He moved in.

The kitchen clean, bright yellow and blue. A wire vegetable rack with yams and okra and Chinese cabbage and root ginger. The washing machine on but silent. No clothes in it. The kettle hot. A teabag in the sink tidy, still steaming. The old lady must be sitting down, having a cup of tea. Yes. He moved into the hall.

The noise of a TV coming from the front room. It was some morning show, sounded like an *Oprah* re-run. And then, louder, booming out full blast from a room upstairs, Ice T. Then diminishing. The guy adjusting the volume. Yes. Down then up again. He could see the guy loving it. One hell of a good system and the bass was massive. He moved along the hall, lightly, rapidly up the stairs, good thick swirly-patterned carpet but still timing the steps to the angry thudding power belting through the house. Everything getting closer. Everything getting louder. Yes. It was right.

The door open. Through it, he could see the guy had his back to him. He was sitting on a chair facing the window, his tall lanky body hunched over talking on a mobile with a finger in his ear saying, I know man they been here they everywhere all over the fucking place man.

Nigel took the things out of his pocket and looked kindly on the guy's back. It wasn't the guy's fault, it wasn't Nigel's fault, it was nobody's fault, they were all innocent. He was only an instrument. It was wrong to kill any living thing because they were all created holy but all the same there was the equation to be balanced. The guy knew that. He knew that. Yes. It was only right. He went in feeling good and centred and committed justice.

22

Nigel leapt for the top of the fence, hauled himself over the crumbling wire and took a diving rolling header into the cutting. Behind him the old lady was yelling and screaming for God to help her help her, and two black guys were shouting and running down the gardens on either side. He ran crashing through the rotting stalks. Up ahead, between him and the culvert, two other black guys were swarming over the fence looking real fucking ugly. He wanted to stop, explain to them, hey man it's cool no problem, but there was no time, he had to get back to Pauline and tell her. The deal between him and the guy responsible for her death was done.

One of the black guys slid down the slope and made a grab for his legs as he wriggled through the bent iron bars but he lashed out with his combat boot and got the guy in the face. There was a soft crunch of cartilage and the guy screamed and let go.

After that, easy. Speeding winding ducking through the alleys that ran through the gardens and allotments back up to Montpelier.

Back into his foxhole.

He'd done it, shaken them off. He turned on his back to contemplate the low cathedral of thorns arching above him, thin sun lancing through thin branches, and felt the long calm high of something promised and then delivered.

All he had to do now was lie up, rest, eat, drink and

move out in good order under cover of darkness. Yes. He laid his cheek on the rucksack and put his arms round it. Oh Pauline.

Frank had done lunch and been congratulated on his performance time and again. A natural spokesman, said the Chief Constable, and DCI Barnard said promotion to Chief Inspector was as good as in the bag. Frank, still feeling nothing but the elation of soon being with the nurse, watched the Brass and the TV mob laughing and posing for stills and sucking up to each other over a couple of glasses of Australian Sémillon Chardonnay with quiche and salad. He kept up his modest but serious act then made the excuse of work to do; after being air-kissed by Maggi and then half on the mouth by the busty PA who also pushed herself against him he left feeling there was a definite smell of cunt in the air.

Forget it, Frank.

As he came out of the Well a patrol car came sirening in with its windscreen smashed and the two guys looking shaken, one holding a bloody handkerchief to his face.

Nothing to do with you, Frank.

By the time he was walking up Maudlin Street all hell had broken loose in the Well and riot gear was being issued.

Ellie talked to the sister on the fracture ward and got her to put the screens round the little old guy in the next bed to Winston.

'He's called George,' she said.

George had the look of an old-time fairground scrapper long gone on cider. A cheery vicious little scrunched-up red crab-apple of a face, close-cropped

296

white hair, no teeth and eyes like chippings off a grave. He was virtually senile, the sister said, and apart from his broken hip he had no lungs to speak of. Emphysema, but it didn't stop him gabbing filth all day.

'Hallo,' he said, 'What's this then, more buggeration? Who's he? Hey, you. I tell you what, my son, I ain't had my bollocks washed by a woman since I was a nipper. I tell you something else and all, it's bloody marvellous. Look at that.' He threw back the bedclothes to expose a thick belt of padding on his thigh and a knobbly, bent erection. He had no pubic hair and the area was scratched red raw. 'How's that for seventy-eight years of age?'

'Oh cover yourself up, George.'

'Why? Who is he? A copper is he?' The toothless mouth went into a Mister Punch curve and the hard little eyes said I ain't totally fucking puddled yet, mate. 'Hey, listen. Come here. She's got lovely soft hands kid, you wants to get her to give you one, might put a smile on your face you miserable-looking bastard.'

Vic tried to get some sense out of George and the subject of Winston's visitors but George said all that lot did was yabber yabber yabber and you couldn't coco that, could you?

Steel-tipped motorcycle boots came skidding down the ward and Cromer stuck his head through the screen.

'Sorry Vic.'

'One of 'em had a suit and tie,' George was saying, 'head like that blackie does the pantos but without the build on him.'

'Excuse me, George.'

'Hand-gallant I was,' said George, waving his wasted forearms about in front of his face like a stick insect. 'Hand-gallant!' The little red face twisted up in rage as

Vic walked out ignoring him. 'Hey you you great long useless streak a piss I'll fight the fucking lot of you!'

'Now then, George,' said the sister.

Outside the screens Cromer said, 'Ellard's dead.'

'Oh shit,' said Vic. *Yeah but I ain't fucking bullet-proof.* 'How?'

'Can of oven foam in the face and garrotted with a steel guitar string. Mother says she saw a little white guy running like fuck. Jungle greens.'

Nigel. It had to be Nigel – but why Ellard? Nigel and Ellard. Vic tried to put it together, tried to make it make sense, but nothing made sense. Maybe it would in time, everything made sense if you waited long enough. Sense of a sort anyway. But Nigel and Ellard. And Pauline –

'Whole place is going fucking berserk,' said Cromer.

'Not surprised,' said Vic. 'What the fuck are we supposed to do about it?'

'They want us up Nigel's squat. House to house and search.'

On the way down to the Escort they left Ellie in Gynae reception and Doctor Chaudhury's secretary came out and told them that was fine, the appointment had already been confirmed.

Just after two o'clock Frank walked into the hospital in full uniform and carrying his briefcase to see Winston Winters. He made an appointment for 2.30, and that was his cover set up.

By 2.10 he was coming out of Gynae staff-only male toilets in surgical greens, a silly pale-blue patterned disposable mob cap on his head, a surgical mask over his face and a pair of silky-thin plastic gloves in his hand.

Cutting it fine, Frank.

They were exiting from the car park into St Michael's Hill when Vic said, 'Stop the fucking car, for Christ sake!' A student cyclist swerved round them V-signing and mouthing as Vic piled out. 'You go on!'

No Ellie in reception. 'Who confirmed the appointment?' said Vic, heaving for breath as the secretary flicked back through the pages of the diary. Christ woman, come on –

'Yes. Here we are. Inspector Collins, extension 3232.'

'Collins?' Collins was in fucking Traffic –

Dr Chaudhury said hallo to Ellie then there was a sharp bright white exploding light inside his head and everything swam and blurred and he was falling and the bright white light was going out and a muffled fading voice was saying Don't you dare say a fucking word.

Ellie had her head down and her feet up in the stirrups. Her rough creamy-white cotton op shift was up round her waist. She opened her mouth to scream but her throat closed up and she was gagging, no sound coming out.

Frank looked at the nurse as she thrashed her legs about trying to disentangle herself. How pretty it was. Mouth watering, he took the chisel from his pocket.

This is it, Frank.

Vic smacked into Dr Chaudhury's assistant outside the door, she was saying No you can't go in there and Vic said Sorry and charged into the examination room and all but fell over Chaudhury's face-down body. Shit. The fucker had a chisel to her neck bending low over her between her legs which were still in those round hoop things and he was fiddling with himself inside the green trousers. Vic threw himself at him trying to pin both arms from behind, trying to pull him off her, and feeling his grip breaking as the fucker heaved them both backwards, slamming them over Chaudhury's body against the door and automatically locking it. Oh shit – Vic grabbed at the green tunic again and hurled them both sideways across the room crash into the autoclave or steriliser or whatever it was, some fucking glass and steel fishtank thing –

It fell with them and shattered into metal, glass and steam as they hit the floor, showering and clattering the silvery instruments all over them like a shoal of metal fish. Christ the bastard was strong, watch out for the fucking chisel. Rolling over. Punching kicking kneeing. Elbows feet fists everything. Broken glass all over the floor and now water pissing out and spraying everywhere and glimpses of Ellie screaming and the door thudding against Chaudhury's head as the people outside threw themselves against it – and the thought going through Vic's mind, Don't do that you'll make it fucking worse –

Vic's hand scrabbling around among the glass for something, anything to get hold of as the bastard twisted round to face him and drove the chisel into his shoulder aiming for his neck, his face, his eyes, God knows. Shielding himself with one arm, feeling round with the other. Shit you're getting the worst of this, Hallam, then his fingers closing round something, three or four things, Christ they were scalding hot, some bit of surgical rubber round them, one longer and thinner than the others, picking them up and jabbing and slashing at the bastard. Rolling over and slipping and sliding in the water on the floor and flailing out at the bastard not knowing whether the warm wet feeling was blood or just fucking hot water. Then the bastard lunged and slipped and Vic dug the long thin thing at him. Into his neck, just under the mask. The bastard glugging and going bug-eyed as the slim flat shiny pencil-thin piece of steel slid easily through his flesh cutting him from his windpipe to his jugular. Then everything slowing down, and Christ the thing was so fucking sharp it just slipped a thin red line through his flesh, then the flesh spreading and suddenly the red line bulged and gushed and the bastard's bright-red life-blood spouted past him.

As Frank died he felt something wriggling in his throat, filling it, blocking it, and then it felt like it was leaping out of his mouth screaming and laughing, something reddish and black and long and wriggly like a lizard or a gecko or an axolotl or some leggy fucking horrible thing, and Frank sinking, feeling funny and light in the head and seeing, thinking he was seeing, it had a head like a knob or a blind foetus and it was screaming and laughing and it had sharp little yellow curved-back teeth like needles and it was leaving him, abandoning him. The voice. Making its last dry fading papery little chuckle. *Heh heh heh.* Frank going down. Oh God. Dark. Cold. Wet. Black. Oh God.

Too late now, Frank.

All Vic saw was a flying gout of thick red blood spurting out and splashing against the grey wall to leave a dark blot with dribbling legs. The guy's windpipe was wheezing air through the slit and his mouth, moving behind the mask, was silently going dugh dugh dugh as if he was trying to call God in reverse through all the blood and then he was shuddering flat out and hot and sticky and dead, blood still leaking out of him and mixing with the water on the floor, steam hissing every-where and then a quick shivery draught of cold air and Vic, exhausted, on his hands and knees, head hanging down like a well-knackered dog, realised Ellie had opened a window and sunlight was hazing in.

They were tearing up the floorboards, ripping the staircase and plaster-and-lath walls apart. Uniforms and Forensics, making a terrible racket and keeping themselves well busy, all happy to have missed the next steel-grilled bus to St Pauls but telling each other not to worry they'd all get stuck in soon.

Cromer stood on the top landing looking out over the back garden and down the hill into St Pauls. Red and orange and blue lights flashing here and there, blinking up off the walls and roofs when you couldn't see the vehicles. Sirens blaring yowling and whining. Police, Fire, Ambulance. No human sound at all and the whole thing wrapped up in a cocoon of traffic noise.

It would be dark soon. More cars would be burned, more shop fronts looted, more heads cracked, more stabbings, beatings, punch-ups. The containment plan relied on the railway lines to the north and east, and blocking off Stokes Croft and Stapleton Road to the west and south but it never completely worked, gangs of troublemakers always got through. More overtime, more police bussed in from twenty miles around, endless bloody mayhem till it burned itself out. Then an inquiry, rafts of articles What Were the Police Doing, case after case coming up in the courts and then some Special Commission throwing well-meaning money at it but it all getting slowly worse anyway. Or at least no better. Maybe Vic was right. Maybe they should just leave them alone.

Mist was starting to settle in the hollows. The sun low and orange, the hum of traffic building as the infant schools turned out, ordinary life going on, sparrows flitting, a cat watching them crouched flat on the stone wall between the two gardens and then bunking off as a thin waft of steam rose out of the briar patch into the cold air.

Steam?

Nigel zipped himself up and looked up through the thorns at the reddening sky. Not long now. He'd had half an hour's kip and could have done with longer but the need for a piss had woken him up. He watched the lights blazing in every window of the squat and blue-overalled bodies moving about. They had a portable generator going, had to because the electricity had been cut off yonks ago –

One of them was out the back door and running down the garden, guy in a leather jacket and biker's boots all over the place on the slippery, tussocky grass. Shit, that young CID kid what was his name, Cromer. Three or four overalls following him with spades and long-handled lumphammers. What to do? Take the rucksack? Leave it? He collapsed the sides of the fox-hole on to it, and backed himself out through the thorns. Don't worry love, I'll be back.

Nigel dropped into the alley. There were black guys at each end.

There was no way Cromer was going to get through the briar patch. Black guys shouting. Fucking useless slippery steel-tipped motorcycle boots. Clambering up on the garden wall, crawling along to the end overlooking the alley.

He stood up to see a couple of black guys running. Knives and cleavers out like fucking Zulus. 'Juke him, man!' Nigel up the wooden fence opposite like a scalded cat. Cromer launched himself across the alley and hit the fence as Nigel was straddling it. The fence collapsed under Cromer's impact and when the black guys came up he was sitting on Nigel, keeping him face down with an armlock on his neck, and trying to get his cuffs out before Nigel got his wind back.

'He ours, man,' said a black guy with a cleaver.

'Oh no he's fucking not,' said Cromer, cuffing Nigel to him. 'He's mine.'

The black guys were coming for him when three blokes in overalls dropped over the wall.

23

When Vic walked into Chief Constable Royston Perry's
office with his arm in an elbow sling and his left sleeve
dangling it was like opening the door of a fridge. The
temperature fell to zero and conversation round the
satinwood conference table stopped in mid-word.
Cromer was already there, looking strained. He had
ditched his biker's gear for a plum-coloured sports
jacket and tie. DCI Barnard was sitting beside the Chief
Constable at the head of the table, and DI Parnes was
next to Cromer, his dark round head bent over a pile
of files and a shorthand pad. On the other side, on
his own, was the Super from the Murder Squad, Sam
Richardson. He was a big heavy-jawed Northerner with
thinning blond hair and pale eyebrows who had joined
the same year as Vic. The Saxon type, slow and patient
and stolid until they go berserk; Vic had seen it a
couple of times. He moved to sit next to him.

'How's the arm, Hallam?' said the Chief Constable.

'Suit got the worst of it, sir.' All peering at the jagged
tear from the lapel to where the shoulder joined the
limp sleeve.

'Make a claim.'

'Yes sir.'

'Right,' the CC stood up. 'I've said all I've got to say
so I'll leave you to it, Barney, and I'll persevere with
St Pauls. Well done you two.' A nod but no smile and
he was gone.

'Well Sam,' said DCI Barnard, 'if it's all right with

305

you I propose we dispense with all distinction of rank for the particular purposes of this discussion, so feel free gentlemen. Vic. And – '

'John,' said Cromer.

'Course,' said the DCI. 'Well it's been a busy day and it's going to be an equally busy fucking night so if Parnesy here keeps a few notes we shall all stand a reasonable chance of remembering what we said in the morning.'

'What's going on?' said Vic. 'What is this?'

'This is a discussion, Vic. Entirely unofficial as I've already indicated. Anything else?'

'I see.' It was a fucking stitch-up and they knew it.

'Right.' DCI Barnard hitched his chair forward. 'If we're all sitting comfortably we can begin.'

The DCI said nothing had been settled yet but both the CC and he himself would like Vic to consider the following relevant facts. He laid a finger on the list in front of him. One, the black bloke was dead. Ellard Wesley Atkins, twenty-four. Two, while Vic was being patched up in hospital the white kid who did it, Nigel Evens, twenty-one, had topped himself in his cell, no thanks to John here because had the kid been thoroughly searched the piano wire or whatever it was he'd concealed in the waistband of his trousers would have been found. Wouldn't it, John? Cromer going beetroot and agreeing.

'Three. As you already know, Vic, Inspector Frank Webber, thirty-two, is also dead. I've talked it over with Sam here and it's either manslaughter in self-defence stroke murder stroke accidental death whilst in the performance of his duties.'

'The fuck are you talking about?'

'Four,' said the DCI, continuing down his list, 'and this is something I don't think you've yet had chance

306

to become aware of Vic, but it has been confirmed to us that Mrs Webber, Mrs Rae Webber, twenty-six, is approximately eight weeks pregnant. She went to the doctor this morning feeling bilious and that was the happy little outcome. Looking forward to telling Inspector Webber when he got home tonight. Do you happen to know Rae Webber, Vic?'

'No, no I don't.'

'I've met her once or twice socially. A very nice young woman. Very attractive.'

'Does she know her husband was a rapist and would-be fucking murderer?'

DCI Barnard paused, gave Vic a lipless smile. 'Why, would you like to fucking tell her?'

'Just asking.'

'The correct reply to that, Parnesy, is that DCI Barnard told DS Hallam that Mrs Webber was still in a state of shock and it had not been deemed advisable to fully inform her of the circumstances surrounding her husband's death.' He waited for Parnes to catch up. 'And that this had been agreed prior to DS Hallam's arrival for humanitarian reasons.'

'Humanitarian reasons,' said Parnes. 'Right.'

'Such as?'

'We don't want another death, Vic. We don't want her to lose the baby do we?'

'Fair enough,' said Vic.

'On this being explained to him, Parnesy, DS Hallam found himself in agreement with the decision not to inform Mrs Webber at this present time. That all right, Vic?'

'Fine.'

'Good.'

'When?' said Vic.

'Pardon.'

'When?'

'I think you'll find we're coming to that now.'

'Good.'

'Five, DS Hallam's investigations, allegations and testimony as and when they become available. Anything to say so far?'

'Only that I wouldn't call this a fucking discussion.'

'Call it what you fucking well like, son.'

'How about a fucking stitch-up?'

Sam Richardson laid a hand on Vic's arm. 'Best listen first, Vic.'

'Right.' glancing up at the DCI. 'Sorry.'

'DS Hallam understandably still disturbed and upset after his ordeal apologised for his outburst,' said the DCI.

'Outburst,' said Parnes.

'You kept it all under your fucking hat though, didn't you Hallam? You had the fucking evidence, so-called, and you wouldn't tell me when I put it to you last night what the fuck was going on, and you only told John here this morning, didn't you? Didn't you, Vic? Is that right? Come on, for Christ sake answer the fucking question!'

'What d'you mean,' said Vic. 'So-called?'

'I'll tell you what I mean by so-called you useless fucking article –'

'Steady Barney,' said Sam Richardson.

'I'll tell you what I mean by so-called, Detective Sergeant Hallam. So-called evidence is evidence which is not investigated, not confirmed. You deduced something from this Italian restaurant business, you deduced something from your phone calls to the Rugby Club, and no doubt you deduced something else quite fucking different from sleeping in the same room as the chief female witness in a fucking rape case. Well I

308

just hope she was fucking worth it! Was she? Well was she? Was she?' Hammering at him, trying to push him over the edge.

Vic's temper surged up to flashpoint, pushing him to plant his fist in the middle of that fucking meaty red face, then his arm and shoulder started to throb like fuck and stopped him. 'I've already explained my reasons for that.'

'Not to my fucking satisfaction you haven't! Or anybody else's! You Sam?'

'Not so far, Vic.'

'You Parnsey?'

'No.'

'You John?'

'Well. Not really no, not yet anyway.' Cromer fumbling, trying to say sorry Vic.

'You're on your own, Hallam.'

'I had gathered that.'

'All deduction, no conclusion. You could have had a list of fifteen, thirty men we could have hauled in and cleared overnight. All but one. And that man would be alive today –'

'And would he be facing any charges?'

'Meaning what?'

'Meaning you know there'd be a fucking cover-up same way you know this is a fucking stitch-up.'

'You can't say that, Vic,' said Sam.

'Yes I fucking can.'

'Your evidence,' said the DCI, ignoring him, 'is all suppositional, all circumstantial. You deduce things you don't follow up and what have you got? Evidence which is not evidence. So-called evidence. That answer your question?'

'I didn't deduce the bastard who tried to kill me, did I?'

'What are you trying to do, hound the fucking dead? Ruin his fucking family, the life of a kid not even born yet?'

'It doesn't look like it, does it, the way this is going?'

'You're a cold-blooded fucker Hallam, you know that? I'm going for a piss.' The DCI shoved his chair back, glared at Vic, shoved his hands through his stiff grey hair, shook his head and left.

Sam Richardson waited for the door to close and then turned his chair round to Vic.

Here it comes, thought Vic.

'How long have we known each other, Vic? Twenty years?'

'Yeah, about that.'

'You want to hear my twopennorth? From the sidelines, as it were. Just say if you don't.'

'No. Go on.'

'Just to take the murder side of things for a minute, Vic.' Scratching his scalp, looking honest and puzzled and trying to give the impression he wished he wasn't there at all. 'Wouldn't it have been better to have gripped this Evens kid in the first place?'

'On sus?'

'You had the blood group.'

'He had the witnesses.'

'Travellers, Vic. And you let John here do them didn't you? Less than a week on the job, still wet behind the ears. No offence John.'

'None taken,' said Cromer.

'Your mate Billy,' said Sam. 'What was his alibi?'

'Ellard.'

'Exactly. What was Ellard's?'

'His job. He was on the door. Where he was supposed to be.'

'Anybody see him?' said Sam.

'Customers,' said Vic. 'Can I ask you something, Sam?'

'Fire away.'

'What were your lot doing all this time?'

'Interviewing Billy. Until you tipped him off.'

'Billy was put out the frame by Forensic. Your lads told him Ellard got him off on a question of time.'

'All right,' said Sam, 'fair enough. We all push the punter. Take Evens again. You could have had him lifted at Stoke, but no. You could have left him kicking the fucking cell door down, but no. What happens? You take him out and lose him and he does Ellard. A fucking riot breaks out and then John here heroically tackles him but unfortunately he tops himself whilst in police custody. Doesn't look good does it? Without all this bloody Webber business.'

'Looking good is what this is all about is it?'

'Just normal damage limitation, Vic. The tabloids and TV'll have a fucking field day, Vic. This is just a normal damage limitation exercise.'

'Come on, Sam.'

'It's not just you in the shit, Vic, not just you and John here, it's all of us. We're all in it. What we're doing is just trying to get out of it, that's all. Save everybody's arse, yours included. No question of getting anyone stitched up.'

Vic looked round for an ashtray. There wasn't one.

'All settled then?' DCI Barnard came back in with a couple of dark patches on the thigh of his tight blue suit where he'd wet his leg. He sat down quickly. 'Well?'

'You could say I've presented the view from my side,' said Sam.

'And?' The DCI looked at Vic.

'I can see what Sam said makes sense,' said Vic.

'From the Force point of view. But I've still got no fucking idea what's going on, where all this is going.'

'Right,' said the DCI, rubbing his hands. 'At least we're getting somewhere so let's see if you can enlighten him John. Let's have your version.'

According to Cromer, Nigel was so jealous of Pauline he followed her everywhere. He wouldn't admit to it but that was what he did. 'Even Billy said he saw him hanging around in the rain outside her bedsit, remember?'

'Yeah.'

'Then Pauline starts going down the Kit Kat because Billy's screwing her, and Ellard sees his chance to move in on the white man boss.'

'Why?'

'Part because he's black, most because he's a fucking dealer, man. We know that now.'

'Do we, John. How do we know that?'

'Nigel told me.'

'When?'

'On the way down here.'

'What did he say, John?'

Cromer leafed through his notebook. 'He said "I executed that man because I considered him to be responsible for Pauline's death. The body is the temple in which we worship the spirit and if we defile the temple we defile the spirit and we deserve to die." '

'Yeah,' said Vic. 'That sounds like Nigel. What else?'

'He said he followed Pauline and saw her several times with Ellard hanging round cars outside the Kit Kat. He said he came to the conclusion Ellard was feeding her lines. First for nothing then for the odd fuck then for money.'

'Why?'

'That's how they work it.'

312

'No, John. Why should Ellard go to all that trouble?'

'Nigel said Ellard wanted to get her to push stuff on commission to the travellers because through them he could get to the students and get into the real money.'

'Nigel said all that, did he?'

'Then he said that on the night in question, Saturday last, he saw Billy giving Pauline one in the back of the car, then Ellard giving her another for three lines of coke up on Brandon Hill. Enough was enough and he went up and strangled her.'

'Nigel said enough was enough?'

'Words to that effect.'

'Then he said he went up and strangled her? He actually said straight out in front of you and other witnesses "I went up on Brandon Hill and strangled her"?'

'I told you, Vic.' Looking in the notebook again. ' "If you defile the temple you deserve to die." '

'That was Ellard. What about Pauline?'

'Same thing.'

'He said the same thing?'

'Word for word.'

'So you put it to him: did you kill Pauline?'

'Yes.'

'And?'

'He said he didn't want to talk about it.'

'I bet he did.'

'They all do that,' said Sam. 'The ones who are going to cough. The others rave on about their fucking rights and their fucking lawyers.'

That was a point. 'Did Nigel rave on, John?'

'No. He just went on chanting that stuff about the temple on and on right into the fucking cell.' Cromer looking distressed now, harassed, losing it. Good. ' "You defile the temple you deserve to die." I go to the

desk, it goes quiet, come back, he's topped himself.'
Cromer looking for sympathy, understanding, pity
even, and getting nothing. All four faces saying you
fucked it, John.

The kid wasn't exactly lying, he wouldn't have the
bottle to blag this lot, but he was holding something
back, bending it here and there. Either to save his own
neck or because he'd been asked to bend it. 'What you
mean is you think he went up and strangled her
because you think he was jealous?'

'That was what he did, what he did to Ellard – '

'Not with his bare hands – '

'Not the point,' said the DCI. 'The point is Evens is
a right little arsehole causes all this shit in St Pauls
and then craps out by topping himself in his fucking
cell – '

'And you go along with that do you, John?'

'I think that's what happened yes – '

'You think but you don't know?'

'From what Nigel told me – '

'Because he was jealous?'

'Yes.'

'But he never said that, did he, John?'

'No, not exactly.'

'What did he say exactly? Come on John what did
he say? There's something else, isn't there? It's written
all over your face. When you charged him with Pauline
what did he say? The exact words.'

Cromer looking unhappily from the DCI to Sam and
back to the DCI.

'Tell him,' said Sam.

'Doesn't make any fucking sense anyway,' said the
DCI.

Cromer took a torn page from his notebook and

unfolded it. 'He said "For the answer to that see page 157." '

'He said what?'

'Page 157.'

Vic held his hand out for the piece of paper. Nothing else was written on it and nothing had been erased. For the answer to that see page 157. Weird to the fucking end, poor kid. 'How was he when you brought him in, John?'

'Sullen. Sort of gone inside himself.'

Yeah, that was Nigel. 'He have his rucksack with him?'

'No.'

'For Christ sake, Vic,' said the DCI. 'Was it Nigel fucking Evens or wasn't it?'

'Could have been Nigel, could have been Ellard.'

'Nigel, Ellard, Pauline, who gives a fuck,' said the DCI, 'they're all dead. Now for fuck sake can we get on.'

On balance it probably was Nigel. Cromer was probably right. Jealousy was probably right. It was the sort of thing Nigel would never admit. The sort of thing he considered a weakness. What had he said about Billy? Something about not wanting to be contaminated. 'Old men's shit diseases.' Bit of a puritan, young Nigel. But who wasn't when it came to some other bloke screwing your bird. Your missis. One reason he was so determined to get that fucker Webber. Come off it, Hallam. *The* reason.

But why were they all so keen to paint Nigel so fucking black?

'What we'd like you think about now if you will, Vic, is pensions, reputations, that sort of thing. Rae Webber could end up with nothing, less than nothing given the meal the media are bound to make of her

315

husband, and it won't be too pleasant for you either, Vic. Or she could end up with something. A pension for one thing – '

'What the fuck are you trying to say?'

'What I'm trying to say, Hallam, is that considering your own fuck-ups and their effect upon the reputation of this Force you might find it in your heart to be a little fucking charitable for once in your life.'

'How?'

The DCI leaned his elbows on the table. 'What do you think about pinning Pauline, Ellard and Inspector Webber on this little toerag Evens?' When Vic didn't reply the DCI picked up the CC's intercom. 'We'll take the coffee now please, Sandra.'

Vic took his in the corridor outside. Nobody came out to join him.

When he went back in and asked what about all the witnesses, Dr Chaudhury, his assistant, his secretary, all the people pushing at the door, the DCI said as far as he was concerned the door was shut.

'Not at the end when they all came in – '

'During the struggle the door was shut,' said the DCI. 'That is vital point one. When they all came in the window was open. Vital point two. Evens had gone, legged it – '

'Holy shit, he was never fucking there in the first place – '

'If I could just come in here,' said Sam Richardson. 'My lads have been down there taking statements and nobody is really sure what they saw. They heard the struggle certainly – '

'Thanks,' said Vic.

'One thinks they saw one thing, another thinks they saw something else, several of the ladies didn't look, either because they couldn't or didn't want to, and Dr

316

Chaudhury was out cold. So whether the window was open or shut either all of the time or some of the time, or who opened it, is neither here nor there – '

'Ellie opened it, for Christ sake, the place was full of steam – '

'All I'm saying, Vic,' said Sam, 'is it doesn't fucking matter who did what. We all know what witnesses are like, we've all been through it enough times, even the lad here. Nobody ever throws the first punch and nobody ever sees the same fight. You know what these things are like Vic, we all do – '

'For fuck sake Sam he was out to kill her – '

'So?'

'What d'you think she's going to say?'

'Have a word with her,' said Sam. 'Mention Mrs Webber's condition, see what she says. She's a nurse, isn't she? Bound to be sympathetic. All you have to do it put it over right.'

'Jesus Christ, Sam, whatever happened to you?'

'The point is,' said the DCI, 'Whatever the ins and outs it all comes down to you and the nurse. Ellie, isn't it?'

Vic stood up, shoving his chair back. 'Nigel didn't kill that fucker Webber did he? I did!'

'Yes well,' said the DCI, giving him the lipless smile, 'as far as that's concerned it's a known fact you and Inspector Webber never got on, to put it mildly – '

Vic lunged across the table. Sam Richardson was on his feet in an instant, jerking Vic back down heavily into his chair. 'You're not helping yourself, Vic.'

DCI Barnard eyed Vic, willing him to have another go, and settle the matter for good. When Vic did nothing, the DCI picked up his papers and tapped them together. 'Well, it's up to you, Hallam. You want to take it to trial, that's your privilege. But it's either man-

317

slaughter, murder or accidental death and if you hated Inspector Webber's guts, who's to say they won't see that as a motive? Plus you won't get any help from anybody here, that I can tell you.' Another lipless smile, then the DCI stood up. 'Anyway, you've heard what we've got to say and we've listened to you. Now it's up to you and what you think is best for all concerned. For yourself, naturally, and your future in this Force. Should you find yourself after due reflection able to go along with what has been discussed here, and setting aside the obvious emotional stress under which you find yourself, I would like to emphasise, as I did at the start, that this discussion has been entirely unofficial – '

'Entirely unofficial,' said Parnes.

'And I can unofficially add that should you at any time wish to present yourself for promotion to inspector again the outcome could very well be different. At least we all hope so.'

'You mean,' said Vic, lighting a cigarette anyway, 'a vacancy has suddenly come up?'

'I don't consider that remark to be in particularly good taste, Hallam.'

'Try this one then. Stick your offer up your arse.'

'Put that down verbatim.'

'Verbatim,' said Parnes.

'Not me you cunt, him.'

'Oh, right. Got it,' said Parnes.

'So what's it to be then, Vic?' said the DCI. 'Go for trial? Put your nurse friend through all that? Then what are you looking at? Early retirement? Because there'll be nothing here for you, I can promise you.'

'You could lose your pension,' said Sam.

'No,' said Vic.

'What d'you mean, no?' said the DCI. 'Come on,

318

Hallam, I need to get this clear. What is it exactly you're intending to do?'

'Nothing,' said Vic. 'Well, you know, apart from work.'

'I see,' said the DCI. 'Just keep quietly ticking over, ticking away, is that it?'

'Can I go now?' said Vic.

They showed the interview with Frank on the early evening news. It was introduced by a serious-looking Maggi Reed who said it was being shown in commemoration of a brave young officer killed in the performance of his duty whilst attempting to arrest a murder suspect. Inspector Frank Webber, a married man of thirty-two, was brutally stabbed to death when he recognised, pursued and courageously tackled an armed and dangerous man. The man, Nigel Evens, twenty-one, was believed to be a traveller, known to be disturbed, and had a record of violence and drugtaking. After his arrest Evens was found hanging from the bars of his cell. He had used a length of wire – it was decided not to specify guitar string because of the danger of a possible copy-cat effect among teenagers and children – which he had concealed in the waistband of his combat trousers. Evens was believed to have been wanted for the murder of Ellard Wesley Atkins, a twenty-four-year-old bar manager from the St Pauls area, using a similar method. The motive was no longer being seen as racial, and the outburst of rioting caused by the incident was now thought to have been contained; police officers were meeting with members of the community. The interview with Inspector Webber, who was due to receive a second commendation for bravery, was being shown after consultation with his wife Mrs Rae Webber who had tragically found

319

out that very morning that she was pregnant with the baby she and her husband had long awaited. Mrs Webber, who wished the interview to be shown as a tribute to her husband was now being cared for and consoled by her parents at their home in Henleaze, Bristol.

Even though Pauline wasn't mentioned because her case was officially deemed to be still under investigation everyone concerned agreed it made a good story and Frank looked terrific. Vic and Ellie didn't see him. They were in bed in Vic's place trying to forget.

24

They started off in the kitchen and got through a couple of bottles of Côtes du Rhône talking and arguing about it. He told her everything, for once: all about him and Webber; how he never even knew it was Webber until after he was dead; all the police business, right up to the job he was supposed to do on her to get them all off the hook. Then they got on to Rae Webber, and what she and Ellie would have to go through if it went to trial. When Vic said he'd just like to see the woman's pregnancy confirmed, that's all, Ellie put her head in her hands and felt drained and hopeless.

'I've had enough, Vic, don't go on any more, please.'

He lit another cigarette and looked around the cold black and grey kitchen, the piled-up sink, the overflowing waste bin. 'Yeah, you're right, so have I. Sorry.' He finished his glass and stood up, and for a moment he looked at her as if he was considering taking her home. Then he stubbed his cigarette out and said, 'Fuck it, it'll all sort itself out in the morning.' He took her in his arms, lifted her up, and said, 'Let's go to bed.'

Lying naked and awkward with each other for the first few moments in the unfamiliar cold sheets, she could see he was still full of self-hatred for what he'd been forced to do; she pulled his head to her breast, soothing him as he suckled at her, feeling warm and generous, but curiously uninvolved.

They began to make love. She thought he was a bit frantic and wild and woolly at first, even with his strapped-up arm, but then he got gentler as the rage came out of him; the second time she felt that she really needed to let go and yell and scream her heart out. When she did, she could tell she'd surprised him, despite the pleased little boy look that spread over his face because he thought he'd made her come when it was something she was desperate for anyway. For a long time they lay in each other's arms, their bodies stuck together and their minds drifting like clouds. Then he began to play idly with her until she felt lazy and safe and at ease with him, and the next time they made love it was as if they'd been doing it all their lives.

During the night, Ellie woke from time to time and luxuriated in sleeping next to him, in feeling his hard solid body curved round her, and his prick rising unconsciously now and then between her buttocks, and making her smile to herself, as she lay there, lax with sleep; what a blind mad idiot it was. She eased herself back against it until it was resting, pulsing along with his heartbeat, just inside her.

Later, as he came out of his first long deep sleep, she could tell his arm had begun to ache and throb: his body was hot and feverish, he was grunting and breathing through his mouth with his teeth closed, and he was shifting himself all over the bed looking for a cool place. She debated whether to wake him, give him some paracetamol, find somewhere else to sleep. But then he went off again, lying on her like a log, his good arm thrown across her, his hand cupping her breast, and she drifted off herself.

But after that she woke every couple of hours, to look at him, listen to his breathing, or shift his weight off her, and so in the end it was an awkward, restless night; as much, she supposed, from both of them being

322

out of the habit of having anyone in bed with them as anything that had happened in the day. She hoped so anyway.

Then it was morning and they were lying naked in each other's arms, kissing and nuzzling and saying nothing much, but looking into each other's eyes and knowing the chisel was still there.

They made love again, and felt closer, and lay together listening to the sounds of morning coming in, traffic, plumbing going, people getting up, going out, driving off, and then he said, 'What would you say to bacon and eggs?'

'Yes please.' He was right, she thought, forget about it, just get on with it. 'Got any mushies?'

'Haven't even got any bacon and eggs – '

The bedside phone rang, it was a quarter to eight, and by the second ring she knew she'd lost him.

It was Cromer. 'They've found the rucksack.'

'Where?'

'In the bushes down the bottom of the garden. He'd got a little den in there, in the brambles.'

'And?'

'Haven't seen it yet.'

'Oh Christ, John – '

'What?'

'Nothing. Ring me when you do.' He put the phone down and turned back to her, determined to show her how much he still wanted her. She said she didn't feel like any more at the moment thank you very much, she was a bit sore and she'd sooner have a bath or a shower if he hadn't run out of water as well –

He put his hand over her mouth and said shh.

They listened to the front door snicking open. A pair of heels clacked on the loose lino inside the door and

323

a woman's voice called out uncertainly, 'Vic?' Then more assertively, 'Victor are you there?'

It was '*Victor*' that got Ellie. She lay rigidly in the bed, his hand still across her mouth, shaking with silent uncontrollable laughter, but at the same time thinking please God don't come in, oh please God don't let her in, knowing who it was immediately from the shut look on Vic's face. He removed his hand from her mouth, and, fierce and bedraggled, put his finger to his lips to warn her. She turned on to her belly, stuffed the pillow in her face, her whole body shaking with the effort of not laughing out loud.

'Victor?' said the voice. 'Is that you?'

She felt him pull the sheet roughly over her, and climb out of bed. She poked her head out from under the sheet and saw him trying to pull the dressing gown on over his strapped-up arm.

He coughed, then cleared his throat again, loudly. 'Who is it?'

'Who d'you think?'

Vic was searching for his cigarettes and lighter. Because of his arm, he couldn't tie his short boxer's dressing gown, and his dick was hanging out. He looked at Ellie, angry and hopeless; she clambered up on the bed, tied it for him and kissed him like a child going off to school.

'What d'you want?' he shouted, shoving Ellie back into bed.

'Victor, I have not driven one hundred and twenty-six miles to talk to a door.'

'All right, hang on.' He looked at Ellie – this is all I need – and walked out of the door, closing it firmly behind him.

She looked different; thinner, sharper, more expensive. She was wearing a square-shouldered russet-brown velvet two-piece thing with a curly lump of gold costume jewellery on one of the big lapels. The skirt was split up the front to above the knee and she had clunky suede high heels tied crossover style above and below the ankle. She was wearing lip gloss, brown eye make-up, and her long blonde hair was cut short and tinted a deep chestnut colour. Even the perfume that came wafting off her down the hall was different, sharp and lemon-grassy. Vic had imagined meeting her dozens of times, but never like this. She had transformed herself: one-tenth tart, nine-tenths businesswoman. Cold-eyed, self-possessed, out to get her own way and determined to be fucking sniffy about it by the look of her. Six months. Why had he ever married her? She was nothing to do with him.

'You're looking well.'

'More than I can say for you.' She looked him up and down, and then with more blame than sympathy, as if he'd broken something that still belonged to her, said, 'What have you done to your arm?'

'Nothing. You used to have long fair hair.'

'So?' She turned to look at herself in the hall mirror. It wasn't there. 'Where's that gone?'

'On the floor behind you. Black plastic bag.'

A man appeared at the door, coughing into one fist, holding a Wintermans slim panatella in the other. He was in his late forties, dark-haired, shiny-faced and jowly. He had a big thickening upper body which made his legs look short, and he wore a double-breasted blazer and flannels with a pink shirt and a dark blue tie with a BMW symbol on it. Vic noticed he was careful not to step over the threshold.

'This is Ross, my area manager. He's come to help me.'

'Good for him.'

'We've got a breakfast meeting in the Royal at half-past eight.'

'In that case,' said Vic, turning back towards the bedroom, 'you'd better get on with it.'

'Victor. I haven't finished yet.'

She was walking towards him, fishing in her burgundy leather shoulder bag and producing a long, thick, white legal envelope. As Vic took it, he noticed Ross moving his bulk to one side to see what was happening more clearly.

'What's this?' As if he didn't know.

'Divorce, Victor.' She managed to make her voice sound as if he had just thrown up on her shoes.

'On what grounds?'

'Irretrievable breakdown.'

'Sounds about right,' said Vic. 'They've got it down to six months now, have they?'

'And here's something else.' She presented him with another legal envelope, manila this time. Ross was leaning forward, one shiny black loafer over the front step. When Vic looked pointedly at it, he drew back. Vic felt no antagonism towards him, all that had gone with Webber, but there was no point in letting the guy think he could push it.

'More good news?'

'It's a solicitor's letter,' she said. 'It concerns you not delaying a sale on this place.' She glanced back at Ross. 'You saw me deliver it.'

'Absolutely,' said Ross.

'I need my half, Victor, I can't go on living rented.'

'Fair enough,' said Victor. He saw Ross drop his shoulders and relax his chest muscles, relieved not to get involved. 'Anything else?'

'I think that's all, don't you Ross?'

Ross hitched up his flannels. 'Definitely.'

'Fine,' said Vic. 'Close the door on the way out.' He went back into the bedroom, tossed the envelopes on the bed, and stood for a few moments with his back to Ellie, his hands thrust deep into the pockets of his boxer's dressing gown.

'What is it?' she said.

He turned round, looking at the swagged cobwebs in the corners of the ceiling. 'Fuck it, I never liked the place anyway.' As soon as he said it he knew it was true; he began to feel free, and light, as if he'd just dumped a heavy rucksack. If you waited long enough, he thought, things always sorted themselves out. He sat down on the bed, and played with her hair, and then, as the shoes clacked industriously in and out of the hall and up the basement steps, they began to get silly and giggly, like a couple of kids. Ross in particular was making heavy weather of it, coughing and clomping like an asthmatic bullock as he ferried things up the basement steps. Not a word was spoken; all Vic and Ellie could hear were the sounds of a car boot lid and doors opening and closing.

Then clack clack clack and she came in. Pat. Trish. Took one look. 'I thought so,' she said, looking from Vic to Ellie's naked back. 'Well. Look what the cat's brought in.'

Ellie leaned up on one elbow. 'I am looking at it.'

'Listen,' said Vic with dangerous amiability, 'why don't you just fuck off quietly like you did before?'

'Don't worry, I'm going!' She slammed out and they listened to her heels stabbing along the hall. Then they stopped. There was a hard little grunt from the kitchen like Capriati's serve and then a 'bosh' of glass against the wall. Seconds later, a cutlery drawer went crash-clatter-jangle. The heels clacked again, the front

327

door banged shut, then there was the noise of a car driving off, fast.

When they got up they found the cutlery drawer was broken-backed, there were knives and forks glittering all over the floor and she'd smashed the only thing Vic had left in his fridge, a large, mouldering, semi-fermented jar of Dolmio Pasta Sauce, up against the lintel over the kitchen window. There was a big splat of red and green slime and bits of it were slowly legging it down the wall and splodging into the sink. They were both naked and there were blobs and exclamation mark streaks of red sauce and chunks and slivers and millions of tiny needles of glass everywhere like demolished Christmas decorations. Ellie began to shiver.

'Come on,' said Vic. 'Back to bed.'

She was lying gazing mindlessly and lovingly at him while he told her what a magnificent fucking woman she was, she really was, like nobody else ever was or ever could be, and how did she feel about going round the corner shop for some bread and milk and bacon and eggs, when the phone rang again. This time she didn't give up but lay there listening and nuzzling and licking him. You're mine. Mine mine mine. Mine mine mine mine mine. They were talking about some book Cromer had found in Nigel's rucksack.

'What does it say, John?'

'It's in the chapter called "The Politics of Assassination".'

'It would be. What does it say?' Putting his hand between her legs and playing with her. She slid her hand down over his lovely silky belly hair. Yes, he was getting hard again. Good. Mine. Mine mine mine.

'It says, "In the end when a man realises as he must that life is nothing more and nothing less than a series

328

of gross betrayals of the flesh and spirit the only question of morality left is how that man shall deal with those betrayals without betraying himself." '

'Not a happy lad, was he? Doesn't prove anything though.'

'There's something else, Vic. He'd got her handbag and some of her clothes and underclothes in there as well.'

Vic put the phone down and folded his arms round Ellie and held her tight. Poor old Nigel. I know how you feel, mate. When somebody you love goes, dies, whatever, that's all you've got left. Bits and pieces and a fading smell. He buried his face in Ellie's neck, breathed in her warmth, and hoped it wouldn't happen this time.

A Selected List of Thrillers available from Mandarin

While every effort is made to keep prices low, it is sometimes necessary to increase prices at short notice. Mandarin Paperbacks reserves the right to show new retail prices on covers which may differ from those previously advertised in the text or elsewhere.

The prices shown below were correct at the time of going to press.

☐	7493 0054 X	**The Silence of the Lambs**	Thomas Harris	£5.99
☐	7493 1091 X	**Primal Fear**	William Diehl	£4.99
☐	7493 0636 X	**Bones of Coral**	James Hall	£4.99
☐	7493 1749 3	**Mean High Tide**	James Hall	£4.99
☐	7493 1398 6	**The Immaculate Conception**	Patrick Lynch	£4.99
☐	7493 1528 8	**The Minstrel Boy**	Richard Crawford	£5.99
☐	7493 1324 2	**Call of the Lion**	Christopher Sherlock	£4.99
☐	7493 1323 4	**Eye of the Cobra**	Christopher Sherlock	£4.99
☐	7493 1968 2	**The Tick Tock Man**	Terence Strong	£4.99
☐	7493 1972 0	**The Cruelty of Morning**	Hilary Bonner	£4.99
☐	7493 1713 2	**Kolymsky Heights**	Lionel Davidson	£5.99

All these books are available at your bookshop or newsagent, or can be ordered direct from the address below. Just tick the titles you want and fill in the form below.

Cash Sales Department, PO Box 5, Rushden, Northants NN10 6YX.
Fax: 01933 414047 : Phone: 01933 414000.

Please send cheque, payable to 'Reed Book Services Ltd.', or postal order for purchase price quoted and allow the following for postage and packing:

£1.00 for the first book, 50p for the second; **FREE POSTAGE AND PACKING FOR THREE BOOKS OR MORE PER ORDER.**

NAME (Block letters) ....

ADDRESS ....

....

☐ I enclose my remittance for ....

☐ I wish to pay by Access/Visa Card Number

Expiry Date

Signature ....

Please quote our reference: MAND